Praise for
ANITA KELLY

'An essential read'
USA Today

'Kelly crafts an absolutely engrossing love story . . . It's a
celebration of living our lives fully as ourselves – the courage
that requires but also the abundant rewards. Can you give
a book a Michelin star? A+'
Entertainment Weekly

'This chef's-kiss debut . . . brilliantly explores the idea of being
true to yourself with insight and compassion. In between all the
deliciously snarky wit, simmering sexual chemistry, romantic
yearning, and quippy banter, Kelly also delivers some moments of
romantic hope and happiness that will long resonate with readers'
Booklist, starred review

'A delicious confection of a story: savory, succulent and also a bit
salty in spots . . . The only bad thing about this book is that even
after you've gorged on the whole thing, it'll leave you wanting more'
Bookpage, starred review

'Kelly will whet your appetite from the first page, capping off the
wonderful feast with the absolute sweetest of happy-ever-afters'
Kirkus, starred review

'A stunning debut'
Library Journal, starred review

'This debut is delicious in every way'
Buzzfeed Books

'*Love & Other Disasters* is by turns funny, sweet, and hot, but Anita Kelly's emotional river runs deep – this romance will stay with readers long after they've turned the last page. A deeply emotional yet buoyant romantic comedy about finding love and self'
Shelf Awareness

'A sweet debut . . . a nonbinary protagonist in a mainstream romance is cause for excitement and the characters spark with chemistry'
Publishers Weekly

'A buzz-worthy debut romance novel'
Scary Mommy

'Kelly writes wildly charming, exquisitely vibrant, and achingly tender prose and has a unique gift for making readers feel safe, loved, and understood within their pages . . . Fantastically fun and crack-your-heart-wide-open vulnerable'
Rosie Danan

'Anita Kelly writes with tremendous warmth and care, and these pages shine with joy'
Rachel Lynn Solomon

'Sweet, steamy, and absolutely delectable! This is a book you both want to savor and consume in a single bite'
Alison Cochrun

'With only one book, Anita Kelly has landed among my all-time favorite authors'
Meryl Wilsner

Originally from a small town in the Pocono Mountains of Pennsylvania, **Anita Kelly** now lives in the Pacific Northwest with their family. A teen librarian by day, they write romance that celebrates queer love in all its infinite possibilities. Whenever not reading or writing, they're drinking too much tea, taking pictures, and dreaming of their next walk in the woods. They hope you get to pet a dog today.

To learn more about Anita and their books, visit **anitakellywrites.com**, or follow Anita on Twitter **@daffodilly** and Instagram **@anitakellywrites**.

By Anita Kelly

Love & Other Disasters
Something Wild & Wonderful

Something Wild and Wonderful

ANITA KELLY

HEADLINE
ETERNAL

Published by arrangement with Forever
An imprint of Grand Central Publishing

First published in Great Britain in 2023
by HEADLINE ETERNAL
An imprint of HEADLINE PUBLISHING GROUP

1

Cataloguing in Publication Data is available from the British Library

ISBN 978 1 4722 8606 2

Offset in 10.8/14.8pt Adobe Garamond Pro by Jouve (UK), Milton Keynes

Printed and bound in Great Britain by Clays Ltd, Elcograf S.p.A.

Headline's policy is to use papers that are natural, renewable and recyclable
products and made from wood grown in well-managed forests and other
controlled sources. The logging and manufacturing processes are expected
to conform to the environmental regulations of the country of origin.

HEADLINE PUBLISHING GROUP
An Hachette UK Company
Carmelite House
50 Victoria Embankment
London EC4Y 0DZ

www.headlineeternal.com
www.headline.co.uk
www.hachette.co.uk

For Kathy,
who taught me love through laughter
but still loves me in my quiet

Paths, like religions, are seldom fixed.... Both the religious path and the hiking path are, as Taoists say, made in the walking.

—Robert Moor, *On Trails*

AUTHOR'S NOTE

While this is a romance and contains all the ideals I most love about romance—humor, heart, and hope—this book also contains difficult subject matter, including familial estrangement due to queer identity. Homophobic language is also used in chapter 16. A full list of content warnings is available at anitakellywrites.com.

Thank you for your trust in taking this walk with me.

Something Wild and Wonderful

I

The Desert

Miles 151 to 702
Spring

CHAPTER ONE

The first rattlesnake made Alexei's heart stop.

Just one uncomfortably long missed beat: a gasp stuck in his chest.

The *woosh* of cars on the Palms to Pines Scenic Byway had faded, replaced by the not-quite-silence of the Southern California desert and the sound of Alexei's pulse jumping in his ears. The day was already warm, his pack heavy on his shoulders.

His first steps on the Pacific Crest Trail had felt surreal, his senses muzzy, like walking through a strange fog of sunshine and sand. But almost an hour in, he had started to ease into the familiar clarity of solitude. Before the quiet around him broke, abruptly, with the distinctive rattle. Tightly wound scales, vibrating in warning.

Alexei's feet stopped automatically.

The snake slithered across the trail in front of him.

Paused exactly where Alexei's next footfall would have been.

For a long moment, they both waited: a fragile standoff.

Until another series of noises filtered through Alexei's brain. The huff of breath working hard through a set of lungs. The soft pounding of shoes on sand.

Alexei's arm shot out on instinct, hitting the solid plane of the stranger's chest. Even as his mind raced, the movement filled him with a strangely comforting sense memory of every time he'd done the same for his younger sister: each time Alina got too close to the edge of the sidewalk in downtown Portland; whenever she leaned too far over the edge of an embankment on their family hikes through Gifford Pinchot National Forest.

But Alexei was far away from the Pacific Northwest now, and the person he was currently protecting from the rattlesnake was definitely not Alina.

For the first time since he'd heard the rattle, Alexei tore his gaze from the ground to glance at the man next to him. The stranger had dark hair, wrapped up in a bun, lightly tanned skin. And earbuds stuck in his ears, which was probably why he'd thundered up to Alexei and the rattlesnake so carelessly. Inch by inch, he lifted a hand to remove one of the small white pieces from his ear while he stared down at the snake, chest heaving against Alexei's arm.

Which, for some reason, Alexei seemed unable to move.

"Snake," the man said.

Alexei's eyes returned to the trail before them.

"Snake," he agreed.

They stood frozen there for another long second—Alexei, the stranger, and the snake. Alexei was contemplating how to get his brain to send the signal to his arm to remove itself from the stranger's chest when the rattlesnake moved its head.

And stared directly at Alexei.

Its tail gave another sharp rattle as its long, thin tongue slithered out between its teeth.

Before Alexei could stop himself, his extended arm turned, so his hand could more easily grab a fistful of the stranger's T-shirt. He would have been more embarrassed about this if the stranger hadn't moved even closer to Alexei in the same instant, his shoulder shoving behind Alexei's back. Alexei couldn't quite focus on anything other than his pounding heart, which was making up for its earlier skipped beat by parading double time against his rib cage.

"Snake," the stranger said again, a whisper this time, brushing against the sun-heated shell of Alexei's ear.

What was the phrase about human reactions in emergencies? Fight or flight? Well, that was clearly untrue. Alexei was fully incapable, at the moment, of either fighting the rattlesnake or flying away from it. A more apropos phrase would be...panic or piss yourself.

And while Alexei might have been clutching a stranger's T-shirt in his fist, at least he hadn't pissed himself.

He was pretty sure.

He'd have to further assess the situation later.

If he made it to later.

But miraculously, the snake turned its head a beat later. Slithered into the chaparral, smooth and silent. Out of sight in half a second.

Alexei almost screamed out loud when a hand clamped around his other shoulder, a scratchy beard shoving its way next to his cheek.

"Hey, boys," the new stranger said. "Why're we cuddling?"

Alexei, finally, dropped his arm and stepped away, sucking in a deep, dusty breath.

"Shit, Faraj," the original stranger said, rubbing at his forehead. "There was this huge rattler right across the trail—" He shook his head, looking up from the ground to meet Alexei's eyes. A slow smile grew on his lips, eyes dazed with relief. "This guy saved my life."

"Damn," Faraj said. "Sounds exciting."

That was, Alexei supposed, one word for it. He had to look away from the original stranger's smile, because now that Alexei could fully see his face, and the way that smile transformed it—those eyes, deep brown and warm, the skin crinkling around them—

It was simply sensory overload for Alexei, right then.

Faraj clapped a hand on Alexei's shoulder again. "Thanks, man."

Alexei opened his mouth before snapping it shut, unable to figure out what to say.

"Hey!" Faraj shouted over his shoulder. "Watch out for rattlers!"

And with a friendly smile to Alexei, Faraj kept walking down the trail. He was followed a moment later by three other men, each of whom gave Alexei a nod, a smile, and a "Hey," on their way.

Alexei blinked back at each of them, still struggling to cool his adrenaline. He rubbed absently at his chest after they'd passed.

"Thanks again."

Alexei nearly jumped. He hadn't realized the original stranger, with the brown eyes and the long hair and the smile, was still there.

"I'm Ben."

Ben held out his hand. After a second, Alexei shook it.

"Alexei."

"You can hike with us if you want." Ben tilted his head toward the trail, where the others had gone.

"Oh." Alexei shook his head. "No, that's okay." After an awkward pause, he added, "You probably shouldn't hike with earbuds in."

He bit his tongue, immediately recognizing how chiding it had sounded. This was possibly one of the reasons why Alexei didn't have very many friends. But, well. The desert was a frightening place. Ben needed to look out for himself.

To Alexei's relief, Ben laughed, hands on his hips.

"My mother would thank you for the reminder."

They stared at each other for another long moment, until Ben adjusted the trekking poles wrapped around his wrists and nodded toward the trail.

"All right," he said. "See you out there."

With one last disarmingly attractive smile, he, too, was gone.

Alexei bent over his own trekking poles, taking a moment.

He was officially one mile into his 2,500-mile hike. This huge thing he had planned for months suddenly taking form in the dust already collecting on his trail runners, the wind battering his face, the sun beating on his neck. He had been prepared for this solitary journey, had looked forward to months spent walking along the rocky spines of California, Oregon, and Washington, alone. A chance to say good-bye to his old life. To this wonderful, wild coast. To find a bit of peace before he started over.

In a way, Alexei had been preparing for this moment for years, ever since his father had started taking him on serious trails when he was seven years old. Thinking of his dad pinched at Alexei's chest, but it was a pinch he had expected, one he was familiar with now. A pinch he had felt, too, when Ben had said, *My mother would thank you for the reminder.* Alexei hoped, eventually, by the time he reached the end of the trail in Canada, that he'd have perfected feeling that pinch. That he would have gotten so used to it, this pinch of his mother and father, that he'd barely even notice it anymore.

It was hard to imagine, truthfully. But he was hopeful anyway. Hope was why he was here.

Either way, something about stepping onto the trail this morning with nothing but his pack and his thoughts had felt...anticlimactic, even once his senses had adjusted. There had been no welcoming party, no spreadsheet for him to consult—he had made so many spreadsheets, in his preparations—no boxes to check in satisfaction. Nothing to announce that this was actually happening.

Until the rattlesnake.

The rattlesnake knew Alexei was here.

And Ben. He knew Alexei was here, too.

Alexei straightened. Stared ahead at the undulating brown hills, the blazing sky.

He had promised himself to take in the lessons the natural world always seemed ready to give. When he thought about it now, rattlesnakes were a rather kind species. There were scarier prospects ahead of him, he knew: mountain lions and bears, dried-up water sources and dehydration. Snow-filled mountain passes to traverse, roaring rivers to cross.

Rattlesnakes at least gave you a warning.

Mostly, like anything else, they just wanted to exist.

Mostly, they just wanted you to listen.

Alexei had survived his first rattlesnake.

He had received a warm smile from a handsome man.

And—he completed a quick pat-down of himself to make sure—he had not pissed himself.

He had been taught from an early age to take small bits of grace where you could find them.

His stride a little stronger, his pulse a little calmer, Alexei turned and walked past the rattlesnake's path, farther into the heart of the desert.

The next time Alexei saw Ben, it was thirty miles later, and Ben's face was full of shaving cream.

"Hey!" Ben's voice stopped Alexei in his tracks, the friendly, unexpected greeting almost as surprising as that first rattlesnake. "You're the guy who saved my life."

Alexei stared at Ben's reflection in the mirror of the bathroom, the small space and bright lights above the sink making Ben's smile even more inescapable than it had been in the middle of the desert.

"I don't think—" Alexei cleared his throat, dry after days of disuse. "I didn't actually save your life."

"Oh." Ben rinsed his blade, tapped it against the side of the sink before bringing it to his face. "I was oblivious and dehydrated. I would have stepped on that sucker, one hundred percent. You most definitely saved my life." His smile in the mirror faded, the hand holding the razor pausing as he turned to face Alexei. "I'm so sorry, though. I don't remember your name."

"Alexei," Alexei introduced himself again.

"That's right." Ben smiled. "I'm Ben."

Alexei definitely remembered Ben's name. While Alexei had passed plenty of other hikers over the past few days, Ben was the only person he'd exchanged more than two words with. Alexei thought he would probably always remember Ben's name.

"Anyway"—Ben returned to his shave—"it's good to see you again. And hey!" He pointed at the counter with his blade. "Sinks!"

The thirty miles since Alexei had last seen Ben had not been the best thirty miles of his life. Past the initial triumph of not getting bitten by a rattlesnake, Alexei's body was full of more aches than he had ever before experienced. His shoulders and hips were bruised from the weight of his pack, his pale face sunburned no matter how often he slathered on sunscreen, his feet blistered and painful even though the guy at REI had assured him they wouldn't be. He had been so enthusiastic, that guy, about how with the right shoes, one wouldn't get blisters, no matter how far you were traveling.

Alexei had spent the last twenty miles or so wishing he could go back to REI and have a serious conversation with that guy. He imagined most of the conversation would simply involve Alexei crying, while the REI guy stood there looking ruggedly handsome and upbeat, like any human who had ever been employed by REI. But for some reason, Alexei liked picturing it anyway.

On top of it all, Alexei's stomach seemed to be rejecting the PCT entirely. He could barely keep anything down. And if there was one thing you needed on a long-distance hike, it was calories. He hadn't planned on making this side trip to Idyllwild, several miles off the official trail, but the prospect of real, freshly prepared food at the restaurants here had proven too great. Hence, his current arrival at the restroom of Tommy's Kitchen. And while he knew it was the right decision, he'd still been frustrated with himself, disappointed, the whole side trail down. Traveling to Idyllwild would set him back half a day, at the least.

Yet when Ben smiled at him and said, *Sinks!*—improbably, the corner of Alexei's mouth couldn't help but twitch into its own half smile. Sinks truly were exciting when you'd spent the last four days walking through the desert with barely a single freshwater source available.

It also felt like a funny echo of their first monosyllabic conversation. *Snake.*

Alexei had never been able to master the art of casual conversation, with anyone, really, but especially when it came to objectively handsome men. But maybe, just maybe, he could handle these single-word discussions with Ben.

"Sinks," he agreed. And then, after another moment of realizing he had likely been staring at Ben's half-shaven face too long, he added, "Okay, well. I'm going to use the restroom now."

Embarrassment swept in as soon as the words left his mouth, the tips of his ears warming as it occurred to him that this had likely not been a completely necessary thing to say.

But Ben held both hands up in the air. The grin on his face spread. There was a small, straight gap between his lower front teeth.

"Toilets!" Ben shouted, jubilant.

Alexei stared at that gap in Ben's teeth. His stomach gave a sharp, painful tug.

Hunger pangs, probably.

"Toilets," he agreed.

"And trash cans! Man." Ben returned to his shave. "Bathrooms. Fucking incredible."

"Um." Alexei's shoulder hit the corner of the closest stall as he backed up. "Yes."

And then he swiftly turned and hustled into the next stall. Which he barely fit into, with his pack. After one, two, three—oh, and four—loud bangs against the sides of the stall, he finally successfully dropped the pack off his shoulders. He only hung his head in his hands for a few horrified seconds.

Luckily, two other men soon entered the bathroom, chatting loudly with each other at the urinals, creating a distraction. And when Alexei returned to the sinks, Ben was focused on his phone, typing and smirking at its screen. He'd finished his shave, and it was striking, the clean jaw, the tender skin of his chin. His hair was down now, and that, too, looked remarkably clean, the shiny dark locks almost hitting his shoulders.

Alexei turned away to aggressively wash his hands, in an attempt to remove four days of desert grime from his fingernails.

Ben's fingernails, Alexei couldn't help but notice, looked as flawless as the rest of him, neatly trimmed, lacking any hint of dirt. Alexei's eyes wandered without his exact permission, studying the veins that popped along Ben's hands as he tapped at his phone, the way the tendons along his wrist and the muscles of his forearms stretched and relaxed with each subtle movement. He was wearing the same sky blue T-shirt he'd been wearing the other day, the only thing on his person that betrayed signs of the trail in its slight wrinkles, its faint streaks of dust.

Alexei remembered what the T-shirt had felt like, bunched in his hand.

He turned off the tap. He had planned on refilling his water pouches while he was in here, but he'd come back later. He had been wrong before. He did not possess the capacity to converse with Ben after all.

It was a relief to escape, he assured himself as he made a silent exit, unscathed by another one of those smiles.

He took a deep breath before he stepped outside.

The patio of Tommy's Kitchen was nearly full, but Alexei spotted a few empty tables in the back corner. He slid off his pack at the farthest one, rested it against the railing. Placed his order number at the edge of the table. Eased his swollen, blistered feet from his trail runners, slipping his toes into the cheap sandals he'd packed for camp. He'd been trying to give his feet breathing room anytime he took an extended rest the last few days, hoping it would help ease their pain.

Once he was settled, he cracked open the bottle of apple juice he'd grabbed from the cooler inside the restaurant. The first sip was even better than taking off his shoes. It was so cold and so sweet. Like the plums in the icebox. The first thing his body had accepted with joy since he'd stepped onto the trail. He almost cried.

"Hey, buddy."

Alexei choked on his next sip, so lost in his liquid sugar reverie that he hadn't realized someone had approached him. When he was able to look up, he recognized the dark beard on the tall, thick man hovering above him. That beard had brushed his face three days ago.

"Do you mind if we crash your party? Not many other seats left, unfortunately."

Oh. Alexei didn't really—but he supposed—

"Here, have a beer for your troubles." The bearded man placed a sweating can of Pabst Blue Ribbon next to Alexei's apple juice. With effort, Alexei resisted wrinkling his nose at it.

"Sure." He managed a small smile.

"Excellent. Hey, I'm actually glad to run into you again." The man plunked his pack down behind them with a *thunk*. "Sorry we kept on trucking so fast the other day. We were lookin' to make some big miles, and it was hot as hell out there; didn't want to lose our momentum, you know? Anyway, thanks for saving Ben from the rattler. I'm Faraj, by the way." He held out a calloused brown hand.

Faraj. That was right. Funny how Alexei hadn't been able to remember that.

"Alexei."

After they shook, Faraj pushed the neighboring table alongside

Alexei's, its legs stuttering across the worn wood of the patio. The other men who had been hiking with Faraj that day soon joined them, lining their own packs up against the railing, cracking open their own cans of beer. Including—because right, of course—Ben. Who sat directly across from Alexei, holding a plastic cup of water.

Alexei swallowed. His plan to eat real food in Idyllwild while feeling sorry for himself was turning into...not that. But this was okay. He would have to talk to strangers more in his new life, as Alexei 2.0. He could do this.

The other men introduced themselves—a Black man with short locs, Ryan; a sunburnt redhead, Tanner—and their food arrived shortly thereafter, cutting off the need for conversation. Everyone at the table had ordered burgers, except for Alexei, who had a turkey club. Ben had added on a salad; Ryan had ordered onion rings for the table. It was all greasy and fresh, a marvel after four days of granola bars and freeze-dried meals, and Alexei's social anxiety settled as he ate.

Halfway into the meal, Ben caught Alexei's eye. He held up a crispy, golden steak fry with another gap-toothed grin.

"Fries," he said.

"Fries," Alexei agreed with a smile, more natural this time.

In fact, with each bite, Alexei felt something returning to himself. Energy. Gratitude. The belief he could keep walking without dying.

The bread of his sandwich was perfectly toasted, the tomato slices fresh and juicy. And the cheese—the *bacon*—

He tried to slow down. He hadn't eaten much at all in the last two days; didn't want to make himself sick. He tried to savor each remaining part of his meal, every fry, each delicious bite of sourdough. And he hadn't even yet picked up—

An idea. A small one, but one that still took effort.

He looked at Ben until Ben returned his gaze. Slowly, pointedly, Alexei lifted the pickle in his hand.

"Pickle," he said.

Ben's smile this time was gentle, almost intimate. Like Alexei had really earned it.

"Pickle," Ben agreed.

It was the best pickle Alexei had ever tasted.

He should have known the whole thing was too good to last.

"All right," Faraj said once his burger was demolished, leaning back and taking a long sip from his beer. "Ryan. It's time, man. Tell us what the hell happened with Leon."

Alexei studied the men at the table. Reached back in his memory and realized there had been another person, another part of their crew who had walked by when he first met them, who was missing.

Ryan started laughing, holding his stomach.

"Shit. I keep forgetting I haven't told y'all yet."

"Yeah, because you've been weirdly holding out on us all day," Tanner said.

"Well, it's a damn good story, and I was cranky as hell this morning," Ryan replied. "Wanted to wait until I could tell it good."

"You definitely were that," Tanner muttered as he loped an onion ring onto his finger.

"Screw you. Anyway, so last night. All you losers are sleeping." Ryan shoved his empty burger basket away, leaned his forearms across the table. "Somewhere towards midnight, I hear a noise coming down the trail."

Alexei's head started to buzz, an indistinct itch creeping beneath his skin.

He had felt good while they were eating. Had been able to handle the introductions. But as Ryan commenced his tale about how he and Leon had met a night hiker high on shrooms outside their campsite last night, Alexei began to dissociate from the conversation.

It was a familiar feeling. Alexei didn't *want* to be an antisocial person; he just . . . didn't have anything to say about shrooms. For so much of his life, he simply didn't have a lot to say about the things people around him often wanted to talk about.

Ben, for his part, didn't participate much in the conversation, either, sipping his water across from Alexei, occasionally distracted by his phone on the table. Alexei felt disappointed in himself as he became more and more uncomfortable, as the guys next to them became more and more animated—something about coyotes, and looking for aliens; Alexei had lost the thread. But he had been proud of himself for a minute there. Talking with a guy like Ben, even if it was only in small syllables. Feeling semicomfortable in his skin.

Now, all he could think about was getting away. Being alone again. He probably wouldn't even be able to muster a decent good-bye.

He was halfway into a mental spiral when he was saved by the call.

It was a fast, repetitive staccato, and it sounded like relief to Alexei's ears, something natural and pretty. He turned his head toward it, away from the conversation, away from Ben's smile, away from blisters and swollen feet, toward the lawn at the side of the patio, the large tree there. He focused on hearing the sound again, to make sure. If he had been alone, he would have brought out his monocular.

But bringing out his monocular seemed... not quite the thing to do, here, in this moment.

"Oh my God." Tanner covered his face with his hands. "Leon is such a fucking idiot."

Alexei's stomach started to churn. He prayed the food would settle.

The bird in the tree was a junco, he thought. Or, no. Hm. Maybe—

He closed his eyes to listen more closely.

CHAPTER TWO

B en knew he was in trouble the moment Alexei closed his eyes.
He had watched Alexei retreat further and further into himself as the meal wound down, as Ryan's story got more and more ridiculous. Had seen him look away into the distance a moment ago, furrow his brow in concentration. But when he tilted his head and closed his eyes—

He was listening to something, Ben thought. The bird, most likely, that was trilling in a tree next to the patio.

All the other fools at this table were laughing about being fools, and this guy—this gorgeous, kind of awkward guy who had saved Ben's life—was listening, hardcore, to a bird.

Ben had lifted his fork to finally make work of his salad, but he paused now, glancing around to see if anyone else was noticing the supremely hot guy who appeared to be meditating at the end of their table. Alas. Only him.

So Ben ate his salad. Stared at Alexei. Watched the sun dance across his eyelids, throw highlights in his very blond hair, along the honey-gold scruff that graced his chin.

He was distracted from the sight only when his phone buzzed on the table.

Julie: YAY BEN YOU'RE STILL ALIVE YAY

Julie: London says hi!

Julie: London is also currently being a giant stress monster and a pain in my fricking behind so I understand if you don't want to say hi back! I wouldn't!!

Smiling, Ben dropped his fork and picked up his phone.

Ben: hi London! *waves* Why are they being a stress monster?

Julie: they're trying to hire a director for the nonprofit. it's a whole thing

Julie: WOW okay they are not a fan of being called a stress monster

Julie: anyway, show me your grossest blister

Ben was actually doing decently in the blister arena these days. He had bit it a while back, though, near Warner Springs, where he'd first run into this group of guys. He'd landed awkwardly on his side on top of a log. He found the picture he'd taken of the bruise that had bloomed on his stomach and sent it to Julie. He had documented it for this exact purpose: impressing his best friend.

Julie: SAUCY, CARAVALHO

Julie: also—GNARLY. WELL DONE.

Ben glanced up from his phone just in time to see Alexei's eyelids finally blink open.

His phone buzzed again in his hand. But Ben couldn't look away, no matter how his brain yelled at him to do just that. When Alexei fully returned to the world of the living, turning his head toward the table again, Ben waited until he caught his eye. Smiled at him.

Alexei's face flushed, pink creeping around the edges of his sunburn, like he'd been caught doing something naughty.

His eyes were so blue. Like the sky above the Cumberland River on a sunny summer day.

Ben used every ounce of restraint he possessed to keep himself from plopping his chin on his palm and fluttering his eyelashes at him.

Another buzz from his phone, and Ben finally looked down. The newest text was from his mother, in response to a photo he'd sent of the sunset last night over the Coachella Valley: cacti and Joshua trees surrounded by peachy-golden light.

Ma: Oh, Bento. It's gorgeous.

Those shimmery still-typing dots appeared. And disappeared. Another dot party. And gone.

Ben frowned.

Finally—

Ma: Please be careful.

A lump formed in Ben's throat. She'd finished every text exchange with him over the last two weeks this way. Every time, Ben could hear the restraint in the words, how hard she was trying. Typically, Iris Caravalho did not bite her tongue.

God, he missed her.

He missed Ma, and Dad, and Julie, and his baby sister Carolina, and his old roommate Khalil, and London, and practically everything about Nashville, Tennessee.

Another text popped up, from Jeremy, an old coworker from the coffee shop. The one who had hiked the Appalachian Trail shortly before getting hired, who never shut the fuck up about it, who had planted the seeds of this trip into Ben's brain years ago.

He'd sent Jeremy the same photo he'd sent Ma, of the Coachella sunset.

Jeremy: fuck yeah, man. you're doing it

Ben blew out a breath.

In truth, the seeds of this hike had been in Ben's brain for a long time. Jeremy's incessant storytelling about the AT only helped germinate them. He had been a rambunctious kid, full of too much energy, barely contained in his small body. All the Caravalhos were full of restless energy, in a way, but while his older brother Tiago had put his into sports, and Carolina had put hers into ruthless academics, Ben had bloomed in the outdoors. He felt truly, fully at ease only when he was on the move in the open air. Exploring. Discovering.

Once he grew past the age where playing in the dirt wasn't an acceptable form of daily activity, though, his restlessness had amplified in other, less cute, unhealthier ways. Almost the entire decade of his twenties had been a string of bad decisions: failed relationships, missed family obligations, messy hookups. Strings of jobs that paid the bills but didn't satisfy much else.

Until two years ago, when Ben had finally been able to focus enough to go back to school and get his nursing degree. Which he was proud of. He had worked harder than he'd ever worked at anything to get that degree, and he was excited to start a legit career he truly cared about.

He was also nervous as hell.

So when he passed the NCLEX, instead of applying to jobs right away, he came here first. To the West Coast, the PCT, an outdoor adventure unlike any he'd ever experienced before. One last chance, on the precipice of his thirtieth birthday, to get his restlessness out. To commit to better decisions. To see something new, something grand, while he prepared his new, responsible life.

Ben stared at that text a few minutes longer.

Jeremy was right. Of course Ben missed Nashville. He was tripping over logs and barely avoiding getting bitten by rattlesnakes. Questioning, most days, whether he'd actually make it all the way to Canada.

But damn, at least right here, right now—he was doing it.

"All right, boys." Faraj stood from his chair, its legs scuttling backward. Ben startled, realizing he'd been as lost in his phone as Alexei had been with his birds. "We should get a move on if we're hoping for twenty-two today. And hopefully catch up with Leon at some point, the dumb fuck."

Ben held in a sigh. These guys were all right, but they were gung-ho thru-hikers, into making big miles every day. Honestly, Ben thought Faraj was being a little wild, trying to push for a twenty-two on a day when they'd already lost a lot of time walking into town. But Tanner and Faraj had both had resupply boxes to pick up from the post office here, and Ben never said no to the chance of hitting up real food and bathrooms.

But now that the rich food was settling in his stomach—now that he'd had decent service for the first time in a week and could reconnect with his people—Ben didn't see what the big rush was.

Tanner and Ryan collected their packs. Faraj gathered everyone's empty cans. Until he got to Alexei's.

"Cool, man." He placed it back in front of Alexei after picking it up and feeling its weight. "Take your time. Maybe we'll see you out there?"

A crease appeared in Alexei's forehead, but he smoothed it away as quickly as it had appeared.

"Yeah." He clearly forced a smile. "Thanks."

Ben took another sip of water. This poor guy probably didn't even drink beer.

Tanner, Ryan, and Faraj clicked hip and shoulder belts into place.

"You all right there, Ben?" Ryan asked after a minute.

It was a fair question. Ben himself didn't quite know what he was doing, exactly, as he continued to sit where he was. Probably making a bad decision. The exact kind of bad decision he'd come to the PCT to finally start avoiding.

Because 95 percent of Ben's bad decisions usually started with beautiful men.

But... it was so nice here at Tommy's Kitchen. Watching Alexei. Listening to birds.

So Ben kept sitting anyway.

"I think I'm gonna rest awhile longer. You guys go on ahead. I'll catch up."

"All right, man." Faraj nodded, unbothered. Hiker groups came and went all the time on the PCT. "See you soon."

Ben moved his empty salad plate to the side. Stacked his sandwich basket on top of Alexei's.

The air around them felt different after the others had gone. Quieter. Closer.

Alexei's eyes darted toward him, then away, hands fidgeting. Ben kept thinking about the way he had half smiled at Ben in the bathroom, almost like he was confused that he was smiling. The serious look on his face when he'd said, with gravitas, *pickle*.

He remembered, too, the way Alexei's arm had felt across his chest, strong, stable. The frown that had been on his face when he'd scolded Ben about his earbuds. It had been so sincere, as if Alexei was truly worried for Ben's well-being, a stranger he'd just met, that it had made Ben laugh.

Ben had probably been in trouble, he thought now, since before that bird started singing.

He was about to say something to make Alexei feel more at ease when Alexei shoved the PBR across the table.

"Do you want this? I'm actually not that big of a beer person."

Ben took the can but waited to take a sip.

"What were you listening to out there?" he asked instead.

"Pardon?" Alexei blushed again.

"Out there." Ben motioned with a nod of his head toward the tree in the yard. "While the guys were busy talking nonsense, you spaced out and were listening to something. I assume a bird."

After a moment, Alexei answered, slow and careful.

"Chipping sparrow." He swallowed. "At least, I think so."

Ben leaned back in his chair. This was what he had always loved most. Meeting new people. Finding out what made them tick. It was what he loved most about nursing. People told you so much, if you were ready to listen.

"Tell me about the chipping sparrow," he said, finally taking a sip of the beer.

And before he answered, Alexei watched Ben take that sip.

Alexei's very blue eyes undoubtedly lingered on Ben's mouth.

Which was…an unexpected development.

Alexei looked away, clearing his throat.

"Its call is a trill. Repetitive, long. They're common all over North America, but are mostly migratory in the US. So they could maybe be starting to migrate north at this time of year, or we could be close enough here to their nesting grounds in Mexico." He paused. "Or it could've been a dark-eyed junco. I didn't get to see it. I like juncos more, actually."

Damn. Damn, damn, dammit.

Alexei had undoubtedly stared at Ben's mouth.

And Alexei was undoubtedly a *nerd*.

It was like a one-two punch. Ben's heart flapped helplessly in his chest. Like a big, dumb gay bird.

Ben was in so much trouble.

"Why do you like juncos more?" he asked anyway.

"Their markings can vary a lot, but in general, I find dark-eyed juncos...prettier. Than chipping sparrows."

Alexei hung his head. Examined a thread on his shirt.

Ben was quiet a moment. Ignored his responsible brain, currently shouting inside his skull that if he moved his ass right now, he could still catch up with Faraj. Let that word, *prettier*, said in Alexei's deep, serious voice, roll around in his head instead.

"I'm sorry about those guys," he said eventually, "if they made you uncomfortable at all."

Alexei shrugged. "Are they not your friends?"

"I only met them at Warner Springs. They're good guys, decent to hike with. That story Ryan told really wasn't typical." He took another sip of PBR. "But I wouldn't call them close friends of mine, no. Are you hiking with anyone?"

"No."

Ben drained the beer while a silence settled over the table. Alexei seemed to relax after a bit. Leaned over to his pack, dug out a journal and pen. Started scribbling words on a blank page while Ben thought about what to do here.

If only Alexei hadn't looked at his mouth like that. If only Alexei weren't so beautiful, and strange, and intriguing, the answer would be easier.

He probably could still catch up with Faraj.

Ben added the empty can to their stack of dishes. Crossed his arms over the table.

"How would you feel about walking together for a while?"

Alexei didn't look up. Tapped his pen against the paper.

"I'm not the best conversationalist."

Ben smiled. He'd gotten that.

"After seventy miles with those guys, I could use a bit of silence." Which was true. Ben didn't mind silence. His blood pressure already felt lower, his mind quieted, in the fifteen minutes he and Alexei had sat alone at this table together.

"I have to refill my water. And do some first-aid things."

Ben shrugged, his grin growing. "I'm tired as hell, man. Let's stay here all day."

That crease reappeared in Alexei's brow. "Oh. Well, I didn't budget for a hotel here. I'm already kind of off track—"

Ben cut him off with a gentle laugh. "No, I'm just saying, take your time. I'm good if you're good." After Alexei didn't respond, he tried to put care into his voice when he asked, "Are you good? You don't have to hike with me."

Because this was the most important bit, really. What Alexei wanted.

Alexei was quiet a long time.

Finally, softly, he said, "I'm good."

Ben worked to make his smile slow and steady.

"Let's clear the table; you can do what you need to do. Meet by that tree whenever you're ready?"

Alexei nodded. Five minutes later, Ben settled himself at the base of said tree, passing the time by convincing himself that hiking with Alexei was totally, maybe, possibly, most likely not a bad decision. Probably.

He also stared at his phone, willing a text from Carolina to come through while he still had service.

Even though he knew she was probably still in fifth period at East High. AP Gov. And while his baby sister rarely broke the rules, she *really* didn't break the rules in her favorite class.

He chatted with Julie instead, about her annoying coworker Lorraine, about London and their new nonprofit summer camp for LGBTQ kids, about London's partner Dahlia who had recently moved to town. It made him feel at home, talking to Julie. By the time Alexei arrived, Ben felt almost fully himself for perhaps the first time since starting the trail. The beer had given him the slightest buzz. It was nice to have a moment alone.

And then Ben put down his phone, and looked up.

It was unfortunate, really, seeing him again from this angle. Eye level with Alexei's impressive thighs. He was tall, Alexei; his broad shoulders hovered above Ben in a way that made Ben's mind go immediately quiet, his stomach quiver.

Ben hauled himself up from the ground.

Good decisions.

He was going to make sure this was a good decision.

As they left the streets of Idyllwild, Alexei didn't speak, and Ben kept his eyes steadfastly to himself. He focused instead on his shins protesting the unforgiving pavement, on the sounds of civilization, bit by bit, fading behind them.

When they were almost out of town, Ben stopped.

"You hear that?" The call was high-pitched. Sweet sounding.

Alexei listened for a moment, brow furrowed. And then he said, "California towhee."

Ben grinned. Remarkable.

A bit of quiet. Some lessons on birds. Before eventually, Ben was sure, Alexei would beg off, and Ben would meet back up with Faraj.

Where could the harm be in that?

CHAPTER THREE

A lexei was not panicking.

Okay. He was panicking a little.

Fine. He was panicking a lot.

It had been unlike him to agree to this. It just...it had been impossible to say no to that smile.

Plus, Ben had listened so kindly to Alexei's ornithological knowledge. No one ever cared about Alexei's ornithological knowledge. Well, except for his dad, as his dad was the one who had taught him bird calls in the first place. Which was a topic—a great big *pinch*—for another time.

But as Alexei and Ben hiked farther away from Idyllwild, back toward the PCT and the sandy, rocky forest surrounding Mount San Jacinto, Alexei assured himself his wish for 2,500 miles of peace and quiet was still, in fact, on track.

Because as they walked mile after mile, Ben proved he had meant what he'd said, back at Tommy's Kitchen. That he was okay with silence.

He stopped every now and then to take pictures with his phone. Exchanged friendly greetings with other hikers they passed by. Hummed to himself, sometimes, which should have annoyed Alexei, but somehow he only found it endearing. They shared a few more five-syllables-or-less conversations.

"Great tree," Ben stopped at one point to say, staring up the thin trunk of a lodgepole pine.

Alexei was starting to feel a little silly about this game, at this point, but the thing was, it *was* a great tree. The way it reached so valiantly toward the sky. Any tree that existed in the desert seemed a bit of a miracle to Alexei. So...

"Great tree," he agreed.

Other than these brief cameos of spoken language, though, Ben seemed right as rain, walking in absolute quietude with Alexei.

It was a little weird.

Every moment, Alexei's brain filled with questions.

Starting with, *Who are you and what is even happening?*

Also: *I have enjoyed staring at the backs of your calves. Did you know?*

Alexei couldn't quite figure out why Ben hadn't kept hiking with Faraj and the other guys in the first place. Why he had stayed at the table. Why he was here, now, with him.

Third question: *Seriously, who are you?*

The questions continued to build that night as they set up camp together, just off the trail. As Alexei stared into the darkness from the comfort of his sleeping bag, after his nightly prayers. Knowing Ben was on the other side of Alexei's tent, asleep in his own.

It wasn't bad, he had to admit. Knowing someone else was out there.

Maybe it was okay not to be alone. If only for a little while.

When Alexei awoke the next morning, he wondered, for a moment, if he had hallucinated the previous day. But when he stuck his head out of his tent, there was Ben, sitting on the hard ground. He looked up, grinning with those sleepy, chocolate eyes, like there was nowhere else he'd rather be. He was wearing a navy hooded sweatshirt that was too big for him, bunching and billowing at his wrists.

Alexei allowed himself, for a tiny moment, the fantasy of crawling over and resting his head in Ben's lap.

"Morning," Ben said.

"Morning," Alexei replied. And then, "Coffee." He pointed to the steaming mug in Ben's hands. This didn't really make sense in the rules of the game, because Alexei actually hated coffee, and in his head, one only nonsensically said five-syllables-or-less to the other person when it was a mutually enjoyable thing. But he said it anyway, because he knew Ben would say—

"Coffee!" Ben agreed, lifting his mug with a smile.

And somehow, a half-asleep Ben smile was even more charming than a fully awake one.

Alexei turned and walked into the manzanita.

When he returned from his morning business, Ben was standing, stretching his arms high above his head, eyes closed to the lightening sky. His sweatshirt had risen with the movement, exposing a small ribbon of smooth stomach and dark hair.

Alexei closed his eyes and asked a small question of God. He knew he had to get used to meeting new people, that a bit of companionship was not bad. Good practice for Alexei 2.0.

But did it have to be *this person*? This cheery, handsome specimen of a person?

God, shockingly, did not answer.

"Ready to go?" Ben asked once they had packed up camp, Ben's instant coffee consumed, Alexei's breakfast of oatmeal shoved down his throat with minimal nausea.

"Yeah." Alexei attempted a smile. "Let's go."

He could do this.

Really, he rationalized as they began to walk in silence once more, it wasn't the most soundproof plan in general, walking through the middle of the desert with a person you knew absolutely nothing about, was it? He should ask the questions in his head so they could establish at least a few baseline facts about the other. Whom Alexei should contact if Ben happened to topple off the side of a ridge. Or if Ben was allergic to anything. What was his last name? Why was he hiking the PCT? How much of the trail was he hiking? How long did he expect to hike with Alexei, exactly? Where was he from? Was he gay?

Okay! Perhaps not all of these questions were relevant. And obviously Ben wasn't gay. He'd fit in naturally with those other very straight seeming guys at Tommy's Kitchen. *Alexei* was being super gay, but this was fine, too; he would analyze this surprising level of gayness later in his journal, where he had planned to process all of his gay feelings anyway. Everything was still going according to plan.

Except life in the desert, again, foiled his best intentions.

The day started in a steady climb, forcing Alexei's energy to be refocused on the weight of his pack, his pacing, the air wheezing through his lungs. And he didn't want to open up a round of friendly, normal, not overly gay questioning when he was out of breath. By the time they stopped beside a boulder to stare down at Tahquitz Rock—a bright pinnacle of granite rising above a canopy of conifers, the whole scene sweeping and humbling—Alexei wondered if it was too late. If the silence had stretched too long and everything was weird again.

But no. He had to ask something. He *had to*. They had been walking together for *hours*; it didn't even make sense; how was Ben so relaxed!

"What's your favorite color?" Alexei blurted out.

Because of course. The one question that finally popped out of his mouth was the one most commonly asked of kindergarteners. Cool. Awesome. This was great.

But Ben only looked at him with a smile and said, "Blue."

And then Alexei realized that Ben's sweatshirt was navy. His T-shirt, sky blue. His tent was blue. Even the mug he'd drunk his morning coffee out of had been... blue.

Alexei finally got the nerve to ask Ben a question, and he asked the one question he *already knew the answer to*.

"What's yours?" Ben asked as he turned, striding back onto the trail, his shoulder accidentally brushing Alexei's arm.

Alexei walked behind him after a beat, after his arm had stopped tingling. He stared at the back of Ben's head, at the dark hair sticking messily out of the hat Ben occasionally wore to keep the sun out of his face, and Alexei wondered what it would feel like if he reached out a hand and plunged his fingers into it, and probably, it took him too long to answer, "Green."

"Solid choice," Ben said. Alexei wondered if he should clarify, explain that while he actually found some shades of green hideous, his true favorite color was, specifically, the color of moss in a Northwest forest. Which was a green so bright, sometimes it almost seemed to glow.

But Ben didn't say anything else, and the words wouldn't have come out right anyway, because they never did, so after that solid failure of a conversation starter, Alexei clamped his mouth shut.

The questions kept dancing in his head anyway.

When they stopped to slip microspikes over their shoes after spotting patches of icy snow, Alexei was absently munching on a bag of nuts, staring into space and wondering what Ben's favorite class had been in school, before he even realized the entire atmosphere around Ben had changed.

Alexei almost choked on a cashew when he heard Ben clear his throat.

"I feel I should tell you," Ben said, the first words he had spoken in an hour, "that I am a bit nervous about the snow."

Alexei looked at him, more surprised to hear Ben's voice than anything, and that was when he saw it. Ben's jaw was clenched, those open, joyful eyes now reserved.

The snow indicated they'd reached Fuller Ridge, a notoriously tricky stretch near the peak of San Jacinto. Being anxious about the snow was natural—Alexei himself wasn't necessarily excited—but

Alexei was thrown by this sudden evidence that Ben was not perfect. What a dangerous thing to know.

"Yeah?" was all Alexei could think to say.

"I'm from Nashville." Ben shrugged. "And it does snow in Nashville, sometimes. But I've never *hiked* on snow before. You know, like, on the side of a mountain. So."

Nashville! He had thought Ben had a slight accent. Fascinating, though. Alexei desperately wished he had access to his computer. He could mark a check box in his spreadsheet of Ben Questions.

"If it makes you feel better," he said, "I'm terrified of the desert."

Ben turned toward him, and Alexei could tell this fact *did* make Ben feel better. Because he was grinning again. Which made the admission 100 percent worth it. Alexei felt almost proud of himself for creating that grin.

"I've found it to be almost absurdly beautiful myself," Ben said.

Alexei remembered a road trip his family had taken when he was in the fifth grade, from Vancouver, Washington, to Salt Lake City. How much of those twelve long hours in the car had been consumed by flat, barren landscapes. It had been the first time Alexei felt that sense of unease about open spaces, the lack of anything between the soil and the sky leaving his skin hot and uncomfortable.

"It is. Beautiful," Alexei confirmed after a moment. "It's just that . . . I'm from the Northwest, and I need . . . trees. Big ones. Like, everywhere."

Ben smiled, as if Alexei had not just sounded like a doofus. Alexei's feelings about nature always sounded better in his head, or when he wrote them down, when he had time to find the right words. Out loud they came out like such: Birds are pretty. I like trees!!

Ugh.

"I'm stoked to see the Northwest," Ben said, genuine and kind, sounding close to Relaxed Ben again. Which was a relief. Still, Alexei glanced at him, concerned.

"There's going to be a lot of snow between here and there."

Ben breathed out, nodding.

"Better get on with it then."

At first, the snow was a hassle. The snowbanks came and went, sometimes at surprising heights, requiring Ben and Alexei to climb up and down their sides like stairs. Larger patches obscured the trail, making the transition back to dry land confusing. On open passes under the high sun, the snow's brightness made them squint, while furious swarms of insects buzzed around their faces. When it hid underneath the shelter of trees, it was icy.

But after the heat and dust of lower elevations, the coolness of the snow was also wondrous. Every now and then, Alexei removed the red bandanna he wore around his head to keep sweat from getting in his eyes, and rolled it around in the snow. Returning the wet, cool bandanna to his skin brought an almost painfully enjoyable relief. Another bit of surprising grace, here in the middle of the desert.

The snow slowed their pace, but it was doable.

Until they came to the last stretch of the ridge.

The trail wrapped its way along a steep path, yards from the very top of the pass, and it was completely covered in white. One slippery misstep would send a person careening down a slope that appeared to end in large, sharp rocks at the bottom. A bottom that looked awfully far away from here.

Ben and Alexei paused on the last bit of visible dirt trail before the snowy expanse began. Alexei stuck his trekking poles in the ground, leaning his weight forward, examining the path ahead. It was a long stretch of snow. They'd have to take it slow and steady.

He looked behind him at Ben, who had taken a small step backward. And the look on Ben's face wasn't low-level anxiety anymore.

This was wide-eyed, pale-cheeked, all-out terror.

"So this is what we'll do," Alexei said, his mind reverting instantly to a need to help, to problem-solve, to calm. All verbs he had been good at once, when he had still been a good older brother. When he had helped lead camping trips with his youth group. When he had run varsity cross-country in high school, helping the younger runners get over their struggles and disappointments.

"I'll go first." He forced his voice to sound as confident as he could. "We'll face the snowbank, walk sideways so we don't have to look down. We have our spikes on and it looks pretty well packed from other hikers. We'll take it as slow as we need to. It'll be okay."

Ben swallowed. Gave the barest hint of a nod.

Alexei turned back around. If he'd learned anything about perilous situations in the outdoors over the years, it was that hesitation would only make it worse. Alexei stuck a trekking pole in. Took a step out onto the ridge.

The trick was not to think too hard, never to pause too long.

But Alexei was forced to pause when he realized after a few steps that Ben was still standing at the edge of the snow, yet to make a move.

"You got this," Alexei said. When Ben still didn't move, he thought about what Alina would have needed in this moment. "Ben. Look at me." He waited until Ben's brown eyes met his, still too wide with fear. "It's not too slippery. Trust your feet. Trust your poles. Don't look down."

Ben nodded, a little harder this time. He took a deep breath and stepped onto the snow.

And stopped.

Alexei waited.

Ben stepped his left foot toward Alexei.

He stepped it back and shook his head.

"I don't know if I can do this." Ben's voice was pinched, small in the wind. It sounded unnatural to Alexei's ears. Like there was an entirely different person standing at the edge of the snowbank than the one he'd met twenty-four hours ago in Idyllwild, shouting about the glories of sinks.

"Ben." Alexei decided to try a new tactic. He opened up the spreadsheet of questions in his mind. "Tell me what you are most excited to see or do when you finish the trail."

Ben was silent a moment before he closed his eyes. Oh no. Closing your eyes on a steep slope of snow was not a great idea.

"Ben," Alexei said again. "Open your eyes. Look at me."

"Ma." Ben snapped his eyes open. Cleared his throat. "My mom," he said, louder. And then, glancing nervously down the slope, "She would be so fucking pissed at me right now."

Alexei took a deep breath himself, another *pinch* hitting his chest. But this wasn't about him.

"All right," Alexei said. "Focus on what's in front of you, and only on what's in front of you. One step at a time." He took another step left. "What else?"

Ben followed, taking a step forward. He completed the movement without backtracking this time.

"Carolina. My baby sister."

Alexei took a step. After a minute, so did Ben.

It would take an hour at this rate to reach the end of this ridge. But if it took an hour, it took an hour.

"Great," Alexei said. "You're doing great. What else?"

"My dog."

Goodness. Alexei had not even contemplated, in his endless list of wonderings about Ben, the possibility of pets. But of course Ben had a dog.

"Tell me about your dog." Alexei took another step.

"Her name's Delilah. A Rottie. I love her."

Step.

"What else?"

"My brother. Tiago."

A pause.

"Don't ever tell Tiago I listed Delilah before him."

Alexei smiled into the snow. And took a step.

It was slight, but he thought Ben was sounding steadier.

He also no longer needed prompting.

"My dad. And my cousins. I have twelve of them, so you probably don't need to know all their names."

"We have time, Ben," Alexei said, concentrating on his trekking poles. "How about this: one step for every cousin."

Ben complied immediately.

"Beatriz." Step. "Adriano..."

Alexei felt breathless by the end of the list, and he hadn't even been talking.

And the roll of Ben's tongue on some of those names, different from his regular accent, had been intriguing to Alexei's gut. He didn't even know what the accent was, felt too stunned to ask.

"Fuck, I have a lot of cousins. Are we at the end yet?"

Alexei glanced to his left. They were about halfway.

"No. But that was good. That was great. Keep going."

"My friends. Julie. Khalil. Laynie Rose."

They took a few steps in silence. Alexei wanted to prompt him again, keep the conversation and their progress going, but he was starting to feel his own blood pressure rise, the shaky exhaustion in his legs climbing to consciousness in his brain.

And then, thank God, Ben kept talking.

"And I am going to crush a Big Mac." He laughed. "How gross. I never thought *that* would be what I crave. Factory farms win, I guess."

"I want Taco Bell," Alexei blurted.

"*Yes*, holy shit, Taco *Bell*," Ben enthused. "I want a Crunchwrap Supreme. And a Cheesy fucking Gordita Crunch."

Alexei smiled.

"Tell me what other gross things you want, Lex." Step. "Does anyone ever call you Lex?"

Alexei almost stumbled. Which wasn't helpful for his blood pressure. If he had helped Ben across this entire ridge only to be the one who actually tumbled into the abyss, he would be extremely displeased with God.

"No," he answered. No, no one had ever called him Lex. Alexei had never had a nickname in his life.

"Is it okay if I call you that?"

Lex.

The single syllable lit up pleasure centers in Alexei's brain he hadn't even known existed.

"Yes."

Step.

And then, to distract himself, because they were so close to getting off this ridge, he added, "I want those tiny tacos from Jack in the Box."

Good God. Why were tacos apparently the only thing Alexei could think about right now? Jack in the Box was objectively disgusting. He was losing his mind.

But Ben only laughed and said, with feeling: "Fuck yes, Lex."

And then—thank the heavens—they reached solid ground again. This was a fortunate development, because Alexei's watery legs almost gave out at *Fuck yes, Lex.*

Ben released a weird noise from his throat, like he was either going to shout or vomit. He took off his hat and leaned forward onto his trekking poles, hanging his head between them.

Alexei looked at him for a few seconds. How the sun highlighted cinnamon highlights in the hair Alexei had previously thought only brown. How the muscles in the back of Ben's neck were ... present.

"Shit." Ben looked up. "My legs are shaking. Can we rest for a second?"

Alexei looked at the muddy mess of a trail around them. He needed to rest, too, but there were no good options here. "Let's walk for a bit more. We'll go slow. Rest at the next decent spot."

Ben nodded and stood, breathing out. "Okay."

"See?" Alexei smiled at him while the fading adrenaline still gave him courage. "You did it."

Ben smiled back, lopsided and relieved.

"I did." And then, "You fucking saved my life again, man."

Alexei blinked. After an awkward moment of not knowing what to say, he turned back to the trail. He hadn't actually done much. Faraj likely would've gotten Ben across the snow faster.

He took a few steps down the trail.

"Hey," Ben said. "Lex."

Alexei stopped short. For some reason he'd thought the nickname had just been an adrenaline-fueled, trekking across a treacherous snowbank thing.

He turned.

"Thank you," Ben said.

"Sure." Alexei nodded.

"Sorry to tell you, but you're stuck with me until Canada now," Ben continued. "I am not doing that without you again."

Alexei stared at him. Ben was still leaning on his poles, gathering his strength. Clearly, the lack of oxygen at this elevation was affecting his brain.

And then Alexei heard a familiar call. He listened, letting it calm his pulse before he tilted his chin toward the slope. "Mountain chickadees down there."

Ben grinned. "Yeah?"

"Yeah. They're everywhere."

Alexei turned and walked until he heard the slosh of Ben's trail runners stepping through the mud behind him. He did not think about that Canada comment, or the muscles in Ben's neck, or the gap between his teeth.

Alexei walked down the ridge and thought very resolutely about nothing at all.

CHAPTER FOUR

A n hour later, they came across a small clearing that offered dry logs to rest upon. Ben almost shouted with relief when he saw it.

Except one of the blessed logs was already occupied by a small woman with light brown skin and short dark hair, head bent over a large sketch pad.

"Hi," Ben said gently, not wanting to startle her. "Do you mind if we join you?"

She did not look up from her drawing.

"Sure," she said, voice flat.

Ben liked to think he was pretty good at reading people's vibes. He'd met plenty of patients like this woman in his clinicals: people who did not give a flying fig about your small talk. They were his favorite.

But thank heavens this woman said yes. Ben was absolutely going to collapse face-first if he didn't get to sit down soon.

"Logs," he said to Alexei as he dropped onto one with a groan.

"Logs," Alexei agreed.

Alexei settled much more elegantly onto his own log, directly across from the woman. To Ben's surprise, Alexei stared intently at her, her sketch pad and scarred knees, the knit of her brow as she worked.

Every other time they'd met a stranger during the short time they'd hiked together, Alexei had appeared uncomfortable: shoulders stiff, avoiding eye contact. Ben was floored when Alexei asked, "Can I see what you're working on?"

The woman looked up. Gave Alexei a hard, assessing stare. He didn't flinch.

"Sure," she said, eyes back down on her work.

Alexei moved across the clearing. Sat right next to her, leaning in. "Wow," he breathed. "Gorgeous."

The woman paused the scratching of her pencil. Turned to him. "Let me see your hands."

Alexei held up both hands, palms flat. The woman squinted in inspection, making sure they were clear of grime. He flipped them, front and back, until with a small grunt, she nodded.

And handed over her sketch pad.

Alexei touched the pages with his fingertips, light and reverent, a faint smile on his face.

"My little sister likes to draw, too," he said, almost in a whisper, as if they were speaking in a church.

Ben realized then. How little he still truly knew about Alexei.

Which—well, obviously. They'd hardly talked. The interesting thing was, it wasn't simply that Ben had been trying to respect Alexei's space over the last two days, although he had. More than that, though, it was the truth that somehow Alexei's quiet had seeped into him.

And it was fantastic.

Even though Ben had been on the trail since the Mexican border, so many of those previous 150 miles had been spent in a state of semi-panic, his body trying to adjust to a harsh landscape he'd never experienced before, trying not to die, trying to keep up with the other, faster hikers he'd met up with.

It was only when Ben had started hiking with Alexei that he'd started to actually relax. Like he suddenly remembered why he had wanted to do this in the first place. Able, in Alexei's calm silences, to fully absorb the natural world around him. The curiosities of the desert, the wonder of it all. His mind free to wander wherever it wanted to go.

There had been moments, these last two days, when Ben hadn't felt weighed down by his past mistakes, by his worries about the future. Hadn't even thought about any of it. He'd only felt free. Like the kid playing in the dirt again.

But something about learning this—that Alexei had a little sister who liked to draw—made Ben snap out of it.

Alexei had even tried, hadn't he? To start a conversation? Back when he'd asked Ben's favorite color. Which had been—okay, kind of hilariously cute and random. But then Ben had seen this badass lizard run across the trail, which for some reason made him think about how he and Tiago would chase tadpoles at Old Hickory Beach when they were little, and his mind had wandered again.

He hadn't even asked, he realized now, in his snow-fueled fear back on the ridge, what Alexei's Taco Bell order was. Which was, frankly, an egregious oversight.

Alexei flipped through several pages of sketches before he turned toward the woman, who was sipping water, looking into the distance with an aloof look on her face.

"I'm Alexei," he said, holding out his hand. After a moment, she shook it.

"Ruby."

"Ruby, can I show these to Ben?"

When Ruby assented with a shrug, Alexei moved to Ben's log, sitting just as close as he had to Ruby, knees knocking into Ben's. It was like his excitement about the drawings made Alexei forget, momentarily, his discomfort with the human world. And for a wonderful moment, Ben was let into his orbit.

"Look at these yucca." Alexei pointed to the plant on the page, its sharp green blades surrounding large, creamy white blossoms. "And the yerba santa." Alexei flipped to another page, the cups of the purple-blue flowers splashed there in bright color, drawn with a slightly dreamy hand. Ben was impressed with the color—a full palette of drawing pencils weren't typical items found in a back-packer's pack—and with the fact that Alexei knew it was called *yerba santa*.

"Are you a botanist?" Alexei asked, looking back at Ruby. Who snorted a little, shook her head.

"I like plants," she said simply.

Alexei looked back down at the page. "An artist, then."

"It's a hobby."

Alexei's head jerked up again, a sharp frown on his face. Ben was reminded of when he had been scolded after the rattlesnake. "This is not a hobby, Ruby. D&D is a hobby."

"You play D&D?" Ben interrupted, fascinated.

Alexei glanced at him, ears pinkening. "Sometimes."

And as if he'd revealed too much, he moved away, back toward Ruby's log. Ben's knee immediately felt lonely.

"Do you have any books of your art I could buy when I get home?"

Ruby laughed at that. "No."

"Well." Alexei handed her back the sketch pad. "You should publish these."

Ben thought about how much Alexei had helped him back there on Fuller Ridge, how naturally he had talked Ben through it. How almost oddly sincere he was being to Ruby right now about her work.

He was a bit of a strange duck. Definitely a nerd.

But it was clear to Ben now. That mostly, Alexei was deeply kind.

Ruby studied him. After a moment, she said in a pained tone, "I have an Instagram."

"Oh." Alexei scratched at the back of his head. "I don't have one of those."

Ben bit his lip to hold back his smile.

Ruby only nodded. "Respect," she said.

Alexei's brow creased in thought before he marched over to his pack, still leaning against his abandoned log, and took out his journal. "Can you tell me your username?" he asked.

Ruby did. Alexei wrote it down.

"Thank you."

"Sure," Ruby said.

Alexei looked at the sky. The sun was beginning to stretch toward the horizon. "We should probably keep going," he said with a hint of regret. "Try to make it a little farther before we camp."

"Agreed." To the protest of his knees, Ben stood. He felt a little awed, and delighted, at how little he had been part of this entire interaction. He turned toward Ruby. "Do you want to hike with us for a while? If that's okay with you," he added with a glance at Alexei.

"Okay with me," Alexei said.

"No, thank you," Ruby answered. Another shrug. "I sort of fly solo."

"Respect." Ben grinned.

And Alexei sounded like he truly meant it when he agreed, "Respect."

They continued on, Ben in the lead. It was a pretty walk now, the wind calm, the path manageable, the late evening sun painting the desert hills in hues of ochre and rust. By the time they found a camping spot, a gem of a hidden clearing behind a small copse of pines, the sun had already disappeared behind those hills, the golden pastels at the horizon reaching toward a deeper blue at the top of the sky.

Quickly, before the dark descended, Ben and Alexei set up their tents, got out their tiny gas stoves to heat water for their dinners. Ben threw on his sweatshirt when the air cooled, slipped his feet into his camp sandals.

He was settled on the ground, sticking his spork into his mac-and-cheese-in-a-bag, when he decided to make his attempt. To see if he could get back in Alexei's orbit again.

"So you have a baby sister, too, huh?"

Alexei looked up from where he was rooting around in his own freeze-dried meal-in-a-bag.

"Yeah," he said with a ghost of a smile. "Alina. She's a paralegal in Portland."

"And that's where you live, too?"

A long pause.

"Yeah," Alexei eventually answered. "Although I'll be moving when I get back."

"Yeah? Where to?"

Another long pause.

"I don't know yet." Alexei bit his lip. "Was thinking I'd figure that part out while I'm out here."

Interesting.

"We're originally from Vancouver, though," Alexei added, "in Washington. Not the one in BC. It's a smaller city, right across the river from Portland."

"Cool." Ben took some more bites of mac and cheese. Waited to see if Alexei would reveal anything else. He was rewarded only a few minutes later.

"She's the only one who knows I'm here. Alina," Alexei clarified, staring down into his food. "Well, and you," he added with a glance toward Ben, a small smile on his face that Ben received in the very center of his chest. But—

"No one else?" he asked, careful and confused. He'd gathered Alexei wasn't super social, but damn. Everyone Ben knew was aware he was here. It was sort of a big deal, hiking thousands of miles, being gone from civilization for months. Even if Alexei wasn't hiking the whole trail, being here at all was an accomplishment. Hell, making it across Fuller Ridge was an accomplishment. Ben was pissed he didn't have service, so he couldn't text Julie and Carolina all about it right now.

Alexei crumpled his trash, stuffed it into a Ziploc bag. Sat with his arms clasped around his knees. His forehead had that signature furrow; Ben could tell he was pondering something.

"Six months ago," Alexei said slowly, "I came out to my parents as gay."

Ben bit his tongue. Held his breath, stomach tensed.

"I was raised in a very conservative, religious family, so I knew…" The furrow deepened. It was getting darker; Alexei's face was half hidden in shadow. Ben wished he could see those summer blue eyes more clearly. "My parents said that if I actually planned on living that way…" Alexei trailed off again. Ben wanted to reach across the clearing, squeeze his hand, tell him he was doing just fine. "Anyway, they cut me off."

"You mean, like, financially?"

Ben was pretty sure that wasn't what Alexei meant. He didn't even know why he'd asked it. It had just been a funny way to phrase it, and damn, Ben felt sick.

"No." Alexei's voice sounded calm, steady now. "My family believed you earned what you needed. They never gave me money for anything past high school."

"So when you say they cut you off…"

"They said I'd no longer be their son."

"Lex." Ben's voice sounded the opposite of steady and calm, tinny and far away to his own ears.

But Alexei only dropped his head back. Looked up at the emerging stars.

Ben licked his lips, trying to figure out what to say. He should know what to say here. "You said this was six months ago?"

Alexei nodded.

"And you haven't talked to either of your parents since?"

"No. Which is why they don't know I'm doing this. Which feels a little strange, since my dad was the one who got me into hiking as a kid." Alexei swallowed, head falling toward his chest again, the slightest dash of emotion flashing across his face before he smoothed it away. "I still talk to Alina sometimes. I don't know if they know she still talks to me. She feels…confused, I think. I feel bad that she's in the middle."

"God. Lex," Ben said again. *Shit.*

"I felt like an awful person at first. Like I was essentially choosing the ability to have sex over my family, and who does that?"

Ben almost fell over.

"Alexei, that's not—"

"I know, I know." Alexei waved a hand in Ben's direction. But Ben was deeply worried Alexei *didn't* know. That that wasn't how any of this worked at all.

"Then the company I worked for had a big merger. I got laid off, got a small severance. So I had some time on my hands, and thought this would be a good way to…work out some things for myself. So." His head dropped back again. "That's my story."

"God," Ben muttered. He could only stare at Alexei gazing serenely at the stars. Fuck, how hard must it have been for him to come out to his family? Had he only recently figured it out? Or had he always known, hiding his whole life, until he finally got the courage, and then—

The despair in Ben's gut began to bloom into a hot, heavy anger.

"My parents aren't bad people," Alexei said, as if he could sense the fire rapidly taking over Ben's senses and wanted to put it out. "They're not. I'm sure they're suffering, too. I know they loved me.

I'm more trying to figure out...how I feel about a world that can make them believe what they believe. That what they did was the right thing. And where I fit now, in that world."

Ben wanted to tell Alexei that he fit. That his parents were assholes. That he was gay, too.

Except Ben's entire system felt frozen. He knew, of course, that even with every corporation in America shooting rainbow confetti out of a cannon every June, things like this still happened all the time, but—hell. Would anything about Ben's experience actually help Alexei right now? *Hey, mate, I'm also a homosexual! Except the last time I went to church I think I was six years old and my family has always been super chill about everything. So. It gets better?*

"You know." Alexei faced forward again, hugged his knees tighter into himself. A small smile played at his lips. "It felt okay, telling you all that. I hope it was okay I told you all that."

"Yeah." Ben's voice came out as a croak. He swallowed. "Yeah, Lex. Thank you for telling me."

"Okay." Abruptly, Alexei unfolded himself, stood, and stuffed his hands in his pockets. "I'm going to go to sleep now."

He was still smiling somehow, but Ben could only nod.

Alexei walked toward his tent. Frantically, Ben tried to think of what to say to stop him. But after a few steps, Alexei turned on his own.

"Hey," he said. "What's your last name?"

"Caravalho. Why?"

"I figured we should know each other's full names. In case something happens on the trail and we have to contact someone."

Ben inhaled deeply through his nose. So cute and thoughtful. Ben wanted to punch Alexei's parents in the face.

"You can contact Iris Caravalho in Nashville if anything happens to me."

Alexei hesitated. "Your mom?"

Ben nodded.

"Is that . . . Spanish?"

"Portuguese."

"Oh. Sorry."

"Don't be sorry."

"You can contact Alina Lebedev in Portland if anything happens to me."

Ben nodded again. He was a nodding machine. "Alina Lebedev," he repeated.

Alexei had turned back, was a step from his tent, when Ben finally stumbled up.

"Listen," he said, stuffing his own hands in the pocket of his sweatshirt. That comment about last names was sinking in a bit more. Ben had known, from the moment they left Tommy's Kitchen in Idyllwild, that Alexei could take off at any moment. The dude, like Ruby, clearly liked being alone. But maybe, if he cared about Ben's last name, if he was thinking about looking out for each other on the trail, he didn't completely hate hiking with Ben.

And if he *hadn't* been hiking with Ben right now, he would be . . . what, hiking thousands of miles to punish himself for being gay? Being alone and sad and figuring out where to exile himself because his parents sucked?

No. That was a completely unacceptable prospect to Ben.

Hiking was a weirdly intimate thing to do with another person. But it really had felt easy with Alexei Lebedev from the start. Maybe, Ben thought, they had met again at Tommy's Kitchen in Idyllwild for a reason.

Ben just had to get Alexei to stay.

"I meant what I said earlier, on Fuller Ridge," he burst out. Even though he hadn't; anything he'd said on Fuller Ridge had been nothing but adrenaline, but he meant it now. "Can we make a pact? We don't have to walk all the way to Canada together. But unless we meet other people we want to hike with, we should stick together. There's no way I'm making it over snow again by myself, and Lex, you seriously shouldn't hike by yourself in the desert. Your fear of it is real; it's too risky to be out here alone. There was a day a few weeks ago, before Idyllwild, when I was hiking with those guys, and the only water source we passed all day was dried up. We would have been totally fucked if Faraj hadn't rationed out his water better than the rest of us, and we were able to share it until the next source."

Ben took a breath.

"Anyway," he said. "I'm just saying."

Alexei stared at him.

"At least through the desert," Ben said. "We should at least stick together through the desert."

Alexei's face twitched.

The desert went on for hundreds of miles. Ben knew this was...possibly a big ask.

He bit his lip, waiting.

And then—

"Okay."

It sounded uncertain, but Ben felt himself smiling like a dumbass anyway, his stomach finally lifting.

"Awesome. Night, Lex."

Ben clambered into his tent before Alexei could change his mind.

He still could change his mind, of course, the next day, or the day after that, or the day after that, and Ben would let him. He wouldn't actually hold Alexei Lebedev to anything he didn't want to do.

But Ben liked helping people, and he knew what he could do for Alexei now. He would curb his thirst for the guy—Alexei was processing heavy shit; he didn't need Ben's messiness. And Ben had promised himself he'd stay away from men for a while anyway. The trail wasn't for all that. The trail was for good decisions.

No, Ben wouldn't touch Alexei.

But he could be his friend.

He could show him that he could trust people. That the world Alexei's parents believed in wasn't the real world at all. At least, it wasn't the world that mattered. And there was so much good in the world that did.

Ben was still terrified of the snow. He missed his family all the time and he doubted, even on his good days, whether he would make it all the way through this thing.

But he knew he could show Alexei that.

CHAPTER FIVE

A crunchy peanut man, huh?"

Alexei looked down at the protein bar in his hand and shrugged.

"Most fat and most protein." While Alexei's stomach had settled since Idyllwild, he had yet to experience the hiker hunger he had read so much about. Most of the time, Alexei forced himself to eat only because he knew he needed the calories. With the exception of his trustworthy stash of gummy bears. But he knew he couldn't survive the PCT on gummy bears.

"I see your fatty protein, and I raise you"—Ben held up the shiny wrapper of his own protein bar—"deliciousness." He took a big chomp, spoke with his mouth full: "I fucking love these lady granola bars."

Alexei had already observed that Ben preferred the bars that were marketed toward women. Like everything about Ben Caravalho, it made Alexei want to smile uselessly into space for a long time.

"Is that your favorite flavor?"

"An excellent question, Lex." Ben swallowed before continuing. "This Peppermint Bark was, indeed, how they first sucked me in. But it was when I tasted Lemon Zest that I became a convert for life. I've been saving my Lemon Zests for special occasions out here, though."

Ben and Alexei were eating their protein bars under a scrubby patch of manzanita. After leaving the forested slopes of San Jacinto this morning, the trail had transitioned back into full-blown desert. While the open landscape offered dramatic views of the arid valley floor and surrounding San Gabriel Mountains, an angry, dry wind had whipped at their faces all day, the sun scorching and inescapable. Alexei desperately missed the comfort of trees.

At least he had the distraction of Ben.

Even though guilt had eaten at Alexei all morning. He hadn't truly meant it when he'd agreed to Ben's pact last night. Which was unlike him. Alexei Lebedev was not a liar anymore. But Ben had seemed almost nervous when he'd made his plea, strangely vulnerable in the moonlight for reasons Alexei didn't quite understand. And once again, it had been impossible to say no to that face.

Not that it hadn't been pleasant, walking all this time with Ben.

It simply wasn't what Alexei had anticipated, and Alexei liked sticking to his plans. He had things he had to think about, lists he had to narrow down. And, well. With Ben at his side, all Alexei found he could think about was . . . Ben.

It would all work out, though. Ben had said *unless we meet other people we want to hike with*. Ben was perhaps the most amiable person Alexei had ever met. He would find another group of hikers to join soon, and Alexei would pretend to do the same, assuring Ben he'd be safe in the desert, and they'd say a very nice good-bye. Meeting Ben Caravalho would be a wonderful story to look back on later. And it had been important, too, Alexei knew. He was proud of the fact that he'd told Ben everything he had last night, that he'd opened up to a stranger and the sky hadn't fallen. No, meeting Ben had given Alexei lots of moments to be proud of.

They called it *trail magic*, the things that appeared on the trail when you needed them most. Caches of water, snacks left at trailheads by local strangers out of the goodness of their hearts. People offering up their homes, giving rides for free.

Maybe meeting Ben was Alexei's first taste of magic.

"Like, not to be all men's rights about it," Ben went on as he crumpled the protein bar wrapper in his hand, "but I like happiness. I deserve the tangy refreshment of a Lemon Zest, too."

"I agree."

"I knew you would, Lex."

He had to admit, the *Lex* thing still got him. Every time Ben used it, this warm, funny buzzing flashed through Alexei's gut. The buzzing was a reminder of why, eventually, Alexei would have to leave this bit of magic behind.

"Oh man." Ben cracked his knuckles. "This dude looks *amazing*."

Alexei tore his gaze from Ben's face to see a beanpole of a man approaching down the trail. He slowed when he saw Ben and Alexei, taking off his hat to wipe at his forehead.

"Hey, man," Ben called out.

"Howdy ho, folks."

The man must have been in his seventies. One of those fit, tan seventy-somethings who hiked the Pacific Crest Trail instead of doing...whatever else seventy-somethings should be doing. Playing canasta with their grandkids. Donating to their local public radio station.

It took Ben approximately two minutes to discover that this particular seventy-something lived in New Mexico, was a retired real estate broker, and his name was Tumbleweed.

Except obviously this skinny white man's name was not *Tumbleweed*.

Trail names were bestowed on thru-hikers by other thru-hikers. Some people were real serious about them, but they stressed Alexei out a bit. He had no idea what kind of trail name someone would even think to call him. What one word could possibly sum up his essence.

He thought about how much the sun was making his skin itch

today. How much he had been randomly blushing in Ben's presence. Tomato, maybe. Or something about being quiet? Mouse.

Except Alexei didn't want to be Tomato Mouse.

He only liked Lex.

Anyway, the point was, Tumbleweed was a silly name.

And Ben had just learned this was Tumbleweed's second time thru-hiking the PCT. Because of course it was.

Alexei fiddled with his pack. He didn't know why he was thinking unkind thoughts about Tumbleweed.

He had never quite been able to figure it out, the science of why some strangers made him uncomfortable and some didn't. If he made a pie chart out of it, the Bens and Rubys of the world would be a tiny sliver, while the Tumbleweeds and the Farajs would make up most of the whole.

Ben let out a low whistle. Alexei looked up.

"How many sutures?"

"Sixteen."

Ben was examining a jagged white scar, far up on the old man's thigh. Tumbleweed let the thin fabric of his black shorts fall down again.

"And that was when I had to say good-bye to the Continental Divide. But the PCT keeps drawing me back somehow."

Ben was leaning forward, elbows on his knees, rapt, and—

Oh God.

Alexei shoved his trash into his pack.

He was totally jealous of Tumbleweed.

Alexei was acting delusional and ridiculous.

He needed to get back to hiking alone, like, stat.

"I've always wanted to go to Albuquerque," Ben was saying now, just like he'd said he was excited to see the Pacific Northwest, and okay, Alexei was spiraling. He yanked his journal out of his pack and tucked his head down. He'd learned it helped sometimes, when he started dissociating, to let himself focus on something that made him feel calm. Like lists.

He had notes to catch up on from yesterday anyway; it had been a big day, and talking to Ben at the end of it had wiped him out. He'd barely been able to stay awake for his nightly prayers once he'd collapsed into his tent. He scratched down the data he'd been trying to document each day.

> Miles hiked. Elevation gained/lost. Weather. Trail conditions.

Below each set of data points, he always left room for other notes, usually listed by bullet point. There were a lot of bullet points to fill in for yesterday.

- Ruby; yerba santa
- Fuller Ridge
- Lex
- Lots of chickadees
- Came out again

He paused here before he added, in a dash underneath:

> —Went better this time

Because Ben had treated him exactly the same all morning as he ever had. Like nothing had changed. It had felt…Alexei tapped his pen against the journal. Maybe he didn't have to summarize it in words. Even if he was possibly being delusional about Ben in general, he knew how that had felt.

Before he forgot the other thing he wanted to note, he flipped to the back of the journal. The list on the first back page was titled "Alexei 2.0."

Not many people got a chance to truly start over. But after Alexei had lost the foundation of his world—no parents, no church—he'd realized, eventually, that he should take advantage of this clean slate.

He wanted to be different, this time around. Braver. Happier.

Alexei added a new bullet point:

- Make an Instagram

And after some thought:

- Figure out what to post on Instagram

Ben and Tumbleweed were back to discussing Albuquerque real estate. Idly, Alexei flipped to the list he'd started a few pages behind "Alexei 2.0."

CITY IDEAS

Boston
Providence
Washington, DC
Ann Arbor
Pittsburgh
Ithaca
Chapel Hill
Madison

He'd been trying to think of a mix of larger cities, where he knew there'd be a variety of job options for a data analyst, and college towns, since he'd always kind of wanted to work at a university.

He dreamed, too, sometimes, of owning a small farm in the middle of Montana, Colorado, Vermont. Always having trees and bird calls close at hand.

But Alexei 2.0 was going to try not to isolate himself. Which he knew he would do if he wasn't near some kind of city center. So for now, the list was cities and towns.

The only other requirement, really, was that it be far away from the place he had always loved most.

"Anyway," Tumbleweed said loudly enough to snap Alexei's focus back to the world around him. "You boys take care of each other, you hear? This desert is no joke."

"We will; promise. Hope we run into you again sometime," Ben said.

"Absolutely." Tumbleweed tipped his hat. "You take care."

Then he was gone, floating easily on down the trail.

Rather like...a tumbleweed.

Darn it.

"Now *that* right there..." Ben leaned back behind the not-quite-shade of the manzanita. "That's why I want to go into geriatrics. Old people are the fucking best."

"Geriatrics?"

"Oh. Guess I haven't mentioned it." Ben looked over at Alexei. "I just passed my nursing exam before I came here. Hoping to go into geriatric nursing when I get back."

Alexei took this in. It made perfect sense. Ben as a nurse. Ben working with the elderly. But...

"Won't that be sad?" he couldn't help but ask.

"Because I'll have to watch a lot of old people die?"

"Yes."

Ben took a moment to answer.

"I know people think that. But it feels like an honor, really. To make their last days a little more comfortable if we can. To listen to their stories. And if they're not physically able to tell their stories anymore, I can at least *be* there. Be a human presence for them, especially if they're all alone. It took me a long time to figure out what I want to do with my life, but that seems like something I can do." Ben shrugged.

Alexei thought: *Mom would really like him.*

It was probably the biggest pinch he'd felt yet.

He tried to think of something to say, about Tumbleweed, about Ben helping ease people's pain during their last days on earth.

In the end, he could only stare into the distance and try to quiet his beating heart. He thought he heard a slight trill.

After several quiet minutes, he said, "Brewer's sparrow."

He was still staring into the manzanitas, away from Ben's face, hoping he could get a glimpse of tail feathers, wings, the streaked nape.

But like always, he could still feel Ben's smile somehow. It flushed through him, bright and warm, and like a fool, Alexei let himself feel it, until the pinch faded away.

Tomorrow, Alexei told himself. Ben Caravalho could find a new group of thru-hikers tomorrow.

For now, Ben and Alexei picked up their packs once more. Ben took the lead.

"When was the last time you took a zero day, Lex? I have to say I'm hurtin' for one."

"I actually haven't taken one yet."

Ben stopped short before Alexei's legs could process it. His chest barreled into Ben's pack. For a brief, overwhelming moment, his lips dived into Ben's hair.

Ben stepped away and turned, appearing unbothered by the body slam.

"Wait, what?"

"What?" Alexei had forgotten what they were talking about.

"You haven't taken a zero day yet? When did you get on trail?"

"Oh." Alexei rubbed at his chest. A zero day was a day off: zero miles hiked. Zero days were necessary to rest sore muscles and prevent injury. They were often scheduled to coincide with visits to towns, to recharge in actual hotel beds, to resupply at stores or pick up prearranged resupply boxes from post offices. Alexei had planned his first one soon, near I-10. "I got on at Route 74. Right before I first met you, with the rattlesnake."

"Got it." Ben scratched at his forehead. "So are you just section hiking then? I thought—"

"No," Alexei interrupted with a sigh. "I'm hiking until Canada. I just...wanted to skip some of the desert."

Even though he knew the decision was odd, it had been a bit terrifying, studying all that beige on the map around the Mexican border, when he'd been planning his trip back in Portland. It had eased the anxiety in Alexei's chest to stick his finger on the first patch of green, decide to start there instead. San Bernardino National Forest. Route 74: Palms to Pines Scenic Byway.

"Oh, right." A smile overtook Ben's face again as he understood. "That makes sense." Did it? Alexei was pretty sure it was weird, starting 150 miles in instead of at the beginning. Why was Ben so nice to him? It was also weird. "So you've been walking for..."

"Today is my sixth day."

"Lex!" Ben pushed him in the shoulder. Alexei's gut buzzed. "What the hell. God, you must be dying. The first week is *the worst*. Your body's, like, in shock basically."

"I—" Alexei tried to find the right words. Relief filled him, almost heady, at this confirmation that the way he was feeling wasn't out of the ordinary. "I am...sometimes uncomfortable."

"Okay." Ben clapped his hands. "That's it. Zero day tomorrow."

Alexei frowned. "I had planned to push on to I-10." Darn, stopping in Idyllwild really had put him behind.

"Nope." Ben popped the *p*, shook his head. "Hiking seven days in a row without a zero is a dumbass idea. Let's make sure we find an excellent camping spot tonight. And tomorrow?" Ben grinned. "We sleep."

With that, he twirled on his heel and moseyed down the trail.

Alexei stared after him. When they were walking, Alexei always had the distraction of the trail, of planning their next steps. It frightened him a bit, imagining a full day of being still with Ben Caravalho.

For now, Alexei kept walking. Focused on what was in front of him, right here, right now: eyes on the trail, ears open to the sky.

CHAPTER SIX

Alexei stretched his swollen bare feet in his sleeping bag. The sun shone high overhead, trickling through the needles of the trees and the mesh of the tent above him. He had no idea what time it was, and he didn't quite care.

The list of things Alexei could not indulge in as a child ran long. But as an adult, he did let himself enjoy certain simple pleasures.

Dark chocolate. A hot bath after a long day of work. Not washing new sweatshirts until something dire occurred, keeping that fuzzy inner lining as soft as possible for as long as possible.

But nothing compared, he now knew, to sleeping in.

He hadn't done much of it in his life. As kids, he and Alina were expected to be up early, regardless of things like "summer" or "weekends," for chores or church. The habit must have been ingrained into him, because even through college and adulthood, Alexei needed to rise early. To get to the gym, to be one of the first people at the office. To make sure his days could be as productive as possible.

But the trail must have changed something in Alexei already.

Because this? This was the best.

As he lay on his mattress pad and listened to the soft whistle of the wind, he couldn't quite remember the last time he had felt this good. He didn't even care that Ben was out there somewhere, with his distracting smiles that made Alexei think delusional things. Alexei didn't care about plans today. His head felt almost mysteriously light and empty of grief. Filled instead with the slight scent of sage. The physical realities of this very moment. Nothing more, nothing less.

Being still was powerful.

Eventually, Alexei did crawl out of his tent. He stepped into his camp sandals and stretched, a painful, deeply satisfying thing. Ben had been right, now that he had the time to truly catalog his body's complaints. That day they'd met in Idyllwild had been the height of Alexei's pain, of his body responding to the sudden, sustained stress of traveling through the desert on foot. He was slowly adjusting, now. He still hurt. But underneath the soreness, his body felt...strong. Alive.

Ben's tent was empty. Alexei glanced around, more curious than worried, until he saw him, twenty yards away. Butt in the air, face—and iPhone camera—focused on a rock.

Alexei felt himself grinning.

Ben was always taking photos. Of the big things, the vistas and landmarks, but also the small things. Often, Alexei would realize Ben was lagging behind, and turn to see him crouched over a strange bush paces back. Sometimes, Ben would be staring right at the middle of the trail, nothing but sand to see. Alexei would tromp back over to him, and Ben would look up and say, "Dude, look at this *bug*."

Alexei found himself noticing more, too, the longer they hiked together: the colors that dotted a spring desert in bloom, the yellows and pinks that hid among all that brown and beige. His eyes lingered longer in the crevices of boulders, wondering what tiny details lurked there that would please Ben. That Ben would want to study and take a picture of. That Ruby, perhaps, would want to draw.

Presently, Ben stood and sauntered toward where Alexei was still standing, even though Alexi rather desperately had to pee. When Ben looked up from his phone and noticed him, his face exploded in a smile that Alexei worried, possibly, might haunt him forever.

In lieu of *good morning*, Ben held out his phone and said, "Lex. Dude. Look at this *rock*."

Alexei squinted at the photo in the glare of the sun, trying to understand why he enjoyed it when Ben called him *dude*.

"I've been meaning to say"—Ben took his phone back—"thanks for letting me stop so much to take pictures." A dapple of sunshine surrounded his left eye. "Those other guys I was hiking with before were so into making big miles every day that I felt weird stopping to stare at shit like this, you know?"

"Well," Alexei said, clearing the sleep from his voice, "now you have all day to take pictures of whatever you want around here."

"*Right?*" Ben beamed. "It's awesome. Except"—he shook his head and put the phone in his pocket—"I would probably kill the battery of this thing in an hour. It's already almost dead, and my portable charger is all the way dead."

"You'll have to reserve it for top-tier rocks only."

"Exactly."

Ben tilted his head, examining Alexei for a moment. It felt like Ben was standing at least an inch too close to him. Right? No, like, three inches too close. Four. God, Alexei had to pee. His bladder was super confused about why Alexei was not moving right now and his brain didn't even have a good explanation. Why could Alexei never walk away from Ben's face?

"Lex, wait. I don't know why I've never thought about this, but…why don't *you* ever take any pictures? I don't think I've seen you take out your phone once."

"Oh." Alexei shrugged. "That's because I don't have one."

Ben's brow furrowed. "You don't have a phone?"

"I mean"—Alexei grimaced, not wanting to look like a completely out-of-touch human being—"I *have* one. I just canceled my service for a while and left it home."

Ben's jaw dropped.

"You left for months...in the middle of the wilderness...with no way to contact anyone?"

"I have an emergency GPS locator," Alexei said, a bit defensively. "It has texting options, so I can let Alina know if something happens. I'm not completely irresponsible."

The emergency GPS locator had been expensive. But more necessary, in Alexei's mind, than a phone. Alexei was good at numbers, at cost analyses. It made no sense to carry, and keep paying for, a device that would have spotty service at best, when there was no one he truly needed to be in contact with. Except for Alina. And he'd given her the information for his GPS locator. The only other people he might like to contact every now and then were his online D&D group, and well, they'd be on a totally different campaign by the time he got back anyway.

It had made sense in his head.

"No, Lex. I wouldn't take you as irresponsible." Ben gave him a small, inscrutable smile.

And then Alexei realized.

How truly, utterly pathetic it was to have no one he needed to be in contact with.

His blush burned his ears.

"I know it's probably weird. To not have a phone. It's just—"

"No, no." Ben waved him off. "Not weird. It's...hardcore. You're like, *actually* off the grid. You're a badass, Lex."

Sure.

They could call it that.

Alexei managed a small nod before he bolted into the bushes.

An hour later, back in his tent and splayed out on his stomach, Alexei stared at a different journal. He chewed absently on the top of his pen.

This journal was slightly smaller than the other. It had a weather-proof orange cover.

On the first page, only one heading was written. He'd written it back in Portland, before he left.

GOOD THINGS

He could do this. He felt good enough today, and alone enough to focus. He knew Ben wouldn't mind if Alexei stayed in this tent all day.

He had researched what you should do. How to best cope with the loss of loved ones. That was how he was choosing to frame it. His parents were lost to him, and grief was natural after loss.

Accept your feelings as valid.

Talk about the deaths of your loved ones.

Remember and celebrate their lives.

Alexei considered pen and paper talking. Words were involved. It counted.

The thing was, Alexei's life had been a good one. He didn't want to be this tragic figure now, someone to feel sorry for. He wanted to document the memories that made him happy. The *remembering and celebrating* part. He hoped remembering the happy stuff would let him accept the past as the past, and eventually, put it all behind him.

And then he'd be fully ready. For Alexei 2.0.

His pen hovered over the paper. His stomach made a loud gurgling noise.

It was just...where did one start, in trying to document a life?

Whenever Alexei tried to think about his dad, all he could see was his lanky frame leaning against the doorway of Alexei's childhood home. The home where he and Alina had run through the yard and the neighboring woods their entire childhoods, the home where he'd celebrated every Easter and Thanksgiving and Christmas and New Year's. The home with the attic that scared him, that Alina always dared him to enter; the one with the creaky third stair, the family pictures framed above it, marching up the wall. The one where his old bedroom was tucked into the back corner of the second floor, looking out onto the trees, where cross-country medals and math department awards hung above his desk. The home where Alina had stuffed cake down the back of his pants on his eleventh birthday when he'd spilled milk on one of her paintings and she hadn't believed him when he'd said it had been an accident.

Alexei should have been able to write about all these things. But it was all still overshadowed in his head, frustratingly, by his dad that day in the doorway, hands in his pockets, head down. Unable to make eye contact with his only son. One of the buttons on his cardigan sweater had been unbuttoned.

Whenever Alexei tried to think about his mom, all he could see was her standing next to his father in that doorway. But she was leaning forward, a hand stretching out. Before she stopped, her fingers curling in on themselves.

"We'll see you soon, okay?" she had said. "We'll see you soon, moyo soltnse."

Because surely, the son she had raised would make the right choice.

It had haunted him for six months, the simple phrase of affection he'd heard his mother say so many times, the one he would likely never hear again. Moyo soltnse. Мое солнце. My sun.

It had been so quiet, losing his parents. They hadn't even asked questions. No *How long have you known?* They hadn't asked whether he'd talked to the church, whether he'd tried to receive counseling. Alexei had thought he'd at least get a talk about that.

He might have, he thought now, if he had been younger. Perhaps it was the fact that he was a grown adult, admitting this forbidden thing, that had made his parents so bereft.

But when his father had looked over his glasses at him and said, "You know what this means, Alexei, if you choose to live this way," Alexei, immediately, *had* known. Of course he had known. He should have known from the moment he walked into his parents' house that day, naive and determined. He had been living away from home for too long. Had been playing too much D&D. He had learned a surprising amount of queer people played D&D. Getting to know his fellow adventurers had made him feel more normal. Like maybe it *wasn't* that big of a deal. Bit by bit, he'd forgotten. That no matter what, it always would be to his parents.

Details of that sunny afternoon seemed foggier in his mind by the day, but if Alexei had to guess, he'd say the whole conversation took less than twenty minutes.

Alexei clenched his jaw, staring fiercely at the blank page, resisting the urge to curl into himself. This was why he had come here. He could do this.

He wrote:

Cake down my pants.

And then he realized how ridiculous it sounded, resisted a scream, and quickly scribbled it out.

Okay, well, and now the page was ruined.

With a huff, he ripped it out as neatly as he could. Crumpled it into a ball. Wrote the heading again.

GOOD THINGS

Maybe he could glide past his parents, specifically, for now. Maybe he could focus on bigger picture things, all the things he had loved about his church and his community as a kid. The comfort of coming together every week. The closeness of their shared Russian heritage. The softness of the leather hymnals under his fingertips, well used and well loved. The way a particularly emotional hymn made his body shiver. His hands on piano keys in his teen years, when he accompanied the choir. The power and peace in those songs, in those buildings, high ceilinged and holy.

Half-heartedly, instead of a list, Alexei doodled a piano. Black and white keys, even and smooth. Doodles felt easier than words.

Except Alexei had never been an artist like Alina. His doodles looked childish.

He was starting to feel anxious, and the knowledge of this, his hyperawareness of how his mind was drifting unproductively, made him even more anxious in turn. He closed his eyes and rested his head on his forearms.

Eventually, Alexei gave in and thought of Alina. Just Alina, their parents shoved away. Because thinking of Alina always made him smile.

She had always worn her hair long, the blond a shade darker than Alexei's but still bright as sunshine, often in a braid. Preferably, a French braid done by Alexei. He had gotten rather good at it, he thought, after years of practice, separating the silky strands into three proportionate sections, making the loops tight and clean. It was what she had been most upset about when he left for college. "But Alexei," she'd pouted, like an actual child, even though she was a high schooler by then. "Who's going to do my hair?"

Alexei opened his eyes and wrote it down, under the appalling sketch of the piano.

Braiding Alina's hair.

He chewed on his thumbnail. There was probably something he could have done, over the last six months, to make things less awkward between them. He still wasn't 100 percent positive how Alina felt about the gay thing, but at least she didn't seem repulsed by him. Most of their interactions in the last six months had just been . . . *weird*. Alexei felt guilty he'd put Alina in an uncomfortable position with their parents, guilty he was making anything hard at all for Alina, whom he was supposed to protect. Alina, in turn, felt guilty Alexei felt guilty, that there wasn't anything she could do to salvage it, that she still talked to their parents. It was a mess.

Still. Alina wasn't lost. Alina was, hopefully, the one thing he thought he might be able to keep. And he worried, the more he wrote about her in this journal, this journal he wanted to use to remember and grieve and heal, the more it would feel like she had left him, too.

With a sigh, Alexei closed the thing and shoved it to the corner of his tent.

He had thousands of miles to hike. Surely this would come more naturally at some point.

He withdrew a battered, dog-eared paperback from his pack.

"Leeeeeeeeeeeeeex."

Ben's whine broke through the silence, sending a signature *buzz* all the way to Alexei's toes.

"Yeah?"

"I'm bored."

Despite himself, Alexei smiled.

He opened the flap of his tent. Ben's was set up only a few yards away. He had scrambled himself partly out of it, his head propped outside its blue nylon walls. His bundled-up navy sweatshirt served as a makeshift pillow between his dark hair and the ground.

Alexei wrangled himself into a similar position, angling his body so his head and shoulders stuck out of his humble abode to better see Ben. Who was squinting over at him, a funny look on his face.

And maybe it was because Alexei's mind had just been stuck

in the past, but suddenly, he felt a little proud of himself again. For allowing himself to admire the back of Ben's neck, his legs, his elbows when Alexei hiked behind him. For daydreaming about crawling into Ben's lap when he wore that sweatshirt, looking so comfortable and inviting. For cataloging the endless expressions that daily painted Ben's face. For allowing himself to look at that face now, and admit how much it pleased him.

For so much of his life, Alexei had never let himself think, look, notice such things. So much had been squashed, hidden inside places he pretended weren't there.

Alexei had spent so much of his life holding himself back from wanting.

And while he knew this particular wanting was temporary and useless, he felt good, in some small way, that he was letting himself feel it.

"We still have over half the day left," he noted, entertained at Ben's *bored* status. They spent hours every day doing nothing but walking and breathing. Hiking was entirely monotonous. If anything, having time to simply sit in your tent and do whatever you wanted was downright exciting.

"I know." Ben stuck out his lower lip while he huffed a breath, sending the locks hanging around his forehead flying. "What are you up to?"

Alexei looked down at the book in his hands.

"Reading."

Ben turned on his side, propping an elbow on the ground, resting his cheek on his palm.

"Ah. You did strike me as the bookworm type."

Alexei hesitated, debating how much to explain himself to Ben. "We weren't allowed to watch TV when we were kids. So I spent a lot of time reading. Like, a lot."

"No TV at all?"

"Didn't even own one."

"Holy shit." Ben's eyes went wide. "I was practically raised by TV."

"Yeah." Alexei looked at the cover of his book, the sandy ground beneath him.

"So were you like...Jehovah's Witnesses? Or Amish or something?"

Alexei flipped through the yellowed pages with his thumb.

"No. Although my church probably has similar principles. I went to public school; we weren't completely cut off from society. We were just supposed to keep our minds pure for God."

"The same God who supposedly approves of your parents disowning you for being gay?"

Alexei sucked in a breath.

"Sorry, man." Ben sighed. "I'll try to keep my mouth shut."

Alexei studied his book a moment more. And then he spoke aloud, for the first time, the one thought that had kept him going these last six months.

"No," he said quietly. "I don't think God approves of that, either."

In a way, Alexei's faith had been shifting since the day he left home for college. There was a branch of his church outside Seattle he could have gone to, that his parents believed he attended. But most Sundays, he had found himself in the University of Washington's nondenominational chapel. He increasingly felt safe there. Fewer strictures, fewer punishments. More of the things that made his heart feel open and loved.

When he'd returned to the Portland-Vancouver area after graduation, and resumed going to weekly services with his family, things chafed at him that hadn't before.

No longer attending church these last six months had left Alexei feeling a confusing mix of horribly empty and deeply relieved.

"Okay," Ben said a minute later, the easygoing tone returning to his voice in a rather obvious but merciful way. "Is it a good book so far?"

Alexei's muscles relaxed. He looked again at the worn cover of *Alanna: The First Adventure*.

"It's actually one of my favorites from when I was a kid. I've already probably read it twenty times."

Alexei still wasn't sure if it was a silly choice, bringing a nostalgic favorite instead of something new. But the Tamora Pierce paperback was small and light, and he had thought it might be a tiny comfort for nights when he was feeling lonely.

"Tell me about it."

Alexei glanced again at Ben. He was still on his side facing Alexei, but had let his head drop back onto his sweatshirt-pillow. He looked snuggled in, ready for a bedtime story, even though it was the middle of the day.

"It's silly," Alexei said, feeling self-conscious. "It's for, like … middle schoolers."

"Perfect. I didn't read jackshit in middle school. It'll be an education."

Alexei laughed.

"Seriously, what's it about?"

"Well, so. It's Tamora Pierce's first book."

"You say that like I should know who Tamora Pierce is."

Alexei gave Ben a look. "You should."

Ben smiled. "Right."

"She's an epic fantasy writer, and this book was the first in the *Song of the Lioness* quartet—"

"Quartet!"

Alexei frowned. Ben looked utterly delighted.

"I've just never heard anyone use that word so casually in a sentence before."

"It means there were four books in the series. It's not that strange."

"Of course. Please, continue."

Alexei, for perhaps the first time since they'd met, felt like scowling at Ben. But Ben was smiling so wide, Alexei also sort of wanted to kiss him.

He focused back on the book.

"It was readers' first introduction to Tortall, the universe where a lot of her books take place. And...I don't know, I loved it when I was twelve. And—"

Alexei chewed on his lip. How much did Ben really want to know about Tamora Pierce?

But he'd said he was bored. He appeared interested. And Alexei wanted Alexei 2.0 to be comfortable talking about these things. To do more than just come out. To talk about these parts of him, out loud, when he could find the courage.

"I mentioned yesterday that I play D&D?"

"Yeah."

"It's super nerdy, I know. But I like it because it reminds me of these kinds of books that I loved so much as a kid. They always let me escape the world for a while. And during a D&D session a while ago, some of the other people in my group started talking about Tamora Pierce. About Alanna, the main character of this book, in particular." He paused. Took a deep breath. "They called her a queer icon."

"Yeah?" Ben was still smiling. "Tell me more."

"She's this girl who pretends to be her brother, Thom, so she can live her dream of becoming a knight. Thom never wanted to be a knight anyway, so he's, like, sure, you be a boy, and I'll run away to be a magician, and we'll both be happy."

Alexei pressed his lips together.

"I don't think I necessarily understood that as queer when I was twelve, at least not consciously. But when my D&D friends talked about it...I felt it. How Alanna and Thom both reject society's expectations of them. Alanna's refusal to live as someone she didn't want to be. She was so...fearless." Alexei swallowed. "I was always a shy kid, and...yeah, I think I loved Alanna so much because I always wished I could be a little more like her."

The space between them filled with the sound of the wind whispering through the pines.

"Tell me more," Ben said again after a long moment, his voice quiet.

"Do you seriously want to know the whole story?"

"I do." Ben adjusted himself on the ground, fluffed his sweatshirt before resettling. "Read it to me?"

"What?" Alexei stared at him.

"I told you, I'm bored. And Alanna sounds pretty badass. You don't have to, though."

"No, I..." Alexei trailed off.

He shot Ben another glance.

"You won't make fun of it? It really is, like, fifth-grade reading level."

"I promise. I won't make fun of it."

And the thing was, Alexei knew he wouldn't.

But he still couldn't quite believe he was going to do this anyway.

He opened *Alanna: The First Adventure* and paged past the title page, the map of Tortall. He cleared his throat.

"Chapter One: Twins."

He tried to make his voice sound normal as he read through the first page, but God, this was bizarre. Reading Tamora Pierce to Ben Caravalho in the middle of the desert, at the age of twenty-nine.

But as he kept reading, he got into a bit of a rhythm. With a small thrill, he felt himself slipping back into the magic of Tortall, even now, even here.

Ben closed his eyes halfway through the first chapter. Alexei didn't mind if Ben fell asleep. He looked peaceful, and happy, so Alexei kept reading, because he rather felt the same.

And then, on page thirteen, when Alanna dropped her cloak,

revealing herself to be Alanna and not Thom, and her companion Coram choked on his brandy—Ben laughed.

It wasn't even *that* funny when Coram choked on the brandy. But it was a little funny. Ben's laughter was soft, but genuine, like it always was, and it lit up Alexei's insides like a firecracker.

Ben was listening. He was on Alanna's side.

Alexei smiled into his paperback and took another breath. And then he kept reading about Alanna's travels to the capital, on the way to her destiny, while the desert sun traveled overhead, blazing into the bleached, sandy earth of Southern California, sinking into Ben and Alexei's skin.

CHAPTER SEVEN

Ben couldn't stop smiling from the moment he woke up.

His body was rested from the zero. He and Alexei had been hiking together for enough time now that their routines were starting to feel natural, melded together: how long it took each of them to pack up camp; when they each liked to eat their biggest meals; how to balance their pacing. Alexei was talking more, sharing more, seeming more at ease. The wind was calm this morning, making their early first hours of hiking easy as pie.

And it was dinosaur day.

Ben hummed as they walked. He often sang inside his head as they walked, sometimes a little outside, too; you needed something mindless in your brain to survive this damn trail. But he figured humming out loud, continuously, would annoy Alexei. And there was no better way to tell your friends you cared—or that you had something you really, really wanted them to ask you about—than to annoy the shit out of them.

An impressive mile and a half into the morning—Ben had made it through at least 40 percent of Tom Petty's oeuvre—Alexei finally broke.

"Ben." He stopped in his tracks, and Ben almost crashed right into him. "For the love of God. What is happening."

Ben beamed. "We're only a hop, skip, and jump away from I-10," he announced.

"And...?"

"*And*," Ben answered with a flourish, "the dinosaurs."

Alexei's brow furrowed. "The dinosaurs?"

"The Cabazon Dinosaurs, Lex! A-plus ridiculous roadside attraction! They're not *right* at the trail, technically, but only an exit away on I-10. Like a five-minute hitch. Done."

"Oh." Alexei scratched under his bandanna, somehow not appearing further enthused by this information. "Um. I am sort of terrified of hitchhiking."

"Don't worry about it," Ben waved this off. "I'll do the actual hitching part. You just sit pretty. I think there's fast food there, too. Which means bathrooms. Sinks, Lex! Trash cans!"

With that final argument, Ben twirled to maneuver around Alexei and take over the lead.

Alexei would see. Because while Ben had been excited about seeing the Cabazon Dinosaurs ever since he'd found out about them in his trail research, he felt particularly jazzed about them now. Because he was 90 percent sure they would make Alexei smile. And finding things that would make Alexei Lebedev smile was rapidly becoming Ben's favorite part of the PCT.

An hour later, they were stuffed into Jasmyn Carbajal's Toyota Corolla.

Or rather, Alexei looked stuffed, his long legs bent in front of him, his knees sticking into the back of Jasmyn's seat, his and Ben's packs crammed next to him. He looked distinctly uncomfortable, but Ben had to admit that he was having a rather fabulous time in the front passenger seat, Jasmyn's rattling AC blowing onto his face. Being in a car felt like flying after weeks of traveling on foot, in a way that made Ben both giddy and slightly terrified. He watched the highway sail by as Jasmyn gabbed about the girls trip in Palm Springs she was returning from.

"We've been doing it every spring for the last forty years." The bangles on her wrist clacked as she talked, her curly hair ruffled by the straining AC. Ben loved her immediately. "There have been a few years here and there where someone had to miss, but it's just about my favorite thing in life, other than my sons. It's important to catch up with your friends, you know? Even if it's only once a year."

"That sounds lovely, Jasmyn." And Ben meant it.

"Important to catch up with your folks, too, of course," she added with a light smack to his shoulder. "In case you boys need the reminder. It's truly not that hard to call once in a while, you know."

"If we have service at the dinosaurs, I promise I'll be calling my own mother shortly."

"That's right." Jasmyn nodded approvingly, the hoops in her ears nodding along with her. "Your poor mamas must be worried sick about you out here! I have to say, I've never quite understood wanting to walk through the wilderness like y'all are doing, but God bless you."

A twinge hit Ben's chest, a multipronged thing. Because he knew his poor mama *was* worried sick.

And because he now knew Alexei's mama didn't even know he was here.

"I wish I could take you home and make you both a good home-cooked meal, but it's still a ways to home from here."

"Don't worry about it, Jasmyn; it looks like we've got—" Ben leaned toward the windshield as the exit approached. "Burger King!" He let out a loud whoop. "And there are the dinos! Hot damn, Lex!"

Jasmyn let out a hearty laugh. "If I couldn't already tell from your accent, I'd know you weren't a local from your excitement about these dusty old dinos. Where you from anyways?"

"Tennessee. Where"—Ben craned his neck to try to glimpse the entire T-rex as Jasmyn pulled into the mostly empty parking lot—"we have a lot of pools shaped like guitars, but not as many dinosaurs."

They did have *some*, to be clear. George Boedecker back in Nashville had installed a bunch of dinosaur statues on his property in Bellevue. Which, like many things in Nashville, was weird, and great. But still, even those weren't like *these*.

Jasmyn kept chuckling as she put the Corolla in park.

"Well, I certainly hope you continue to enjoy yourselves out here. You quiet one back there, take care of this charmer, will ya?" Jasmyn waved a bangled arm as Alexei and Ben retrieved their gear.

"Oh, he will," Ben promised. "Thanks again!"

With a sputter of exhaust, she was off.

And Ben and Alexei turned to face them.

There were two: a T-rex and a brontosaurus, standing watch over the Burger King.

"Yikes," Alexei said.

And okay. Ben could see what Jasmyn was saying. Their paint was faded and chipped, clearly worn down by time. But—

"Come on, man." Because faded paint or not, they were *huge*. Someone had decided they were going to build these things, and by God, they did. Human beings were the weirdest, and Ben loved everything about this. "This is amazing."

Alexei gave a skeptical tilt of his head.

"They're kind of...depressing?"

"Oh my God." Ben threw his hands up in despair. "The fact that the federal minimum wage hasn't changed in over ten years is depressing. Not having a cure for cancer is depressing. This is..." More hand waving. "Charming vintage Americana!"

Alexei added a dose of dubious squinting to his head tilt. "Charming?"

"Okay, just Americana then. Bigass dinosaurs in the middle of the desert, just for the hell of it. Yes."

Alexei squinted some more. Until the left side of his mouth shifted, and—yes, *victory*, it hid a bit under all his scruff, but that was most definitely a smile. A smile that was poking fun at Ben, not necessarily a pure product of the dinosaurs themselves, but like the Burger King, Ben would take it.

A moment of silence passed as they stared. And then—

"God bless America?" Alexei hedged, and it was the closest Ben had witnessed Alexei come to a sense of humor. He could have cheered.

"Exactly," he said.

"So do we sing the national anthem now, or...?"

Jokes! Alexei Lebedev was attempting to make jokes!

"No, even more American than that," Ben answered, grabbing his phone from his pocket. "We take selfies. Come on," he added when Alexei simply stood on the sidewalk, unmoving, as Ben backed toward the dinosaurs.

"Oh." Alexei's smile faltered. "You want *me* in them?"

"Of course I want you in them, Lex! Or else the moment won't be properly documented!"

"Oh," Alexei said again. But after a moment, he stepped forward, and leaned his shoulder toward Ben, and Ben angled his phone in twenty different directions in an attempt to get both their faces and the dinosaurs in the same frame. Which was difficult because, again, these dinos were huge.

To Alexei's credit, he did smile through every attempt. And maybe Ben couldn't exactly tell if it was forced or not, but damn, it was still cute, and it was nice, Alexei's shoulder brushing against his, and—friends! Ben would definitely post this photo on Instagram of his new good friend he wasn't attracted to at all.

"I'll email these to you?" he asked once he thought he'd finally gotten a few decent ones. He stepped away, typing on his phone. "I have a bar or two of service here to send them through before I forget."

"Oh. Um. Sure." Alexei, again, seemed almost surprised by this request, but gave Ben his email address nonetheless. Even though Ben could have guessed it. It was obviously alexei.lebedev@gmail.com.

"All right." Ben stuck his phone in his pocket and clapped his hands. "Let's do this."

They entered through a door set in the brontosaurus's tail, walking up a set of stairs to a dusty gift shop. It was super weird and perfect and Ben sent Julie a postcard that looked like it'd been printed in 1989.

He made Alexei send one to Alina, too.

Ben waited until they were outside again, walking across the cracked pavement to the Burger King.

"Tell me something more about her," he said. "Alina."

Ben still enjoyed Alexei's silences. Felt more at home on the trail, somehow, inside them. But he'd discovered that, sometimes, simply asking Alexei to talk produced the loveliest results.

Alexei, as he often did, took a moment before he answered.

"We spent a lot of time outside when we were kids. There was this patch of woods behind our house. She would..." They paused outside the door of the Burger King. Alexei adjusted the strap of his pack, trekking poles dangling from his wrist. Another small smile twitched at the corner of his mouth. "She would always pretend to be these outlandish things. A llama was one of her favorites. Or a sloth, or a butterfly. Or sometimes"—Alexei's voice grew more animated— "she'd insist on being like...a dandelion. Or a jellyfish."

"What about you? Did you ever pretend to be a favorite creature?"

"Yeah. I was always a fox."

Ben bit the inside of his cheek to keep himself in check. "Always?"

"Yes," Alexei said emphatically. "A fox made sense. Most of the things Alina made up weren't even native to the Northwest, or any other reasonably similar woodland habitat. How could you be a jellyfish in a forest? I swear she did it just to frustrate me."

Alexei sounded frustrated even as he was saying this. But he was still smiling. It seemed almost like Alexei was struggling not to laugh at himself. Ben wanted to hear Alexei laugh, real and loud. He'd laughed a few times these last few days, always soft little chuckles, but Ben wanted to hear Alexei unrestrained. He wanted to reach up and discover how Alexei's beard would feel against his palm. He wanted to run his thumb down the line that formed in the very center of Alexei's forehead when he was uncomfortable. Wanted to stick his hands fully into that wheat blond hair, growing a bit shaggier by the day, that shone in the desert sun.

But that was not why Ben was here.

"Thanks for telling me that, Lex," he managed.

They stepped inside the restaurant, into the comforting blast of AC.

"AC," Alexei said. Ben's shoulders relaxed.

"AC," he agreed. "I'm going to hit the bathroom. You can go ahead and order. I'll be out in a minute."

Alexei nodded, moving to study the menu.

Ben took a deep breath before retreating to the restroom, where he could splash his face with beautifully cold water from a beautifully human-made tap.

They were almost finished with their meal when Delilah popped onto Ben's phone.

"Oh my God," he said, almost yanking it out of the wall where it was plugged in. He brought the screen all the way up to his face so he could take in her soulful brown eyes, her slobbery Rottweiler smile.

She misses you! Ma had texted.

"Everything okay?" Alexei asked.

"Yes," Ben answered. "My dog is still cute. Everything is fantastic."

Alexei smiled at the last of his fries.

"Do you mind, actually, if I call my mom before we go? I can step outside, if it makes you uncomfortable."

Alexei shook his head.

"Please, go ahead. Talk as long as you want."

Ben hesitated before he pressed Call. He thought about Jasmyn, shouting about calling your folks back in her car. How it must have made Alexei feel. He should step outside.

But... the AC in here *was* pretty spectacular.

She picked up on the second ring.

"Bento!"

"Ma."

"Meu Deus, is it wonderful to hear your voice. Where are you? Are you safe?"

"Yes, I'm safe. Currently, I am in a Burger King. In..." Was Cabazon a town? All he could see out the window were the dinosaurs and billboards along the highway. "Down the road from Palm Springs."

"Ooh, fancy! Take pictures of celebrities!"

"We are not actually *in* Palm Springs. We are in a Burger King."

"Still closer than I've ever been to Palm Springs."

"It's good to hear your voice, too, Ma. Are you at work?"

"I stepped out. They'll survive."

Ben smiled, unsure if they actually would. Iris Caravalho objectively ran the East Nashville High main office.

He noticed Alexei had brought *Alanna* out of his pack.

"Hey." He covered the bottom of his phone with his palm. "You better not be reading about what that bastard Ralon is up to without me."

Alexei looked up, his face indecipherable.

"And how is Faraj?" His mother was asking. "Ryan and Leon? That jackass one?"

Alexei put *Alanna* back in his pack. Brought out his journal instead.

"Tanner." Ben almost added, out of an inherent need for harmony, that Tanner wasn't *that* big of a jackass. But he'd heard Tanner say some pretty sexist shit. So he kept his mouth shut and filled Ma in on the rest.

"I assume they're good, but I'm actually not hiking with them anymore. I have a new trail family now. His name's Alexei."

A beat of silence on the other end of the line.

"Alexei and . . ."

"That's it."

Another beat of silence, somehow more suspicious this time.

"A trail family can be one person, Ma."

Alexei wasn't looking at him. But Ben noticed his pen pause, hovering over his journal.

"Tell me, Bento, how good looking is this new trail family of yours?"

"Ma."

"Is he nice? He better be nice. You've dated some real stinkers, you know."

"Ma."

"And you're already calling him your family, before he's even met your mother! I don't know how I feel about this."

"It's not—" Ben sighed, rubbing a hand down his face. "Ma, please stop."

"You better send some photos so I can assess his suitability for you. I know they say you can't judge a book by its cover, but sometimes, you can."

"I literally just uploaded some photos on Instagram. You can look at them later. And you don't have to assess—" But he couldn't finish the sentence with Alexei sitting right across from him. Could Alexei hear this whole thing? Ma was loud. Ben definitely should have stepped outside first.

"Ack, I'll have to get Lina to show me later. I think someone's hacked my Facebook again, and aren't they connected now?"

"Ma, you always think someone's hacking your Facebook."

"Because they are! Someone really needs to give that Zuckerberg a talking to; he's made a real mess of things. Although even he's probably not as bad as that Bezos these days. His mother cannot be proud of what he's become."

"Being one of the world's most successful businessmen? I bet she can, Ma."

A cluck of Iris's tongue. "That is not success."

"*Anyway*," Ben said pointedly, "what else is happening at home that I've missed?"

"Well"—a loud sigh—"speaking of jackasses. Your uncle Jaco has gone and injured himself again."

"What did he do this time?"

"Broke his leg on a gig. Out for six weeks."

Damn. Jaco had been working in construction for a while now, but he was an independent contractor. That likely meant six weeks out, unpaid.

"I hate being so far away," Ben said. "If I had just—" *Stayed at home and started working*, was what he was going to say, but Iris talked over him before he could.

"Ben. Nuh-uh. I told you because you asked, but don't get all upset. Uncle Jaco is not your responsibility."

"I know."

Another tongue cluck. "You've wanted to do this for years, Bento. Let yourself enjoy it."

Ben held in another sigh. If his mom, who by all Iris Caravalho measures was stressed to hell about his doing this, was telling him to enjoy it, he knew he should believe her.

It was just that, over his last decade of dumbass decisions—and fine, Iris was right, stinker boyfriends—he'd often missed out on things that were happening with his family. It was one of his biggest goals, in his new Good Decisions Lifestyle, to change that.

At least he had been there, he told himself, when Aunt Birdie started misplacing her shoes. Hiding one under her bed, one under the kitchen sink. When she was confused more often than she wasn't.

"I hate being so far away," Ben eventually repeated himself.

A small, rueful laugh from Ma. "I hate it, too, meu filho. But you *are* having fun, no? It helps me to know you're having fun."

Before he could stop himself, his eyes flicked to Alexei. Whose head was down, his hand moving fast across the page now.

"Yeah," he said, quiet. "I am. Make sure you have Carolina show you the pictures," he added.

"I will." Iris muttered a curse under her breath. "Okay, the Doc is calling me inside. I should go."

"Tell her I said hi." Ben smiled. The "Doc" was the principal of East High, Dr. Jones. Ben had always liked Dr. Jones, even when she was staring him down for doing something unfortunate. Like almost failing sophomore English. And geometry. And civics.

"I will," Iris said again. "Thanks so much for calling, Ben. Te amo."

"Te amo."

"Everything all right?" Alexei asked as soon as Ben hung up, pausing his writing.

Ben filled him in on Uncle Jaco. He looked out the window, jiggling his knee under the table, that restless feeling he felt so often niggling at his skin.

"Do you need more time to write?"

Alexei looked at him, that crease appearing in the center of his forehead once more. "No, I—"

Ben's phone beeped.

Unable to resist the hit of dopamine, Ben reached for it again. He grinned, texting back immediately.

"Julie is very glad I am still alive," he informed Alexei, "and *very* pumped about the dinosaurs." He shot Alexei a look. "As most people with taste *would* be."

Alexei, to Ben's delight, rolled his eyes. His forehead crease disappeared.

> **Julie:** speaking of ancient creatures
>
> **Julie:** ben, you would not believe this dog london & dahlia just adopted
>
> **Julie:** it is the most hideous thing i have ever seen

She sent a picture of a small, hairy, one-eyed mutt with a severe overbite that made Ben laugh out loud.

> **Julie:** don't tell either of them, but i am OBSESSED WITH HIM AND KINDA MAD I DIDN'T GET TO ADOPT HIM FIRST
>
> **Ben:** you know Snoozles would never allow a dog in her realm

Julie's cat barely allowed Ben into her realm. Or Julie, for that matter.

> **Julie:** ugh. I know. What a bitch
>
> **Julie:** i love her so much

A thought struck Ben.

"Hey." He looked up from his phone. "I know you said you didn't grow up with TV, but do you have a TV now?"

"Yeah." Alexei's ears went pink. "I do."

"Do you watch *Chef's Special*?"

"I've...heard of it?"

"Ah." Ben shrugged, some of his excitement fading. "Well, last summer, Julie's twin, London, was on it, and they kicked ass." He shook his head. It was still hard to believe this event had actually happened. "It's pretty much my closest brush with celebrity. Thought you might think I was cool."

Ben unplugged his phone and his portable charger as he talked. They had wasted enough time here already.

"What are you writing, by the way?" he asked as he wound the charger cords, stuck them back in his pack. "If you don't mind me asking."

Alexei blinked down at his journal. As he closed it, Ben realized it had a different cover than the one he'd seen Alexei writing in previously.

"I never mind you asking," he said. Ben's heart might have fluttered. "I was writing about this beach house in Long Beach we used to go to. Long Beach, Washington," he clarified as he put the journal in his pack. "And birdhouses. Separately. Actually," he segued without a pause, "do you mind if I write down one more thing?"

"Sure."

Alexei retrieved the other journal Ben was more used to seeing. Ben tried not to look at what Alexei was writing; he really did. But he'd already stuffed all his things away, eaten his last onion ring. There was nothing to keep him from seeing Alexei flip to the very last page and write, at the bottom of a list titled "Alexei 2.0," "Watch Chef's Special."

Ben didn't know what it meant. Alexei 2.0. And while he knew Alexei had just given Ben express permission to ask him anything, something about it felt too personal to ask about here, in the middle of Burger King.

Because Ben already knew there was nothing wrong with Alexei 1.0.

And he worried this list meant Alexei didn't feel the same.

"Okay." Alexei shoved the journal away. "Let's go."

They were back on the trail a half hour later. The sun and wind were relentless once more, the path a never-ending cycle of inclines and descents over brown hills, the landscape even more barren of significant vegetation than yesterday. The heat wore at them, the sky a hazy shade of blown-out blue, and too soon, the excitement of the Cabazon Dinosaurs seemed far away.

They stopped frequently for small water breaks, to wipe the sweat out of their eyes. Lizards skittered by their feet, over and over. Ben paused to take a picture of a flowering silver cholla cactus. It was only then, when Ben shoved his phone back in his pocket, that Alexei spoke for the first time since their hitch back to the trail.

"You do know," he said slowly, "that I already think you're cool."

Ben blinked, trying to piece together where this comment had even come from. Finally, he remembered what he'd said about London and *Chef's Special.*

"Thanks, Lex," he said, trying to keep his voice neutral. "I think you're cool, too."

Alexei didn't say anything. Only turned and kept walking down the trail.

Ben took another long breath before he followed.

CHAPTER EIGHT

They set up camp that night not far off the trail, a grand view of a dry valley at the edge of their tents. They'd refilled their water at Whitewater Creek a few miles before and were somewhat saved from the wind in this little alcove. All things considered, it had been a solid thirteen-mile day, even with the side trip to the dinosaurs.

They managed to get through another chapter of *Alanna* after dinner, before they both collapsed into their tents.

After his nightly prayers, Alexei settled into his sleeping bag. Tried to clear his mind. He was 95 percent successful, except for that thing Ben had said earlier, the one thing, out of all the strange, unexpected things that had happened today that Alexei couldn't stop thinking about. *A trail family can be one person.* It felt engraved on his organs at this point, even if he still couldn't articulate, precisely, why it affected him so much.

Still, he didn't think that was the reason he couldn't sleep. Even in the warm safety of his wildly expensive sleeping bag, the trail plagued him tonight. His face felt more sunburned than usual, or maybe overly whipped from the wind. The discomfort of his angry skin made it hard to fully give in to his exhaustion; every small move seemed to scrape at him, his nerve endings raw.

He was grateful to be here. He was getting used to the desert.

But tonight, he missed his bed.

Alexei wasn't sure how long he tossed and turned.

How long he had submitted to restless sleep before the howling started.

It was so loud, he jerked awake, breathless and confused.

Alexei had heard coyotes at night on the trail before. He understood this was a common occurrence in the desert.

But this noise seemed so *close*, close enough to raise the hairs on Alexei's arms, the back of his neck. Like it was stalking down the trail, headed straight toward them. Alexei's blood swirled in a panic, pounding against his temple as another long, mournful call sounded straight to his gut. Had they left out any food? No, of course not, they—

Crunching. Outside Alexei's tent.

There was no doubt in his mind now, he wasn't making this up, he had spent all his time worrying about bears and instead—

"Lex."

Ben's voice was low and wheezy, and Alexei nearly screamed.

"Lex, let me in."

There was a frantic punching of Alexei's tent. A small scream *might* have escaped Alexei's lips for real. And then, instinct moving his limbs more than coherent thought, Alexei unzipped the flap.

He barely had it halfway open before Ben tumbled inside.

"What the *fuck*?" Alexei managed before Ben's elbow smacked him in the jaw.

Alexei didn't have time to even contemplate how easily *fuck* had just flown out of his mouth—even in adulthood, he had never gotten the hang of cursing—because then Ben's knee was in his gut, and Ben's legs were—God, Ben's legs were everywhere, dangerously close to dangerous things, and his arms were frantically, *loudly*, trying to rezip Alexei's tent. When he finally accomplished this feat, Ben flopped around and down with a thud.

Their heavy breaths filled the air, a practically tangible presence. Alexei couldn't see anything very well, considering it was some godforsaken hour in the middle of the night. But he knew from the heat of Ben's breath that their faces were very, very close. There was nowhere else for their faces to go.

REI did not lie, at least, when they called this a one-person tent.

"What are you *doing*?" Alexei hissed, pulse racing.

"Um." Ben swallowed. "There's something out there."

"Yes, and if it didn't know where we were before, it *really knows now*."

Ben's breath hitched. "I'm sorry," he whispered. "Fuck. I was scared. And...I guess I panicked."

Alexei huffed out a sigh, unsure whether he should punch Ben or, perhaps, hold him forever.

"Listen," he said instead, forcing his voice into a calmer octave for Ben's sake, "coyotes rarely attack people. Okay? Just think of them as, like, wild dogs."

"Dogs that sound *really fucking scary*."

Two minutes ago, Alexei's own nerves had been rattled in a way they had never quite been rattled before. But he couldn't help smiling. Soothing Ben—it calmed Alexei, too. His blood pressure simmered to a slightly less lethal level.

"Yeah. I know."

"Sorry," Ben whispered again.

They were quiet a moment, and so, noticeably, was the night. The coyote was either being very, very stealthy, or—

"I think it's gone," Alexei said.

"Lex," Ben said after a beat. "I think...I am bad at the PCT."

A small laugh escaped Alexei's lungs.

"I don't think that's true."

"Can I stay here another minute?" Ben asked. "To collect myself from monumental embarrassment?"

"Uh. Sure."

And even though he could still barely make out Ben's face, Alexei flipped over to his other side out of pure self-preservation. It was better to stare at the dark wall of his tent than the mass of dark hair and tiny nose and brown eyes and gap-toothed smile he could envision being right there, inches away. It was simply too much, this whole ridiculous chain of events.

It was almost funny, with how fast Alexei's heart was still pitter-pattering around in his chest, that it was able to then stop itself completely five minutes later, when Ben's arm flopped over Alexei's side.

As with the first rattlesnake, all systems came to a halt. Breath stopped pouring from his lungs. He was pretty sure he stopped blinking.

How . . . what? What was Ben *doing*?

Was he just messing with Alexei? Because he knew Alexei was gay? That seemed like a very un-Ben-like thing to do.

Then again, Alexei still didn't really know Ben *that* well. Even though, in his gut, he felt like he did. But . . . no. He blinked hard into the night, his brain trying to talk sense into his gut. He'd known Ben for, what? Less than a week? A spontaneous, temporary trail friendship. Maybe Alexei didn't know him at all. Or maybe Ben was just . . . a straight guy who liked to cuddle with his friends when he was frightened?

That was probably a thing.

Fuck.

Oh. It happened again. Alexei, for the first time in his life, was full of f-bombs.

Whatever this was, Alexei had to put a stop to it, and now. Because this—Ben's breath on his neck, his chest warm against Alexei's back, the underside of his arm flush against Alexei's bicep, his curled fingers whispering ever so gently against Alexei's wrist—it wasn't fair.

It wasn't how two men who barely knew each other responded to a close call with a coyote.

Alexei was pretty sure, from every societal clue he'd ever received, that he and Ben were supposed to slug each other in the shoulder and laugh this whole thing off before Ben stumbled back to his tent. This would merely be a funny story they'd relive later.

They were most definitely not supposed to...do this. Hold each other.

And Alexei could not imagine laughing about this later.

He could smell Ben. His sweat. But there was something else, too, something fresh and clean somehow, something close to pine, even in this dusty, hot desert.

Ben's pinky twitched against Alexei's wrist. Alexei held back a growl.

He was already half hard.

He was about to throw his body back around, maybe not-so-accidentally shove his shoulder into Ben's face, and tell him politely but firmly to get the hell out of his tent, when he heard it.

A soft, adorable rumble.

Ben was snoring.

Ben was *asleep*.

Ben had crashed into Alexei's tent in an all-out panic less than ten minutes ago, and now he was sound asleep, his body taking up half of Alexei's single-person mattress pad, his arm curled around Alexei like it belonged there, and Alexei was pissed off and turned on and too confused and exhausted for this.

He should kick Ben out anyway. Wake him and tell him to go back to his own tent. Because, seriously, Alexei barely fit in this one *by himself*.

But he didn't.

Alexei squeezed his eyes shut. Ben's breath continued to flush warm against his neck, more steady and rumbly now, and the pleasure it sent through Alexei's system was deep-seated and un-deniable. How Alexei longed to be the little spoon to a body like Ben's, a solid, hardworking body made of decency and trust. Maybe he could steal one night of it. It hadn't been his idea. He was doing nothing wrong.

Except it felt wrong. Everything about it felt wonderful and awful all at once because the weight of Ben's arm around him felt realer than anything he'd ever felt but there was no consent in any of it. He squeezed his eyes shut even tighter against the sudden prick of tears.

Alexei focused his mind on simple things he understood.

Birds in flight.

A neatly formatted spreadsheet.

Scales on a piano.

A quiet Northwest forest full of moss.

Braiding silky blond hair—over, under, over again.

And eventually, fitfully, Alexei fell asleep.

When he awoke in the morning, Alexei's first thought was that he was cold.

A beat later, he realized this was because his sleeping bag, meant to zip tightly around his head, was open and askew across his torso.

He remembered his sleeping bag was askew because Ben had tumbled into his tent last night.

He understood now that he was cold because Ben was gone.

Alexei tried to think of an appropriate word to describe his feel-ings toward Ben at that moment. He remembered last night, when curses had magically appeared in his brain in the shock of being surrounded by Ben Caravalho.

But all that came to his mind now was *dorkbutt*, which was what Alina used to call him when they were kids and she wanted to really piss him off. Alexei was cold, and hard again, and there wasn't a damn thing he could do about it, and Ben was a massive dorkbutt.

As soon as he could get his dick to calm down, he was going to storm out of this tent and confront the massive dorkbutt, and tell him to—to what?

Alexei had no idea.

He scrambled into a sitting position. Ran a hand through his hair and his lengthening beard.

It was just that . . . Alexei wanted the fantasy of what happened last night—a comforting arm wrapped around his while he fell asleep—so badly. He had wanted that for so long, before Ben, before he came out to his parents, before he even fully accepted his identity.

And even if it had been in a messed-up way, he had gotten it last night.

And still—*still*—Alexei had woken up alone.

Alexei's sexual history was this: four anonymous swipe-rights over the last two years.

He had never possessed the ability to approach an actual human being he was attracted to in real life of his own volition, even once he'd moved away from home, even during college. But two years ago, he grew fatigued with his own longing.

He viewed it as an experiment. Data collection. Alexei understood data.

When his first swipe-right led to an actual date, he was so nervous he threw up.

Each of his four dates had led to some form of sex. Some of it had been embarrassing, whenever Alexei's inexperience had been apparent. Most of the men, though, had been kind enough.

One man was . . . not so gentle. Not so kind.

But each encounter, in a way, served its purpose. Confirmed what Alexei already knew, in his heart of hearts. But . . . it was still good, he always thought, to have data.

None of the data ever led to further dates.

Not one had led to more than brief moments of cuddling. And while Alexei had loved the lead-up to each of those four times, the dropoff always left him empty.

The careful redressing of clothes. The awkward good-byes. Waking the next morning, the muscles of his body remembering the events of the night before, while his solitude on his pillow reminded him none of it had mattered.

He hated it. He had hated it so much every time.

And now he knew what it felt like not just in his own bedroom, but in a tent. With someone whom he actually knew—because dammit, he *did* know Ben, his kindness and his curiosity and his fears—who wasn't a random swipe-right. Maybe it shouldn't matter at all, because Ben was straight, and they were just friends, and they could laugh it off, like Alexei knew they should. He shouldn't even be framing it around the swipe-rights. It wasn't the same thing at all. They were friends, and it had been an accident. Alexei assumed everything about last night had been an accident.

But no matter how hard he tried to logic it away, somehow, waking up alone this morning seemed to matter even more.

It was quiet outside his tent. Alexei's anger faded to something more gray and heavy. No matter his own confusing feelings, he knew Ben wasn't actually a dorkbutt, not even a little bit.

And as the quiet outside his tent stretched, Alexei was suddenly struck with the fear that Ben was gone. Like *gone* gone. Like he had felt too awkward and embarrassed after spooning Alexei all night that he had packed up early and walked away.

Which...was what Alexei had wanted. He had never planned on sticking to the pact, right? He'd wanted Ben to walk away so he could get back to planning Alexei 2.0, back to saying good-bye in his own private way to the best coast. But—

Alexei peeled back the flap of his tent.

Ben sat cross-legged on the ground, the hood of his sweatshirt over his head, bare toes sticking out of his camp sandals. Staring into his mug of instant coffee. *Thank God*, Alexei thought, sighing inside himself.

Ben looked up at the rustle of Alexei crawling out of his tent.

Alexei sincerely cursed the reality that there was no elegant way to get oneself out of a one-person tent.

He was able to glance at Ben's face for only a fragment of a second. It looked grim, Ben's full lips diminished into a flat line. So Ben wasn't in a laughing mood about last night, either. Darn.

Alexei promptly excused himself to go take a piss behind some sad, scraggly plants.

Alexei couldn't wait for real trees again. What he wouldn't give right now for the solidness, the strength of a redwood.

When he returned to their campsite, Ben still hadn't moved.

"Hey."

The single syllable from Ben's mouth felt unnaturally loud, even though Alexei knew he had actually said it rather quietly. It stopped Alexei short, cutting him off from the path he had been steadfastly focused on: piling straight back inside his tent to change his clothes, get ready for the day, and never talk about last night again.

Gathering his strength, he turned toward Ben.

Ben's hands twisted around his mug.

"So here's kind of a weird thing about me." Ben paused to take a deep breath. "Sometimes, when I'm really stressed, I...fall asleep."

Alexei took a second to process this. He supposed...that would explain last night. If it was even true, if that was even a thing.

Ben rushed to fill Alexei's silence.

"Ask Julie, or my old roommate Khalil, or pretty much anyone in my family. I learned in high school I couldn't wait until the last minute to cram for a test because every time I was lights out as soon as I opened a textbook. I slept a *lot* during nursing school. Like, I have fallen asleep in a *lot* of weird places. I am actually shocked, now that I think about it, that I didn't fall asleep on Fuller Ridge. It's a pretty solidly unhelpful quirk."

Ben's gaze had skittered away as he rambled, focusing on a random point in the horizon. He hazarded a quick glance back at Alexei now before taking an awkward sip of his coffee.

"Anyway, are you mad at me? You look like you might be mad at me. It's okay if you are. I seriously invaded your space, Lex. I'm sorry."

Alexei rubbed a hand over his face, trying to rub away any trace of whatever he was accidentally displaying there.

"No," he said eventually. Because it was the simplest thing to say. And he wasn't mad at Ben. He was frustrated at himself. For being so relieved Ben hadn't left. For saying yes to walking with Ben in the first place.

"So . . . we're cool?"

"Yeah, we're cool."

Alexei dropped his hand. Ben's shoulders slumped forward in relief.

The silence that ensued still felt strange, fraught. Ben opened his mouth a few times, like he was going to say something else, but he never did.

A thought struck Alexei then. A solution, immediately soothing.

They would finish *Alanna*.

They would finish *Alanna*, and then Alexei would tell Ben everything. That he was too attracted to him to keep hiking together, that he needed time alone, that he had had a lovely time and was grateful. Ben would be understanding; Alexei knew he would. And Ben wouldn't have any trouble finding other people to hike with; Alexei knew that, too.

Alexei breathed out, feeling infinitely better. He walked closer to his tent. Time to move on, start the day, keep walking again. They would both feel better, he knew, once they started walking again.

That was the beauty of a trail. All you had to do was walk, and like a prayer, it healed you.

Something caught his eye several yards over, past the peak of his tent's poles.

"Over there," Alexei said, pointing with his chin. No call rang out, no songs to hear here, but their body movements were unmistakable. Remarkable.

"Roadrunners."

Before Alexei fell back into his tent, he watched Ben swivel his head to see, a small smile taking over his features, like a breath of fresh air after you'd been stuck too long underwater.

CHAPTER NINE

Here's a question, Lex." Ben's pack hit the floor of the motel room with a thud. "What first? Bed or box?"

Alexei stared at the Priority Mail Flat Rate box he'd dropped onto his bed, hands on hips. Alexei's name, written in his neat handwriting, straight block letters in thick Sharpie, was the most orderly thing Ben had ever seen. Ben tried, sincerely, not to be turned on by it.

In any case, Alexei was taking too long. While he deliberated, Ben made his decision, moving his own unopened box to the table in the corner before taking a flying backward leap onto the mattress. With a dramatic sigh, he closed his eyes, arms splayed wide at his sides.

It was four days and fifty-seven miles after Ben and Alexei's late-night almost-run-in with the coyote. They had finally reached Big Bear City, home base for their next zero day. A zero day that included *beds*. And a private bathroom. And a rattling AC in the window.

It was so blissful, Ben could almost forget how he'd almost screwed it all up.

He had wanted to die, for a variety of reasons and in a number of ways, when he'd woken up in the middle of that night with his arms around Alexei.

He had attempted to make up for it over the following days by regaling Alexei with every memory he had of falling asleep at inappropriate times and places.

"When I was a freshman in high school, Tiago was a senior, and his basketball team made it to the regional championship," he'd started as they'd carefully picked their way down sandy switchbacks through Hatchery Canyon. "Ended up going into overtime on free throws, after this call from the refs the other team didn't agree with. Some parents started getting into a fight in the bleachers. Ma was yelling up a storm."

He kept walking; stepped over a log.

"I fell right asleep. Missed Tiago's overtime winning shot. He's literally never stopped giving me shit about it."

"I do believe you, you know," Alexei had said. Ben believed him, that he believed him. But he also heard the amusement in Alexei's voice, the smile that he hoped was underneath that beard as Alexei tromped along behind him. So he told another one.

"Junior prom," Ben said. "My crush I didn't think I'd ever have a chance with asked me to dance, and then whispered something, like, shockingly dirty in my ear. I walked over to the wall where Julie was afterward. Passed out on the floor."

And it happened, just as Ben had hoped it would.

Alexei laughed.

"Okay, I don't know if I actually believe that one."

"Swear to God. You can ask Julie, next time we have service."

They walked in silence along the dusty trail. The landscape, slowly but surely, was starting to transition from the wide-open desert that surrounded I-10 to the more forested, mountainous terrain that surrounded San Gorgonio, Onyx Peak.

"I never went to prom," Alexei said a few minutes later. "Or any school dance, really."

Ben tried to picture it. A slightly slimmer, ganglier Alexei, in a buttoned-up shirt and khakis, standing stiffly at the edge of a dance floor. Ben's chest ached to walk over to that boy and give him a hug.

"Did you want to?" Ben asked.

More quiet steps as Alexei considered his answer.

"I don't know," he eventually said, voice quiet.

They didn't talk again until Alexei recognized the song of a mountain bluebird.

The hills had been alive with bird songs the last two days as they approached Big Bear, the trail entering San Bernardino National Forest once more. Ben could almost feel the tension draining from Alexei as the density of trees increased, the availability of shade a balm as they walked under the boughs of white firs and Jeffrey pines.

At night, Ben and Alexei followed Alanna as she triumphed over the vicious, petty Ralon, as she impressed all in the capital with her resilience, as she began to tap into the deep well of her magic.

And Ben pretended, each night, that he cared about Alanna nearly as much as he cared about the cadence of Alexei's voice, the way it pitched when he got to a part he was particularly excited about. Ben pretended, with each chapter, that his heart did not purr inside his chest like a kitten.

They'd gotten into town today right on time to catch the post office before it closed and retrieve their resupply boxes, always a fortuitous sign of a good zero to come. Organizing resupply boxes had been one of the most time-consuming parts of Ben's trail preparation. New food, first-aid supplies, all prepared and mailed in advance, as finding grocery stores along the trail wasn't always a guarantee.

It was such a satisfying accomplishment, reaching another re-supply box, waiting at another post office. Telling the past version of yourself who had packed it months ago: *Look at us. Made it to another one.*

Ben and Alexei had slung their near-identical boxes under their arms and secured a room at this small, mountain town motel. If it could even be called that. It was more like a large cabin with a few rooms for rent, seemingly run entirely by a portly man named Mo. The decor appeared to be straight from the 1970s, wood-paneled walls and heavy tartan curtains. The bases of the bedside lamps were made of gnarled wood, carved into the likenesses of bears and chipmunks and deer. A small, squat TV that belonged in a museum of technology from days past sat on top of the dresser, a yellowed, handwritten piece of paper taped to the side: *DVDs available in office.*

The two full beds were visibly droopy in the middle, the comforters matching the tartan pattern of the curtains but made of a scratchy, worn polyester.

Ben couldn't remember the last time he'd felt this happy.

They would stay in this scrappy little town for the next twenty-four hours, resting, doing laundry, loading everything from their resupply boxes into their packs.

But first, they'd clean themselves up and hit the Mexican place they'd passed on the way to the motel.

Ben heaved himself off the bed with effort. "All right, I'm hitting the shower before dinner, or else I'll fall asleep right here and the bed will smell like hiker trash the rest of the night."

Alexei was working methodically through his box, sitting cross-legged on his bed. He barely nodded, focused on his task, as Ben grabbed his toiletries bag and left the room.

When the first blast of the shower hit Ben's skin, he let out an audible groan that, belatedly, he worried would carry through the walls to Alexei. But shit, he hadn't taken a shower since Warner Springs, and goddamn, it felt good. By the time Ben emerged from the bathroom, freshly washed from head to toe, face shaved, nails trimmed, he felt like a brand-new human being.

And tomorrow, after they found a place to wash their trail-stained, overworn clothes, he'd even be able to throw clean underwear into the mix. What a world!

Alexei stared at Ben from his spot on his bed, a Snickers bar frozen in his hand.

"Feels fucking *good*." Ben smiled, rubbing a palm down his face. "I love being in town."

He threw himself back onto his bed, the mattress creaking in protest. He closed his eyes, damp hair fanning across the pillow beneath him.

After a minute, the silence in the room began to feel odd. *Too* silent. Ben ventured open an eyelid, looking over to find Alexei still staring at him, mouth slightly open.

"Lex," Ben said calmly. "Do you want to hit the shower next? Not to rush you, or anything, but tacos are waiting."

"Right." Blinking, Alexei turned away, grabbing his own toiletries bag before rushing out of the room.

Ben let out a slow, deep breath and stared at the stained ceiling.

The thing about Alexei...was that he was rather obvious about everything, in a way Ben wasn't sure Alexei was even always consciously aware of. Ben didn't know, for instance, if Alexei was aware that he often stared at Ben's mouth, or at Ben in general, for a beat or two too long.

It was obvious, too, when Alexei was uncomfortable, how his shoulders stiffened, how he normally dug out his journal and retreated from the world for a while. It was obvious when Alexei was tired and cranky. When he felt a little goofy and smiled more easily. It was obvious when he was excited about something, all the walls that usually surrounded him disintegrating like magic.

Alexei's near inability to hide what he was feeling was one of the things Ben loved most about him. Ben had spent far too much time in his life around people who appeared to be one thing, only to turn out to be another. It was refreshing, being around Alexei's honesty.

Wait, a voice in his head said. *Did you just say you* loved—

"Shut up," Ben said out loud. To himself.

And then he smothered his face with a pillow.

Ben loved lots of people. He loved his friends. Alexei was a friend.

A friend who read him fantasy novels, who had saved his life at least three times. A friend who had taught him so much about birds. A friend with tree trunk thighs. A friend with eyes that melted him almost every time Ben looked at them, so earnest and kind. A friend with a scruffy blond beard Ben wanted to feel against—

Nope. *No bad decisions.*

He had been so happy ten minutes ago. Then Alexei looked at his mouth too long, and he felt...like this.

Maybe...this had all actually been the worst decision from the start. Choosing to walk with Alexei when Ben knew, when he was honest with himself, that there had never been a moment Ben hadn't wanted him.

He should have known he wouldn't be able to stop.

It just still didn't feel right, wanting Alexei that way. Didn't feel like what Alexei needed. And they had such a good thing going. God, they were such good hiking partners by now. Ben wouldn't be able to explain it to anyone who hadn't gone through something like this, but that partnership felt so special, unlike anything he'd ever experienced before. Giving that up would feel like giving up the PCT.

And where would fully falling for Alexei truly get him anyway? Alexei might let his walls down around Ben sometimes, but Lord knew he still had walls aplenty. Ben had been down that road before, with extremely mixed results. Alexei had serious things to work through. Alexei lived very far away from Nashville.

A noise sounded from the shower. Alexei dropping something, maybe.

And now Ben was picturing Alexei in the shower, and—

Shit. Shit, okay. Ben had never been great at doing hard things—like excelling in school, or getting a real job, or saying no to men who were bad for him—but he was trying to get better at being an adult. Walking away from Alexei would be hard as fuck, but maybe he had to do it, for both their sakes. Maybe they should have a conversation. Maybe Ben should finally be more honest. With himself, but also with Alexei.

But…he'd made Alexei make that pact, about sticking together through the desert.

What would Alexei do if he was left on his own again? Keep making that Alexei 2.0 list, which Ben still didn't completely understand but which filled him with rage anyway? Who would be there to force him to smile sometimes?

Had Ben done enough? To show Alexei that the world was decent? That he deserved friendship and trust, exactly as he was?

His mother's voice this time: *Not your responsibility, Bento.*

Ben's phone buzzed where it was charging on the floor. He let it buzz, clutched the pillow to his chest instead.

Alexei emerged from the bathroom. His skin was rubbed pink; his normally neat hair sticking in all directions as Alexei ruffled it with the thin motel towel. Ben's entire body ached.

"You were right," Alexei said with a small smile. "Feels good."

Ben was filled with a flashback to the night before.

Alexei had studied his maps, as he did every night, before he made his notes in his journal, before he cracked open *Alanna*. He had shared, with a tentatively proud smile, that he'd officially walked a hundred miles.

A hundred miles through the desert. Across a landscape that scared him.

Ben didn't know what to do with his feelings, with the want that threatened to choke him.

But he knew Alexei deserved a night out in Big Bear City.

Maybe he'd figure out what to do tomorrow.

Maybe, for now, they could both have a well-deserved night out on the town.

The Mexican restaurant, like their motel, was small and wood paneled, the walls strung with Christmas lights and papel picado. Ben and Alexei settled into a table in the middle of the room and opened their laminated menus.

It had felt strange walking here from the motel, free of their packs, their bodies light. Ben worked to make his heart feel the same way.

A waitress with sleek brown hair dropped ice waters in plastic cups in front of them, asked if they wanted a drink. Ben quickly scanned the placard on the table for beer options.

"A Pacifico would be great."

"Water's fine, thanks," Alexei said.

"Do you not drink?" Ben asked once the waitress had walked away. "I hope that's okay to ask. It's fine if you don't. I just don't want to make you uncomfortable if I do."

Alexei took a sip of his water.

"My family believed it was a sin. So yeah, no keggers for me growing up."

Ben's mouth tilted. It was a good sign, he thought, that Alexei was attempting to make jokes about his family.

"But I don't care if you drink." Alexei shrugged. "I've *tried* getting into beer, since moving out on my own—it's sort of, you know, a thing in Portland—but I can't do it."

"Yeah, beer's not for everyone. Have you ever tried anything else?"

"Some liquor. Whiskey and stuff." Alexei winced. Like the whiskey had wronged him. Which Ben imagined it probably had.

"Got it. But have you ever had…" Ben flipped to the back page of the menu, holding it up to highlight the brightly colored drinks displayed there. "A Big Bear City margarita?"

Alexei frowned.

"Are you making fun of me?"

Ben's smile fell. "What?"

"Because, you know." Alexei took another sip of water, his movements too fast, shoulders tight again. "Gay guys like margaritas. Or whatever."

Oh, geez. Ben suppressed a sigh. This poor guy.

"Lex," he said, trying to infuse his voice with sincerity, make it clear he wasn't making fun of Alexei, for reasons homophobic or alcoholic. "Anyone with taste buds likes margaritas."

"You didn't order one," Alexei refuted immediately, stubbornly, and Ben smiled.

"The night is young, my friend." Ben leaned back in his chair. "We are a quarter mile away from our motel and have nowhere to be tomorrow. This"—he tilted the beer bottle the waitress had just dropped off—"is merely my appetizer."

Alexei looked at him for another dubious second before staring back down at the menu. He turned to the last page.

"Anyway, Lex, sorry. Drink what you want. Just…" Ben shook his head. This conversation had gotten away from him. "You're in Big Bear City, and the only person here who knows you is me. The world is your oyster." Ben flipped back a few pages in his own menu. "Fight the patriarchy and let yourself enjoy a margarita if you want to."

When the waitress returned, Ben ordered a smothered burrito. Alexei ordered enchiladas.

There was an odd pause. Ben glanced across the table.

Alexei was staring at the back of the menu, frowning.

"I don't know which margarita to choose," he muttered. "It's like the Cheesecake Factory of tequila back here."

Ben barked out a surprised laugh. He smoothed away his giggles with his palm before turning to the waitress.

"This fine gentleman will take a peach margarita, blended. Sugar on the rim."

As she left, Alexei shot a rather menacing glare Ben's way. Or maybe it was closer to a pout. Either way, it was a look Ben hadn't seen before, and it tickled him in every possible way.

"I may have been a repressed child, but even I know a margarita normally comes with salt."

Ben shrugged, grinning. "You'll like the sugar better."

He knew Alexei had a sweet tooth. The only thing the guy ever seemed genuinely excited to eat on trail was his stash of gummy bears.

Alexei scowled. Or attempted to scowl. The corner of his very serious mouth twitched.

"Well," he muttered, fiddling with a napkin, "who wants a big swallow of *salt* in their beverage?"

Ben laughed.

"I wouldn't have taken you as a Cheesecake Factory fan," he said.

"There was one in the suburbs outside of Portland. Kind of far from Vancouver, but we went there for special occasions sometimes. Like my sixteenth birthday, or when I graduated high school." Alexei shrugged. "Cheesecake is awesome."

Ben was dying to know what Alexei Lebedev ordered at the Cheesecake Factory, but was interrupted from inquiring by the arrival of Alexei's blended peach margarita.

Ben couldn't help himself. He propped his chin on his palm, staring as Alexei took his first sip.

"Stop that," Alexei admonished, reaching for the complimentary chips and salsa the waitress had dropped off with the margarita.

"Well?"

"I like it. Okay?"

Ben reached over and grabbed the heavy glass.

"Hey!"

Ben took a loud slurp.

"Oh, *come on*," he practically shouted. He dragged his tongue along the side of the glass to lick up a bit of sugar. "That is fucking fantastic."

Before Alexei could retort back, Ben's phone beeped on the table. He glanced at it before flipping it over.

"Julie?" Alexei asked.

"Tiago," Ben answered. Tiago always texted him the randomest shit. Right now it was: remember how you used to be so bad at minecraft lol

Alexei twisted the margarita glass between his fingers.

"You don't talk about Tiago as much."

Ben's eyebrows rose. He supposed this was true. It wasn't that he and Tiago weren't close; he just talked with Carolina—and worried about Carolina—so much more these days.

"Tell me something about him," Alexei said. It was a funny echo of the times Ben had pushed Alexei to tell him something about Alina. And something about it—Alexei, forcing Ben to share this time, not as a method of distracting Ben from the trail, but just because Alexei wanted to know—made Ben's heart give another small flutter. Whether in appreciation or in warning, Ben wasn't quite sure.

"Tiago was always super into sports," he eventually said. "He and Julie bonded over it, because Julie was a basketball star, too. They'd shoot hoops at our house, watch UT games together." Ben took a long sip of his beer. "He's a sports journalist now," he added. "And...he's really good?"

He didn't mean for this to come out as a question. And yet.

Alexei smiled. "You sound surprised."

"No, it's just—" Ben scratched at the back of his neck. Something embarrassing prickled there. "I always knew he knew sports, but he was always such a goofball. I never knew he could *write*. But I read all of his columns, and they're..." Ben shifted on his chair. "Like, I don't even pay much attention to sports, but he makes you feel like whatever it was, whether it was a high school volleyball game or the Titans going to the Super Bowl, was important. It's impressive."

It *was* impressive. Ben was proud as hell of Tiago.

It really was totally, completely fine that Ben's class clown of a brother turned out to be way smarter and more successful than Ben likely ever would be.

Alexei studied him. Like those summer blue eyes could see straight into Ben's childish insecurities. Which was mortifying.

He was saved, thankfully, by the waitress delivering their food.

Alexei broke his stare and casually ordered a second margarita.

"I'll have one of those, too," Ben said before the waitress left. "Except, uh, just a house one. On the rocks."

"With salt," Alexei supplied. Ben grinned, sheepish.

"Of course." The waitress flashed a smile.

"What about you?" Ben asked as he picked up his fork, more than ready to turn the conversation back to Alexei and away from how Tiago spent his twenties building a respectable career instead of working in coffee shops and dating people who always broke his heart. "You do something with business, right? Or finance? Or you did. Sorry, I forgot you said you got laid off."

"No, it's okay. I'm a data analyst. Which is kind of a generic term, really. I worked at a company called Atlas Athletics after I graduated from UW, until I was laid off, like you said, a few months ago. Which was okay. It was a good place to work, but I'm kind of looking forward to finding something new."

"So you like it? Being a data analyst?"

"Yeah," Alexei said. "I made a lot of reports. Recommendations. I am really excellent at charts."

Ben smiled.

"Did you major in math, then, in college? Or business?"

"Statistics, actually."

Oh. *Statistics*. Well, that made sense. He thought about Alexei's fastidious notes, how he studied his maps every night. Of course Alexei was smart. He was probably a genius.

The waitress brought over their margaritas. Ben took a long gulp. His brain was being annoying.

"I should have minored in computer science, though," Alexei mused as she walked away. "My first year of work was basically a crash course in how little I actually understood coding."

"Yeah," Ben said, putting his glass down and shoving in a huge mouthful of food to cover for how little he had to say about fucking coding.

"Sorry," Alexei said after a moment of silence. "I am... truly, horribly boring."

Ben almost choked on his burrito.

"Lex," he got out. "Trust me, you are not boring."

Ben took a deep breath. He thought about Alexei staring up at the stars that night, telling Ben about his parents. Even if they wouldn't always be, right now they were still trail family. Ben could be vulnerable, too.

"I didn't go to college."

Ben knew, logically, that it was okay not to go to college. He'd had other friends, like Khalil, who had gone to trade schools or apprenticeships, or straight into work.

The difference was that Ben had never had a plan. For a career, for his life. He hadn't been smart enough for college, and then he'd spent a decade being a fuckup. He wondered sometimes. What his twenties would have been like if he'd gone.

Alexei frowned.

"But... don't nurses have to go to college?"

"Yeah, no." Ben ran an anxious hand through his hair. "I mean,

I did. But I didn't go to college right away, like after high school. I wasn't a stellar student in school, and then I spent a while just…fucking around. Doing whatever, watching time go by. It wasn't until my aunt got sick and I spent a lot of time in doctors' offices and nursing homes that I started thinking about nursing. And even when I decided that was a thing I wanted to do, I didn't have the academic background, or the money, to get into a four-year nursing program. They're pretty competitive." Ben's knee bounced under the table. "I went to Nashville State instead, this local community college, and honestly, it was a miracle I even got into *their* program, which is competitive, too. So anyway, I only have an associate's. And most RNs these days have a bachelor's. Fuck, a lot of them have a *master's*."

Ben took an agitated sip of margarita.

"But you passed that test, right?" Alexei's brow was furrowed, that line on his forehead deeper than Ben had ever seen it.

"The NCLEX." Ben said it on this big woosh of air. Even though it was over, it still stressed him out. "Yes. Thank fucking God. By the skin of my teeth somehow."

"And is that all you need? To be a nurse?"

"Technically, along with some type of degree, but Lex…" Ben leaned forward onto his forearms. "I had to work harder than I've ever worked on anything during that nursing program. I almost failed pharmacology. When I was doing my prereqs, before I applied, I had to take A&P twice. What if…" Ben paused. And then he finally said it. "What if I'm not even *good* at it?"

"Bullshit," Alexei said, sharp and immediate.

It was so shocking that Ben's eyes widened, his mind stuttering to a halt.

And then he started to laugh. After a second, so did Alexei.

"Damn," Ben said, tension draining out of his system. "That was a beautiful curse, Lex."

"Thank you."

Alexei took a sip of his margarita, his cheeks flaring pink. But he was smiling.

"When you told me why you wanted to be a nurse," he said after he'd placed the margarita back on the table, "that time we met that old guy on the trail, Thistlewhistle or whatever, you were so passionate and eloquent about it. You are better with people than anyone I've ever met before. It's magic, how you make everyone around you so comfortable."

Alexei was doing a funny, wavy gesture with his arms Ben had never seen him do before. Ben had never seen Alexei talk this animatedly before at all, about anything. Even birds.

Ben found himself holding his breath. This dinner, so far, was not going at all how he'd expected. *It's magic*, he repeated to himself.

"Who cares about your test scores?" Alexei went on, sounding almost angry. Defiant. "If I'm sick, or in pain, or someone I love is, I'm not going to care whether the nurse who's helping me has a master's degree or not. I would just want…someone like you."

Alexei dropped his hands to the table. Dropped his eyes back to his food.

Ben knew he had felt lots of foolish things over the years, especially when it came to attractive men.

But he was pretty certain, right then, that he'd never felt so lovesick in his life.

For many moments, he didn't know what to say. Eventually, he picked up his fork, returned to his abandoned burrito.

"Thanks, Lex," he said quietly to his plate. And then, after a beat, "Sorry. Apparently being on the PCT makes me a lightweight. Although I'm not usually a morose drunk, so I don't know what's happening."

"It's cool, Ben," Alexei said, light and casual and entirely comforting. "It's cool."

CHAPTER TEN

S ilence settled over Ben and Alexei as they finished their meals, as it so often settled over them on the trail.

But Alexei found he didn't want the silence here, in this bright restaurant where the food was rich and spicy and delicious and Alexei was finally hungry enough to truly taste it, and Ben Caravalho was open and uncertain and beautiful.

The truth was, Alexei had felt melancholy about Big Bear City ever since he'd realized, yesterday, that they could easily finish *Alanna* here.

Alexei would say good-bye here.

It felt right, if bittersweet. Tomorrow, during the zero, Alexei would explain himself. He really was getting too attached to Ben, in a way that was starting to feel disconcerting. There would be other hikers in town Ben could meet up with, new trail families to keep him company. Alexei would return to his plan.

But tonight, as Alexei indulged in the sweet alcohol and the filling food of this restaurant, as he listened to Ben spill new, surprising truths, something flushed and freeing spooled down Alexei's spine. Maybe it was the tequila. But his melancholy steadily faded away, replaced by a funny tingle, buzzing underneath Alexei's skin. A different buzz than the one that normally rested there, that made him want to hide away. This buzz felt like his brain cells expanding, discovering new territory. Like he could open his mouth and ask anything and it would be okay.

Another nugget from Ben's revelations snapped in his memory, delayed but important.

"You said you had an aunt who was sick? That's why you wanted to be a nurse?"

As soon as the questions hung in the air, Alexei knew this probably wasn't quite the cheery kickstart this conversation needed.

But amazingly, Ben seemed to relax a little.

"Yeah. Alzheimer's. It runs in my family—my grandmother, my mom's mom, died of it before I was born. My aunt started to show signs about five years ago. Her husband had left a long time ago, and her only kid, my cousin Alice, had moved to Chattanooga and was busy with her own family. So my aunt was kind of alone, other than having my mom. Alice was super stressed about all of it, not being there enough. But I was around, so"—Ben shrugged—"I helped."

He tapped the tines of his fork against his empty plate.

"It's awful. Just a fucking awful disease. I'm terrified of it happening to me one day. But all of her doctors and nurses were incredible. Compassionate and calm, even when she'd get into these rages. I'm still not sure if I could work full-time in an memory care unit, because it's...a lot. It was helpful, though, being on the other side during my clinicals—the helping side, not just the sit-in-a-chair-and-wait-for-someone-to-get-sicker side, you know?"

Alexei wanted to say: *I don't. You are incredible.*

But after a pause, for some reason, what ended up dropping out of his mouth instead was: "That's one thing I worry about, with my parents."

Ben looked up in surprise.

"You have a history of Alzheimer's in your family, too?"

"N-no, I..." *Why* had Alexei brought up his parents? "Just...if they get sick, in general. Or if something happens to them. It feels weird that...I might not know."

"Oh," Ben said softly. "That's hard, Lex."

"I mean"—Alexei winced—"that was a little dramatic. Sorry. Probably I'll know, because Alina will tell me. But like...if they were in the hospital for one reason or another...would they want me to come visit them?"

Ben was quiet a moment, spinning the base of his now-empty margarita glass.

"And you would want to visit them?" he asked carefully.

"Of course," Alexei answered immediately.

Ben only nodded, and Alexei was grateful.

Maybe if Alexei had grown up in a different type of family, in a different kind of world, this whole process would have been easier. But for Alexei's entire life, it had been drilled into him. There were only two things that mattered: family and faith. Without them, he was a drifting ship at sea. And Alexei liked sturdiness. He was trying to be hopeful about the future, his new plans. But in the deepest parts of himself, he simply didn't want to be out on these riotous waters at all.

He knew Ben didn't get it, the fact that Alexei couldn't make himself fully hate his parents. Maybe no one would ever get it, because it was probably the wrong thing to feel. Alexei didn't know, at this point, if he knew how to properly feel anything.

"Sorry," Alexei said. "I feel like I made everything heavy."

Ben shook his head. "Nah, Lex. I believe I was the one who brought up fun topics like my insecurity about my future career and the joys of Alzheimer's, so I think we're even." He pushed his empty plate to the side. "Okay, no more family talk. Do you want to try another drink? Or are you ready to get out of here?"

A group of teenagers entered the restaurant, brash and bustling.

"Another drink," Alexei heard himself saying.

"Something new? I feel confident you've got a handle on margaritas now."

Alexei shrugged. His body felt loose and jangly. *Please shrug like that all the time, it's fun,* he felt his shoulders say.

"Hey, Izzy?" Ben called to the waitress as she walked by. Because of course Ben remembered her name. "Do you think the bartender could make us a Malibu Bay Breeze?"

Izzy smiled, nodded, kept walking.

"What's a Malibu Bay Breeze?" Alexei asked.

"Sunshine and summer and happiness. And rum."

And when Izzy handed it to him, Alexei learned Ben was, again, absolutely correct.

"Whoa," he said.

Ben laughed, and it was bright, just like the sharp, sugary liquid sliding around Alexei's tongue. It broke apart whatever lingering tension was still at the table, dissolving Alexei's parents and Alzheimer's and associate's degrees, replacing them with the tang of pineapple and cranberry and the sweet space between Ben's teeth.

"I'm glad you like it. Although I am officially cutting you off after this; three cocktails is plenty, so long as you don't want to spend your zero day tomorrow with a hangover."

Alexei wasn't so sure. Sampling colorful cocktails he'd never tasted before with Ben for the rest of the night sounded like a solid plan to him.

"I wonder, actually, if we should move to the bar, open up this table," Ben mused. The restaurant had indeed filled up, with more newcomers waiting by the door. Ben waved Izzy over, and soon their plates were cleared and they were moving. It was only when Alexei stood, on two legs that should have been strong from over a hundred miles of hiking but instead felt wobbly and strange, that he truly processed the effects of tequila and rum.

"Huh," he said to himself, standing still for a moment, taking stock of the tingling in his skull, until Ben gave him a powerful, knowing clap on the shoulder. Refusing to be embarrassed—he felt good, he was acknowledging his desires and trying new things, totally on the road to Alexei 2.0, nothing to be embarrassed about here—Alexei grabbed his Malibu Bay Breeze and slid onto the brown leather stool next to Ben in the corner of the room. He shifted his hips, twirling the stool, back, forth, back.

Fun.

Stools were fun.

"Oh my *God*," Ben groaned, taking his buzzing phone out of his pocket. "I swear, it's like she *heard* me say 'no more family talk' and wanted to hound me."

"Ma?" Alexei smiled, feeling light. He loved saying it. It didn't always pinch, when Ben talked about her. *Ma*. Such an affectionate word, so much love in two little letters.

"Yeah." Ben grimaced. "I'll make it quick, promise."

"Ben." Alexei laughed. "I don't care. Talk to her for an hour; I'm good."

Ben brought the phone to his cheek. His smooth, freshly shaven cheek, slightly hidden behind his free-falling hair.

Alexei faced forward as Ben talked. Stared at the bottles of liquor along the back wall, the twinkle of Christmas lights that hung haphazardly above them. He nibbled absently on the bowl of chips Izzy had placed in front of them, his mind feeling sort of floaty, in a hazy, happily empty kind of way.

Until the moment when, an indeterminate number of minutes later, he heard Ben say his name.

He glanced over to see Ben looking at him, a palm cupped over his phone, his mouth twisted in what appeared to be a half laugh, half grimace.

"She wants to talk to you."

"Me?"

"You can say no."

But strangely, Alexei did want to talk to Ma.

He had learned so much about Ben tonight. It felt like a good final puzzle piece, getting to talk to Ma.

"No, it's okay. I'll say hi."

Ben stared at him for a beat, one skeptical eyebrow half raised, before he removed his palm. "Okay, Ma, one second. And be nice."

He handed over the phone.

"Just tell her you're taking care of me or whatever and she'll be happy."

Alexei held the phone in his hand for a moment before raising it to his ear.

Just tell her you're taking care of me.

Christmas lights reflected through the glass of his Malibu Bay Breeze, a distorted rainbow, and Alexei thought about snow, and coyotes, and how sometimes, when they walked through particularly hazardous stretches of trail, he liked Ben in the lead, so Alexei could lag behind him and keep watch, make sure he didn't fall.

"Hello, Mrs. Caravalho."

A peal of laughter invaded Alexei's eardrums. It was different from what he'd expected. It wasn't until he actually heard Ben's mother's voice, high pitched and breezy, that he realized he had expected it to be lower, rumbly, like what you'd expect from someone who gives really strong hugs.

"So polite! Please, call me Iris. Or if you want to be like my kids at school, Miss C."

"Um. Okay. Miss C."

Another bloom of laughter.

"I just wanted to talk to the boy who's keeping my son company, make sure Ben's taking care of himself out there."

"Yes, ma'am—"

"Lordy, *definitely* don't call me ma'am."

"Uh, right." Alexei looked over at Ben, who was hiding half his face under a palm, his eyes still doing that half-cringing, half-laughing thing. "Yeah, no, Miss C, don't worry; I'm making sure your Benjamin is safe."

He wasn't quite sure what made him say that, *your Benjamin*. Maybe some semiconscious thought that by lengthening Ben's name, he could impart the way Ben's shortening of his own made him feel.

But as soon as he said it, he knew he'd made a mistake. Because Iris released a loud *cluck* of her tongue, and Ben's eyes went wide. He waved his hands, shaking his head, his body language screaming *Abort! Abort!*

"Alexei, honey, can you put my dearest son back on the line, please?"

"Uh, sure, of course. Um, nice talking to you, Miss C."

He threw the phone back at Ben like it was a hot potato, having no clue what was happening, but feeling a strange desire to giggle about it anyway.

"*Ma*, I—" Ben started, a hand dragging over his eyes. He was clearly cut off by the loud, fast crackle of noise coming through the receiver from Iris.

And then something remarkable happened, and any laughter remaining in Alexei's throat died away.

Ben was talking to his mother in another language. It took Alexei's brain a minute to remember what it was. Portuguese. Ben had said his family was Portuguese.

For some reason Alexei had never expected that Ben spoke the language, at least so fluently.

Alexei had studied Spanish in school, had been pretty good at it, as a mission trip to Central America had been scheduled in his future. Until he'd stumbled onto a Reddit thread about missionary work his senior year of high school that helped crystallize his own secret anxieties. Alexei barely even liked talking about his faith to people he knew, outside of youth group. It was personal, not something he wanted to sell, like the guys who always stopped by their house to convince them to change cable providers.

He had convinced his parents to let him delay the trip until after college. And then he kept promising, after college, that he'd do it soon, even though he knew he never would. But what was one more lie to his parents on top of everything else?

On the plus side, he still liked Spanish. And so Alexei thought he comprehended a few words of Ben's Portuguese, here and there, but it was mostly like trying to understand a conversation through a cheese grater, rough and full of holes. Alexei had never heard anything so wonderful. Like the words were richer, their edges fuller, their loops swoopier, than anything that had ever reached Alexei's ears before.

Ben caught Alexei's eye and gave an eye roll.

Alexei wanted to put his mouth over Ben's, open and hungry, and swallow down every syllable.

Eventually, Ben switched back to English, but Alexei was in such a fog by that point, he couldn't follow the conversation then, either.

"You just made my mother's entire day," Ben said when he finally ended the call.

Alexei swallowed, his tongue feeling heavy in his mouth. *Get a hold of yourself, Lebedev.*

"How's that?"

"My name's Benedito, not Benjamin."

The way he said that. *Ben-uh-jee-tu.* Alexei couldn't get enough air in his lungs.

"I'm so sorry. I didn't know."

Ben laughed.

"Of course you didn't know! Why the fuck would you know my name is *Benedito*? Anyway, the fact I hadn't already told you my name was Benedito *clearly* shows my lack of respect for our culture and gave her a chance to go all Portuguese mother on me, so good work. She loves that shit."

"Uh." Alexei's brain was rapidly losing the ability to form coherent sentences.

"And you called her Miss C!" Ben shouted. "So cute! God, she must have loved that."

"Well. I wasn't going to call her *Iris*," Alexei managed to say.

Ben laughed again, lifting a newly delivered beer to his lips.

"Why not?"

"It's such a beautiful name," Alexei said. "It felt...intimate."

Ben gave him a funny look, a smiling-but-slightly-puzzled look, and Alexei snapped his mouth shut.

Except after a beat, he opened it again.

"She said the kids at school called her that. Is she a teacher?"

Ben shook his head.

"Secretary. Head secretary, actually, at the high school I went to. Or as she not-so-humbly puts it, 'The only person who actually knows what the hell's going on at that damn place.'"

Alexei smiled. "I bet that's true."

"It is. Everyone knows Miss C." Ben grinned into the distance with fondness. "She says she's going to retire after Carolina graduates this year, but we'll see. The school wouldn't be the same without her. She obviously deserves to retire, but it makes me a little sad. That all the kids coming through East High next won't get to know her."

Alexei wished he knew what she looked like, so he could fill in the details better. But he could picture most of it anyway, a rough sketch of a bustling high school office, Iris's energy filling the room.

Ben picked at the label on his beer bottle.

"I give her a hard time, but I am glad she taught us Portuguese, even if I only ever get to use it when she wants to yell at us. It was how she and my dad fell in love, or so the story goes."

Alexei held his breath, rapt. All he knew about his own parents was that they had met at church.

"I know I said I wouldn't bring up depressing stuff again, but remember I said my grandma had passed from Alzheimer's? So my dad came into the school office one day, way back when, looking to apply to be a bus driver, around the time my grandma, Iris's mom, was starting to get pretty bad. She'd lost language. Ma said it happened so fast. That one day she was talking, and the next she simply...wasn't. My grandma was second-generation Portuguese American, knew the language pretty well from her parents. My mom and her siblings, though, never really learned it. Just bits and pieces here and there."

Ben took a long swig of Pacifico.

"So when she heard the name Caravalho, when my dad came into the office, she asked him if he spoke Portuguese. And when he said yes, she decided, all of a sudden, that she would truly learn it, so she could feel closer to her mom, who was fading by the day. And my mom is...my mom, so of course she convinced my dad to teach her, right there and then, even though they barely knew each other." Ben shrugged. "The rest, as they say, is history."

Alexei was pretty sure this was the most romantic story he'd ever heard.

He wanted more. His Malibu Bay Breeze was long gone, and Ben's second Pacifico was almost demolished, too, but Alexei didn't want to leave the bar yet. Alexei wanted more stories. More whatever this was.

So after a few minutes, he said, "My parents made Alina and me go to Russian school for a while, when we were kids."

"Yeah?" Ben turned his head toward him. "And what does Russian school entail?"

"It was connected to my church, so...church stuff, sometimes. Academic stuff sometimes—math tutoring. But mainly language."

"So you speak Russian?"

"Yeah. Mostly because we spoke it at home, though. Alina and I hated Russian school." Alexei grinned, remembering. "It was all day, every Saturday, and it was boring as all get-out. It actually wasn't that hard to convince my mom to let us stop going. My dad didn't like it, but I think my mom's always had complicated feelings about Russia. I mean, we all have complicated feelings about Russia, but my dad is first generation. Moved here when he was six. So he's more..." Alexei waved a hand, as if the gesture could encapsulate his dad. "Anyway, going to Russian school was just what you did. So when Alina and I were whiny about it, my mom chalked it up to our family friends as us being rebellious. But looking back at how adamant she was about things she *did* believe in, I don't think there was a lot of love lost there."

"How very rebellious of you and your sister. Wanting to have Saturdays to yourselves as children."

"Yeah." Alexei grinned into his empty glass. He knew Ben was teasing. But it *had* felt pretty rebellious, at the time.

"All right," Ben said, a smile in his voice. "Say something in Russian."

Alexei stared at the dark countertop, contemplating.

It wouldn't sound sexy and romantic like Ben's Portuguese had.

But after a few moments, he opened his mouth and said, "Mne nravitsya tvoye litso."

Alexei immediately dropped his head to the counter then and began to laugh, before Ben could ask what it meant, because Alexei felt so ridiculous, downright *silly*, about the fact that he had just said *I like your face* to Ben Caravalho in Russian at a Mexican restaurant in the middle of nowhere, California.

His laughter eventually turned into hiccupping giggles as he rested his forehead on the slightly tacky bar, and God help him, Alexei didn't feel anything in that moment but a light-headed happiness.

A burst of laughter from Ben joined Alexei's giggles, and Alexei looked over at him.

"You were being too nice to me for me to really absorb it at the time," Ben said in between his laughs, "but I'm just remembering how you called Tumbleweed *Thistlewhistle*."

Alexei laughed harder.

He laughed until his stomach hurt, and Ben clapped him on the back.

"All right, Lex. Now that"—Ben scribbled his signature on their bar tab before sliding off his stool—"is the sign of margaritas and rum well had. Let's go sleep for twelve hours."

CHAPTER ELEVEN

B y the time they'd breathed in the fresh air of Big Bear City again, strolling through the early evening twilight back to their motel, Alexei felt better than he had in a long time. Alexei, maybe, felt the best he had ever felt in his whole entire life.

This *place*. This trail, this state, this world was so mind-guttingly *gorgeous*, full of more than you could ever know, peaks and valleys and seriously, *so much* sand, and Alexei was almost starting to feel affectionate toward the desert. And each day they inched closer to the Northwest, to moss and ferns and redwoods and trilliums and roses and banana slugs, and oh, he couldn't wait to see it again. Everything about the natural world made sense to him, from bedrock to oceans to an entire sky filled with birds, and paying it respect was the only responsibility in the world Alexei truly had at the moment. A moment of grace, a blessing made visceral. His body felt stronger now. He couldn't wait to get back on trail.

Only a few minutes had passed when they walked by a gravel parking lot filled with hikers. The crowd was gathered around a man sitting atop a picnic table outside a shuttered café, strumming a guitar.

Alexei stopped abruptly.

"I can play the guitar," he said. "Did you know that?"

Ben's mouth twitched. "I did not."

"I'm better at the piano, though."

Ben's smile grew. "Naturally."

They watched the guy, playing an old Dispatch song, for a few seconds more.

"I'd love to hear you play sometime," Ben said.

"Think that guy'd let me borrow that?" Alexei asked. Ben wanted to hear Alexei play; he'd hear him play.

Ben looked at him, a funny look on his face. "You serious, Lex?"

The scruffy bro finished his song ten seconds later. Alexei stepped forward and cleared his throat.

"Hey," he said. The crowd turned toward him. "My friend doesn't believe I can play." Alexei pointed at the guitar. "Would you mind if I borrowed that for just one song?"

The guitar player looked up.

"You guys on the PCT?"

Alexei nodded. "Yeah."

"Then of course, man."

As Alexei adjusted the strap around his shoulder, strumming a few chords to get his fingers reacquainted with the instrument, he glanced at Ben.

"I honestly have no idea if this song is cool or not, or whatever," Alexei said quietly, just to him. "But you know I didn't have much access to pop culture, so."

And without further ado, Alexei launched into "Wonderwall."

It was almost funny, how not-nervous he felt, even as he opened his mouth to sing the first verse. He felt good. He felt *really* good.

It didn't matter that Alexei hadn't touched a guitar in months. He had played this song a million times, in secret in his old bedroom, even though he was only supposed to be practicing the guitar for church. He knew it like the back of his hand. He knew it like he knew the skin around Ben's eyes was crinkling right now.

Alexei swiveled his eyes as he sang, over to Ben's to confirm. The alcohol was still strong enough in Alexei's system—it had to be the alcohol—that he even managed to maintain eye contact for a line or two, singing about wanting to say something to a person but not knowing how, before he switched back to looking down at the guitar, at his fingers on the frets, remembering on instinct what to do.

At the break after the first chorus, when a moment of silence hung in the air before the second verse, one of the bros called out, "Fuck yeah, man!" and Alexei looked at the crowd, a bit surprised to find they were still there. Everyone was looking at him. Nodding their heads. Smiling.

Alexei had never felt gayer, singing this song to Ben. And at the same moment, he had somehow won the approval of bros.

What a weird, wild world.

He returned his gaze toward his fingers and the strings, focusing in on the line he always sang the hardest to himself as a lonely teenager, the one about realizing what you weren't supposed to do.

Alexei, of course, had always realized.

And here he was, in a circle of wanderers in the middle of California, doing it anyway.

He strung the last chord. It warbled out through the parking lot as the sky darkened around them, hanging there, resonant and perfect, before the sound broke, and the crowd let out a respectable spattering of applause.

Alexei unwrapped the strap and handed the guitar back to its rightful owner, giving a nod of thanks.

"You guys want to stay and play awhile?" the owner asked with a smile.

"Nah, we're good. Thanks again." Alexei held up a hand in a short wave before turning to leave. He heard Ben follow.

The song had opened up a part of himself that was so easy to forget sometimes, when everything else felt too heavy. The part that loved music, strings and chords and keys. It was easy to show emotion in music.

Acceptable. Admired. It was hard for Alexei to express things when they weren't wrapped in melody, but at least he allowed himself that.

And he had always allowed himself that. He had learned "Wonderwall" as a kid, even though he knew he wasn't supposed to love "Wonderwall."

He had kept his guitar, and then he had swiped right as an adult, even if it had been difficult. He had come out to his parents, and he had walked away instead of asking for forgiveness. He had tried a margarita tonight, not because Ben told him to, but because once he let himself, he wanted to.

They walked in silence back to the motel and Alexei grappled once more with the strange sensation of feeling proud of himself.

"I believed you, by the way," Ben said.

"Huh?"

"You told that guy I didn't believe you played."

"Oh, right. Well, I needed to make up some reason for him to give me the guitar."

"You are full of surprises, Lex."

Alexei only smiled.

Ben entered their room first. He sat on the edge of his bed, running a hand through his hair.

Alexei plopped on the bed next to him, unthinking.

And then he huffed out a small laugh.

"Oh," he said. "This isn't my bed."

Alexei was simply so used to always being next to Ben. Even when they slept, Alexei still felt Ben's presence, mere feet away. Alexei knew he was supposed to say good-bye to him soon. But goodness, it felt hard to hide from the truth tonight. And the truth was Alexei was galaxies away from what it felt like to be without Ben Caravalho.

He didn't move from Ben's bed. He would, in a minute. But he was comfortable here, right now.

Ben turned his head toward him.

Alexei looked back and smiled at Ben's face, still suffering slightly from "Wonderwall"-inspired elation.

"Hi," Alexei said.

"God." Ben shook his head, looking down and wiping a hand over his face, releasing a small, almost sad-sounding laugh. "Of course, you are the cutest fucking drunk."

"Am I?"

Ben looked at him again, and Alexei wasn't sure he had ever seen him look so serious. It happened quickly, Ben's eyes turning a shade darker, his jaw clenching. There was a strange beat of silence that felt heavy and light all at once, and then Ben reached up and ran his knuckles down Alexei's cheek.

"Yes," he whispered.

Ben was touching Alexei.

And he was awake this time.

Alexei realized he did not feel strange about this.

At that moment, he only felt like Lex.

The words burst out of him.

"Can I kiss you?"

The words seemed to dance in the air, invisible but loud, and Alexei held in a gasp at himself. He couldn't process Ben's face; his heart was thundering too loudly in his ears, clouding all other senses. A ghost of humiliation waited in the wings, ready to hit fully once the adrenaline of this night was over.

It took his brain a moment to realize Ben was saying something.

"What?" he blurted.

Ben bit his lip. "I said yes."

Alexei blinked.

"What?" he said again.

Finally, that very serious look on Ben's face broke a little, so he could laugh a little, and Alexei exhaled in relief. He always felt better when Ben was smiling.

"Yes," Ben said, louder this time.

"But—" Alexei broke off, brow furrowing. Because, wait. But—

Ben leaned forward and kissed Alexei on the mouth.

It was a quiet moment of almost stillness, just the softness of Ben's lips, so full and gentle against his own. Alexei's brain gave up and clicked off. Let itself have this. Absorbed the feeling of Ben's lips into memory.

And then Ben made a soft noise, somewhere between a gasp and a sigh, and his hands pressed forward, thumbs caressing Alexei's cheekbones, and *oh God*, Ben was kissing him now. Like, *kissing* him. Ben smelled so good, like pine and the lemongrass of the motel shampoo, like sugar and tequila, and underneath it all, that unmistakable hiker smell, of dirt and sweat and skin, and Alexei let go, let go, let go.

He moved a hand to Ben's hip, pressing a palm over the hem of Ben's ridiculous oversized sweatshirt he'd put on during the walk back from the restaurant, the one he wore at camp, the one he wore to keep warm. Everything about Ben was soft and comforting, always had been, but now that he was actually, literally at Alexei's fingertips, everything about him felt extra precious and special: soft cotton and campfires, the warmth of hot chocolate and spring sun. Ben was moss and redwoods, everything that called Alexei home.

When Ben's tongue nudged at his lips, Alexei opened for him helplessly, the first clash of that tongue against his doing sharp, dangerous things to Alexei's gut. Repressing a moan, he did the only thing he could think to do, the thing he had been secretly itching to do ever since he'd met Ben. Alexei's fingertips wrapped around Ben's neck, inched up the base of his skull. And then he plunged both hands into that hair, smooth and ticklish. And on an almost unconscious instinct, Alexei tightened his fists and pulled.

Ben broke away to gasp. Alexei was so electrified by the sound of it, the raw openness, that he forgot to feel guilty that the gasp might have been from pain. But from the way Ben was looking at him, breath shallow—even if it did hurt, Alexei didn't think Ben minded. It was dizzying, knowing he had made Ben look like that. Alexei wanted more, just like that. He wanted to witness Mr. 100 Percent Chill come undone. He wanted to be the cause of it.

Through a series of awkward scrambling, of mouths hitting chins and elbows hitting sides, of shoving off shoes, Ben and Alexei navigated themselves farther back on the bed, until Alexei was hovering fully over Ben, Ben's head resting on the pillows.

"Wait," Ben said as Alexei moved his mouth to Ben's jaw, to his neck. "Fuck," he groaned when Alexei hit the soft skin behind his ear. "Wait," he said again, and Alexei actually processed it this time. He lifted his head, resting his weight on an elbow.

"Yeah?" he asked, a bit breathlessly. If Ben was going to tell him to stop, he would understand, of course, completely. He would also probably die. He would try to accept his death with humility.

"Are you still drunk? You must be. I don't want—"

"No," Alexei cut him off. "I'm not."

And it felt true. The reckless giddiness that had filled him earlier at the bar had dissipated on the walk home. When Alexei had to focus on chords, on finger configurations over guitar strings, on remembering lyrics, it had brought his system back to attention. Right now, Alexei's head felt as clear as the water in Crater Lake, Oregon: sparkling, crystalline blue.

"I'm good," Alexei assured Ben again, when Ben continued to look at him with uncertainty. "I promise."

Ben stared at him a second longer, until, apparently, he believed him. Because suddenly, Ben's hands were—God, Ben's hands were just...*everywhere*, his lips firmly back on Alexei's. Alexei sank himself farther down, covering Ben's body with his own, chest to chest, settling one thigh between Ben's legs, and—

Even with Ben's willing kisses, with his aggressive hands, it was all still a little shocking.

But mostly it was thrilling. Mostly it was transcendent.

And Alexei couldn't bear one more transcendent second with Ben while his elbows scraped along this pilled, scratchy comforter.

With a grunt of irritation, Alexei sat up, yanking at the comforter beneath Ben's body until Ben got the picture. He canted his body upward, as much as was needed for Alexei to rip the polyester nightmare from underneath him. In one fluid motion, Alexei flung the whole affair onto the floor.

"Whoa."

Alexei's motions stilled when he realized Ben was staring at him, leaning back on his elbows, his mouth smiling in a kind of amused awe.

"What?" Alexei said. "That thing was awful."

"Agreed. You are just...intense."

Alexei froze further. He supposed he did feel a little intense. Which wasn't different, on a normal day, but it was when it came to this. When it came to this, Alexei felt so, so different.

"I like it," Ben clarified at Alexei's hesitation. And then Ben reached up and began unbuttoning Alexei's shirt.

Alexei looked down, watching Ben's progress, and he wondered why everything about this was so vastly superior to any sexual encounter he'd had before. Every time Ben's knuckles grazed his skin, pleasure sizzled deep into his bones.

He wondered if it was because of the trail. Because never in his life, even in his cross-country days, even throughout all the hours he'd spent at the gym these last few years, had Alexei been more aware of his own body.

Every second on the trail was about the body.

Blisters. Bites, scratches.

Stretched muscles, overworked tendons.

Sunburned skin.

Maybe it was this hyperawareness of every part of himself that made each slide of Ben's fingers, every whisper of Ben's lips, feel like Alexei was on fire.

But maybe it didn't have anything to do with that at all.

Maybe it was just because it was Ben.

So attentive to the small details Ben.

Ben, who was easing Alexei's shirt over his shoulders, whose palms were sliding back down over Alexei's chest, his abdomen, his sides.

"Damn," Ben's voice, shaky and low. "Lex."

Alexei closed his eyes, unable to watch Ben admire him. Alexei knew...about his chest. About the shape of his torso. Some of the definition had already changed these last few weeks of hiking, his body adjusting to the rigors of the trail versus the targeted exercises of the gym, but he understood what Ben saw. He had always liked wearing his body down to exhaustion, whatever the method. It was a simple, understandable thing, working his muscles and his lungs. He could focus when he worked out, calm and even and productive. The gym was the one space, these last six months, where he never felt sad.

It wasn't admirable, really, at least not in Alexei's eyes. It wasn't something to brag about, that his shoulders were sculpted because the endorphins that raced through his body in exercise were often the closest he felt to happiness. That he had defined obliques because he was lonely.

Because the endorphins always faded.

Ben's light touch across his skin became too much. Alexei opened his eyes, tugging on Ben's sweatshirt so he wasn't the only one exposed. Ben slipped the sweatshirt off along with the T-shirt underneath before lying back on the pillow again. Alexei looked down at him then, really looked at him, Ben's lean body and his open, patient face.

And Alexei knew he had slipped into the danger zone of getting too into his head, thinking too much about all the nights spent at the gym because he had nowhere else to go, the swipe-rights that always left him empty, the overwhelming unexpectedness of this man below him. He worried, heart thrumming anxiously in his chest, that all the windows that had opened within him would soon start to close.

"Say something in Portuguese," Alexei heard himself say.

Ben smiled. And he did.

His arms reached up again, his hands on Alexei's skin firmer this time, fingertips reaching around to his back, trailing down his arms as sultry sounds fell out of his mouth, thick consonants and long vowels, and Alexei closed his eyes once more, let it wash over him, the language and the touch, until Ben's words ran dry.

Alexei opened his eyes again, pulse calmed. He had no idea what Ben had said. He didn't particularly care. All he could think about, as he stared at this beautiful, bilingual perfection of a man, was that he couldn't believe Ben didn't think he was smart enough, or good enough. Alexei had never met anyone worthier of everything. He was going to be the best goddamn nurse this world had ever seen.

Alexei sank down and kissed him, pressing into the heat of his mouth, moaning at the touch of Ben's bare stomach against his, heart fully opened once more. He yanked in impatience at Ben's shorts and his own until it was all gone, nothing but skin on skin, muscle against muscle, each sensation ringing like a drum in Alexei's chest: *right, right, right.*

They arched against each other, struggling to somehow get closer, touch more, feel more, each shift of their torsos alive with friction, Ben's hands tracing down Alexei's lower back, cupping his butt, gripping at his hips.

"Fuck," Ben gasped between kisses. "God, Lex, you feel so good."

Alexei answered with a grunt, moving his mouth to Ben's collarbone. He couldn't handle Ben's curses, his breathy encouragement, this mindless dry humping. He was going to lose himself before he could even get to what he really wanted. And for a wild half second, he almost said it out loud.

He couldn't. He wasn't there yet. But he said it to himself as he planted his palms on the bed to ground himself, as he leaned his body away from Ben's and focused on his mouth making its way down Ben's chest, and that, too, was revolutionary.

I want to make you unravel. I want to feel you in my mouth.

I want to see your face when you come.

Alexei pulled up short, though, when he reached Ben's hip.

Not because of Ben's dick being inches from his face, although Alexei was very, very aware of that. No, it was the cartoon figure on the very top of Ben's thigh, right before the muscle dipped into his hip. Alexei ran his finger over the faded ink. The figure was short and wore a hat. He had pointy ears. He was winking at Alexei, pointing a sassy finger.

"What is this?"

Ben looked down. "Oh God." He winced before throwing his head back onto the pillow, chest heaving. "You found Link."

"Link?" Alexei glanced up, questioning.

"You know, from *Legend of Zelda*?" Ben swallowed, shaking his head. "I played that video game nonstop when I was a kid. I was bad at school but I was, uh, kind of a nerd."

Alexei couldn't stop running his finger over it, his lust temporarily frozen in the surprise of it. It was so...funny. And cute. It was...entirely like Ben.

"Anyway, I blame Tiago. The fucker actually took me to get it when I was eighteen, instead of telling me it was an incredibly bad idea, like any respectable older brother should have."

"I've never played a video game," Alexei said absently, placing a chaste kiss on Link's ears. Alexei had never even thought about getting a tattoo. Leviticus was pretty clear on that one.

"Really? Never? I mean, no, never mind, that makes sense."

He'd watched other people play video games over the years, and some of his D&D friends insisted there were ones Alexei would like. But even venturing into the world of tabletop and RPG had been a lot to take in.

Maybe he'd add *Legend of Zelda* to his list, though. Maybe Alexei 2.0 could learn to play it, and think of Ben.

"I'm just wondering," Ben said softly, running a hand through Alexei's hair, "how you occupied yourself as a teen, without TV or video games."

"I read a lot."

"Oh yeah," Ben said. "Right. Sorry, I knew that."

"And, you know." Alexei finally tore his eyes away from Ben's silly, intriguing tattoo, running his hand down Ben's other thigh. "I jerked off a lot and hated myself."

"Lex." Ben's hand stilled on his head.

The *Lex* made Alexei get down to business. Because this wasn't the time for all that.

This was the time to kiss the base of Ben's dick. To slowly run his tongue, flat and heavy, up the length of him, satisfaction seizing his system at Ben's shudder. He stayed at the tip for a minute, swirling his tongue while his fingers danced around Ben's inner thighs, flirting with his balls, monitoring Ben's breathing, the twitches of his body, the clench of his fingers in Alexei's hair, slightly frantic and wonderful.

He had done this only a couple times before, but he wanted to do it right for Ben. The noises Ben was making made him feel like he was doing an okay job so far. Encouraged him to keep going.

Alexei took a breath. And he took as much of Ben into his mouth as he could.

"*Jesus Christ*, Lex. Oh, fuck, I probably shouldn't have said that to you. Lord's name in vain. I'm so sorry. I—oh fuck, that feels good."

Alexei released his suction for a moment to laugh, which made Ben whimper, and a bolt of happiness pinged through Alexei's heart. He started to lose himself soon afterward, in the stream of curses leaving Ben's mouth, the rhythm of Ben's hips, Alexei's own muscles taut and vibrating.

Ben's breath came faster, heavier, as his lower body lifted off the bed, pushing shamelessly farther and faster into Alexei's mouth. Alexei slid a hand around Ben's backside, squeezing and steadying his movements, feeling the tension coiling in his thighs, the urgency in how Ben grasped at his shoulders. What a gift, to bring someone pleasure, to learn how bodies reacted to every variation of touch. Alexei felt overwhelmed with it. When Ben came, Alexei couldn't watch his face as closely as he had hoped, but he could hear Ben's breathy cry, and that felt like a wonder, too.

He planted soft kisses along Ben's side as he clambered upward, falling contentedly onto his side. Ben's arms were raised, his forearms crossed over his forehead, eyes closed, chest rising and falling. Alexei ran a hand over the soft hair there, feeling Ben's heart beneath it, studying the physicalness of him here, next to him. Their bodies were both painted in vivid hiker tans: their necks, faces, hands, and calves darkened from the sun, the rest of them pale as winter. Well, Alexei was a frostier shade of winter than Ben, Ben was—

Alexei's train of thought was cut short by Ben throwing himself on top of Alexei rather suddenly, flattening his back against the mattress, Ben's forearms locked around Alexei's shoulders.

"My turn," he said.

"Oh," Alexei said, dumbfounded. And then, "You don't have—"

"Stop it." While the words were aggressive, the kiss Ben planted on Alexei's lips was gentle, reassuring. "I want to."

Alexei swallowed, a heady anticipation crashing into his system, scrambling all of his wires. He had already been so happy. He had thought—

But then he really looked at Ben's face, and Alexei laughed. Because Ben looked slightly out of his mind. His eyes were unfocused; he struggled for breath.

"You could, you know, take a minute," Alexei said, reaching up to run a hand through Ben's hair. It was damp at the scalp but felt light and clean between his fingers. He still couldn't quite believe, even after what they'd just done, that Ben was letting him touch it.

"No," Ben said, and his hand reached down between them, clamped itself around Alexei's dick, "I don't believe I can."

Alexei's breath caught in his throat. "Don't—"

Ben let go immediately.

"Sorry," Ben pulled back, frowning. "I shouldn't have assumed— should have asked—"

"No, it's—" Alexei closed his eyes. How to explain you were more turned on than you'd ever been in your life? "I'm just literally about to go off any second."

"Oh," Ben said on a heavy exhale. He leaned down again, resting his forehead against Alexei's, noses touching. "Fair."

They stayed like that a moment, and Alexei's eyes fluttered open to take in the sight of Ben's eyelashes, the light freckles on his cheeks, his parted lips.

When Ben moved, he was slower, deliberate, started at Alexei's neck, made his way down Alexei's chest. Alexei's head lolled back on the pillow. There was no wrong or right way to be in this liminal space: no sin; no guilt; no hurt. Only Ben's hands, Ben's mouth, so tender and attentive, and the way they made Alexei feel, like he was made of fireworks: hot, thrilling bursts of color.

Alexei tried to make it last as long as possible, he really did, but holy hell, Ben was *good* at this. His hair tickled Alexei's thighs; it was hard to believe that Ben—that Ben was—oh God, Ben was making Alexei feel so good. It felt like approaching the top of a waterfall, the thundering roar getting closer and closer, until you finally got near enough to see the drop-off, and it felt like the whole world cascaded off the edge.

His fingers gripped the sheets, stars dancing behind his eyelids when he reached that edge, obliterated. When he finally blinked his eyes open, Ben was still between his legs, lips kissing the inside of Alexei's thigh, his hip bone.

This was the moment. This was when the emptiness always poured in before, at almost the exact instant the orgasm receded, everything that had felt so good and powerful in the moments leading up to it replaced with shame and awkwardness. Alexei had never known how best to proceed at this juncture, how to reconcile the riotous feelings of his body with his mind.

But now, here, Ben, who was smaller than him, turned Alexei's boneless body onto its side. Ben wrapped an arm around him, holding him tightly, with intention, taking control, giving Alexei everything he had ever wanted, the space for his body to ride this out, to rest in it. Alexei fumbled for Ben's hand. Finding it, he brought it to his mouth and kissed its palm before twining his fingers through Ben's and returning it to its resting place, on Alexei's chest.

He felt Ben kiss the back of his shoulder.

He knew he wouldn't wake up alone.

Alexei's chest expanded larger than Alexei had ever felt it, a brand-new entity inside himself. Large enough for joy.

And large enough for a single shard of something else, something composed of unease and fear, to rear its head, resting easily next to Alexei's heart. It pressed there, small but persistent, until Alexei's body overrode it all, and he fell asleep.

CHAPTER TWELVE

B en woke slowly, as if still tucked neatly into a dream. Sunlight streamed through the gauzy curtains, warming his face. His body was relaxed, supported by the cozy mattress.

Beds. God bless them.

He turned with a lazy stretch, a low groan.

He still felt mostly asleep when he saw Alexei.

Who was perched at the edge of the bed, propped tensely on an elbow, his other arm stretched across the mattress, as if half reaching toward Ben, half preparing himself for launch. His eyes were wide and wild: the most beautiful and terrified version of blue Ben had ever seen.

Last night returned to Ben in vivid detail, waking him abruptly all the way up.

"Lex—" Ben reached for him, but Alexei had already snapped out of his stupor. He snatched his hand back, blinking furiously.

Ben's heart, which had been so wonderfully sleepy and content moments before, crushed like a fist inside his chest.

Alexei fumbled out of the bed, running a hand through his rumpled hair. He stepped toward the chair by the wall, where his underwear was, and slipped it on, and Ben could only watch him and remember. That body over his, under his mouth. It was the best body Ben had ever witnessed. And not just because of the muscles or because of the...*everything*, but because it belonged to Lex, this strong, kind, fascinating human being.

Who had just scurried into the bathroom and slammed the door without a second glance back.

Oh God.

Ben scrambled to a sitting position and hung his head in his hands.

He had *told* himself not to do this. Over and over. And then, at the slightest invitation—

Oh God, and it had been so good. Better than Ben even could have imagined. And despite his best intentions, Ben had imagined a lot.

And now Alexei was freaked the fuck out.

They could talk it through. Work it out. Because Ben thought he could say good-bye to this, but clearly, Ben was an idiot.

Alexei emerged from the bathroom with his toiletries bag, neatly packed.

He walked to his pack in the corner and hefted it onto his still-made bed. Found his shirt on the ground and pulled it over his shoulders, buttoning it over his magnificent chest.

He did not look at Ben once.

Alexei was leaving.

Ben knew it in his gut. As the realization sank in, he almost couldn't speak at all. But he had to say something. Had to try.

"Lex. Listen. Last night was—"

"Ben, it's fine." Alexei pulled on his shorts. "It's cool."

He had said this last night, too, at the restaurant, and it had been so funny then. A phrase Ben had never heard Alexei say before, yet it had sounded so natural when he'd been comforting Ben about his life. Now it sounded ridiculous, like Alexei had turned into some kind of neutral-phrase-spouting robot.

"It's cool?" Ben repeated, with confusion. Because also, this response didn't even make sense.

"Yes. It's cool."

Ben stared at Alexei's back as he turned to pick up his trailrunners.

"Alexei," he said softly. "It's not cool. I mean, that's not—" He rubbed a hand over his face. "We should talk about it. I'm sorry, Lex, if—"

"I'd prefer to not talk about it." Alexei collapsed into the chair where his underwear had been, unrolling his socks. "Ben, I'm sorry. I meant to talk to you about this in a better way, but I think I'd like to get back on the trail sooner rather than later." He bent down to slip on his shoes. "Alone," he added, speaking to the floor.

As if Ben didn't know. As if this wasn't obvious.

But Ben still flinched anyway.

"Alexei," he tried again, but it came out as soft and feathery as before, like he was about to burst into tears. Which it was possible he was, but that definitely wouldn't help this situation. He cleared his throat. "Lex, if you want to stop hiking with me, that's fine, although I really wish you'd hear me out. But either way, this is a bad decision. You need the full zero. I know we had a relatively light hiking day yesterday before we got here, but your body needs—"

"Ben." Alexei held out a hand, as if to physically stop Ben from speaking. Which Ben supposed was fair. Lord knew he was already regretting letting the words *your body* escape his mouth. "I know what you're saying. But I feel good. And I'm already behind on my mileage goals, so I need to catch up now if I want to make it to Canada before the snow."

Alexei stood and did a quick scan of the room, looking for anything he'd missed.

Except for Ben. He still hadn't made eye contact with Ben.

"Come on, Lex." It sounded weak and defeated, even to his own ears. "You should at least stay until we can do some laundry."

"I'm okay. I'll only get anxious hanging around here today anyway."

Even though both Alexei and Ben knew this was patently untrue. It was Ben who had gotten anxious and bored during the last zero day; Alexei had clearly been at peace. It was Alexei who had put Ben at ease by reading to him.

Oh. Ben swallowed.

He wouldn't find out what happened to Alanna.

"If that's . . . what you want," Ben managed.

"It is."

He sounded so certain. And Ben knew he was.

Alexei wanted to be alone. Ben had always known it. He just maybe hadn't actually respected it until now.

He turned to the window and listened to Alexei put on his pack. The shifting of fabric as Alexei adjusted it against his hips, the click of straps put into place. The tinny clang of Alexei's trekking poles banging together.

And then, a moment of silence.

"Ben?"

Ben closed his eyes. Alexei finally sounded like himself, voice gentle, a little uncertain. And it set Ben on the very edge of cracking.

"Yeah?"

Another beat of quiet.

"Thank you." Alexei's pack shifted against his back. "For walking with me."

Ben nodded, his throat too thick to say any more.

He waited until he heard the click of the door.

And then he fell back against the pillow. The mattress only felt droopy now. Too soft.

He fell promptly asleep anyway.

The next time he awoke, the sun shone even higher in the sky, Ben's body felt far worse than it had before, and he desperately needed to pee.

After that matter of business finally propelled him out of bed, he paced the room, hands in his hair. He should get to the Laundromat, pronto. He should take another shower. He should finally open his resupply box.

He sat down on the bed and called Julie.

"What happened?" she asked, breathless, after picking up on the third ring. "Did you hurt yourself? Did a bear attack you? Fuck. Was it a rattlesnake?"

"Julie." He almost cried at the sound of her voice. "I'm fine."

A frustrated sigh. "Then why the *hell* are you calling me, Caravalho? You know what an actual phone call means. The IRS has a very legitimate concern about my taxes, or someone very dear to me has died."

"I fucked up, Jules." He rubbed a hand over his forehead. "I wanted to hear your voice. And maybe cry a little. I don't know."

"Oh." Her voice softened immediately. There was an indistinct shuffle. "Okay. Hold on."

"Wait, are you at work? I'm sorry. I honestly have no idea what day of the week it is. I can call you back."

"It's Tuesday, objectively the worst day of the week, and stepping out to talk to you is going to be the best part of it, so shut your mouth."

More shuffling. A small *whoosh* Ben thought was a door swinging shut. And then quiet.

"Okay, so how'd you fuck up? I'm thinking you either broke your leg or something happened with that hunky hunk in all your Instagram photos."

"Are you sure I'm not interrupting? I'm on a zero day, so I'll be around. I really can call you back."

Julie snorted. "Bitch, please. Lorraine sent a real trip of an email this morning, and I've been very angrily telling myself I don't care about it for two hours. I'm begging you. Interrupt me."

"Ugh. Fuck Lorraine."

"I agree. Now, what did the boy do?"

"What if I told you I actually did break my leg?"

"I would be very mad at you for lying and saying you were okay when I picked up the phone. Come on, Ben. Tell me what's wrong."

Ben sighed.

"Well. So. I slept with him."

"Obviously," Julie said. "I'd been assuming you were sleeping with him this whole time."

"No, no. We were just friends. Hiking partners."

Silence. Ben could picture Julie, in whatever closet she was hiding in, trying very hard to think of something kind to say.

"Is that so," she finally said.

"It is!"

"Same dude you posted a photo of three days ago, just the side of his face while he watched the sun set, with no caption? You weren't already banging that dude."

Ben sighed. "He's going through some shit. His parents fucking disowned him, Julie. For being gay. He came to the trail to deal with it."

"Shit," she muttered.

"Exactly." A pang of guilt hit him for spilling Alexei's secrets, but he told Julie everything. And he was still reeling from this morning, and God, he missed telling someone everything. "And from the moment I met him...I don't know. I think I've been waiting for him to walk away from me this whole time, even though I made him make this pact—"

"You made a *pact*?"

"Yeah. To walk through the desert together. He's scared of the desert."

"Oh no. Oh, my dumb little heart is melting. Please, continue."

"Well—" It suddenly felt like a lot to tell, the last couple of weeks with Alexei. "Basically, we got to this town last night, Big Bear City, and went to this restaurant. And..."

Ben swallowed.

"And it was great. I sort of word vomited a bunch of stuff at him, but it was nice, and—and we were drinking. Except Alexei doesn't drink, because he was raised in some kind of super strict religion, and I think I maybe pushed him to? Oh God. It's just that he's had this really hard time and I'm really proud of him and I just wanted him to let loose and let himself have fun and—oh no, Julie. I'm one of those people they warned us about in all those D.A.R.E. videos."

"Ben."

"I am! I'm a bad influence, Julie! I'm a drug pusher!"

"Wait, did you do *drugs*, too?"

"Alcohol counts as drugs."

Julie sighed. "So then you banged."

"Yeah. Well, actually, no—Julie, oh my *God*." Ben fell back onto the bed. "First, we started walking back to the motel, and we pass this group of people playing music in a parking lot, and Alexei just, like, takes this dude's guitar and plays 'Wonderwall.'"

"Shut the fuck up." Julie laughed.

"I *know*." Ben curled his legs in front of him, unable to hold back his sigh. "It was so, so unlike him and so *dreamy* and he can, like, really sing? And he was *looking* at me, and *ugh*—"

"My poor Benny poo," Julie soothed.

"I know." Another sigh. "Yeah, so then we banged."

"Obviously."

"Obviously."

"And was it bad or something?"

"It was *incredible*."

"Gross."

"You asked."

"So then what happened? I'm waiting for the *you fucked up* part here."

Ben frowned.

"Did you not hear me when I said I plied a sweet, sweet man with alcohol and then sucked him off when I knew that was the last thing he probably needed, like, emotionally?"

"*Gross*, you know I don't like details—"

"You love details."

"But why is having a bit of fun and then getting off not what he needs emotionally? It sort of sounds like that's exactly what he needs."

Ben closed his eyes.

"It wasn't. Because if it was, he wouldn't have bolted this morning as soon as he woke up."

"Oh." Ben could picture Julie's frown. "And you just let him go?"

"Yeah. It was the right thing to do."

Julie was quiet a moment.

"Well, that fucking sucks."

"Yeah. It's going to be so lonely hiking without him. I just felt safer with him there, you know? And he knew all this stuff about birds and—"

"I can't believe you just let him go!"

"He seemed pretty determined, Jules. He needs time alone to sort his head out, I think. And—"

"Wait, I'm sorry, he looks at you like he's looking at you in those Instagram pictures and fucking serenades you and then he just leaves?"

"Julie."

"No, I get it, he needs to be alone and sad for a while, but—" A heavy sigh. "Goddammit, Ben. I just . . . want this to stop happening to you."

A hole opened up in Ben's chest.

"I know," he whispered, trying and failing at not sounding pathetic. "Me too, Julie. That was how I fucked up, too. I shouldn't have ever hiked with him in the first place. I liked him from the moment I saw him. I had already been telling myself, before last night, that I needed to step away. I just—" He squeezed his eyes shut. "What if I can never grow up?"

"Hold up. What do you mean?"

"I spent the last decade of my life making bad decisions, and I came out here to *stop* making them, and what is literally the *first* thing I do?"

Okay. Maybe that wasn't technically accurate. He had hiked 150 miles before he met Alexei. Maybe he could still be proud of those 150 miles he somehow got through without throwing himself at a boy.

"Ben." Julie took a deep breath. "Okay. Can I be honest with you right now?"

Ben snorted. "You're always honest with everyone, Julie."

A pause that ran a little too long.

"Not always," Julie said softly.

"Okay." Ben felt his chest puffing up in defense before he could stop it. "Go for it, then."

"I worry about you, Ben," she said. "I've been worried about you for a long time." Before Ben could say anything, she added, "Especially since Robbie."

Ben sucked in a breath between his teeth. God. You date *one* possessive prick who isolates you from your closest loved ones for a year, and your best friend never lets you forget it.

"But it's not *just* Robbie," Julie went on. "You've always been too hard on yourself, Ben. Always thinking you're making these...'bad decisions.'" Her voice turned angry, the air quotes clear over the line. "You never believe in yourself as much as you should. I don't know why, because you're fucking amazing, so honestly, it pisses me off most of the time."

She did sound pissed off, and Ben welcomed it. Would much rather Julie yell at him than speak in that gentle, pitying voice that didn't fit Julie at all.

"Like, you put yourself through nursing school after taking care of your aunt Birdie, and now you're doing this incredible thing only point-two percent of the human population probably even thinks about doing, and you're worried about not being grown up enough? What the fuck."

Ben curled himself into a tiny ball. As he often wanted to, whenever the word *Robbie* entered a conversation.

"And Ben, actually, now that I said all that, it makes me think . . . Birdie started getting sick right after you left Robbie, didn't she?" Julie's voice got soft again. "Ben, I don't think you've even given yourself a chance to breathe since Robbie."

"I'm breathing just fine," Ben responded. "That's all there is to do on the PCT. Walk and breathe."

"Yeah. Yeah, no, that's good." Julie took another big breath. "Anyway, I think what's happened is you surrounded yourself for a long time with shitty people who reinforced that you weren't enough. But the thing is—"

Another frustrated huff.

"You haven't made bad decisions, Ben. You open your heart to everyone, which, sure, isn't always a *wise* decision, but it's not necessarily something to be ashamed of. It's the people who haven't treated that heart with respect who have been the bad decision makers. Do you get it?"

Ben stared out the window, eyes hot. He *wanted* to get it. He knew Julie was trying to be nice. But he still felt so deeply embarrassed about all of it. That he'd stayed with Robbie so long, that Julie had to talk to him in gentle tones about his life when he was nearing thirty and should've been able to figure out his shit himself.

Plus, even if not *everything* about the past decade was his fault, a pattern was still a pattern. He did have some responsibility for his mistakes here.

"They weren't *all* shitty people," he managed after a long pause. "Hugh was nice."

It was weak, and beside the point, he knew, but he felt exhausted suddenly and didn't know what else to say.

"He was," Julie agreed. "Until he wanted you to do something you didn't want to do."

Hugh had been after Robbie; Ben had thought Hugh was a good decision. One of the last people he'd dated, at least in a serious way, near the start of nursing school. But after a few months, Hugh had wanted to open up their relationship. Which, at the time, had felt like an almost surreal turn of events, considering Robbie hadn't even liked Ben hanging out with other people. Ben had wanted to be cool with the idea, but when he was honest with himself, he simply didn't know how he felt. He was a whole mess then anyway, struggling to keep up with school, and it just felt like too much.

It didn't matter in the end. Because by the time he'd decided to tell Hugh he couldn't do it, Hugh had already fully moved on to the guy he'd wanted to be more open with anyway.

He really had been nice, though, while they were together. And hot.

It was possible Ben still stalked Hugh's Instagram sometimes.

"And this guy," Julie pushed on after another long pause. "Alexei. Is *he* nice? Does he believe in you? Does he respect you, treat you with kindness, act like you're perfect exactly as you are? Does he make you feel like you can do anything?"

Ben laughed a little. "Julie, have you become a romantic?"

Julie had never dated anyone in her life, as long as Ben had known her. Since the fourth grade. It felt a little funny that she was pressing him like this.

"Shut up, Caravalho." Oh good, angry Julie again. "I'm fucking serious. Does he?"

Ben's laughter faded. He tried to be serious, too.

He thought about Alexei at the restaurant. When he'd talked about Ben, and nursing, and being good with people. How he'd said: *It's like magic.*

Ben started to cry.

It was possible he'd already been crying for a while now.

"You don't have to answer those questions right now if you don't have an answer. But if he doesn't do those things, then yes, let him go, Ben. *Let him go*," she emphasized. "You can do it. Keep kicking ass on that trail all on your own. I know you can. But..." A smaller pause. "You look happy in the photos you've been posting lately, Ben. Like, really, genuinely happy. And Ben?" That soft, un-Julie-like voice again. "It's not a bad decision to be happy."

Ben bit his lip.

"Even if he lives in Portland?" he let himself ask. "Even if he decides he doesn't want to be with me, after the trail? If he even wants to be with me now?"

Julie sighed.

"Those are questions for you and Alexei to answer, Ben. But I feel like spending some time at least thinking about them isn't a bad idea."

Maybe she was right.

But Ben already felt himself resigning to the fact that he might not ever see Alexei Lebedev again. Alexei was already back on the trail; Ben had barely gotten out of bed. Alexei was strong, would likely be hiking even faster now. He would be far away by the time Ben returned to the trail. If Ben returned to the trail. Maybe he would just sleep forever in Big Bear City instead. Move in with Mo. Mo seemed nice.

Alexei, for all intents and purposes, was simply a painful, if familiar, ache in the middle of Ben's chest now. He felt silly he'd even asked those questions to Julie out loud. If Alexei wanted to be with him, he'd still be here.

"I miss you so much, Julie."

"I miss you, too."

"Can you go give Delilah a hug for me sometime, maybe?"

"You bet your ass I can."

"The trail is really hard," Ben whispered. "I think I'm really bad at it sometimes."

"How many miles have you hiked so far?"

"Two hundred and fifty."

"Well, Caravalho, even if you quit today, that would still be two hundred and fifty more miles of the Pacific Crest Trail hiked than anyone else I know."

Ben smiled. "Do you want to talk about Lorraine's email?" He felt bad for dominating the conversation so thoroughly.

"Fuck no I don't."

"I have to go do laundry." Ben was still whispering, for some reason. "And repack my pack."

"And I have to go attend some boring meetings. But look, Ben? It was really good to hear your voice."

Ben smiled again.

"Find the boy if you want. But take care of yourself first, okay?"

"Okay. I love you, Jules. Thank you."

"You're welcome. Send me more pictures of weird shit."

She hung up.

Slowly, Ben got himself together. He supposed he wouldn't move in with Mo. He already knew what a hassle it was, moving in with a guy. He took another shower. Brushed his teeth. Opened his resupply box. Threw his dirty clothes into a bag to drag through town. Rinsed his water filter. Charged everything he needed to charge, texted everyone he needed to text.

It was only later, when he was doing a final sweep of the room, that Ben noticed Alexei's empty resupply box, broken down and tucked neatly behind his bed.

He leaned down to grab it. Stared at the return address in Portland, Oregon. The street where Alexei Lebedev lived when he wasn't on a trail.

Ben had always pictured Portland full of hipsters and queer people. He'd always wanted to visit. It was funny, picturing someone like Alexei there—a sincere, quiet data analyst, among the tattoos and dyed hair.

Ben snapped a photo of the address with his phone before returning the box to its place on the floor.

CHAPTER THIRTEEN

Hiking was hell.

Alexei didn't know why anyone did it.

A casual stroll through the woods? Sure. But backpacking? Carrying around fifty pounds on your back through dangerous wilderness, day after day, when civilization was *right there* as a viable option? Having to transport your trash in a dirty Ziploc bag? Spending half of your days stressing about finding clean water? Getting sunburned no matter how many times you reapplied your greasy sunblock? Not to mention! The constant, persistent, infuriating bugs! Every damn day!

Why. *Why.*

Plus, Alexei felt like junk. Less than twenty-four hours off trail, and it was like his body had forgotten how to walk. He had a headache. Had lost his appetite again. And his newly resupplied pack felt like it weighed a million pounds.

There were trees, once he was back on trail, and wonderful views, and Alexei would have loved this day, probably. Before.

After three shin-crunching, mind-numbing miles through town, Alexei pushed uphill for two more miles to Bertha Peak before he stopped for a break. It was a perfect place to stop, with an unimpeded view of Big Bear Lake. Alexei stared down at the sparkling blue waters far below. Shoved a granola bar in his mouth. It tasted awful.

A trill sounded from farther down the hill, followed by a series of long, clear notes. Alexei's body stilled automatically. It was Alexei's favorite thing about listening for birds. It forced you to be so very still.

After a few minutes, he was sure. Lark sparrow.

He almost opened his mouth. Almost turned to Ben to tell him, before he remembered.

He kept walking.

Another mile down the trail, he almost passed right by a tiny woman sitting in the dirt, head hunched over a large sketch pad.

Alexei stopped in his tracks.

"Ruby."

She looked up. She was wearing the same outfit as the first time he'd met her: black Lycra biking shorts, a racerback tank top. Bright pink socks.

"Alexei."

Something about the fact that she remembered his name—

He collapsed next to her, pack crashing at his feet.

"You're alone this time," she noted, going back to her drawing.

"Yeah." Alexei sucked in a shaky breath. He pressed his palms to his eye sockets, staring at the indistinct swirls of white against the black of his eyelids. His headache was starting to fade, but his stomach felt worse. He felt light-headed, off balance.

Ben had been right, of course. Alexei's body was tired. He needed the zero day. And he *really* wished he could have done laundry.

"Want to talk about it?" Ruby asked, never pausing the smooth motions of her drawing hand.

"Yes," Alexei answered, dropping his hands. "But I don't know how. So . . . no."

A moment of silence.

"That's a big mood, my dude," Ruby finally said.

"Yeah," Alexei agreed. "Yeah, it is."

And then he hung his head between his knees and began to cry.

So. Maybe Ben was gay. Or bisexual. Or something.

It was just—when Alexei woke up next to Ben and remembered it all—

His first thought had been, maybe he wasn't.

Because there had been so many opportunities for Ben to tell him that he liked men. So many. And Alexei knew straight people experimented sometimes. Like being gay until graduation. Alexei had spent most of his college days at the University of Washington alone in his dorm room, or the library, or the college chapel—making new friends in college had, unfortunately, been exactly as difficult as Alexei had worried it would be—so he didn't have much personal experience with the practice. But anyway, he'd heard of it. Maybe some dudes on the PCT got gay until Canada.

Even though that made no sense to Alexei. But a lot of things about the world didn't make sense to Alexei.

Or maybe Ben just felt bad for him. Poor disowned gay boy. Maybe Ben thought he was being nice. And maybe he was.

Alexei just felt so *dumb*. He wished he were different. That he could've shoved Ben's shoulder this morning, that they could have joked about it, that they still could have taken the zero day together.

Or—okay, in retrospect, he wished he could have been calm enough to at least talk it through with Ben. Let Ben clarify things.

But in the moment, all Alexei had known was that he wouldn't be able to handle it. Hearing Ben say last night had been *fun*.

Because it hadn't just been fun for Alexei. It had been everything.

Alexei was going to think about last night for a long, long time.

In the end, he'd gotten what he wanted. The good-bye had been far more abrupt and awkward than he'd planned, but here he was. Alone again.

Eventually, Alexei's tears dried. He lifted his head. Dug in his pack for tissues.

"Sorry about that," he said to Ruby once he'd composed himself.

She shrugged, picking up a different pencil from her side.

"No problem," she said. "Shit's hard sometimes."

"Yeah," Alexei exhaled. "That's true." He turned toward her. "What are you drawing?"

Ruby lifted the sketch pad. "Prickly pear."

"Ah. Could've guessed that." He should have looked before he'd asked, seen the magenta pads she was starting to fill in on the distinctive, famously edible cactus.

"Have you gotten to see any of these?" she asked.

"A few."

"Fucking awesome, right?"

Alexei laughed. He couldn't believe she was talking to him like things were normal, after he'd invaded her space and promptly had a very snotty meltdown. "Yeah," he agreed. "They are." And then, looking at the trail around them, "It's sort of amazing any of this exists at all, really."

Ruby finally looked up. Joined him in his look around.

"Yeah," she said.

She tapped the end of her pencil against the paper. After a moment, she began to collect her things.

"You want to walk together awhile?" she asked.

Alexei looked at her, surprised. He remembered her saying she flew solo. Had felt a kinship with her, as soon as she'd said it.

"I don't ask shit I don't mean," she said when he didn't respond. "But if you want to be alone, I get that, too."

Alexei felt like crying again. He scrambled up.

"I would love to walk with you, Ruby."

And if she heard him possibly sniffling a few more times as they walked that day, she never said anything.

They sat together at camp that night near the shores of Holcomb Creek. It had been a high, ridge-filled, view-filled day, and Alexei was glad to rest now in this quiet, flat spot among the sagebrush.

He knew it probably wouldn't last, hiking with Ruby, and he didn't need it to. But he was grateful he'd found her today. Hiking with Ruby had helped.

"Where are you from, Ruby?" he asked as they cooked their dinners. He knew Ruby wasn't interested in trail families. That their relationship wouldn't be like his and Ben's. But he wanted to remember things about her all the same.

"Queens."

"Like, New York?"

"One and the same. You?"

"Washington State originally."

Alexei waited a minute before he added, "But I'm thinking of moving to the East, when I'm done with the trail. Probably not New York." He rubbed at his beard. "Boston, maybe."

Ruby made a little *hm*. "Big change," she remarked.

Alexei inhaled, let it out slowly. It was the first time he'd said anything about his move, in a specific way, out loud. Naming a destination. And Ruby vocalizing the reality of it—*big change*—made it seem, suddenly, much more frightening. "Yeah," he agreed. "Big change."

Ruby stretched out her brown legs.

"New York's better," she said. "But, you know. Your mileage may vary."

"I've never been to either of them," Alexei admitted. "But I don't know." He smiled a little to himself. "I've always wanted to see Harvard Square."

"Yeah, I can see that. You are a white man," she said. "Boston'll suit you just fine."

Alexei tinkered with his stove. "I am a gay white man," he said. Because if he could write *came out again* in his journal tonight, it'd be at least one bullet point he could be proud of.

"Right," Ruby said. "Like I said. Boston'll suit you just fine."

Alexei laughed, something around his heart easing, just a tiny bit.

"I'm not ready to go back to Woodside yet," Ruby said a minute later, "but man, I would kill for some pancit molo. Or kare-kare."

Alexei looked over, raising an eyebrow.

"Filipino food," she supplied. "Pinoy shit." She sighed. "I'm so sick of my trail food, I could die."

Alexei smiled at that. "Yeah." He pulled up his knees, wrapped his arms around his shins while his ramen cooked. "The only thing I ever really want to eat are gummy bears."

He laughed at himself, how childish this had sounded.

And like a stitch in his side, he suddenly missed Alina so much, it hurt. Her sweet tooth was almost worse than his. Growing up, along with caffeine and alcohol, they weren't supposed to consume refined sugars. But Alina was the best at sneaking home treats she pilfered from kids at school. She had a special box in the corner of her closet where she kept her stash.

She'd moved into a new apartment recently in Portland, finally leaving Vancouver after getting her paralegal job. He hadn't seen it yet, the new apartment, and it was in a different neighborhood than his, up in North Portland. The one safe topic they'd talked about, though, the few times they'd talked over the last few months, was her plans for decorating it. He wondered what her kitchen cupboards looked like now. If they were full of Oreos and Little Debbies.

"You're real cute, Alexei," Ruby said. She didn't say it in a flirty way. Alexei couldn't imagine Ruby saying anything in a flirty way. But it made Alexei's ears burn anyway. He dug into the dirt with the toe of his shoe.

"Thanks," he said. He ate his ramen. Thought about how far away New York felt. How far away it all felt, Portland and Vancouver and Boston and anything that wasn't this desert.

He asked, "Why are you here, Ruby? On the PCT."

She was quiet for a long time. But eventually, she answered.

"Needed to be alone for a while."

Alexei nodded. Rested his chin on his knees.

He figured that was all Ruby would give him. But a minute later, she spoke again.

"And..." She scratched at her neck, "I came here to listen to my body." A small pause. "And to draw."

Those all seemed like pretty good reasons to him.

"Thank you again," he said after another long silence. "For letting me walk with you for a while."

Ruby shrugged.

"Sometimes you need to be alone. And sometimes you shouldn't be. Seemed like you were the second one today."

Alexei breathed in deep, felt the desert air fill his lungs. "Yeah," he agreed.

Shortly afterward, Ruby packed up her pencils. Alexei said his nightly prayers.

It took him a long time to fall asleep.

In the morning, Alexei accidentally slept in. When he finally emerged from his tent, the sun was higher in the sky than he liked it to be at the start of his hiking days, and a bit of anxiety tugged at him. Ruby was sitting on the ground, her pencils surrounding her once more.

He was glad to see her.

But he missed the smell of Ben's instant coffee.

"Morning," she said.

Alexei rubbed his face, trying to force himself into waking up. "Sorry if you were waiting for me," he said.

"Nah. I'm not going anywhere today."

"Zero?"

Ruby leaned closer to her page. "Just don't feel like walking today." She looked up at him. "Listening to my body, remember?"

Alexei stuffed his hands in his pockets. "Right. So you're not gunning it for Canada, then."

"No. I'm hopping on and off where I feel like it. I love this trail, but the human body isn't meant to walk twenty-six hundred miles in a row. You know that, right?"

Alexei smiled. He admired Ruby so much. "I do." He shrugged. "Sometimes we make weird choices anyway."

She made a huff of agreement, head back over the sketch pad. "That's a fact."

Alexei got ready for the day. Took down his tent, packed up his gear. He'd just clicked in the chest straps of his pack when Ruby spoke again. Repeated back the question he'd asked her last night.

"Why are you here, Alexei? On the PCT."

Alexei leaned forward on his poles, testing how his legs felt today. "To say good-bye," he said.

Ruby was quiet until she asked, "Do you feel ready to say it yet?"

Alexei shook his head.

"No," he answered truthfully. It was easy to be truthful with Ruby.

"Well." She tapped her pencil against her lip. "There's still over two thousand miles for you to get there."

Alexei smiled at her. "That's what I'm hoping." He wrapped the straps of his poles around his wrists. Took one last admiring look at Ruby's sketchbook.

And then he said good-bye to her and her pictures, and walked again toward Canada.

It was late morning, many tiring miles passed on alternately rocky and sandy terrain, when Alexei had another unexpected reunion.

A group of hikers rested under a white alder.

Something flared in Alexei's memory when he saw them in the distance, heard their voices weaving over the wind.

His body reacted before his mind could think much further, running to where they sat, as much as it was possible to run under the weight of his pack.

"Hey," he panted, nodding at them. The words flew out of his mouth. "Hi, hey. Have you seen Ben?"

The group's conversation died away. They looked up at him in unison, squinting into the sun.

The ginger-haired one recognized him first. Alexei couldn't remember his name now. It felt like years since he'd met them.

"Hey! You're that guy from Idyllwild!" Ginger's eyes lit up. "The quiet one Ben stayed with!"

"Oh shit!" Faraj said. "How the hell's it going, man?"

"Um. Fine."

A long pause ensued, wherein self-awareness crept back into Alexei's brain, and he blushed. And desperately wished he could disappear into the earth.

It was just, when he saw them—it was this visceral connection to Ben.

And he missed Ben so much.

Faraj cleared his throat.

"We haven't seen Ben since we left him with you in Idyllwild."

Alexei felt the breath in his lungs sink like a crater. "Of course. Sorry."

Of course they hadn't seen Ben. Ben could still be in Big Bear City, for all Alexei knew. What the hell had he been thinking?

"I thought you two would have still been hiking together," Faraj ventured after another awkward silence.

"Right." Alexei lowered his bandanna, swiped at the sweat on his forehead. Tried to think of an explanation for this very illogical encounter. "We got separated a couple days ago. I only thought if you had seen him—I just wanted to make sure he was still all right, was all."

And as soon as he'd said this—oh no. Suddenly, all Alexei could picture was Ben tripping, twisting his ankle, breaking a bone, without Alexei's emergency GPS locator, without reliable cell service. Oh God.

He had promised Ma. That he was making sure Ben was safe.

But surely Ben was safe. He'd probably found another group of hikers in Big Bear City—maybe the people from that parking lot, the ones with the guitar, if they were still around?—and surely one of them had an emergency GPS locator, too. Ben was fine. Ben was totally, probably, completely fine.

"You all right, man?"

Startling, Alexei realized he was still standing in front of the Idyllwild bros.

"Um. Yes. Sorry, sorry to bother you, I'll just—" Alexei started backing up, but a guy he only vaguely recognized interrupted.

"Do you have his number?" Unknown Guy asked. "There's a trailhead coming up, by Deep Creek Bridge. You might be able to get service there."

"I don't have a phone," Alexei said. "It's cool. No worries. Good to see you all again." He backed up another step.

"Hey, man, wait." Faraj stood. "We're about to get going, too. You want to hike with us? I'm sure we'll run into Ben eventually."

"Oh, uh, no, that's okay. I'm going to take my lunch here, actually, I think. Thanks for asking, though."

"Sure." Faraj dug in his pack until he brought out a battered cell phone. "Listen, I don't have service right now, but I can keep checking and send Ben a message for you next time I get some bars, if you want."

Alexei swallowed, jealousy hitting his gut that Faraj had Ben's number, and Alexei didn't. Faraj could talk to Ben whenever he wanted. A year from now, Faraj could dial Ben when he was bored, chat about their favorite TV shows.

Faraj was also being nice.

"Yeah," Alexei said. "That'd be great. Thanks."

"Cool." Faraj typed something and then looked at him. "What should I say?"

Oh. Right. *What the hell should Alexei say?*

"Just tell him...Alexei wanted to make sure he was okay."

Faraj typed it. "Will do." He put the phone back in his pack. "I'm sure he *is* okay, you know."

"Yeah." Alexei nodded, exhaling a breath. He felt a small, curious desire to give Faraj a hug. "Thanks."

The rest of the crew started adjusting packs and picking up poles.

It hit his brain from out of nowhere.

Leon! The fourth guy Alexei vaguely recognized must be Leon. The one who was behind that day, because he'd gotten high and chased coyotes.

Strangely, Alexei felt like laughing. It was possible skipping the zero day was making him delirious.

"Hey, man, if you do end up seeing Ben again before we do, tell that fucker we miss him, okay?" Leon asked.

Alexei forced a smile. He waved as they left.

And then he sat in their place, in the shadow of the alder tree.

He rested his chin on his knees and stared down the trail.

He pretended he was not willing Ben's lanky form to appear. That he did not secretly hope Ben would magically walk up out of the dust, any second now, and hold out his phone, saying, "Lex. Did you even *see* this bug?"

Alexei called it a day shortly after Deep Creek Bridge, past the turn-off for the trailhead. Where he might have been able to contact Ben, if he had had a phone, if he wasn't a lonely weirdo.

The afternoon had passed by in a similar fashion to the morning: a fantastic section of trail Alexei felt unable to truly comprehend.

As Alexei set up his tent, he simply wished he could know for sure if he'd ever see Ben again. Running into both Ruby and Faraj and company over the last twenty-four hours had sparked hope. That maybe it would happen. And Alexei could apologize. For how he'd left that morning. For asking to kiss Ben in the first place.

It was fine, of course, if they didn't see each other again. He knew it would take time to stop missing Ben, but Alexei was already starting to settle back into it, being solitary on the trail. He could feel himself quieting. It was a feeling that was familiar, but in a bittersweet way—like trying on an old T-shirt that felt the same and smelled the same, but your body had changed, and it no longer fell in the exact right way.

It was the golden hour by the time Alexei's camp for the night was set up, the sun preparing for its grand good-bye, painting the desert landscape in saturated, arresting hues. Like God was grabbing you by the shoulders, making you pay attention.

Alexei always loved setting up camp during the golden hour. No matter how hard the day had been, it always felt like a blessing. To be able to stand still when the air smelled the sweetest.

He didn't eat dinner. He stood outside his tent in his sandals, soaking in the light on the rocks around him, thinking.

Eventually, he picked up one of his trekking poles. He walked back to the trail. It was sandy here; any message would likely get covered up by the footfalls of other hikers or blown away by the wind. He knew it was probably pointless to start with, and silly, to boot. If

Ben had taken the zero day back in Big Bear City, which Alexei really hoped he had, he would still be a full day behind him.

But Alexei stuck his pole into the sand anyway and spelled it out, in big letters covering the width of the trail:

B E N

And an arrow, pointing toward his tent.

It was unsatisfying.

Back at his tent, Alexei rooted through his pack for something more tangible, something that might actually catch Ben's eye, make him pause.

He carried the beat-up copy of *Alanna: The First Adventure* to Ben's name in the sand. He found a decent-sized rock, placed it on top of the cover at the edge of the trail, by the upper curved edge of the *B*.

He stared at it for a while. Tried to let the magic of the light wash over the scene. Felt increasingly silly, but hoped the magic could infuse it, somehow, anyway.

And then Alexei got into his tent. He curled over onto his side, pulled his sleeping bag up over his ears. He tried to make his mind blank.

Sleep came easier that day. He gave himself up to it, deep and dreamless and alone.

Until, several hours later, Alexei's eyelashes fluttered open when he heard the crash.

CHAPTER FOURTEEN

If you die doing this, Ben said to himself, *Ma will never forgive you.* He stumbled over a rock and almost screamed. He'd been hiking in the darkness for almost three hours now, and his nerves were past shot.

Ben had practiced night hiking with Julie months ago, at a favorite park back in Nashville. She had screeched about it the whole time, but he had had a rather lovely time back then. In a forest he knew well. With his best friend.

It was apparently a bit of a different experience in a rocky desert thousands of miles away from home, when he was completely and utterly alone.

The thing was, he'd done some calculations during that zero day in Big Bear City, and realized he was behind on miles, too. Maybe Faraj's annoying pushes for big mileage days weren't that annoying after all. Because if you didn't walk fast enough, early season snows in the high mountain ranges of Oregon and Washington could make the trail impassable by the fall. And maybe Ben wouldn't make it that far. But he did have plans to see his family halfway through this journey, and he had resolved in Big Bear City to at least make it that far, even if it killed him.

There was a reason, Ben mused with every footfall, why only

.2 percent of the population contemplated doing this, or whatever Julie had said.

Even though Ben had been trying, over the last two days, not to think too hard about a lot of the stuff Julie had said. Because whenever he did, it made him feel things, and feeling things was the worst.

So Ben was night hiking, because that was what you did in the desert to catch up on miles. And night hiking, as it turned out, was also the worst.

Panic had bloomed, spreading in all directions like a drop of ink hitting water, almost as soon as the sun had gone down. Hiking in a world of shadow was terrifying. Ben questioned every noise, every silence, every step.

He would have stopped a long time ago, but the trouble was he couldn't find a good spot to fucking camp. He had decided to night hike through a patch of trail that was apparently surrounded only by unyielding cliffs and rocky ledges. At least, from what he could see. Which wasn't fucking much.

The Deep Creek Bridge truly freaked him out, hearing all that water in the darkness, unable to fully see it. He wore his headlamp, but it only shone so far, only illuminated so much.

He tried singing in his head, but he couldn't remember any song that had ever been sung in the history of people singing music.

He was losing it.

A pathetic prick of tears had just hit his eyeballs when he saw it.

The beam of his headlamp danced over something on the ground. Something out of place. Something that—his heart threatened to beat out of his chest—he was 95 percent sure he recognized.

Slowly, carefully, he bent over to pick it up.

Poor Alanna. She was covered in dust.

Ben brushed off the cover as best he could. Ran his thumb over the spine.

The other thing was, Ben might have, possibly, maybe considered the fact that if he night hiked to catch up on miles, he might also hike himself closer to Alexei.

He just hadn't thought too hard on what would happen, if that actually worked.

She was such a small, well-loved paperback, *Alanna*. Ben likely would have walked right past her—and possibly, soon, in his exhaustion, straight off a cliff—if he hadn't been searching the ground so desperately for a soft place to land.

But he had been, and Alexei had left her here, to give it to him.

Ben released a quiet sob.

Alexei Lebedev would not stop saving Ben's life.

He looked around. Saw that the ground to the left of the trail stretched smoothly into the darkness in a most hopeful way.

For the first time in hours, Ben stepped off the trail. One step, two. Three, and then—

The beam of his headlamp hit the edge of a tent post. One Ben knew very well.

He scanned the ground before clicking off his headlamp. He didn't want to wake Alexei by flashing this harsh light all over the place. Was this a violation in the first place, setting up camp next to Alexei without express permission? Although he'd left the book. Was it a bad decision, picking up the book?

But Ben needed to rest regardless, and this was the only decent place he'd found to do it. He'd set up camp a respectful distance away and hope for the best in the morning.

Maybe he'd figure out what to say to Alexei in the morning.

He couldn't believe Alexei was here.

As quietly as he could, he dropped his pack to the ground. Placed Alanna inside it and found his tent, rummaging for the small pack of folded posts.

He could set up a tent in the dark. Right? He'd been on the trail

for a month now. Had hiked nearly three hundred goddamn miles.
He could do this.

He was only shaking a bit as he snapped the first pole together.
Now that he wasn't hiking, his body apparently realized how cold it
was in the desert in the middle of the night. He might have to turn
his headlamp on again, just for a minute—

The pole in his hand slipped from his fingers, crashing against
one of his trekking poles with a clang that seemed entirely too loud
for two such small, infuriating things.

"Shit."

Three seconds later, there came the distinct shuffle of someone
wiggling around a small tent in a sleeping bag. Followed by the
sound of a tent flap unzipping.

Ben cringed. He couldn't see him, but he could picture—

"Ben?"

Willing himself not to pass out, Ben stood and faced Alexei's tent.
Where his headlamp shone directly into Alexei's confused, mostly
asleep blue eyes. Alexei squinted, holding up a hand.

"Shit," Ben said again, yanking the headlamp away from his forehead so it hung around his neck, throwing creepy shadows across
the ground. And then, after an awkward second: "Hi."

He stuffed his hands in the pocket of his sweatshirt.

After a few beats, a sound wheezed across the clearing between
them. It almost sounded like . . . a laugh?

Was . . . Alexei laughing? Ben's heart was beating too loudly in his
ears to tell.

"Ben." Alexei was definitely laughing. "You have really got to stop
scaring me half to death in the middle of the night."

Ben looked at the ground, scuffing a shoe in the sand. It was a
good sign, that Alexei didn't seem mad. Right?

But it suddenly wasn't very funny to Ben at all. That he had, in fact,
scared Alexei half to death in the middle of the night twice now.

"Yeah," Ben affirmed. "Sorry."

"Were you *night hiking*?" Alexei's voice was still twinged with disbelief, a hint of amusement. Or exasperation. Or something. God, night hiking had fucked with Ben's head. He couldn't tell up from down.

"I..." Ben scrunched his shoulders up to his ears. "I'm sorry," he repeated.

A silence Ben couldn't read.

"Thanks. For leaving the book," Ben said. "That was nice."

"Sure."

Finally, Ben's legs made the decision for him. He walked to Alexei's tent and sat down.

"Lex."

He was going to say, *Is it okay if I camp here?* Or *Can we talk in the morning?* Or *Sorry for waking you up in the middle of the night. Again.* Or *I'm glad you're okay.*

But once he was there, Alexei right in front of him, his mind went blank. Ben couldn't see Alexei very well in the dark. But he could smell him. And he smelled—well, Alexei had been hiking the PCT for two weeks and hadn't washed his clothes in a long time, so mostly he smelled stinky. But it was a particularly Alexei rendition of stinky.

And then Ben's mouth opened and he couldn't stop anything that spilled out of it.

"I'm so sorry, Lex. I shouldn't have been drinking with you. We should have talked more first, before... We should have talked more afterward, too, but you were so *upset* that morning and I didn't want to push you." Ben's shoulders deflated. "I just...really thought I could keep myself from doing anything with you, but then you were so adorable at the restaurant, and fuck, Lex, fucking 'Wonderwall'! It was like you were trying to kill me."

Ben looked to the side, taking a deep breath before staring back at the ground. He bit his tongue, worried what else his fatigue would let escape.

Finally, after the silence had stretched too long for Ben's nerves, he hazarded a glance up. Alexei was staring at him, a confused look on his face, the halo of the headlamp's glow casting gray shadows on his cheeks.

"Can you say something, Lex?"

Another brutal silence. And then:

"You thought I was adorable?"

Ben strangled a laugh.

"Yes. You are very frequently adorable, Lex. On top of being really fucking hot. A lethal combination, really."

"Uh."

"Oh, come on." Ben shoved his hands back into his hoodie. "You have to know you're hot."

"Wait," Alexei blurted out. "Are you gay?"

After a stunned second, Ben laughed. Which made him feel, at least a tiny bit, like himself again.

"Um, *yes*, Lex," he managed.

Alexei reached out and shoved him in the knee. Ben tried to ignore how much he liked it.

"What the hell, Ben? How come you never said anything?"

Ben's laughter died away when he heard the hurt in Alexei's voice. The glow from the headlamp caught the anger visible on his face. Shit.

"I'm sorry, Lex," he whispered. He added honestly, "I don't know."

Because when he thought about it, while outing himself that night when Alexei shared his trauma with his parents hadn't felt right, Ben probably should have done it later. As time went on, Ben probably should have found a right time to do it.

But maybe...

Maybe it had been easier to protect himself—to keep himself from making a bad decision—if Alexei didn't know.

Ben exhaled slowly, rubbing his forehead.

In his defense, he had probably also thought, after a while, that Alexei would have figured it out on his own.

Because, like, Ben was really fucking gay.

Plus—

"I did think," he said slowly, still processing that Alexei had just asked him this *now*, "that you would at least know I was queer. After the whole, you know, sleeping together thing."

"I thought"—Alexei licked his lips—"that maybe you were just screwing around. Experimenting. Or that... you felt sorry for me. I don't know."

Ben hung his head in his hands.

"Alexei, no, God, that was not—" Ben blew out a hard breath. "That was why you were so upset that morning. Okay. That makes a lot more sense now."

Ben really *had* fucked it up. In so many ways.

He forgot sometimes. That Alexei was likely new at a lot of this, that he likely hadn't had enough queer people in his life, that his head had probably been filled with ridiculous things. Ben had to at least make this clear. He leaned closer to Alexei's tent. Ben had missed that anxious forehead, ached at the sight of it.

"First of all, anyone who *experiments* like that is not straight. Second of all, what happened between us was definitely not an experiment. God, Lex, everything that happened that night was what I've wanted to do with you since the moment I first saw you. At least, the *beginning* of what I wanted to do with you." Ben leaned back, taking a deep breath, trying to reel himself in. "I don't know where we go from here, Lex. If you need time to be alone, if we part ways, I'll understand. But I need you to know that I wasn't screwing around that night. You have to know that I meant every minute of it."

Alexei stared at him. Ben pulled his knees up to his chest. Damn, it was cold.

"Ben," Alexei said after a silence. His voice was shaky, quiet. "Ben, get in here. It's freezing out there."

Ben stilled. He stared back at Alexei for a long minute.

He glanced over his shoulder at his discarded pack, his unraveled tent and fallen poles. He unlaced his shoes. And for a second time, Ben clambered inside Alexei's one-person tent.

Alexei unzipped his sleeping bag, leaning away to make room. Ben tried to slide onto Alexei's tiny mattress pad as elegantly as he could.

But no matter what either of them did, it was an absurd affair.

Ben attempted to tuck his feet into the cozy foot box of Alexei's sleeping bag, but Alexei's own two feet barely fit in there. Alexei attempted to cover them both with the unzipped sleeping bag; it hardly covered their shoulders. Still, Ben was almost settled when he realized he needed to take off his sweatshirt for a pillow. Alexei was already cozied up with the flannel he sometimes wore at camp, folded neatly under his head. The mechanics of sitting up again to take off the sweatshirt without punching either Alexei or himself in the face seemed nearly impossible.

Alexei giggled first.

Laughing felt so good. By the time Ben was fully settled, the tension from the night hike had finally faded out of his system.

They found themselves facing each other, chest to chest, noses almost brushing in the darkness. Ben had turned off his headlamp for good, chucked it into a corner of Alexei's tent. He could only barely make out Alexei's eyelashes, the curve of his cheek. But he felt him everywhere. Ben was pretty sure he was still shivering, the chill of the desert night still ever present, but Alexei's body heat crept in, inch by inch, warming him through.

"I can't believe you were night hiking alone," Alexei said, voice almost a whisper. "Please, Ben, never do that again."

Ben nodded, a small sign of assent. His hands were balled into fists, trapped between their chests.

After a minute, Alexei sucked in a big breath.

"So, you—" he started. "I mean, do you—"

A quiet exhale.

Finally: "You like me?"

Ben counted to three to calm himself before saying, as even and sincere as he could, "Yeah, Lex. I like you." He couldn't help but add, because he was exhausted, and tired of not being honest: "You don't even know."

Alexei remained still, hands tucked under his head. Ben could practically hear the gears turning in his brain. He wanted to reach out a thumb to that forehead. Tell Alexei whatever he was feeling was okay.

But he could only wait.

It's not a bad decision to be happy.

Ben was so tired.

His eyes had drifted closed when Alexei spoke again.

"I meant it, too," he said, voice stronger now. Ben's eyes blinked open. "The other night. I think...I think it was probably the best night of my life. And I'm sorry I left that morning, Ben. I didn't know..." He took a deep breath. "I didn't believe you could actually feel that way. About me."

Ben bit the inside of his cheek. He wanted to celebrate this admission, accept this apology. But he heard the hesitation in Alexei's voice, too. Waited for the *but*.

"Well," he said. "I do."

Alexei cleared his throat.

"And just to...clarify. You would want...more of that. That night. If I wanted it."

Ben knew he couldn't deny it, good decision or not. He groaned. "Fuck, Lex. Yes."

"Um." Alexei's voice sounded a bit breathy now, and fuck if it didn't drive Ben wild. But whatever they were doing here still felt very fragile, and Ben would die before he violated Alexei inside this tent again. He tried very hard to think of the least sexy things he knew. Dryer lint. Wet socks. Cat litter. "Okay," Alexei continued after another throat clear. "This is . . . a lot for me. Is it okay if I take some time to process it?"

"Of course," Ben said. And then he lifted a shoulder, still trying to calm himself. "In the words of the great Unk, we can walk it out."

Silence.

"The great Unk?"

Ben released a small, sleepy laugh. "It's not weird you don't know Unk, Lex. If anything, it's weird that I do."

"I missed you," Alexei said.

Ben closed his eyes. "I missed you, too."

"I would love to walk it out with you, Ben."

If Ben hadn't been so exhausted, he could have cried in relief. He still didn't really know what the hell they were doing, but they could keep walking together. And at the moment, that was all Ben cared about. The last two days of walking without Alexei had been awful.

Ben was almost fully unconscious when Alexei nudged his shoulder.

"Um, I think you should maybe get your tent? So it doesn't blow away? And secure your pack?"

Ben groaned, for much more annoyed reasons this time. He had finally gotten comfortable. Well, as comfortable as was possible with most of his ass still hanging off Alexei's mattress pad. But Alexei was right. Leaving all his stuff out there had been a dumbass move.

"But"—Alexei's voice turned hesitant once more—"can you come back?"

Ben was a doomed fool.

"I promise," he said.

CHAPTER FIFTEEN

The quails pushed Alexei over the edge.

The trail felt reassuring again the next morning, almost normal again: one foot in front of the other, one foot behind or in front of Ben.

Except, of course, that things weren't really normal at all.

Ben Caravalho was gay.

Gay gay gay.

Even though it wasn't a complete surprise—the more Alexei had thought about that night, the more he knew his reaction the following morning had likely been irrational—Alexei still felt slightly stunned by the news anyway.

There was just...so much Alexei had never let himself believe. So much he'd never trusted.

He knew this development was good. No, it was incredible.

He also knew it hadn't been the right thing to do, asking Ben to stay in his tent before Alexei had given him a true answer about anything, but it had been so deeply, overwhelmingly wonderful. The idea, even now as they walked, that Alexei could possibly turn to Ben and hold his hand, that Ben would possibly want him to, that he could lean his head against Ben's shoulder, that he could turn and brush his lips over—

Alexei was terrified.

Would their relationship only last until Canada, if they pursued this? What if it didn't last even that long? Canada was still so far away. Alexei cared about Ben so much. What if Ben got sick of Alexei at some point?

Wouldn't that break his heart?

Alexei realized the sound of Ben's footfalls behind him had fallen quiet. He turned to see Ben hunched on his heels, taking a photo of the red and orange blooms on a torch lily.

Wouldn't it be worth it?

God. No one had ever liked him back before. It had felt okay, admitting his desires to himself when Ben was only a fantasy, but now that it was real, now that Alexei could actually, potentially, truly have him—

They kept walking.

Maybe, Alexei reasoned, he could have Ben and still have Alexei 2.0. He could still take time alone to write in his journals, make his lists and his plans. Ben would give him all the time he needed if Alexei asked. And then he could still fall asleep next to Ben and touch his face and—

Nashville. Ben lived in Nashville. Alexei lived...well, Alexei would be living somewhere after this.

But he needed to reach that decision, where his *somewhere* was, on his own.

And what if he didn't figure it out? What if it was only when they reached Canada and Ben returned happily to Nashville that Alexei finally admitted he was more lost—more alone—than ever?

And then Alexei saw the quails.

Actual quails. A whole *covey* of them. Alexei counted eight. No, nine. Good gravy, *ten*.

He stopped dead in his tracks, thrusting out an arm in case Ben tried to walk past him.

"Gambel's quails," he whispered. Alexei was pretty sure. California quails would be larger; their coloring wasn't as scaled.

They pecked and scratched and strutted across the trail. Ben inched up to Alexei's shoulder to see, and Alexei dropped his arm, turning his body toward him, eyes still on the large birds.

"Look at their topknots. And the crests on the males! Aren't they so weirdly beautiful? The ones with more gray are the females. They don't have the black patches on their bellies, see? But look at the patterning on the males; they—"

Alexei made the mistake then. Of looking at Ben.

It was such a shot of adrenaline, seeing the covey. This was part of what he'd come here for, too, seeing things that made him feel wonder again, and Ben was looking at him like—like Alexei was the smartest, most interesting person in the world.

Alexei cupped both hands around Ben's face and kissed him.

It was a hard kiss, one that encompassed the thrill Alexei felt in that moment, and Ben kissed him back, a small noise rumbling in his throat as he pulled Alexei closer by the straps of his pack.

It took Alexei a minute to realize. That they weren't in a tent, tucked away from the trail in the dark, or inside a safely locked motel room.

On instinct, Alexei pulled back, looking left and then right along the trail.

But the only creatures watching them were a covey of Gambel's quails.

When he found Ben's eyes again, Ben was studying him.

"I'm sorry." Alexei raised a hand to his mouth.

A small smile graced Ben's lips.

But his eyes seemed sad.

"I'm not sorry you want to kiss me, Alexei," he said. "I just want you to be sure it's actually what you want."

Alexei nodded, eyes wide. He couldn't believe he'd done that. He was a little exhilarated he had done that. He…was being unfair.

"I'm sorry," Alexei said again.

"It's okay." Ben broke his gaze. Stepped back, readjusting his trekking poles.

"It's not." Alexei's heart beat hard in his chest. He couldn't stop feeling the ghost of Ben's lips on his. He needed to figure out what to do here. His thoughts continued to scatter, unfocused and loud. "Mind taking over the lead?" he asked after a long moment.

"Sure, Lex." Ben stepped around him. Granted Alexei the grace, for now, of being able to keep walking in silence.

They took a brief break a half hour later. They were close to Deep Creek Hot Springs, listed in Alexei's guidebooks as a highlight of this section of trail. The weather so far today had been mild, the wind quiet.

Alexei watched Ben take a Lemon Zest granola bar from his pack.

"Did the guys from Idyllwild know you're gay?" he blurted out.

"Yeah. They did." Ben glanced down, a small smile playing with the corner of his mouth. "By the way." He dug his phone out from his pack. "These texts came through this morning."

He held out the screen.

> Alexei is looking for you, Benster
>
> Wants to make sure you're okay
>
> You're hitting that, right?
>
> I would.

Alexei's face turned to fire.

"So they were cool with it?" he asked, ignoring the texts.

"Yeah, Lex." Ben's voice grew soft, his eyes lifting to Alexei's as he took back his phone. "Not everyone's an asshole, you know?"

Alexei was quiet.

"Sorry." Ben shook his head. "I didn't mean to imply your parents are assholes."

"No," Alexei said. "It's okay."

He looked away, squinting into the distance.

"Is Faraj gay?" he asked, those texts finally processing in his brain.

Ben laughed. "Honestly? I don't know. I think he was just busting my balls. But"—he shrugged—"maybe Faraj is a little queer. Who knows."

Alexei took this in.

"When did you come out?" he asked next. There was a whole storm of questions inside him suddenly. "Is it okay I'm asking you these things?" he added.

"Yeah, Lex. You can ask me anything. And when I came out the first time?" Ben tilted his head. "Freshman year of high school. I probably knew by sixth grade. But, you know, middle school sucks."

"Huh." *Sixth grade.*

Did Alexei know by then?

No. He never would have allowed himself even to think it.

But maybe.

"And Ma is okay with it? And everyone?"

"Yeah." Ben's voice went soft again. "They are. I'm lucky."

Alexei sat, thinking about high school Ben, out and loved.

Ben stood while Alexei was still lost in his thoughts.

"We should probably keep moving." He picked up his pack. "You can keep asking questions, though."

Alexei nodded. This was enough for now.

Several quiet hours later, they reached Deep Creek Hot Springs. Whatever thoughts still tumbled in Alexei's head were cut short by the crowd.

Which was sizable.

And significantly naked.

Ben barked out a laugh.

"Holy shit," he breathed. "This is..." He trailed off, shaking his head and laughing some more.

Weirdly, Alexei wasn't that thrown by nudity in the outdoors; there were plenty of swimming holes in the Pacific Northwest where clothing was optional. Not that he had ever partaken of the practice himself.

Still, Alexei hadn't seen Ben's eyes this full of glee since the Cabazon Dinosaurs. It eased a weight that had been sitting inside his chest.

"Yeah?" Alexei grinned over at him. "You don't see a lot of this in Tennessee?"

"Nope. Can't say I've ever seen quite so many breasts and balls all in one spot before, but hey"—he shrugged—"I came to the PCT for new experiences, right?"

"Wait." Alexei blinked at Ben's grin, a sudden thought making the blood drain from his head. "Are you going to—"

Ben interrupted him with an even louder laugh. "Nah, Lex. I'm going to keep my drawers on, but I am *definitely* going in. You down?"

Alexei nodded and followed, only slightly unsteady on his feet as Ben stepped around scantily clad people and abandoned packs. They soon found a small pool that wasn't yet overcrowded.

"This look good to you?" Ben glanced over his shoulder as he toed off his shoes.

In fact, it looked perfect. The water was still and clear, the bend in the creek where the hot springs lay surrounded by a majestic outcropping of scarred, golden rock and chaparral covered hills. It was quintessential Southern California wilderness, and it was gorgeous.

And none of it was as distracting as Ben ripping off his shirt.

Alexei averted his eyes, studiously focused on unbuttoning his own shirt, the solidness of the rock where they stood. Until he heard Ben splash into the water, followed by a long, indecent groan.

"Holy shit. This feels *incredible*."

Alexei glanced up to see Ben, wearing nothing but his *drawers*, sink under the water to his shoulders. His hair was down. He lifted his chin to the sky, closing his eyes as he spread his arms wide across the surface of the pool.

Like an angel. A hot, gay angel.

Huffing a breath, Alexei shed his own shirt and shorts and joined Ben in the pool before he could think too hard about it. Which—oh. This *did* feel incredible.

Alexei navigated around Ben's floating form, eventually resting against a smooth, sun-warmed stone. He let his body slowly become light, attuned to the gentle current of the pool.

A small puff of a cloud drifted at the edge of his vision before Alexei's eyes flitted closed. The din of other hikers, onshore and in surrounding pools—their laughter and chattering, tabs cracking open cans of beer—faded to a distant murmur as Alexei's body surrendered to the dark, to the feeling of being liquid.

He wanted Alexei 2.0 to be more honest.

Letting Deep Creek Hot Springs soothe all of his jangled joints—letting them wash away the stress and the adrenaline of the last few days, at least temporarily—felt like one of the most honest things Alexei had ever done.

He wasn't sure how much time passed before he felt the brush of Ben's knee as he leaned in, his breath like a kiss on Alexei's earlobe, intimate and soft.

"I thought I should warn you," he said, "that at this very moment, two very old, very naked men are about to get into this hot spring with us."

And then Ben leaned away to exchange greetings with their new companions.

Alexei tried to hold on to the sensation of sunshine on his face, the healing water surrounding him.

Eventually, he lifted his head and blinked open his eyes.

The men were, indeed, very old.

The one Ben was talking to—about angina, currently, and rather enthusiastically—had brown skin and a decent head of nearly white hair. The one directly across from Alexei was paler, almost bald, his skin looser. Alexei very consciously tried not to look into the depths of the water near either of them.

Bald Guy gave Alexei a nod. He moved his arms underneath the surface of the water, engaging in the simple joy of floating. A thin gold chain circled his neck, a small cross resting on the hair of his chest.

Ben and White-Haired Guy moved on to arthritis. The old man reached out his hand for Ben to examine and Ben took it, pressing gently on the man's wrist, his fingers, his lumpy knuckles.

Alexei watched the care and focus on Ben's face, and his insides went soft.

He glanced back at the man across from him, who had lifted his arms to rest on the rocks that enclosed the pool. His left arm draped behind the back of his friend.

Were these men lovers? The thought seeped into Alexei's skull the longer he stared at the bald man's arm. Had they seen Ben whisper in Alexei's ear before they walked in? They must have. Did they assume Ben and Alexei were lovers, too? What compelled them to walk for miles on a hot, dusty trail to slip into hot springs in the nude at their age? Because they wanted to? Because they could?

They seemed so comfortable with themselves, all of their wrinkles and imperfections. They carried an air of two people who knew each other. Who had seen things together. Who would continue to see things together, for as long as they could.

The longer Ben talked with them, the longer they shared this pool, the more Alexei couldn't stop thinking about it.

How much he hoped he could be like them one day. Share their ease. Their indulgence in a life well lived.

And how deeply he didn't know how to do that.

Ever since leaving his parents' house that day, Alexei realized now, he had been living day to day. He just needed to get through each day, dragging himself out of bed, dragging himself to work, and then, after he was laid off, to the gym, to REI, to the post office, knocking things off his checklists. He just needed to get to the PCT.

And while he'd told himself his journey on the PCT would help figure out his future, that future seemed rather shortsighted suddenly. Where he would live next. A new job, new things he could try, wherever that was.

But what about the whole life he wanted to have? The overarching point of it all?

Who did Alexei want to be when he was eighty?

He startled when Ben's knee nudged his own some time later. He must have fallen asleep. He looked up at Ben from underneath half-closed eyelids.

"Hey, sleepyhead." Ben was sitting up, smiling down at him. He'd put his wet hair back in its bun. Which meant it would be extra wavy later at camp when he took off the elastic to readjust it. "We should probably move on soon if we want to make it to those campsites."

Alexei tilted his chin in acknowledgment. His guidebook promised a couple nice, legal sites a few miles farther up the trail, under willows near the banks of the creek.

Their naked friends had left.

To Alexei's surprise, he felt a pang of regret. That he hadn't talked to them. That he hadn't been able to say good-bye.

He thought of the cross on the bald man's chest. It had both comforted and intrigued him.

Next time, he promised himself. The person he wanted to be would ask more questions next time.

Alexei and Ben lingered in the water, even though Alexei knew they should move on to make it to the campsites before it got dark, like Ben said. Alexei was also pretty sure staying in water this hot for this long wasn't good for you, especially in the desert.

He stared back up at that single cloud.

What, exactly, was keeping him from Ben Caravalho?

What was in his spreadsheets, in his lists, that said he couldn't have this?

How would he live to reach naked-hot-springs-kind-of-eighty without learning how to let himself have things?

"You're always so patient with me, Ben," he said quietly.

Ben frowned.

"It's not hard, Lex. I'm not, like, extra patient or anything." He shrugged, looking away. "I just like being around you."

Alexei's heart swelled.

"Ben," he said. "You're just..." He splashed a hand in the water in slight frustration, breaking the peace of the pool. Why couldn't he ever speak the right words out loud? But Ben laughed at the splash, frown disappearing. So Alexei did, too. "The best," he finished.

Ben caught his eye, gave him a small, private smile.

Honesty. He could do this.

Alexei sat straighter, finally raising his shoulders out of the water so he could do this properly. "Ben," he said again. He took a deep breath. "I want you so much." He knew Ben probably already knew this, what with Big Bear City, and the quails, and everything, but holy crap, it was different saying it out loud. On purpose. "But I'm scared. I'm new at...everything, really. So I'm scared you might have to keep being patient, and I don't know if that's fair to you. But I want..." He searched around his brain again for the right words. "To try. Being more than hiking partners. With you. If you still want to."

Ben studied him. His smile had faded as Alexei talked, his face betraying nothing while Alexei waited for his response. Like Ben was being careful. Hiding something. Which felt odd. Had he changed his mind? Oh God.

"When you kissed me before," Ben eventually said, "by the quails. Was that the first time you'd ever kissed a man in public?"

"Yes."

"But in Big Bear City, that wasn't your first time—"

"No." Alexei blushed.

Ben broke eye contact, looking across the water. "You should figure out your boundaries, Lex."

Alexei furrowed his brow. "Boundaries?"

"Yeah. What you're comfortable or not comfortable with. Like kissing in public or not. That kind of stuff."

"Oh." Alexei bit his lip.

"You don't need to figure it all out now," Ben added. "And if you're just not into public displays of affection, that's okay, too. There's no one perfect way to do any of this."

Ben was being nice. Patient. As always. But…Alexei wished, suddenly and furiously, that he didn't need this hand-holding. That Ben wouldn't have to be worried about Alexei's boundaries, because Alexei could simply be like he was in Big Bear City. Carefree. Acting on his desires.

He knew he'd messed up with the kiss by the quails. He knew he'd messed up at every juncture probably. But he didn't want Ben to hold back. And it felt like that was what he was doing. Alexei wanted Ben, the full, smiling, laughing Ben.

But when he opened his mouth to explain that, the words stuck in his throat.

"All right, Lex. Come on." Ben was smiling at him as he stood, but it still didn't feel right. Anxiety crawled under Alexei's skin. It felt like he had just opened his whole heart—as much as Alexei had ever opened it to another person—and Ben had hardly reacted.

"The trail awaits," Ben said over his shoulder as he made his way out of the pool. Alexei watched him go, frowning, until, with reluctance, he followed.

CHAPTER SIXTEEN

B ack on dry land, Ben and Alexei attempted to dry themselves with the miniature towels they each had in their packs. Alexei searched for dry underwear, trying to think. Everything that had happened in that hot spring had felt important, monumental to Alexei. But he probably just hadn't explained it well enough. He never did.

"Hey," Ben said. "Spot me for a second?"

Alexei looked up. And before he had fully comprehended what Ben was asking, Ben was yanking off his wet underwear. Alexei's brain clicked off.

In a flash, Ben pulled on new underwear and shorts, leaning over his pack to retrieve his sunscreen.

"I'll spot you?" He shook the bottle. "Or watch our stuff if you want to go find a more private spot?"

Ben sounded totally normal, but Alexei could see it. The way he was pressing his lips together. Probably biting the inside of his cheek. Trying not to laugh at the fact that Alexei had very clearly just stared at his dick.

And once Alexei's brain clicked back on, he felt like laughing, too.

Ben had been quick and discreet. They were actually relatively well hidden in this small copse of trees. Half of the other folks in their vicinity were nude. And it felt good, helped ease Alexei's anxiety, to see Ben laughing again.

Ben began to apply sunscreen to his nose and cheeks.

Alexei stared at him. And suddenly, he was picturing it. If they were both eighty. Returning to this very spot. Alexei already had a receding hairline; he would definitely be the bald one. He pictured Ben's long hair, just as it was now, pulled back into a bun but painted in grayscale, full of flecks of white and silver. His eye crinkles would turn into the loveliest wrinkles, a face deepened by a life lived helping people, a life spent being true to himself.

Maybe Alexei couldn't always find the right words. Maybe that was okay.

Maybe he had to show Ben instead. That Ben didn't have to be careful.

Alexei stood and inserted his thumbs into the waistband of his underwear. He stepped out, one foot, the other.

He stood naked in the sunlight and threw Ben a shy smile.

Ben's hands froze mid-application of sunscreen to his forearms.

It was only a few seconds, probably, before Alexei pulled on his dry briefs. His face was on fire. But he was smiling. Alexei felt good.

Before he reached for his shirt, he jutted his chin toward the small bottle in Ben's hands.

"Can you put some on me?" he asked, quiet but sure.

Ben took a slow breath before he stepped forward. "Yeah?"

Alexei nodded. "Yeah."

And then Ben was close, so close. He squeezed sunscreen onto his fingers. Traced them down Alexei's forehead to his nose. Down his cheeks to his jawline, brushing around the edge of Alexei's beard. Alexei tried to keep very, very still.

Ben moved to his neck. The stubble underneath his chin, the space behind his ears. Alexei's breath grew labored as Ben worked down to his shoulders. Alexei didn't truly need sunscreen on his shoulders. But he was still pleased Ben kneaded for longer than was strictly necessary there anyway.

"God," Ben breathed. "You are so fucking sexy, Alexei Lebedev."

Nerves tingled down Alexei's spine. This was what he wanted. Ben's curses, Ben's desire. He felt cared for, and a little sun drunk, a little high on what this felt like, this magical hot-spring-inspired surge of courage. Maybe Ben was right. Maybe Alexei did need to think about boundaries. But he wanted this, too. He wanted *sexy*. He wanted skin and closeness and trust.

Ben's eyes looked slightly dazed, his fingers beginning to trail aimlessly down Alexei's side. Alexei liked that, too, but he was also on the verge of embarrassing himself. He opened his mouth to thank him, tell him he was good now, and—

"Jesus. You can even find fags on the PCT these days."

The voice was close. Loud. Deep.

A second voice followed.

"Seriously. Can't escape fags anywhere anymore, seems like."

"At least have some decency, for Christ's sake."

There was a moment that felt like falling, weightless and disoriented, out of space and time. Alexei was back in his parents' house, pinned under the weight of his father's gaze. Alexei was back in church, twelve years old, ashamed and confused.

"Ignore them," Ben whispered. Alexei blinked back to the present. Saw Ben's eyes widen, his pupils dilate.

The wooden pews and his father's misbuttoned sweater disappeared. They weren't going to get in here. They weren't going to touch Ben.

Alexei's pulse thundered in his ears. But his mind cleared, and he tried to stare back at Ben with meaning, with assurance. Because he knew now, what it looked like when Ben was scared. And he'd promised to keep Ben safe.

"Are you actually serious right now?"

A woman's voice this time.

Alexei's eyes flickered to the world beyond Ben, taking in the scene. The man closest to them was big, American flag patterned shorts stretched over tanned thighs. He was turned toward the approaching woman, her dark hair sticking out of a Patagonia trucker's hat.

"Get the fuck out of here, you small-minded scumbags," she said.

The man with the stars-and-stripes shorts deliberately unclicked the strap across his chest. His companion did the same. They dropped their packs in the sand.

"I think we'll go wherever the hell we want, actually," the skinnier guy said.

The woman narrowed her eyes and opened her mouth, but Alexei was moving now.

"It's fine, we're going," he said, throwing on his shirt and shorts in record speed, scrambling for his socks. "Ben," he instructed, because it looked like Ben needed instruction. He stood in the same frozen position, face blank. "Come on," Alexei said, softer now, "we should go."

As Alexei rammed his feet into his trailrunners, more people walked toward them.

"Hey, Leslie, what's going on here?"

"These homophobic assholes were giving these guys a hard time."

"The hell?"

Alexei grabbed his pack. Ben was still struggling with his shirt.

"Hey, guys, wait," the woman in the Patagonia hat—Leslie—stepped closer to Alexei. Her eyes, blazing with anger a minute ago, only looked concerned. "You guys shouldn't have to leave."

"It's okay," Alexei said.

But no. It wasn't.

Decency. That word stuck on Alexei's tongue, bitter. A word he'd been raised on. Indoctrinated on. *It's not always a sin to have indecent thoughts*, he'd been taught. Over and over. *Only a sin to act on them.*

But Ben and Alexei hadn't been doing anything wrong.

And meeting Ben was the most thoroughly decent thing Alexei had ever done.

He shook his head. "I mean, it's not. But we were getting ready to go anyway."

Leslie nodded.

"I'm so sorry that happened to you."

Alexei looked at her. Her face was full of freckles. Her eyes were green. Her T-shirt had a picture of a bear on it, hugging the state of California.

It was a simple sentence, what she had just said.

But it made the world tilt anyway, just a bit. Like it was showing Alexei colors he'd never seen before.

"Are you going to be okay?" he asked. "I don't want them to retaliate against you."

Because one thing he did understand was the mind-set of those two guys. Who were currently in a heated discussion with the other folks who had joined the fray. And he knew the way Leslie had just talked to them was not going to change their hearts and minds.

"Shit." Leslie sighed, adjusting her hat. "I did fly in pretty hot there, huh? I tend to do that when I see dumb shit. My boyfriend hates it." She looked back at the arguing crowd. Which, to Alexei's chagrin, seemed to be growing by the minute. "But don't worry. There are more of us than there are of them. And we come here all the time. Forest rangers are always coming through here. If they try to start shit, we'll report them for trying to start a wildfire or something."

Against all odds, Alexei laughed. He looked back at Ben. He was almost ready now, struggling into his shoes, but he still looked unsteady.

"Please don't do that," he told Leslie. Wildfires here were no joke. She sighed again.

"Fine. My boyfriend would probably be pissed if I lied to law enforcement anyway. But hey." Her voice turned sincere again. "Sorry if my yelling put you on the spot." She glanced back at the group, worrying her lip. "Didn't mean to call attention to you like that, or talk over you, or anything. Just couldn't keep my mouth shut. Like I said, it's a problem sometimes."

"No." Alexei shook his head. "You were fine. You were great. Thank you for being here."

Ben stepped next to him, poles in hand.

"Try to forget them, okay?" Leslie said to both of them. "They're just dumbass losers."

Alexei laughed again, even though, again, it seemed out of place, after what had just happened. But there was something so playground trash talk about Leslie's phrasing, and he couldn't help himself. He imagined Leslie on a baseball diamond, spitting out a wad of tobacco before throwing a no-hitter. *Dumbass losers*, she'd say from the mound.

"Thanks, Leslie," Ben said, and Alexei's laugh faded as he heard the shake in Ben's voice. Still, he couldn't help but smile at Ben with fondness. Still remembering the names of every stranger he ever met, even now. "Maybe we'll see you around the trail."

"We're locals, but hey. Take care of yourselves, okay?"

With one last serious look, Leslie turned to join her friends.

And Ben and Alexei did what they always did. The only thing to do. They walked.

With each step, the chatter of the crowd at Deep Creek Hot Springs faded behind them, until it grew quiet. Until it was only the crunch of their feet on the ground, the gentle hustle of the wind.

Alexei wanted to reach out a hand. Rest it on Ben's shoulder. Take his palm in his.

But he could sense Ben's anger, Ben's unease, and gave him space.

Alexei focused, instead, on settling his own lingering adrenaline.

After fifteen minutes, Ben stopped.

He stepped a foot off the trail. Stared out at the golden hills that surrounded them everywhere they looked, endless patches of chaparral.

"It's not fair," he said eventually. He yanked the elastic out of his hair, aggravated, and ran a hand through it. "You had just—" He stopped. "You had *just*—we were just—"

"Ben."

"And *that* fucking happens? On the *PCT*? What the *fuck*."

Ben's chest heaved. He stared at the desert like he wanted to set it on fire.

"Ben," Alexei said. "I'm okay."

"Well, I'm fucking not," Ben snapped. He closed his eyes, took a deep breath. "I just…I haven't had anyone call me a *fag* since high school. I mean, I live in Tennessee; being out isn't always a walk in the park, but it's not…" Ben shook his head and turned to look at Alexei. "Alexei, I need you to know that wasn't normal, what happened back there. It's not normal at all."

Alexei studied Ben's face.

He understood every emotion he saw there. Even when Alexei had been talking with Leslie, even when he had somehow been *laughing*, he had still been shaking inside. Muscles tensed, blood pressure raised, mouth dry.

Leslie's kindness and courage didn't make what had happened un-happen.

He felt a bit afraid, too, of what would happen if they ran into those guys again. Those guys had mentioned the PCT, they'd had packs, so they probably weren't only day hikers. There was a very real possibility he and Ben would run into them again. It made this long, legendary, single track trail feel a bit suffocating.

But Alexei didn't know if he agreed with Ben's assessment.

That what had happened wasn't normal.

Because everything about Alexei's upbringing had prepared him for this moment, really.

Of course Alexei would be called a fag.

Alexei *was* a fag.

This felt like an expected part of his reckoning. The only part Alexei hadn't expected, in that whole scene, was Leslie.

Ben, though...Alexei thought about how angry Ben was about Alexei's parents. How he had said, when he talked about being out to the Idyllwild bros, *not everyone's an asshole.*

Ben lived in a world where not everyone was an asshole.

So when assholes did show up, it took him by surprise.

Alexei reached for Ben's hand. Intertwined their fingers. Squeezed.

"Were people mean to you in high school?" Alexei asked, wanting to know. Maybe Ben lived with a more optimistic worldview, but he had also lived in this world longer. This world that called him *fag* but which Ben chose to love anyway.

Maybe what just happened brought up trauma for Ben that Alexei had never been brave enough to live through. Their trauma was different, but they likely each had trauma just the same. It hurt Alexei to realize it, to know this was not the first time Ben had been wounded. The idea of anyone looking at Ben and seeing anything but goodness and light seemed completely illogical to Alexei.

Ben sighed and looked off to the side.

"Yeah, sometimes. It wasn't horrible. People called me names sometimes, like that back there. Or just...you know when people are talking about you or looking at you weird? Laughing at you? Even if it isn't super obvious."

Alexei nodded. This he did know.

"But even if it occasionally sucked, I always had Julie and Tiago and Khalil and my people, so it really wasn't that bad."

Alexei rubbed Ben's thumb. Alexei had never had a Julie or a Tiago or a Khalil. Or a Ma.

And while it didn't erase what had happened, it still felt good to him now. To have a Leslie.

"It sucked sometimes, though," Alexei pushed. Because it also didn't surprise him, that Ben kept reiterating that whatever he'd gone through in high school *really wasn't that bad*. That he chose to see the sunny side, even when there wasn't one. Alexei wanted Ben to know he could be honest with him.

"Yeah."

"That just sucked back there."

"Yeah."

They were both quiet.

"You know what didn't suck, though," Ben said, looking at Alexei again, and Alexei could see it. That little, resilient flicker of life in Ben's eyes. His Ben, pushing past the anger, pushing past everything, to make Alexei smile. "You. Before all that dumb stuff happened." He pulled on their clasped hands, bringing Alexei closer. "Striptease Lex."

Alexei bit his lip. "It was just a second," he protested.

Ben tilted his head. "Maybe that could be your trail name. Striptease."

Alexei rolled his eyes, dropping their hands.

"Technically, you started it," he said.

"Technically, Al and Giovanni did."

Alexei laughed. In the haze of his memory, he remembered the old men in their hot spring introducing themselves to Ben. It felt good to remember them.

"That one guy was very happy to discuss all his ailments with you."

They stepped back onto the trail. Alexei took the lead.

"Old people love a nurse. Giovanni's probably fit as a fiddle, though. Although his joints *did* feel godawful."

Alexei smiled to himself, remembering the way Ben had examined Giovanni's knuckles. They had about five miles to the campsites. He was glad to be moving again.

"I wish I could've said something back to those guys," Ben said ten minutes later. Alexei's lungs deflated, sad Ben was still focused on it. "Defended us. But I just . . . went blank."

Alexei stuck his trekking poles in the ground. Right, left, right.

"Sometimes," he said, "there's nothing you can say to someone who's already decided to hate you."

Silence. Until, miserably: "I hate that."

"I know, Ben."

"I'm glad Leslie was there. I'm glad you talked to her."

"Yeah," Alexei said. "Me too."

Alexei could practically feel it in the following silence, how hard Ben was working to find more words, something else to say to make it better.

"Let's finish *Alanna* tonight," Alexei said after several beats. "We're so close to the end."

A long exhale behind him.

"Yeah," Ben said. "I would love that, Lex."

Alexei stared into the dark, listening to the cadence of Ben's breathing, the gentle lapping of Deep Creek. The swaying of the cottonwood they were camped near. Quiet noises of the desert at night that were starting to feel so familiar.

What did feel strange was sleeping in a tent that wasn't his. Ben's tent wasn't meant for two people, either, but it was a different style, a few inches wider than Alexei's, and Alexei would take it. They had arranged their sleeping bags side by side after eating dinner. They'd talked a little. Kissed a little, gentle and sweet. And now Ben slept next to him, curled up into the depths of his bag.

But while Ben slept, Alexei's mind buzzed.

He reached for his journal, his pen.

He needed bullet points, and he needed them bad.

Alexei squinted in the darkness; he could barely make out the paper, but didn't want to use his headlamp and wake Ben. He kept things simple: basic facts he wanted to remember from this day, when he had lived through so many different things, felt like such a different person.

He paused halfway through, looking over at the dark mass next to him, nothing but nylon with a jungle of hair sticking out of it. It was so precious, he had to bite his lip to prevent himself from bursting into giggles.

He tapped his pen against his chin, collecting himself. Figuring out what else to add to his list.

He had a strange desire to add a bullet point that said: *You can even find fags on the PCT these days.* He didn't, because it had been so frightening at the time. But now, in the safety of Ben's tent on the quiet banks of the creek, something about it almost seemed funny to Alexei, now that he'd lived through it. So many things people said—the things people Alexei had grown up with had said—were so easy to turn around. So easy, with a different inflection, to make celebratory instead.

Gays: Surprisingly common now, even in the outdoors!

Alexei fought another possibly inappropriate surge of laughter.

Eventually, he wrote:

Leslie in the Patagonia hat

Getting some words down to document the day calmed his brain a bit. But Alexei still stared into the near blackness at the page in front of him, for maybe a few minutes too long.

Because soon, a dark thought crept in.

What would Dad have done today? If he had been there?

He wouldn't have been as crass as the two men had been. Wouldn't have been as aggressive.

But he would have thought—would have felt deeply—the same sentiment.

He would have looked at Alexei and prayed.

Alexei flipped to a blank page.

Maybe if he wrote this one thing—not a bullet point, but the words that lived inside him every minute—he could finally sleep.

He lifted his pen once more.

Do they miss me?

Alexei stared at the words, barely visible.

No. Not quite right.

There was a reason he wanted to write this, finally, today.

Alexei chewed the cap of his pen. He listened to Ben breathing. And then he fixed the question, made it closer to what his heart wanted to know.

Does it count if the person they miss isn't actually me?

CHAPTER SEVENTEEN

River crossings had been one of Ben's biggest anxieties when researching the PCT. Some fords in the Sierras and Cascades during high snowmelt years were known to be especially harrowing. But the water of Deep Creek the following morning, thankfully, was shallow and calm. Cold as hell, and their feet would be wet all morning, but on the upside, Ben wasn't afraid of being swept away downriver. Or, like, too afraid.

It was a wide crossing, though, and rocky, with a tall sandy bank waiting for them on the other side they'd have to scramble up. Ben rubbed his eyes and tried to sharpen his senses as they made their careful way across.

They had just about made it there when the mooning happened.

"Hey, Thompson!"

Ben looked up. There was another pair of hikers crossing the creek with them, one of whom had already reached the opposite shore. And who was apparently celebrating this fact by pulling down his shorts and showing his white ass to his companion, who was still in the water, a yard or so ahead of Ben and Alexei.

A series of sounds echoed across Deep Creek in quick succession:

Ben's own laughter. A muttered "You asswipe." A splash. And a sharp yell.

Ben hustled ahead, making his way to the stranger. Thompson, mooning guy had called him.

Thompson steadied himself on his knees where he'd fallen. He lifted his left hand out of the water. It was followed by a cascade of blood.

"Hey, man," Ben said, "I'm Ben. Is it okay if I touch you?"

Thompson stared at his hand.

"Oh *shit*," the guy onshore said.

"Yeah, looks like you got a nasty cut there," Ben said as he reached out, slowly but steadily grabbing Thompson's arms. Helped pull him back up to standing. Arranged Thompson's right hand over his left.

"Can you push? Apply pressure just like this?" Thompson nodded, making eye contact with Ben now. A good sign. "I can help patch you up onshore, but the most important thing is that you don't pass out in this river with that heavy ass pack on your shoulders, all right?"

"All right," Thompson agreed, voice faint.

"What should I do?" Alexei asked at Ben's side.

"Let's get Thompson out of this river and then you can help get my first-aid kit."

"I have first-aid stuff," the guy onshore said as they approached. "I should help him."

"He's a nurse," Alexei said. He nodded toward Ben as Ben and Thompson stumbled onto shore. The mooner got a good view of the blood dripping from his friend's hand.

"Yeah, never mind," he said, face paling. "I'm gonna trust the nurse on this one."

Alexei retrieved Ben's first-aid kit. As quickly as he could, Ben donned surgical gloves and sterilized the wound. Fashioned a small tourniquet on Thompson's arm before he turned and asked Alexei for more supplies.

"I am so fucking sorry, man," the helpless friend said.

"You're a fucking idiot," Thompson said between gritted teeth.

"It's nobody's fault," Ben interjected. "You just had the misfortune of stumbling onto a sharp rock. When I did my rotation in the ER, I learned at least half of the worst injuries are the results of dumb mistakes or bad luck. You just had some bad luck."

"Bad luck I wouldn't have had if Nick hadn't distracted me with his ugly ass," Thompson scowled.

"Hey, dude, I didn't know it would make you impale yourself! At least I distracted you with a nurse nearby!"

"You didn't *know* he was a nurse, you jackass."

While the friends bickered, Ben worked. It was good, actually, that they were bickering; Thompson needed a distraction. Ben irrigated the wound and was finally able to get some gauze on it. He searched through his kit for more supplies with one hand.

"Here's the thing, Thompson," Ben said. "This is a pretty deep laceration. Half of me wants to suture it, but sutures are risky in the backcountry no matter what. So I'm just going to use Steri-Strips and a shit ton of wrap, but you have to be really careful with it." He worked as he talked. "If you see any sign of infection—if there's swelling, or redness, or the wound feels hot, you need to get it checked out as soon as possible. If you see a red line traveling here"—Ben traced down Thompson's wrist—"toward your heart? Get your ass to a hospital, okay?"

"Got it, Doc." Thompson had calmed significantly, color returning to his cheeks. "You're like...a PCT angel."

"Yes," Alexei said, quietly, from behind him.

Ben felt himself blush as he stripped off his gloves.

By the time he and Alexei were ready to go, he felt pretty good about the prospects of Thompson's hand healing safely. Would have a nasty scar, though. Belatedly, he realized he should've asked Alexei to take a picture with his phone for Julie.

"Sit here for at least twenty minutes, okay? Take some ibuprofen and just relax."

Ben had turned toward the sandy bank when Thompson's mooning friend, Nick, attacked him with a hug so hard Ben almost fell over. "Thanks, man."

"Sure." Ben patted his arm. "No problem."

With a final wave, Ben and Alexei scrambled up the bank. Which, shit, was going to be tough for Thompson. Ah, well. Ben had done what he could.

They walked ten minutes before Alexei stopped, abruptly, in front of him.

"Okay," he said as he turned, hands on his hips. "I'm trying to hold it together here, but Ben"—Alexei looked straight at him—"that was incredible."

Ben smiled at his more-than-a-hiking-partner.

"You're cute, Lex. It was just a laceration. I mean..." Ben's smile dropped as he grimaced. "A pretty nasty laceration, but I didn't do anything they couldn't have done themselves. I sort of just took over." He reflected back on the last twenty minutes, how he'd gone into instinct mode. Over a cut. "I hope they didn't mind."

"Didn't *mind*?" Alexei's voice was practically a screech. Ben had only ever heard it reach that pitch when he got real excited about Alanna. "Ben." Alexei threw out his hands. "You *saw* that dude almost burst into tears when you were done, right? I don't even know what half the things you have in that first-aid kit are. That was professional. That was..." Alexei sputtered. "Really hot."

Alexei blushed and stuck his hands back on his hips.

Okay. Well. This had taken an unexpected turn.

Does he believe in you? Julie asked in his head. *Does he make you feel like you can do anything?*

Ben bit the inside of his cheek.

"Yeah?"

"Yeah. Yes. I was half hard the entire time. God, Ben. How in the world could you think you won't be an amazing nurse?"

Ben's mouth hung open. Holy shit.

"Wait," he said. "Were you really?"

Alexei shifted uncomfortably, ears crimson. Holy *shit*.

"So you're telling me, Alexei Lebedev"—Ben took a step closer—"that you are turned on by the size of my first-aid kit?"

Alexei stared back at him, jaw clenching. Their noses almost brushed.

"Yes. And no." Alexei shook his head. "I'm just turned on by you."

Ben had much, much more to say about this.

Before he could, his phone buzzed in his pocket.

He took a slow breath before retrieving it. He normally wouldn't interrupt a conversation such as this, but if his phone was buzzing, it meant he had service, and he couldn't pass that up.

He tore his eyes away from Alexei's to look at the screen, and—

A wide grin grew on Ben's face. He was pretty sure he knew what this gif explosion was about.

With reluctance, he stepped out of Alexei's orbit.

"Do you mind if I call Carolina? I have, like, half a bar but maybe it'll work."

"Of course." Alexei blew out a breath, turning and rubbing a hand over his face.

Yes, Ben was *very* much looking forward to continuing this discussion later.

"Ben, hey," Carolina said on the third ring, her voice deadpan as always, as if she had not just exploded his phone. As if she had not just received the most important news of her life, if Ben's guess was correct.

"Did you get it?" he asked. "BU?"

"Yeah." A smile cracked through her voice. "I got in."

Ben whooped into the forest.

"As if there was any question."

"Yeah. But"—a weird gap of silence—"financial aid"—static—"only—"

Ben frowned. Goddammit. "Lina? I can't—"

He waited through another minute, occasionally saying her name, to no avail.

"Okay," he sighed, "I don't know if you can hear me, but I love you."

He glared at the phone and its cursed single bar of service until Alexei jolted him from his trance.

"Everything okay?"

"Yeah. Yeah, more than okay." Ben shoved his phone back in his pocket. "My baby sister got into Boston University."

"Oh." There was a funny look on Alexei's face. Surprise maybe? But he recovered quickly. "That's great. Congratulations to Carolina."

"Yeah. I mean"—Ben picked his trekking poles back up—"of course she was going to get in." They walked again, Ben talking to Alexei's back about how it was her first choice, how she was probably stressed about money now, but he was sure she'd get scholarships. Carolina was the smartest person he knew.

"That's great, Ben," Alexei said again.

And it was.

Carolina had been accepted into Boston University.

Ben had gotten to use his first-aid kit.

Alexei had talked about being turned on. *Out loud.*

And no one had even called them a homophobic slur today.

This day wasn't just good.

This day was great.

Ben had almost drifted to sleep when Alexei cleared his throat.

When he blinked awake, Alexei was staring at his guidebook, headlamp set on low.

Ben had seen Alexei study his guidebooks, his maps at camp before, but something about witnessing his nighttime routines inside the privacy of the tent really got Ben going. Making those careful notes in his journals. That headlamp on his forehead, his face all serious and cute.

"We hit I-15 tomorrow," Alexei said. "Cajon Pass."

"I know it, Lex," Ben mumbled into his sleeping bag, perking up slightly to shout, "French fries!"

Ben was well aware of the Cajon Pass McDonald's, one of the few restaurants along the whole trail that was literal steps from the PCT, and hence a star attraction among thru-hikers.

"Yes." Another light throat clearing. "There's also a hotel?"

Ben froze.

And then he shoved the sleeping bag away from his face. "Shut the front door."

"It's a bit up the highway, and it would push us back a few miles if we stayed there; we're not scheduled for another zero until—"

"Lebedev!" Ben pushed Alexei's shoulder. Alexei fell against the side of the tent. "You're telling me there's an opportunity to sleep in a *bed* less than a day away? Who cares about miles!"

Okay, so he'd recently literally reminded himself he should care about miles. But still. *Beds.*

"Yeah." Ben could hear the smile in Alexei's voice. "Okay." And then, after a long pause, "So"—hilariously, *another* throat clearing—"when we're at this hotel. You had mentioned that, uh—"

Ben propped himself on an elbow, fully alert now. "Yes?"

"That what we did in Big Bear City was only the beginning. Of what you wanted to do." Alexei twisted his pen between his fingers. "With me."

"Uh-huh." Ben grinned. Alexei scowled. Which looked much more menacing in the exaggerated shadows cast by his headlamp. Ben laughed, shuffling himself closer.

"Well," Alexei spluttered, exasperated. "Would you care to extrapolate?"

Ben laughed harder, shoving his face into Alexei's shoulder.

"Oh, Lex," he said. "Would I."

Alexei made a noise of displeasure in his throat. Ben collected himself after a moment, pulling back.

"But maybe"—he tilted his head—"you should tell me what *you* want to do at this hotel, Lex."

Alexei only scowled harder. But eventually, he took a deep breath. And Alexei did as asked.

Ben had been pretty good up until this point, he thought.

The truth was, when he'd given Alexei that speech about boundaries back at the hot springs, he'd been half saying it for himself.

Ben knew, when he truly thought about it, that boundaries were what he had been missing when it came to relationships. He let them take over his life. He needed...balance. Balance, maybe, would make him better when he got back home. Better at focusing on his career and his family. Better at being an adult.

And so he'd tried to act like his heart wasn't melting when Alexei had looked up at him in that hot spring with such affection in his eyes. He had been letting Alexei initiate almost every touch since then, waiting for Alexei's cues.

But it had been a great day. And tonight, Ben simply felt so happy. He didn't think too much about balance. About what would happen after the trail. About whether having Alexei Lebedev inside his tent was a mistake. Because Alexei wasn't Robbie or Hugh or Wyatt or any of the men Ben had dated before. Alexei was a butterfly, just emerging from his chrysalis, and he was showing Ben his wings. Ben couldn't turn away from that. Like every Joshua tree, every flowering cactus, every strange bug and fascinating rock formation Ben had been lucky enough to witness on this trail so far, he could only cherish it.

And he couldn't stop hearing Julie's voice again as he watched Alexei's blushing face in the dark. *It's not a bad decision to be happy.*

So eventually, Ben leaped out of his sleeping bag. Let Alexei's beard scratch his skin, ran his hands wherever Alexei allowed them to go, which was pretty near everywhere. They could not accomplish everything Alexei had listed; most of it would have to wait for the hotel. There was no room, and they were dirty, and it was dark and cold. Alexei deserved a bed.

None of this was ideal at all in a small tent, but that night, they made do.

CHAPTER EIGHTEEN

While Mo's mountain cabin motel back in Big Bear City had barely had a lobby, Cajon Pass Inn was legit. Two employees stood behind the smooth countertop of the front desk. This was a hotel with a pool, a hot tub. This was a hotel with a cleaning staff.

A hotel with king beds.

One of which Ben had just requested from a smiley man named Aaron, according to his name tag.

Alexei made a choking sound behind him.

Ben bit his lip on a grin. Alexei had made similar noises fifteen minutes ago when Ben purchased condoms and lube at the Circle K next door. Ben hadn't packed any for the PCT, because, well, he wasn't supposed to be doing this. And while the selection had been subpar, he was so thrilled to find supplies at the Circle K at all that saving Alexei from embarrassment had been low on his priority list. Plus, Alexei was so cute when he blushed.

"We do have one available," Aaron said. "How long will you be staying?"

Ben slapped the counter, his grin escaping. "Just for the night, please."

"Um." Alexei stepped up next to him, making eye contact with no one save for a very interesting spot on the floor. He slid a credit card and ID across the counter. "I got this."

"Hiking the PCT?" Aaron asked as he processed Alexei's card.

"Unfortunately." Ben grinned. "I apologize for the odor."

Aaron laughed.

"Have to say I'm used to it, man. You guys actually aren't half bad."

"Aw, thanks. I appreciate that. You ever spend time on the trail?"

Aaron shook his head, placing a set of room keys into a paper pocket. "Nope, and can't say I want to. I'll stay here where there's air-conditioning and TV. Now, you'll be in Room 232, which if you look at this map, is right—"

Alexei snatched the keys and map from underneath Aaron's fingertips.

"We're good, thank you so much."

And he was gone.

Ben watched Alexei dart out the door and held in a laugh. "Thanks, man." He waved to Aaron before hustling after Alexei. Who was halfway up the steps to the second-floor balcony by the time Ben caught up with him.

"I hate you," Alexei said.

"No, you don't." Because even when Ben messed up, he was 95 percent sure Alexei didn't hate him. "Oh man. *Yes.*"

As soon as Alexei opened the door, Ben threw his pack to the ground and flew onto the bed. He swung his arms and legs back and forth as if he were making snow angels.

This mattress was *way* better than the one at Mo's.

Alexei stood at the side of the bed and stared at him.

And then he dropped his pack and started babbling.

"This place probably has a continental breakfast, right?" Alexei paced to the window, pulling open the blinds and staring at the golden hills they'd been walking through for so long. "I love a continental breakfast. We can load up on horrible pastries and inedible apples for the trail. I hope they have a cereal station. I would kill for some Fruit Loops."

Ben paused his snow angel action. Alexei kept talking.

"We were never allowed to eat things like Fruit Loops when we were kids. But starting in middle school, Alina got really good at stealing junk food from her friends at lunch." Slowly, Ben slid himself off the bed and padded over to stand behind him. "She loved those zebra cakes, the Little Debbie things."

Ben slid his arms around Alexei's waist. "The best," he murmured into Alexei's neck.

"Yeah." Alexei swallowed. "One day when she was in eighth grade, she went to a sleepover. When she got home, she came into my room and brought out this Ziploc bag full of Fruit Loops. We never had anything so neon colored and artificial in our house. I loved them."

Ben pulled Alexei closer into his chest, his mouth grazing the back of his neck before he said, "I'm more of a Raisin Nut Bran man."

"I don't believe it," Alexei said on a wheeze.

"Oh, believe it." Ben's hands made a delightful trip up Alexei's chest. "It sounds healthy, but that sugary stuff around the raisins? Delicious. Raisin Nut Bran is the shit. And they never have it at continental breakfasts." Ben's hands lowered back to Alexei's stomach. "A travesty."

He could feel Alexei's body tensing underneath him, his nerves tumbling through every stuttered breath. Ben adored him. He leaned up to take his earlobe in his mouth.

This seemed to do it. Finally, Alexei let his body go fully slack against Ben's, his head lolling to the side to give Ben's mouth better access.

"Ben."

He said it so softly, bending his spine farther into Ben's torso. Ben heard everything inside that one soft sound.

He removed his mouth from Alexei's neck, sinking his forehead onto Alexei's shoulder. Squeezing him tighter, this beast of a man who let himself be a kitten sometimes, when Ben's arms were around him.

"Lex"—Ben slipped a hand underneath Alexei's shirt—"what do you want tonight?"

Ben could feel Alexei's heart, pounding against his fingertips.

"I want you to be inside me."

Ben groaned. "Say that again."

"I want you inside of me," Alexei whispered.

The thing was, Ben was already there.

Ben dropped his hands and took a step back, leaving them both unsteady. He ran a hand into his hair.

"We should shower. You can go first; I have to answer some texts. But—" Ben turned Alexei around, kissing him hard. "Don't touch yourself when you're in there, okay?" Another kiss to that flushed, ruggedly adorable face. "Save it all for me."

Alexei waited on the enormous bed as Ben took his turn in the shower. He felt...what was a good word for this? Wanton, maybe. It was a little obscene, lying there naked and open on top of the covers. He tried to make his limbs languid, his posture relaxed, even as his insides burned.

He had never felt wanton before. He had never done obscene.

He was trying it out.

It wasn't half bad.

In truth, something had been unlocked in him ever since last night in Ben's tent. When he had said things out loud he'd barely even let himself think before. When Ben had jumped out of his sleeping bag, making Alexei laugh. Alexei had craved that. The feeling of letting go.

Still. Alexei wanted to savor tonight. He had to *chill*.

He tried thinking about his old Russian schoolteacher, with her severe, judgmental face, her thick wool sweaters, her complete lack of smile lines.

Even then, his mind started to stray. He wondered if Ms. Chernyshevskaya had been hiding any secret kinks. What if *everyone was hiding secret kinks*.

Okay, okay. He closed his eyes and tried to think about . . . blisters. And rattlesnakes. Scorpions. Bears! Which Alexei still had yet to encounter, but that only made their looming threat even more pressing. There was also the threat of heatstroke, Alexei reminded himself. And insect stings. And . . . Ben's calves. Ben's face when he fell asleep, his sleeping bag scrunched around him, a bundled-up mess of dark eyelashes and long hair.

Ben—right now. On top of Alexei before Alexei had even realized he was in the room, body still damp from the shower, face freshly shaven, hair tied up in a high knot. His mouth on Alexei's mouth, soft but urgent, and Alexei forgot what he'd been thinking about. Let his brain shut off once more so he could give his body over to Ben, Ben, Ben.

"Damn," Ben removed his lips to say. "This bed is a thousand million times better than a tent. Let's stay here forever."

"Okay," Alexei agreed.

They kissed until Alexei felt soft and pliable. They kissed until Alexei felt hard and on fire. They kissed until Alexei felt both at once.

Ben eventually crawled away, reaching for the bedside table. He picked up his phone to put on music before grabbing the supplies: condoms, lube, a towel he laid underneath them. The music that filled the room from the phone's tiny speaker was quiet and folksy, set at a volume low enough to be soothing.

"Here's what we're going to do." Ben rested at Alexei's side, propped on an elbow. His fingers traced down Alexei's chest and Alexei shivered, feeling exposed, wanting Ben covering him again. "We're going to go slow. Until you tell me to not go slow anymore. And if you don't like where things are going, just tell me. The only thing I care about is what you like, and there's no gay rule that says you have to like penetration."

Alexei blushed at Ben's forwardness, at the conflicted feeling inside his chest. His slight frustration, again, that Ben had to talk him through all this.

He almost opened his mouth to say something, to tell Ben to trust him, that he knew what he wanted, even if his only previous time doing this hadn't been great. But then Ben nudged Alexei's legs open wider with his foot and ran a hand down and up the inside of Alexei's thigh, and Alexei's words curled up in his throat.

He grabbed Ben's face with both hands instead, brought him back down to him, tried to express his enthusiastic consent with his tongue. Ben shifted back on top of him, and Alexei sighed, pushing his hips into Ben's comforting weight.

Long-distance hiking involved endless hours of being weighed down, literally, by the pack on your shoulders, by your body battling the elements without respite. But here, their packs on the floor, safe within the confines of walls, the pressure of only Ben's body felt like a gift.

"Alexei," Ben broke a kiss to say, running a hand through Alexei's hair, and *oh*, Alexei wished he did that more often, and *mph*, a small thrill always rushed through him now when Ben used his full name. Which he only ever did when he was serious about something. "I want you to talk to me. I want you to tell me what feels good, okay?"

"Everything about you feels good," Alexei replied, and Ben grinned.

"I'm glad." Without breaking eye contact, Ben reached down

with one hand, and after a quick tug on Alexei's dick, there was a quiet click of the lube opening. "Then tell me what feels especially good. I want to know, and it turns me on."

"I'll try," Alexei said honestly. He thought he was getting better. At trying things.

They were kissing again then, and Alexei thought maybe Ben was kissing him so hard as a distraction from what he was doing with his hands, as his knuckles traced down Alexei's side, his palms caressing Alexei's hips, then farther, farther, pushing Alexei's legs apart, until Ben pressed gently against him with a warm, wet finger, making small circles, going no farther.

"That feels good," Alexei breathed, and it did. It felt safe.

Alexei ran his fingernails up Ben's back, and Ben purred. That felt good, too, making Ben produce noises like that. That actually felt the best.

Ben pulled his lips away, forehead resting on Alexei's.

"Your fingernails were so clean, the day I met you in Idyllwild," Alexei said.

Ben's finger never stopped its circling motion, but a puff of laughter hit Alexei's cheeks.

"Yeah?"

"Yeah." Alexei swallowed. "It's so hard to keep your fingers clean on the trail. I was impressed."

"Huh. I just thought, *This hot guy is hot.* But, thank you?"

"And I loved your smile. Still love your smile. And your eyes. And that small gap between your teeth."

Ben dipped his head, nipping at Alexei's neck. "I hate the gap between my teeth," he said, but Alexei could tell from the quiet laugh inside the words that he was pleased. He moved his mouth to Alexei's nipples, and Alexei lost words again for a bit.

Until a minute later, when he said, "I trust you, Ben."

Ben did pause then. He looked at Alexei. Alexei looked back.

And when Ben whispered, "I trust you, too, Alexei," Alexei felt everything inside him turn to caramel.

"I'm going to go a little deeper now," Ben said a beat later, "if you want to lift your hips a bit." Alexei tried not to clench when he felt Ben's finger move inside him, slowly, slowly. It wasn't as good as the gentle circles, but it was okay. He distracted himself with more kisses until he felt Ben push in another finger, and he broke away to suck in a breath, to concentrate on letting his body relax and adjust.

"Okay?" Ben asked.

"Yeah," Alexei breathed.

Ben dropped his mouth to Alexei's ear.

"Did your swipe-right do this? Did he go slow enough?"

He had told Ben a little about the swipe-rights last night. About the last time he'd attempted this.

"No."

Ben was silent a moment, starting to shift his fingers inside Alexei, drawing them out, pushing them back in, and seriously, sex was so strange.

"Did he hurt you?"

"A little," Alexei admitted.

"Motherfucker," Ben gritted out, low and quiet.

"This doesn't hurt," Alexei said quickly, because who cared about that guy, because this truly was starting to feel better than okay. "That feels good, Ben."

He felt Ben smile against his neck. But it was followed by a pause, a huff of air against his collarbone.

"I wish—" Ben started. "I wish you hadn't swiped right on those guys."

Alexei sighed. "I'd waited for so long, Ben," he said quietly. "I wanted to be sure."

Ben lifted his head with a frown. "Be sure?"

Alexei shrugged, as much as he could. "Yeah."

"But that's not—" Ben closed his eyes before opening them again, looking down at Alexei with that familiar concern. "That's not how it works, Lex. You don't have to have sex to confirm you're queer."

Alexei's frustration returned. "Fine. But maybe I just...wanted to be touched, okay?"

Ben's face softened. "Yeah, Lex. Okay. I know."

But Alexei's frustration didn't disappear this time. He took a deep breath. "Ben," he said. "Remember what you said about boundaries?"

Ben nodded.

Alexei turned his gaze toward the ceiling. "I think one of my boundaries is that you don't talk to me like I'm an idiot."

He wasn't looking at Ben's face. But he heard his soft inhale of breath. And felt Ben's fingers leaving him, his hand resting on Alexei's knee instead.

And he heard the hurt in Ben's voice when he said quietly, "Lex. I don't think you're an idiot."

Alexei exhaled, meeting Ben's eyes again, wincing at the confusion there. "I know. I'm sorry." He ran his hands up Ben's chest in reassurance. "You haven't done anything wrong. It's possible...I am a little defensive about this stuff, about not being more experienced. Which is on me. I just want..." He sighed, rubbing a hand over his face. What did he want? "I just want you to be my partner, not always my teacher. If that makes sense."

Ben nodded. "Yeah, that makes sense, Lex." His voice still sounded a little sad, and Alexei felt guilty, but now that he was saying things, he wanted to keep going, before he lost his momentum.

"Another boundary I've been realizing I need"—he reached his hands out to Ben's body again—"is for you to be clear with me, if you can. Like...me not figuring out you were gay, even though I probably should have."

"Lex." Ben's face twisted. "I really am sorry I didn't tell you."

"No, I know; I promise I'm not trying to make you feel bad. I've just been thinking about it, and realizing I should try to explain. That sometimes it feels like…I don't know, my brain doesn't work like other people's. So I just…need you to be clear about things. About what you want. About things that are happening."

Ben said, "Okay," softly, kindly, like he understood. But Alexei bit his lip.

"I feel like I just told you to not tell me things and then told you to tell me things." He sighed. "I'm sorry." Deciding to be difficult in the middle of sex. Maybe this was what sex with Alexei was like without the lubrication of alcohol.

"No, Lex." Ben ran his knuckles over Alexei's temple. "It makes sense. Thank you for telling me. I'll try to be better."

Alexei shook his head. "It's not about you being better. You're great, Ben. It's just…" He flopped a hand around between their chests. "Me."

Ben grabbed that hand, kissed the tips of Alexei's fingers. "I like you," he said. "All of you."

"Did I just totally ruin the mood?"

"Well, considering we are both still naked, on a big-ass bed in a real hotel…" Ben drew Alexei's thumb into his mouth, sucked on it for a second before releasing it with a pop, and Alexei's dick was immediately at attention again. "And also considering I find you telling me important things incredibly sexy…" Ben ran a finger through Alexei's chest hair. "Yeah, no."

Alexei smiled. "Good. Because I really, really want you to fuck me."

Ben smiled back, slow and wolfish, and Alexei felt rather proud of himself. But before Alexei could enjoy more of that smile, it was gone. Because Ben was suddenly halfway down Alexei's body, his mouth on Alexei's dick, and yeah, okay. Alexei probably should have known Ben wasn't straight, for sure, when he did this in Big Bear City.

A moment later, those two fingers returned to where they had been before, and Alexei could barely breathe. It hurt a little, when Ben entered a third finger, but the hurt barely registered in Alexei's brain, eclipsed by everything else, by Ben's mouth and tenderness and, God, this sweet music he was playing. It took effort to make Alexei's mouth work, to tell Ben he was ready, before he came too early.

Ben kneeled between Alexei's knees to put on the condom, to reach for the lube again, and Alexei watched, fascinated by every little bit of Ben's body, by how radical it felt, letting himself observe and want and see. And then Ben was lifting Alexei's legs, higher, higher, and Alexei laughed, and Ben smiled and said, "Trust me, it's all about the angle."

And then Ben was looking at him, serious, an *Alexei* kind of look, and Alexei nodded, and after some adjustments, some small, murmured instructions, Ben was inside.

Even after Ben's fingers, it felt tight, but once he was finally, fully in, Ben stilled, looking down at Alexei openmouthed and panting, holding Alexei's thighs, waiting. Alexei reached out to rest his palms on Ben's chest. To feel his heartbeat. His hands traveled up to cup Ben's face, pressing a thumb inside that open mouth, because he had liked that before, and Ben moaned, his eyelids drooping closed, some of his restraint breaking. What a wild thing, Alexei thought, as Ben sucked on his fingers, as his body tilted in this strange position, to still be learning new things about your own body, nearly thirty years after you were born with it.

"Ben," he whispered. "Ben, it feels good. You can let go."

On the first thrust, Ben hit a spot that made Alexei lose his breath, lose his words completely. But he wanted Ben to know, wanted to tell him. So he allowed his body to release a kind of cry, a type of sacred proclamation. One that, once he started, Alexei couldn't quite stop. He would've been embarrassed, probably, if Ben hadn't returned the noise with one of his own, one lower and more guttural that only made Alexei feel wilder.

No, this wasn't like that swipe-right at all.

Alexei couldn't imagine being like this—feeling like this—with anyone else, ever, in the history and future of the entire world.

They moved together, that caramel feeling Alexei had felt before deepening along with the tension in his spine, until his whole existence became an intense, underground tremor, looking for fault lines, a chance to break through. His fault lines learned Ben's movements, even as they grew faster, more erratic, Ben's face contorted with concentration and pleasure all at once. Alexei loved being able to watch more this time, this way, couldn't get enough of it, every detail of how Ben breathed, the muscles that strained in his neck.

Finally, when he couldn't take it anymore, Alexei reached down and grabbed at himself clumsily, exploding within seconds, and the whole time, he thought:

only you

only you

only you

Ben came two thrusts later, forehead creased. There was a vein at Ben's right temple that always pulsed when he came, Alexei now knew. He wanted to kiss it but was too disoriented to make it happen. Instead he watched Ben's mouth, slack and open as he rode it through, his thighs trembling underneath Alexei's.

"Fuck," he said softly before he let go of his hold on Alexei's calves, before he dropped down and let his forehead rest on Alexei's chest.

Alexei ran his fingers into Ben's hair, liked the feeling of him there, liked the feeling of Ben still inside him as they both came down, until it became uncomfortable. A whisper of that immediate post-coital shame still breathed in Alexei's head, but it was mostly smothered by Ben's weight, by the smell of him, by the nonsense babbling Ben was currently expelling into his chest—"so good, fuck, *hrmmmmm*, God, Lex, fuck"—that made him laugh.

After Ben had carefully withdrawn, after he'd wiped down Alexei and retreated to the bathroom to clean himself, Alexei curled onto his side and listened to the music still pouring from Ben's phone, the sweat on his skin cooling, his limbs deadweight on the bed. It felt truly indulgent, this wide expanse of bed, and Alexei loved it. Like he could picture himself a prince, something he had never quite pictured for himself before. A gay, sore, happy prince.

And as Ben returned to his side, pulled the blankets up over their hips, as Ben's arm curled around his stomach and Alexei's fingers found his, Alexei wondered if his entire life, he had simply been fed the wrong fairy tales.

CHAPTER NINETEEN

The continental breakfast did *not* have Raisin Nut Bran, as predicted.

Alexei told himself that was why Ben was acting strange.

The morning had been blissful. Alexei had slept better than he had since first stepping foot onto the PCT, evidenced by how relaxed his body felt now. His mind was sharp, fully awake, like he could take on the world.

He thought Ben had been feeling the same, what with the energy he had attacked Alexei with once they were both awake. Alexei was still feeling the effects of Ben's mouth and tongue and fingertips as he sat in this small lobby, shoveling in scrambled eggs and blueberry muffins and—yes, hallelujah, Fruit Loops—making up for the calories he'd lost over the last twelve hours, prepping for all he'd soon need for another day on the trail.

But almost as soon as they'd sat down with their paper plates and tiny plastic cups of juice, Ben had gone quiet. Quiet in a different way than he often was with Alexei on trail. This was a tense quiet: bunched shoulders, a tight, uncharacteristic set to Ben's jaw. Alexei watched him uneasily as Ben sipped from a steaming cup of black coffee, eyes unfocused.

Maybe Ben was tired. Maybe he just needed caffeine.

Maybe Ben had a headache. They were likely both dehydrated.

Alexei tried not to panic as Ben put down the coffee. As Ben stared at the table. Fiddled with his fork.

"So I, um. Have something to tell you. And ask you."

Alexei's mind fuzzed, like radio static. In between stations, no clear signal.

"It's not a huge deal," Ben started, "but I've been thinking about it, ever since you said last night that you want me to be clear about things. So I thought I should tell you now, even though—" He blew out a breath and wiped a hand down his face. "Sorry. I'm probably being overly dramatic about this. I just don't want to freak you out."

"Ben." Alexei worked to keep his voice calm. "You are already freaking me out."

"Right. Sorry." Ben gripped both hands around his cup of coffee and looked Alexei in the eye. "In a month, I'm getting off the trail."

Alexei's stomach left his body. *Woosh*, gone. Good-bye, intestines.

"Temporarily," Ben added quickly. "I have to go back to Nashville. I need to be there for Lina's high school graduation, and my uncle Jaco's having a fiftieth birthday party around the same time. And Caravalho family parties are truly not to be missed."

Ben attempted a nervous, close-lipped smile.

A party.

Ben was leaving the trail for a party.

Okay, and his beloved sister's graduation.

Some part of Alexei's brain knew this was understandable. People often left the trail for major life events. And…Ben said he'd be leaving in a month. More time for Alexei to spend with him, to indulge in this…thing they were doing, and then Alexei could go back to figuring out the rest of his life. An easy, neat resolution.

So why did his insides feel like they were dying?

"I'll be coming back, to finish the trail," Ben said again, with emphasis, like he was making a promise to Alexei, or to himself. "I should have told you about these plans already, probably, but it still feels so far away. Sometimes I forget it's happening. But…" Ben dropped his eyes again, trailed a finger around a drop of water on the table. "I sort of had an idea. But I didn't know if it was out of line or not."

Ben cleared his throat and sat straighter, shoving his hands into the pocket of his sweatshirt.

"I was wondering if you'd like to come with me."

Alexei blinked.

"To Nashville?" His voice sounded funny in his own ears.

The corner of Ben's mouth curved up the tiniest bit.

"Yeah. To Nashville. I was planning to stay for just over a week, eight days or so, before coming back."

When Alexei didn't say anything, Ben rushed on.

"I haven't bought the plane tickets yet, because I wasn't sure exactly where I'd be on the trail. Like, I had a guesstimate, but in case I had injuries, or there were closures, or something happened, you know. But things are pretty on track, so I think I can make it to the Sierras, and then hop a ride to Reno. And…I'm thinking I should buy them soon, before they get too expensive."

Ben swallowed and reached for his coffee again.

"No pressure, of course; I mean, it's a big thing, asking you to buy unexpected plane tickets out of nowhere, to take a break from the trail you weren't planning on, but it would be fun. I think."

Work, brain. Work. Say something.

"But either way, if you don't want to come, which again would be totally fine, you know I'd meet you again when I got back. If you wanted. I'd skip whatever miles you'd hiked while I was gone, start up again where you were."

"How?" Alexei was barely keeping up—he had never felt so

bewildered in his life—but somehow this prompted words out of his mouth. "How would you know where I was? I don't have a phone."

Ben's shoulders drooped. "Your emergency locator. I could find you on that, right?"

"You'd have to download a program, to sync with it." Alexei knew he was being obstinate for no good reason. He was reacting badly. Of course, Ben could find him with the GPS locator. That was why he'd paid so much money for the darn thing. A way to be found. If he wanted to be.

"What, like an app? I can download an app, Alexei." Ben smiled, hesitant but sincere. "I would find you, Lex."

An awkward silence filled the air. Alexei picked at the remnants of his second muffin. His heart thrummed in his ears.

"Is it okay if I need some time to think about it?" Alexei finally asked.

Ben nodded, but his eyes were sad, the set of his jaw tense and disappointed. Alexei wanted to kiss him. Alexei wanted to run out the front door of the Cajon Pass Inn and never look back.

"Yeah, of course," Ben said. He started gathering his trash, crumpling a napkin onto his plate, clearly trying to brush off the weird mood that permeated everything. "Like I said, I knew it was a big ask."

Ben stood and carried his plate to a trash can, draining the last dregs of his coffee along the way. Alexei followed him outside, his insides twisted.

"Look." Ben twirled around when they were outside their room. "Can we maybe forget I even asked you? It was too much. I—" He brought a hand up to scratch at the back of his head. They'd each taken a quick shower before heading to the continental breakfast. Ben's hair was down, in damp, beautiful waves. "Would you even want to—"

He swallowed, looking away, off into the hills.

Alexei couldn't stand it.

He reached forward, resting a hand on Ben's side. But that wasn't quite right, not what he wanted. He slipped his hand underneath Ben's sweatshirt, his T-shirt, until he could feel his skin. Yes, that was better.

Ben inhaled as Alexei drew him closer.

"Ben," Alexei said. "I didn't say no."

Ben looked at him with such hope in his eyes that Alexei could kick himself. But he wanted to keep running his thumb over Ben's side more.

"I only said I need to think about it," he said.

"I know." Ben sighed, hanging his head in his hands. "I know. Which I knew you would need to do. I'm sorry."

"Don't be sorry." Alexei bit his lip. His heart was thundering a little less with each minute that the shock of Ben's question wore off, with each second that he got to touch Ben. "It's . . . it's really nice. That you'd want me to come."

Ben dropped his hands.

"Of course I want you to come, Lex," he said, and Alexei's chest got that sinky caramel feeling again.

"I just need to think about it," he said again anyway.

And as they entered the room, as they gathered their things and prepared their packs for another day on the trail, Alexei's brain finally started to filter through the realities of Ben's question.

Leaving the trail. A week without walking.

Visiting Nashville, Tennessee. An area of the country Alexei had never seen. That hadn't been on his list of cities. But maybe it could be.

Meeting Ma.

Meeting Carolina, Tiago, Julie.

Seeing where Ben grew up. His childhood home.

It meant knowing all of Ben, not just the parts of himself he chose to bring to the trail. It meant…Alexei was still trying to process exactly what it meant. But it meant something. Something big and not at all part of his plan.

Would Ben introduce Alexei to his family as his boyfriend?

Ben had been inside Alexei last night, had made Alexei come this morning before he was barely even awake, but the thought of *that*— being Ben's *boyfriend*—made Alexei's throat run dry.

Was that what Alexei wanted?

Of course it is, a tiny voice in his brain shouted immediately. *It's all you've ever wanted. What is even wrong with you?*

Alexei swallowed. It was true. Alexei had always wanted a partner. God, he'd *called* Ben his partner last night, hadn't he? And Ben hadn't freaked out.

He just…he thought he'd have Alexei 2.0 better established first. That he'd be a steadier, newly resettled, more confident person before he took on contemplating boyfriends.

But he was possibly getting ahead of himself. Ben probably didn't consider Alexei his boyfriend.

It was just a visit. Like a vacation.

Alexei had always loved vacations.

Ben and Alexei bade adieu to their king bed. Alexei dropped the keys off at the front desk.

They made their way across the parking lot, toward I-15. The asphalt absorbed the hot desert sun, tossed it back at them.

A month, Alexei thought as they walked along the side of the interstate, the rush of passing cars and trucks rattling their bones. A month was a long time. God, he'd barely been on the trail a month, and it felt like years.

They found the trailhead. It would be all uphill today, up, up into Angeles National Forest, toward Mount Baden-Powell. Alexei remembered talking Ben through Fuller Ridge, that first day they'd hiked together, how he told Ben to take it one peak at a time.

Nashville.

Alexei repeated the word silently to himself, felt the way it rolled through his mouth.

Alexei knew nothing about Nashville.

He tried to picture it, and all that came to mind were speakeasies. Low ceilings, sweaty bodies. Neon lights; loud, brash instruments. Or were they called honky-tonks? Alexei didn't know. Was Dollywood there? Half his brain flipped over in anxiety.

The other half of his brain danced a little jig. It said: *But maybe that could be fun, with Ben.*

At least through the desert, the first half whispered.

Their original pact.

Alexei hadn't meant his promise back then, but it was one that made sense now, one that allowed Alexei's nerves to settle, his body to relax back into a trail rhythm. Ben was hoping to get off trail once they reached the Sierras, once they left the desert. Alexei had told Ben he needed time to decide about Nashville. He had time.

No matter what, they could still keep that pact. Alexei found solace in that. A boundary he could still keep.

Alexei breathed in and out. Focused on his steps, the even distribution of his weight beneath his pack.

Hundreds of miles left of just this.

Ben Caravalho's smiles. More books to read, more birds to hear. That soft oversized sweatshirt. Ben Caravalho's hair wrapped up in a bun. And the scorching, unforgiving trail under the Southern California sun.

CHAPTER TWENTY

"Wait." Ben smacked Alexei on the arm, startling him from a restful half slumber. "I think I know this one."

Alexei opened his eyes, following the path from Ben's pointed fingertip to the top of a conifer on the other side of the trail. When he finally sighted it, too, he smiled. Impossible to miss, once you saw it. Electric yellow body offset by black wings, complemented by a bright, orange-red head.

"T-t...something. It starts with a *t*. You told me last week. Don't tell me."

Alexei bit his lip to hold back his grin, to keep his mouth from saying it.

Ben sat up from where he'd been reclining on the ground next to Alexei, crossing his legs and resting his chin on his hands, staring intently at the yellow dot in the tree. Like if he only stared hard enough, it would come to him.

It worked.

"Tanager!" he shouted, leaping from the ground and pummeling his fists in the air. "That is a western *freaking* tanager." A beat later, "Right?"

"Exactly right." Alexei let the grin escape.

Ben raised both hands in triumph before collapsing back onto the ground.

"It only took me five hundred miles to actually retain a single piece of information about birds."

When Ben had calculated, a couple days ago, that it had been 500 miles since they'd first started walking together in Idyllwild—minus those two regrettable days they'd been apart—he had burst into that "I would walk 500 miles" song. And kept singing it. And singing it. Until Alexei had threatened to cancel his plane ticket.

When they'd left Cajon Pass almost a month prior, Alexei had spent a good thirty-six hours making constantly shifting pro-con lists in his head.

In the end, the pros won. Of course they did.

Part of it was wanting to meet Ma. Not wanting to leave Ben.

And part of it was the fact that if Alexei was serious about Alexei 2.0, about starting somewhere new, he needed to actually, well, take it seriously. He needed to visit new places. See what fit. Nashville had never appeared in Alexei's radar of possibilities, but maybe the trail had brought him this option for a reason. Maybe he was meant to see Tennessee.

Even if he didn't end up loving Nashville, it was still east of the Rockies. Still something totally different. Other than a trip to Russia for a family wedding when he was four years old, an event he barely remembered, Alexei had hardly been outside of this coast.

Really, he thought saying yes at all to something so unexpected was proof that Alexei 2.0 was well in progress. Alexei had spent his whole life abiding by rules, making plans and following them. Spreadsheets, syllabi, maps. He had thought that was his way out of his grief: the carefully planned route through California, Oregon, Washington, coming out better on the other side of it.

But as he had walked toward Mount Baden-Powell after that night at the Cajon Pass Inn, slowly but surely, it'd dawned on him that maybe it was the detours that actually counted the most. The adventures he met along the way that would actually change him.

Thank goodness all this had come to him, because by the time he'd handed over his credit card in Wrightwood, Ben had become such a miserable companion—pretending to be fine when he clearly wasn't, his eyes closed off, his entire aura un-Ben-ish—that Alexei would have done anything at that point to see a real smile from him again.

"You sure?" Ben had asked approximately twenty-five times, until Alexei had reached over and stolen his phone, typing in his credit card number himself.

But Ben was full of real smiles now.

Ben had become exceedingly cheery, even for Ben, the closer they got to Kennedy Meadows. The closer they got to the hitch to Reno. To the plane ride to his hometown.

And against all odds, with each mile, Alexei had only become more sure.

"I bet you would recognize a mountain chickadee, too, at this point," Alexei said.

"Negatory," Ben said confidently. "Although your faith in me is cute."

"Or scrub jays," Alexei continued. "When we get back and hike more into the Sierras, I bet scrub jays will start popping up everywhere, and believe me, they're obnoxious. You'll start recognizing them for sure."

"Whatever you say, Lex. I'm just going to sit tight with my tanager victory for the moment."

Alexei was going to miss this. These small interludes on the trail when they decided to extend a lunch break, or take a temporary respite from the sun after a particularly crushing incline. They had become some of his favorite moments.

He knew it was barely more than a week—eight days—that they'd be off trail, and then they'd be right back to these moments again. Resting in the shade. Listening to birds. Just the two of them and the open air.

But he was still going to miss it.

Ben turned on his side and squinted toward Alexei.

"Kennedy Meadows tomorrow."

"Kennedy Meadows tomorrow," Alexei confirmed.

Although they had technically been in the Sierras for a while now, Kennedy Meadows was the gateway to the famed High Sierra: Yosemite. Mount Whitney. Sequoia National Park, Kings Canyon. The John Muir Trail. The peaks and meadows that had inspired Ansel Adams and so many others. For most northbound PCT hikers, Kennedy Meadows was the milepost you walked through all of Southern California to get to. The beginning of the crown jewel of the entire trail, by many people's standards.

Ben and Alexei were finally a skip, hop, and a jump away. The landscape had already started to change substantially over the last few miles of trail, the desert finally, finally slipping away, morphing into something different, something exciting.

And they were going to leave it.

Ben had originally hoped to get through more of the Sierras before rerouting to civilization—getting off at Tuolumne Meadows maybe—but it wasn't going to be feasible. Alexei blamed it on himself, for twisting his ankle two weeks ago. He couldn't even quite remember what happened; they had traversed up and down far rockier, more treacherous paths on their journey thus far, and then on a relatively straightforward, gentle section of trail, Alexei had found himself abruptly faceplanted on the ground, a sharp pain ricocheting up his leg.

Ben had made him rest the ankle for a full day, an unplanned zero, and then insisted on lower mileage days for the next week, putting them behind. They had figured out then that stopping at Kennedy Meadows made the most logistical sense. It was a popular starting point for section hikers, too, so Ben thought it would be easy to get a hitch to the highway, where they could then get a bus.

Buses. Highways. Airports.

Alexei had done a relatively decent job of not *really* thinking about it all too hard, for the first hundred miles or so after Wrightwood. Reno had still sounded so far away, and the trail had been tough, requiring their full attention. As they made their way out of the San Gabriels, into Antelope Valley, through the Piute Mountains at the edge of the Mojave Desert, and now into the southern Sierras, Ben and Alexei often fell into a comforting, focused rhythm, even on the hard days. Like well-oiled, thru-hiking machines.

But they had also had their fair share of tribulations. Other than Alexei's twisted ankle, there had been mutual crankiness at various points, especially when they had run too low on water and the stress of trying to find the next viable source was real. Or frustration when they lost the often poorly marked trail and walked in circles in the hot sun, wasting time and energy trying to find it again. Ben had repeated freak-outs on top of particularly steep ridges, snow or no snow, and while Alexei was now a verified expert at talking Ben through them, they were stressful nonetheless.

There had also been the night Alexei pulled a tick out of Ben's butt cheek, which led to more ramblings about Lyme disease from Ben than Alexei truly needed. And most regretfully, there were the two days when Alexei's stomach betrayed him once again, and Ben waited patiently by the side of the trail each time another bout of stomach cramps made Alexei suddenly dash off into the manzanita.

So as Reno got closer, Alexei found that, to his own surprise, he wasn't overly nervous to reenter civilization with Ben at all. He supposed after you had gotten lost together, after someone had waited for you without shame as you repeatedly emptied your bowels, airports and highways didn't sound as scary anymore. They had been around each other at their most exhausted and at their freest. He knew Ben like he had never known another person. Like Ben had simply become part of his DNA. Alexei didn't see how Nashville could change that.

What he did start to worry about, as Kennedy Meadows now

loomed in their reality, were the other people who would be in Nashville. Would Ben's family like him? Would his friends? Would Alexei retreat into his awkward lizard brain as he so often did, forget how to talk to any of them?

"I'm actually a little sad we probably won't run into Faraj and the guys again," he said now, thinking about the people he *had* gotten okay at talking to, these last 500 miles.

They had run into the group of Idyllwild bros again shortly after Wrightwood, and hiked together for a few days this time. Alexei still hadn't been as comfortable with the whole crew as he was with just Ben, but he had ended up feeling almost fond of the group. Tanner, the ginger-haired one, had gotten off the trail for a while to deal with some plantar fasciitis, and Alexei thought the group was more harmonious without him. Leon made poor choices, but he was funny. And Ryan had illuminating stories about being Black in the hiking community, stories that made Alexei reflect on his privilege, think more carefully about his own choices.

And Faraj—well, Faraj flirted with Alexei a lot. Which made Alexei blush a lot. And made Ben hide his laughter in his shirt a lot.

It turned out those guys back at Deep Creek Hot Springs had been right, in the end.

The PCT *was* full of queers, after all.

"Yeah," Ben said, lying back down and resting his palms beneath his head. "They're super-fast hikers at this point. There's probably no way we'll catch up with them."

"Maybe we'll run into Ruby again, though," Alexei said, hopeful.

"Definitely," Ben agreed with a smile.

They had run into Ruby a few other times now, although she never said yes to actually hiking with them. Which made Alexei feel even more grateful for the day she'd let him walk with her when he'd needed it.

She seemed a little happier, though, each time they saw her. It was subtle; Ruby was still Ruby, blunt, quiet. But Alexei thought he could see it. That whatever she needed time alone for, whatever she needed to listen to her body for, she was finding it.

"Will you know all the birds in Tennessee, too?" Ben asked as he and Alexei finally lifted their bodies from the ground, pulling on their packs to resume the trek to Kennedy Meadows.

"Not all of them. I've never really spent time east of Salt Lake City before," Alexei reminded him. "But maybe some." Alexei was rather excited, in fact, to hopefully see some species he had only previously read about. The famed northern cardinal. The lovely eastern bluebird.

"I know the state bird is a mockingbird," he said, almost absently, as he picked up his poles. Ben released an amused puff of air, somewhere between a laugh and a sigh, that Alexei recognized well by now. It always made him happy, this affectionate puff of air from Ben's lungs that felt like it was just for him.

"Of course you randomly know the state bird of Tennessee."

"I think Tennessee might have two actually." Alexei frowned as they stepped back onto the trail. "I hate when states have two. It feels like bending the rules."

"I am assuming, naturally, that you have all the state birds memorized?"

"Obviously. How else would a repressed child without a TV spend their spare time in the fifth grade?"

Ben snorted.

"Excellent," he said, a spring in his step. "This'll occupy us for twenty minutes at least. Hit me with Alaska, Lex."

Interlude

Nashville, Tennessee
June

CHAPTER TWENTY-ONE

H oly crap," Julie breathed, clutching Ben's arm when the coast horned lizard appeared on the screen. "It's like a super tiny dinosaur."

Ben grinned. He knew Julie would like the lizards.

"I can't believe you got such incredible detail with your phone, Ben." Ben's dad, Luiz, leaned forward in his recliner, squinting through the thick lenses of his glasses at the TV. As he had done with almost every photo Ben had projected from his phone thus far. "They're fantastic."

"Thanks," Ben said. "It's really just the macro lens I bought before I left."

"Dinosaurs," Julie whispered again. She was curled at his side on the ancient Caravalho living room couch, head resting on his shoulder. Ben kissed the top of her hair.

"These are the Vasquez Rocks," he moved on, swiping to a photo of the sandstone formations that jutted out of the desert floor, glowing pinkish-red against the sky, like a fading sunrise.

"Whoa," Julie said, voice loud again. "Badass."

Ben glanced over at Alexei, as he had been doing every few photos, to make sure he was still doing okay. Even though over the last twenty-four hours, Ben had been impressed by how okay Alexei had seemed. It shouldn't have surprised him—it was Alexei who was always the rock in stressful situations, Ben who freaked out.

But it was still a small wonder when Alexei's steadiness transferred so smoothly from the trail to the airport, especially after his initial and understandable hesitance about this entire trip. Each time Ben hadn't been able to stop his leg from shaking, chewing the inside of his cheek to shreds from Reno to Nashville, Alexei's hand was always eventually there, resting on his knee, giving his arm a squeeze.

Ben was simply so *excited*. He'd been gone almost two months to the day. It was the longest he'd ever been away from home. It felt surreal, being here with his people again.

The excitement mingled with the strange mental adjustment of being back in the real world, along with the nerves about Alexei's nerves that Ben had never really kicked since Cajon Pass. That Alexei would hate it. That it had been a bad idea to ask him to come. Ben's gut, basically, was anxiety soup.

But Alexei had remained calm even as Ma crushed them both in an epic hug at Arrivals yesterday, when his dad gave him a quiet handshake, when Ben chattered nonsensically through his exhaustion and adrenaline the entire ride home.

It had been late by the time they got to Ben's childhood home, where Ben had been living in his old bedroom in the basement since nursing school. He hadn't been particularly attached to his most recent apartment anyway—he'd basically moved into the first place he could find, after moving out of Robbie's place—and while unglamorous, living at home helped him afford the textbooks and tuition. It was also convenient during the trail, already having all his belongings stashed here, not having to worry about rent or getting a subletter while he was gone.

He'd tromped Alexei down to the basement almost as soon as they'd arrived last night. And only then had Alexei had a surprising reaction.

He'd practically screamed when Delilah licked his hand.

"Delilah!" Ben had thrown his arms around the Rottweiler's neck, and they both, with great zeal, wrestled each other to the floor.

Alexei had steadied himself against the railing of the stairs, hand over his heart.

"The dog," he breathed. "Delilah is your dog."

Ben gave him a funny look. Delilah licked his cheek, wiggling her butt and whining softly.

"Yeah. I talked about seeing her, like, nonstop on the plane."

"I know." Alexei blushed. "But you've talked about so many people, I couldn't place the name, and was too embarrassed to ask once you'd mentioned her for the millionth time. I thought she was one of your cousins."

Ben had laughed until he'd cried, and they'd both curled up under Ben's soft blue comforter, Delilah at their toes, and passed out immediately.

This morning, though, Alexei had met Carolina over breakfast— she'd been at a farewell party the previous night with her Speech and Debate teammates—and Tiago came over, bearing a cup of coffee from All People, Ben's favorite, which was almost shockingly thoughtful for Tiago. A half hour after Tiago arrived, Julie drove up, and then Aunt Joan and Uncle Jaco, and finally, cousins started trickling in: Beatriz, Claudio, Ana. Alice, visiting from Chattanooga for Jaco's party, had slipped in right as Ben started the slideshow.

Ben's house wasn't big. It was possible every inch of it being crammed with Caravalhos, plus Julie, had finally pushed Alexei over the edge.

Alexei's posture now was the opposite of Julie's casual draping. Back straight, hands clasped politely in between his knees. And while he gave Ben a tiny smile every time Ben caught his eye, Ben could see the strain in his jaw that hadn't been there the previous night, how his quiet was different today.

Ben knew his family was a lot.

He knew Alexei was doing his best.

But Alexei was *here*.

Ben couldn't get over it, every time he looked over and saw him on the family couch.

The next shot Ben showed was from the top of a ridge, one he was sure they had known the name of at the time. But after walking along so many ridges, they all seemed to blur together now.

Ma shot out of her chair at the sight of it, clutching at her chest.

"Jesus, Mary, and Joseph," she said. "You *walked* on that? One slip and you could've *died*, Bento!"

"Aw, Aunt Iris, relax. Look at him; Ben's just fine," Claudio asserted.

"But he's going *back*," Ma said, and then seemed to catch herself, taking a deep breath. She settled back into her seat, hands clasped tightly in her lap. "Sorry, Ben." She nodded, as if to give herself strength. "The pictures are lovely. Keep going."

Ben reached over Alexei's lap to grab his mother's shoulder. He gave it a quick squeeze.

His chest felt tight. Competing with his guilt over causing Ma stress, there was a swell of pride. Because she was right. He *was* going back. He'd made it through 700 miles, and there had been plenty of moments during those 700 miles when he'd contemplated quitting. But he'd made it this far without major injury or incident. He was terrified of the Sierras, but he trusted Alexei's instincts more than anything else he'd ever known. Alexei would only carry them across ridges and river crossings they could bear together. Alexei would make sure they were okay.

And even if things didn't go perfectly after this, Ben still felt strong after those 700 miles. Stronger than he'd ever felt. Strong enough to try.

He swiped on his phone. A photo of the massive windmills that had dotted a lonely stretch of desert appeared on the TV.

Delilah jumped onto the couch and rested her head on Alexei's lap.

"I can't believe you actually walked all of this," Julie murmured as he swiped to yet another new scene. "This is amazing, Ben."

And it was.

Ben had been there for all of it. But experiencing it through the eyes of his people made it feel different. The more you got used to something, the easier it became to miss all the details.

But Julie was right, too.

Their walk had been amazing.

"You doing okay?" Ben asked Alexei, low and quiet, once the slideshow was done and everyone had splintered into separate conversations.

"Yeah." Alexei scratched at Delilah's neck. Ben did his best not to explode in joy at the sight of it. "Everyone's really nice," he added neutrally.

Ben leaned in closer, wanting to bring Alexei fully back to him.

"You know what I kept thinking about during all those photos?" he asked.

"What?"

"The foxes."

They had night hiked together not long after Wrightwood, during the stretch of trail that followed the Los Angeles Aqueduct, too bare and exposed to truly hike safely during the heat of day. It still hadn't been exactly fun, night hiking, but it had been far less frightening doing it together. And there had been unexpected treasures. Like the expanse and depths of the wide-open, starry midnight sky.

And the surprising playfulness of kit foxes.

The furry creatures had repeatedly crossed their path somewhere around one in the morning. Once Ben's and Alexei's hearts had stopped pounding and they realized the foxes had no interest in sinking their teeth into their calves, all they could do was giggle like children. Ben had bemoaned his phone's inability to capture the scene in the inky blackness, the inadequate halos of their headlamps.

"Let's just remember," Alexei had whispered, squeezing his hand.

And so they did. Paused in the middle of the trail, they memorized the large triangular ears, the fluffy tails, the keen eyes. Until eventually, the foxes tumbled over each other back into the darkness for good, and Ben and Alexei kept walking toward Canada.

"Thanks," Alexei said now, a small but genuine Alexei smile on his face. And then, as if he understood precisely how Ben was attempting to comfort him, "You're sweet."

"I know it's a lot," Ben said, squeezing his hand. "Meeting so many people at once. Meeting even more people tonight."

This trip was bookended by two big events with downtime between them, starting with Uncle Jaco's fiftieth birthday party tonight. Next weekend was Carolina's senior awards ceremony, graduation, and graduation party. They would run to the airport at the tail end of the graduation party on Saturday, and hopefully be back on the trail by next Sunday.

"I just realized something." Alexei's forehead creased. "Is your uncle's birthday party a dress-up affair? Because...I only have my hiking clothes."

Ben blinked. He knew Alexei's entire hiking wardrobe by now. One pair of cargo shorts and two shirts. Three pairs of socks, three pairs of underwear. A flannel and flip-flops for camp. A bandanna.

Ben burst into laughter, dropping his head back on the couch. "I mean, Caravalho family parties aren't black tie affairs or anything. And you could probably borrow some of my clothes, but you're bigger than me, and..."

Ben sat forward, snapping his fingers.

"Lex. You and I are going to the mall. We can get an Auntie Anne's pretzel. I haven't had one of those since, like, the seventh grade, but now that I've said it, I definitely need one immediately."

The wrinkle in Alexei's forehead had not disappeared. "Do we have time?"

"There's always time for the mall, Lex."

Ben stood and clapped his hands.

"All right, minha família. Who's down for a shopping trip?"

Alexei had been to a few Lebedev family weddings in his lifetime.

None of them even came close to being as fun as Uncle Jaco's fiftieth birthday party.

At least, Alexei comprehended it was fun, extremely so, for everyone else. And so, while Alexei still felt off-kilter from the overstimulation of the day, everyone else's enthusiasm for each other couldn't help but seep into his bones just a little.

The party was held at a nondescript fire hall, linoleum floors and gray walls. But the Caravalhos had strung white lights everywhere, each plastic table adorned with blue-and-white-checkered tablecloths and vases of bright flowers. The back door of the fire hall was open to a lushly green lawn, dotted with party games. The lawn sloped gently toward a creek, the sweet-smelling air filled with the croaks of toads and the chatter of insects. Music filled the air inside and out, a constant beneath the never-ending buzz of conversation.

Ben did his best at introductions in the first hour, dragging Alexei around to meet everyone, letting go of his hand every few minutes to engage in hearty, back-slapping hugs. Alexei's face felt sore from having to smile at so many people, although his decision to simply give up on remembering any of their names reduced his mental workload significantly.

Eventually, as Alexei knew would happen, Ben was torn away into deeper conversations too many times for Alexei to catch up. When Alexei assessed that Ben's constant explanations to keep Alexei clued in were more burdensome than enjoyable for anyone, he slipped away to the buffet table, where he loaded up on potato salad, baked beans, and fried chicken.

Finding a lawn chair outside, he sat and watched various children and adults alike throw Frisbees and play cornhole as he enjoyed his food. It was loud pretty much everywhere, but at a more manageable level outside. Still, no matter where he was, every few minutes, he could hear the infectious peal of Iris's laughter.

It felt rather like bird-watching: sitting in the twilight, observing. He was learning the calls of the Caravalhos, their songs.

"Lex." Ben ran over, breathless. He wore a large, floppy hat that appeared to be shaped like a huge fabric cheeseburger. Alexei paused midchew to stare at it.

"Oh yeah." Ben tracked Alexei's stare. "Burger hat. It's a thing. Anyway, we really *must* play ladderball at some point."

"You must know I have no earthly idea what you're talking about."

"Obviously," Ben said easily. "But ladderball's the best. You'll love it."

An old man walked over and threw his arm around Ben's neck.

"I hope you don't think you get the burger hat all night simply because you've been off in the wilderness for months, Benny boy," the man said. Ben grinned, and five minutes later, he was gone again.

Later, there were speeches roasting Uncle Jaco, during which Ben found Alexei again, slipping in next to him at the table, his hand twisting down to thread into Alexei's. Alexei was adjusting to it, the way Ben had so casually held his hand in front of his family from the moment they stepped off the plane. No one batted an eye, so Alexei went along with it.

Because it was wonderful, holding Ben's hand. Always grounded Alexei, whenever he started to get a bit overwhelmed in this humid, noisy place.

There was pretty much nonstop laughter during the speeches, bouncing off the walls of the fire hall, and Alexei found himself smiling more naturally each time Ben burst out into a laugh next to him. Alexei learned way more about Uncle Jaco's dietary habits than he thought he even knew about his own, along with the fact that Uncle Jaco was a proficient rollerblader. Which he learned first-hand after the speeches, when Jaco rollerbladed in big circles around the fire hall to "Once in a Lifetime" by the Talking Heads—Jaco's favorite song—in celebration of his broken leg being healed, before coming to a quick stop in front of his birthday cake, where he blew out his candles with a flourish.

Only a little different from a Lebedev family party.

Ben disappeared again shortly thereafter. But other than a slightly painful encounter with Tiago, wherein Tiago asked Alexei where he was from and then attempted to make conversation about the Portland Trail Blazers, about whom Alexei knew close to nothing, Alexei really was okay sipping lemonade in the corner alone. Watching. Absorbing. Not so secretly staring at Ben being happy.

And then the sun settled behind the trees, and the dancing started.

Alexei had been keeping track of the songs he recognized—two out of six, so far—and quizzing himself on people's names when Carolina glided into the seat next to his, her cheeks flushed from the dance floor.

"All right, Mr. *Alexei*." She drew his name out, her fist wrapped around a bottle of IPA. "Wait, sorry." She shook her head, frowning. "Do you identify as Mr.? Damn, I need to get better at assuming gender stuff."

Alexei blushed, although he wasn't quite sure why. Maybe it was Carolina's casual acceptance of the idea that Alexei could be different than he appeared.

Alexei hadn't met many trans people before, at least not as far as he knew. But he knew Ben was friends with Reina, Khalil's girl-friend, who used she/her, and London, who used they/them. Alexei would be meeting them both tomorrow at a brunch with Ben's friends. Ben had told Alexei more about them on the plane ride yesterday, so Alexei would know their pronouns.

Alexei felt hesitantly excited to meet Ben's friends at brunch. Which was surprising, after how overwhelmed he felt by all the new people he had already met today. But even though he knew not all of Ben's friends were queer, it seemed like a lot of them were. More than Alexei had likely ever hung out with at once before in person anyway. And the idea of being part of that kind of a community felt like...everything Alexei 2.0 had quietly been hoping for.

"Mr. is fine," he said.

"All right then, Mr. Alexei. Tell me your deal." She took a swig of beer, staring straight at him.

"My deal?" Alexei's pulse started to race, understanding he was about to be interrogated by the person Ben loved most in this world.

"Yeah. Give me your vitals. Background, Enneagram type, party affiliation, devotion level to my brother, stuff like that."

Alexei had no idea what an Enneagram was, and he figured the fact that he had known Ben for less than two months and then flown across the country to meet all of his family and friends was probably answer enough for that last one.

"My family's Russian-American mostly," he said.

"All right." Another swig of IPA. "Next."

Alexei ran a finger under the collar of the blue button-up he'd purchased at the mall earlier today.

"For party affiliation, I guess I'm an Independent."

"Oh Lord," Carolina muttered. "That's fine. You're still young. We have time to change that."

Alexei tried to remind himself that this person was, in fact, more than a decade younger than him.

It didn't work. He still felt nervous around Carolina, wanted to impress her, seem worthy of her brother. He cleared his throat.

"I vote," he said. "And I try to pay attention to local politics."

Both of these things were true. He had tried to educate himself over the last decade, ever since leaving home for college, about political topics beyond abortion and religious freedom. It was almost a completely different world, expanding his viewpoint beyond these things. He always studied his voter's pamphlet carefully, tried to make his decisions based on what sounded like the best ideas for the community, regardless of what his church or his parents would have said.

It felt monumental, sometimes, filling in those bubbles for himself, dropping his ballot off at the elections center. He wanted to tell Carolina that, but when he looked at her, he realized she was smirking.

"Really," she said dryly. "I bet you listen to podcasts, too."

Alexei frowned.

"No," he said, confused. "Should I?"

Carolina's gaze turned thoughtful. She tapped the mouth of the beer bottle against her lips.

"Wait," Alexei said, suddenly *really* remembering that Carolina was only eighteen. And what kind of an eighteen-year-old drank *IPAs*? "Should you be drinking?"

She smiled. She looked so much like Ben when she smiled. It made Alexei feel irrationally, immediately protective of her.

"Give me your phone number." Carolina grabbed her phone from where it sat facedown on the table. "I'll text you some podcasts you should listen to."

Seriously, *how* many times was he going to have to explain himself in regard to this?

"I actually don't have a phone. Or, rather, I used to, but my service is turned off."

Carolina looked at him over the top of her phone case, which read, in bold black letters over a pretty floral background, "INTERSECTIONAL FEMINISM OR BUST."

"Oh my God. Are you one of those survivalist Luddite people? Do you have an underground bunker somewhere?"

Alexei sighed.

"I just didn't think I needed my phone on the PCT."

"So you haven't had a phone for, like, months."

Alexei nodded. Carolina stared at him for a long moment before she started typing.

"I'll text some recommendations to Ben to pass on to you."

"Okay." And then, remembering himself, "Thank you."

Carolina grinned at her phone. "You are welcome."

"Lex!"

Out of nowhere, Ben was there, crashing into Alexei's knee. His hair was in a high bun, his face overtaken by a goofy, lopsided grin. He wore dark jeans, a navy short-sleeved button-up with tiny white polka dots. Every time Alexei looked at him tonight, he felt like he couldn't breathe. Seeing Ben outside of his hiking clothes had been...a revelation.

"Whitney's on," Ben said, chest heaving slightly. When Alexei didn't say anything in response, his eyes widened. "Don't tell me you've never heard this song."

"Yeah, I am a mere youth, and even I know 'I Wanna Dance with Somebody,'" Carolina chimed in.

When Alexei still didn't say anything, she leaned forward, chin propped on her fist, phone forgotten.

"*What?*" Alexei said, feeling strangely exasperated.

"You are...*interesting,*" Carolina said, her voice filled with a sense of curious wonder. At least, that was how Alexei was going to interpret it.

"Come on." Ben pulled Alexei to his feet, leading him away from the table and Carolina. "You *must* dance with other gays whenever Whitney's on," he said over his shoulder as he marched Alexei to the dance floor. "It's in our bylaws."

"You're drunk," Alexei noted, smiling as Ben finally stopped and twirled around to face him.

"Maybe a little. Come *onnnnn*. Dance with me, Lex."

And feeling helpless to refuse, Alexei did.

He felt a little drunk himself, from the happiness radiating from Ben, from the silly bop of the song. And so he danced. It all seemed to happen rather quickly. Alexei had no idea *how* to dance, wondered at this moment if he had ever actually danced in his entire life, but a quick assessment of the dance floor proved none of these other people knew how to dance, either, so he didn't think too hard about what his body was doing.

Ben reached out his hand during a chorus, and while Alexei willingly took it, he still found himself surprised to be tugged so violently toward Ben's chest and then flung outward again. Ben lifted their twined hands and twirled underneath them, encouraging Alexei with another push to do the same. Ben never stopped shouting-singing along the whole time, and Alexei couldn't quite meld together in his brain how this was both endearing and hot. And then Alexei realized *everyone* was singing along, and he realized he was laughing. That his face almost hurt from it.

He leaned in to shout over the music into Ben's ear.

"You said the rule was to dance with other gays." Because suddenly Alexei had a vision. That he and Ben were dancing this exact dance, just like this, but in a dark room where everyone else was like them.

Swipe-right number two had offered to take Alexei clubbing sometime, two years ago, but even the word, *clubbing*, had practically made him break out in hives.

Right now, though, the idea sent a lick of electricity all the way up his spine.

"My cousin Martim is bi," Ben shouted back, pointing across the dance floor to a tall man with curly dark hair, who flashed a smile and waved at them like he knew exactly what Ben was saying. Alexei blushed and looked back at Ben.

"And we're pretty sure Ana is a big lesbo, but, you know, I'm trying not to pressure her too much. I'll find more gays for you," Ben added as he danced in a circle around Alexei, "next time."

Alexei laughed. "This is good," he said. "This is enough."

And as he kept jiggling his hips and jerking his arms, he realized the song had changed. But no one had stopped dancing, and he didn't feel like stopping, either. So he didn't.

Someone walked by and plopped the burger hat on Alexei's head.

"I can't tell if your sister hates me or not," he shouted at Ben.

"Oh, Alexei." Ben smiled, his shoulders jumping, his body loose and in constant motion. "I can't think of a single reason why anyone would ever hate you."

Hours later, Ben and Alexei wished Carolina and Ben's parents a good night after they all tumbled through the front door. Alexei watched Iris, so much taller than her husband, lean down to plant a kiss on Luiz's cheek before they ambled up the stairs side by side, Luiz's arm curled around her waist. Alexei knew his parents loved each other. But they had never shown such casual physical affection. He stared after them a second, entranced by it, before Ben tugged at his arm.

As they walked downstairs, stopping near Ben's bed to take off their shoes, Alexei was filled with a deep, soothing sense of relief at it being the two of them again. Even though he had ended up having a surprisingly good time at the party, it had still been quite the day. Being alone with Ben made him feel normal again, his nerves settled.

Plus, the Caravalhos also did their laundry down here. Ben's bedroom smelled like fabric softener, and it made Alexei feel like he was wrapped in a warm blanket every time he entered it.

He was about to collapse onto the bed to sleep forever when Ben's arms circled around him from behind, flat palms running up Alexei's chest.

"Not to be dramatic about it." Ben's voice was at his ear, his breath hot on Alexei's cheek. Automatically, Alexei's back curled, falling back against him. "But if I don't fuck you right now, I might die."

"Oh," Alexei said, heart thumping, watching in a daze as Ben's fingers made quick work with the buttons on his shirt. "Dying would be bad."

"Hard agree."

Within seconds, Alexei found himself on his back on Ben's tiny twin bed—not even close to a king, but it would do—his shirt on the floor, Ben's tongue inside his mouth, while Ben's fingers worked at Alexei's pants.

"Ben." Alexei broke away for long enough to breathe. "Your family."

"Two floors away," Ben panted. "Benefits of the basement."

And then Alexei forgot about Ben's parents, too, because soon he was naked, and Ben was yanking off his own shirt, and Alexei was so hard, he couldn't think straight.

"Lex," Ben said into Alexei's neck, trailing openmouthed kisses down to his collarbone, "God, I am so glad you're here, Lex."

"You are?"

Alexei knew, in the logical part of his brain, that of course Ben was glad he was here. But the part of Alexei's brain that felt vulnerable and uncertain about all this still felt gratified to hear Ben say it.

"Yes, Lex. God, I forgot how *cute* you are," Ben said, aggressive, punctuating it with a light bite to Alexei's left pectoral that made Alexei gasp. "Being all quiet and polite and sweet all the time. *God.* I've wanted to fuck you senseless ever since the plane landed."

Ben's clothes were now fully removed, too, and he grabbed Alexei's hand and brought it to him, as if to show the proof of this statement. He groaned as Alexei's hand made contact, his head dropping heavily toward Alexei's chest.

"And then tonight," he wheezed, voice strained, "you actually danced with me. I wasn't sure if you would. But you did, and ugh, all I wanted was to drag you to the bathroom and take you in my mouth."

"Ben." Alexei shuddered. "I'm going to come right now if you keep talking like that."

"Good," Ben grunted. "But don't."

His tongue swirled around Alexei's nipple. Alexei closed his eyes, focused on regulating his breathing, on not shoving his hips too violently into Ben's.

"I just love you being here. In my house, in my town. Meeting my family and all my people."

Ben lifted his face to hover above Alexei's, eyes going tender. He ran his knuckles down Alexei's cheek.

"My family is like...they're *me*, you know?"

A gap opened up in Alexei's chest. Like when the first rattlesnake had stolen his breath away.

He wanted to say, *I know.*

I know.

Because my family used to be me, too.

He tried to gasp air back into his lungs as Ben moved again, his mouth moving down Alexei's torso. There wasn't time for this, for his crisis about his family, when Ben's body was moving so frantically, when Alexei wanted this so much, just Ben, just here and now.

"And Carolina loves you, by the way."

"Really?" Alexei blinked, mind whirring. "She does?"

Ben returned to Alexei's mouth for a deep, blistering kiss.

"Oh yeah." He leaned back to grin, his fingers tickling down Alexei's side. "She cornered me before we left. I believe her exact words were, 'That boy is the most earnest person I've ever met. If you weren't already in love with him, I think I might be.'"

Ben leaned back on his heels, nudging Alexei's leg with his hand. "Can you flip over? I think I want you on your knees, if that works for you."

Alexei flipped over without thinking. They had tried this before. They had tried lots of things in Tehachapi, the sole other king bed they had found between Cajon Pass and Kennedy Meadows. They had taken a full zero there, hardly left the bed other than to do laundry and shopping. It had been educational and wonderful.

Alexei had topped once in Tehachapi, and it had been good, if a bit nerve-racking. But Alexei was glad for Ben to be in control tonight. More than happy to be on his hands and knees for him.

It was only when Ben's fingers began tickling down Alexei's lower back did the words he had spoken sink into Alexei's brain.

"Ben," he said, "did you just say you're in love with me?"

"Did I?" Ben rubbed his erection between Alexei's cheeks with a light groan. "Oh, I guess I did. Or rather, Carolina did. Fucking A, let's not talk about my baby sister right now."

"You brought it up," Alexei muttered, head dropping onto Ben's pillow.

"Right." Ben grabbed at Alexei's hips and Alexei pushed back, wanting to get closer to Ben somehow, as close as possible.

"Well, she was correct, as she usually is," Ben said as he reached for his side table, pulling out a condom and lube. "Of course I'm in love with you."

He dropped a kiss on Alexei's shoulder after he said it, and Alexei released a small whimper, emotion battering around his rib cage like a bird caught inside an attic. He found himself unable to form words, or do anything at all, other than hope Ben understood how much he needed him inside him right now, hard and fast and honest.

He must have, because soon Alexei felt Ben's fingers move to grip his hips, and he was easing himself in, and Alexei was ready for him. Wanted those fingers to bruise him.

"Yes, Ben," he heard his lips saying. "Yes, God, please."

It was urgent and inelegant, all muscle and sweat, and after a few brutal thrusts Ben managed to ask, "Are you okay, is this okay," and Alexei immediately moaned back, "Perfect, it's perfect."

Because Alexei didn't know if he could handle tenderness right now. His heart already felt tender enough on its own. He wanted this, the sensation of being almost out of control, of oblivion.

"Lex, I'm close already, God, I hope that's okay, *fuck*," Ben said, readjusting his grip, his rhythm growing erratic.

"Me too." Alexei twisted Ben's sheets in one of his hands, panting, imminent release making black hover at the edges of his vision.

He wondered, somewhere in the back of his mind, how exactly he had evolved from the swipe-rights—nervous, timid, awkward—to this, this type of rough, physical carnality, unfettered and slightly unhinged. But ever since he had started dancing tonight, since he had let himself fall into this world of the Caravalhos, so different yet so comforting all at once, a world of affection and laughter and unquestioning acceptance, Alexei had felt something shift inside him. Like he was examining the contours of a new body he was so close to sliding into, a life he had never seen fully before because it had always been held just outside his field of vision.

And that Alexei loved every second of this.

Soon, Ben was groaning, shuddering, falling over Alexei's back, and when Alexei came, all he could think of was Ben's voice saying, *Of course I'm in love with you*, and it felt like falling headlong into an infinite space filled with sparks, bright and close enough to burn.

After they had caught their breath, a crowded tangle of limbs on the small bed, Alexei felt like saying it back, over and over, into Ben's skin: *I love you I love you I love you.*

He felt like saying, *Please don't ever leave me.*

Instead, what Alexei heard himself say was: "I came all over your sheets."

Ben hummed and nuzzled into his neck.

"I'll do laundry tomorrow," he murmured. "Another benefit of the basement."

He wrapped his arm around Alexei's stomach a little tighter.

"Fuck, that was hot, Lex."

"It was perfect," Alexei said again, at least one truth he was able to articulate, and maybe one truth for the night was enough.

Neither of them moved to stand, or pull the sheets over themselves, or fix the mess they had made. Alexei knew they needed to do all those things. But for a moment, he let himself indulge in it: wrung-out and happy in the dark, sticky stillness.

CHAPTER TWENTY-TWO

B en!" Dahlia Woodson extended her hand. "It is so good to finally meet you!"

Dahlia was very short and very pretty, with a huge pile of dark hair swept onto the top of her head. She had moved to town during the hectic time period when Ben was swept up in the NCLEX and then PCT preparations, and they'd never been able to meet up. She smiled with her whole face, and Ben liked her immediately.

"Ben, you magnificent asshole." Khalil hugged him with a hearty back thump. "And hello, magnificent asshole's companion."

Alexei met Khalil's handshake with a tiny, adorable smile. "Alexei."

More introductions were made all around until finally they were seated: Julie, London and Dahlia, Laynie Rose, Khalil and Reina. And, wonderfully, Alexei.

A waiter filled their glasses with water while another handed out menus. The atmosphere of the restaurant was sunny, full of floor-to-ceiling windows, green plants hanging from the walls, silver fans whirring above, everything open and bright and clean. It all matched Ben's disposition rather pleasantly.

And if Ben wasn't mistaken, it matched Alexei's, too. He had handled the loud, rapid round of introductions with aplomb, his shoulders relaxed, his smiles small but easy.

Ben opened his menu with one hand, reaching down to squeeze Alexei's hand with the other.

"Seriously, Ben," Dahlia said with a grin across from him, chin propped on her hand. "It's a pleasure. London has told me *so much* about you."

London sighed heavily and looked up at the ceiling.

"Wow," they said. "You couldn't wait even two seconds."

"Ooh!" Julie jumped in from Dahlia's other side. "Are we talking about how London had a big silly crush on Ben all throughout high school?"

"I hate you all," London muttered, opening their menu and staring at it resolutely.

"I mean, I get it!" Dahlia said to Ben. "You are pretty dreamy."

London scowled. Ben bit the inside of his cheek.

"You know, it truly is the most typical Ben Caravalho thing to ever happen," Julie said. "That you went to the fucking backcountry and somehow still brought back a hot boyfriend."

She grinned at him as she said it. Ben grinned back.

It occurred to him a second later, though, that while he knew Julie meant this affectionately—she had texted him lots of complimentary, encouraging things yesterday after finally meeting Alexei in person—the statement had probably sounded a little odd to Alexei.

And she had called Alexei his boyfriend. Shit. Out of nerves, Ben gave Alexei's hand another squeeze.

He had never quite known how to describe what they were, him and Lex. Boyfriend didn't even seem to cover half of it. And labels didn't seem to matter on the trail. But they probably should have discussed it before flying here. He knew Alexei had never had a boyfriend before. That the label would be a big deal to him.

Ben squeezed his hand one more time, for good measure.

"Julie," London said, shaking their head.

"Are we disputing the fact that Alexei is hot? Or that Ben's a little slutty?"

Ben choked on his water. Khalil, on his other side, snorted.

"You know I mean it in an empowering way!" Julie protested.

"We're really easing Alexei into the group, huh," Laynie said.

"You know." Reina spoke up from the end of the table, her light brown hair twisted into a clip at the back of her head. "When I met you last year, Ben, I did think, this one seems a little slutty."

Ben laughed at that. But okay. Maybe he should have filled in Alexei about his dating history. At least a little. Before, you know, right now.

He turned his body toward Alexei, finally looking him in the eye. And while he'd expected to see that crease of worry across Alexei's forehead, his face was clear. If anything, it seemed like Alexei's eyes were almost...amused?

Still, Ben should address this, even if he hadn't planned to do so before breakfast, in front of all of his friends.

"I have...dated," he started, "kind of a lot of people. I haven't told you about them because you didn't ask, and most of them honestly didn't even matter. Okay?"

"*Ouch*," Khalil said, a hand over his heart.

"Oh shit, I always forget you guys dated," Laynie said.

"For a *week*," Ben scowled. "In *tenth grade*." He said this to his friends, the jerks, but kept looking at Alexei, his fingers running over Alexei's knee.

"You okay?" Ben asked quietly.

Alexei looked back at him for a beat.

"I think," he said with a smile, "that I am rather proud to be with a slut."

Ben's eyebrows raised in surprise. Dahlia gave a loud laugh from across the table.

"I like you, Alexei," she said.

Ben felt himself blush. With a small grin, he said, "Me too."

Their waiter approached the table as Reina was saying, "Aww," and Julie was saying, "God, everyone I love is gross now," and then they were finally ordering their food, the tension of the moment dissipating.

"Alexei, tell us more about yourself," Dahlia said once the waiter had left. "Where are you from? What do you do?"

"I'm from Washington State originally, but live across the river now in Portland. And I'm a data analyst."

"That sounds smart," Dahlia said. "Numbers stuff."

"Yeah," Alexei confirmed. "Numbers stuff. What about you?"

Both London and Dahlia froze. Ben jumped in.

"Oh! Yeah, I meant to tell you. Alexei has never watched *Chef's Special*."

London exhaled, leaning back in their chair.

"I'm sorry," Alexei said, his face regretful. "That's right. Congratulations on that."

"No," London said immediately. "Please don't apologize. This is awesome."

Dahlia smirked. "You are officially London's best friend now, Alexei."

"It's just," London sputtered, waving their hands in frustration, "the show is *over*. I don't understand why everyone still wants to talk about it so fucking much."

"By the way," Julie chimed in, lifting her chin, "that table over in the corner has been staring at you since we walked in."

London made an indistinct muttering noise.

"Aw, poor baby," Dahlia cooed, patting the top of London's head. "It *is* so very hard to be rich and famous."

London glared at her. But Ben swore their mouth twitched, like they were suppressing a smile. It was possible Ben had never seen London look happier in their life. He couldn't describe how glad he was for them.

"*Anyway.*" London looked back at Alexei. "Extremely weird and surreal television appearances aside, I'm actually a sound engineer at a local music studio."

"Really?" Now Alexei's eyebrows lifted. "That sounds cool."

"Alexei's a musician, too," Ben said, draping an arm around the back of Alexei's chair. Alexei looked at him in surprise.

"I wouldn't say I'm a musician," he said.

Almost at the same time, London said, "I'm just a sound engineer."

Dahlia looked from London to Alexei and back again, leaning her chin on her palm once more.

"*Soul mates*," she whispered.

"Seriously," Ben went on. "This one stole some dude's guitar when we were in town once and serenaded me with a killer rendition of 'Wonderwall.'"

"Oh my God," Reina said from the end of the table. "I'm obsessed with that."

"Yeah, 'Wonderwall' still slaps," Laynie said.

"I know, right?" Ben smiled. "Although word on the street is he's better at the piano."

Alexei blushed, and it lit Ben up inside.

"My darling twin, by the way, is also neglecting to disclose that they run a nonprofit for LGBTQ youth, on top of the music stuff and the TV stardom," Julie hopped in, pride evident in her voice.

"And what *my* darling twin means to say is that the nonprofit is barely surviving, and costing a ton of money, and I've learned I have no idea what the hell I'm doing," London said before taking a long breath. "But sure, QueerOut is a thing. Hopefully. This will be our first summer of running a camp for queer and gender expansive youth in the woods of Tennessee, and I hope it's not a complete disaster."

"It won't be," Dahlia and Julie said together.

"I've actually been meaning to talk to you, London," Khalil said.

"I know your focus is on cooking skills, but how would you feel about maybe offering a session about hair cutting, or styling tips in general? Reina was talking about how she's going to help you out with some counseling and it made me want to help, too."

"*Yes*, Khalil, oh my God, that would be amazing," London said, eyes wide. "We still have programming gaps, like, a concerning amount really, and that's perfect." They dug their phone out of their pocket and started to type. "Can I have Sami reach out to you tomorrow?"

Sami was the new director of QueerOut whom London had recently hired, whom they'd snagged from her previous education nonprofit work in North Carolina. Julie said she was a real trip, and smart as hell.

"Yeah, sure," Khalil said, sounding casual, but grinning wide.

"Khalil's the best stylist in Nashville," Ben told Alexei. Khalil didn't protest. Instead, he ran his hands through Ben's long locks, which now hung past his shoulders.

"Speaking of which," Khalil said, "you know I love the long hair, but this situation is getting a little desperate, babe."

"Which is why I was going to rope you into cutting it this week," Ben answered. Because Khalil wasn't wrong.

"I would actually love a trim, too," Alexei said, leaning over the table toward Khalil, "if you might have another appointment open this week?"

"Aw, but I kind of like how shaggy it's gotten." Ben ran his hands through Alexei's hair, just as Khalil had done to Ben. Alexei blushed again.

This whole scene felt a little unreal. Alexei, talking to Ben's friends so naturally. So much farther out of his shell than he had been yesterday. Ben, getting to tease Alexei in front of the people he loved. Ben never wanted to leave this restaurant.

"Of course," Khalil said. "Why don't you both stop by the shop tomorrow after we close up, if you're not busy. I'll trim your shaggy-ass backcountry selves, and we can have some beers and catch up some more."

"That'd be great." Ben smiled. He had lived with Khalil for the messy first half of his twenties, until he'd moved in with Robbie. They were still close, but he missed it, that everyday kind of closeness they had as roommates. "We'll be there."

The conversation flowed as their food arrived and they all tucked in, as the dishes were cleared, water glasses refilled. Alexei even leaned lightly into Ben's shoulder as they lingered around the table, his face rosy, Ben's arm thrown once more over the back of his chair.

"Hey, Alexei." London leaned their forearms on the table. "Is it true you play the piano?"

"I haven't actually played in a while, but yeah. I accompanied my church choir for a long time."

"I don't know if you guys are busy with other plans after this, but Dahlia and I are just going back to our place. I have a piano there, if you're interested in tagging along. My old roommate Eddy used to play it more than I ever did; I kind of miss hearing it. Maybe you can tell me if it needs to get tuned."

Alexei looked at Ben.

"What do you think? Do we have to get back to your family?"

"Nah, we're good. I'm game if you are."

Alexei grinned. "Cool."

Ben's phone lit up on the table. When he saw the caller, his brows rose in surprise, his arm dropping from Alexei's chair.

"Hey, is it okay if I take this?"

"Of course." Alexei waved him away.

Be right back, Ben mouthed to the table as he stood, hitting the green button as he walked through the restaurant.

"Hey," he said as he reached the sidewalk outside. "How's it going, Ted?"

"Howdy there, Ben! Lordy, it's good to hear ya. It's going swell; how about yourself?"

"Good. Really good." Ben glanced through the window of the restaurant, where he could see Alexei, still smiling, engaged in a conversation across the table with Dahlia.

"That's great to hear, Ben. I have to tell ya, when Farah told me she'd seen you at the mall this weekend, I couldn't hold myself back from calling you. Hope it's okay to be calling on a Sunday."

"Of course."

"You were safe out there on that trail? No broken bones or anything?"

"No, sir," Ben answered, still staring through the window. "I'm happy to report I'm in one piece."

"Well, that's excellent. Because we've missed you here, Ben, and we have a spot open now on our nursing staff. You did pass your NCLEX, didn't you?"

Ben froze.

"I did," he said slowly.

"Of course you did. Truth be told, we've actually had a spot open for a while. Shawna moved on down to Georgia a bit ago now; Frank got a job with Coca-Cola. We've been just hangin' on here, waiting for you to get back. If you'd be open to working for us officially, of course. You might have other things lined up, I reckon, and we'll still have to bring you in for an interview and all, do everything HR tells us, but between you and me, the spot's yours. It'd start as your residency, and I'd take the lead on mentoring you myself, although you know we do everything as a team here. Like I said, I know you might have had a few other offers come in since passing your test, but we'll do what we have to, to fight for ya."

Ben's heart beat in his ears. Working for Ted at Lakeview Hills, a nursing home and rehabilitation center not far from his parents' house, was without a doubt his favorite clinical rotation from nursing school. On top of the experience confirming his interest in geriatrics, the team had treated him with warmth and respect, even though he was a green student. It was a well-run facility, clean, a caring and competent staff. He had learned a lot. It had felt like a family.

This, some part of Ben's brain knew, was a dream come true. Everything he had hoped for.

"How"—Ben cleared his throat—"how soon would the position need to be filled?"

"Well, like I said, Ben, it's been open for a while. We've had a traveling nurse here to cover the loss of Shawna, and she's been real good, but ideally, we'd love you to start as soon as possible. If you've just gotten back and there are things you need to do, I understand. We could wait a couple more weeks, possibly."

Inside the restaurant, Laynie had moved from the far end of the table to take over Ben's seat. She and Alexei were deep in conversation.

"Is it okay if I have some time to think it over?" Ben's brain felt blank. Lost. "I'm . . . I'm flattered, Ted; I am. This—this means a lot." Ben swallowed. "I love Lakeview. But I did just get home, and there are some things—"

"Of course, of course, I know I'm springing all this on you here. Listen, you get back to your Sunday, take some time to think it over. How about you give me a call back by Wednesday, okay?"

Wednesday. Carolina's last day of high school. They were going to dinner at Moto downtown to celebrate.

"Okay. I will."

"Any questions you have before then, just give me a ring or shoot me an email, okay? If I'm not around, Colette can answer your questions, too."

Ben nodded numbly at the window. "Sounds good."

"I'm so glad you picked up, Ben. Talk soon."

"Talk soon."

Ben kept the phone to his ear long after Ted hung up. Ted, who believed in Ben. Ted, who could give Ben a steady job in his chosen field, a job where Ben already felt at home. Where Ben could start the rest of his responsible, grown-up life.

Alexei looked up from the table. He must have felt Ben's eyes on him.

He smiled. Waved at Ben through the window.

And so very quietly, Ben's heart tore in two.

Julie pulled Ben aside as they walked toward their cars, yanking his arm to pause him by the edge of the sidewalk. "Hey," she said.

"Hey." Her strawberry blond ponytail shone in the sun.

Had she been able to tell he'd been off for the last ten minutes? Probably. Ben's brain was barely functioning. He couldn't remember anything that had happened at the table in the brief time since he'd walked back into the restaurant.

Ben hoped Julie didn't call him out on it; he wasn't ready to—

"I like him," she said.

Ben blinked. Breathed out slowly.

"Yeah." He bit the inside of his cheek. "Me too."

"I know I already told you that, but wow, he is even more handsome and quiet and adorable than I expected."

A grin appeared on Ben's face out of reflex, but he could barely feel it. "Yeah."

"It's about time you found yourself someone who isn't an asshole. Plus, I don't know if any of your exes looked at you the way he does."

Ben glanced at Alexei, who was leaning against London's Tesla.

He knew how Alexei looked at him. But out of some sense of masochistic misery, he asked anyway.

"How does he look at me?"

"Like you hung the moon. Like you're the most important person in the universe."

Ben remained silent.

Julie nudged his shoulder with her own. Before she walked away, she said softly, "And you deserve that, Ben."

The Caravalhos' house in East Nashville was small but tidy, full of worn carpet and packed bookshelves. London and Dahlia's apartment in 12 South, in contrast, was the epitome of hipness. Full of high ceilings and hardwood floors, it flowed from the modern kitchen, full of sleek, top-of-the-line appliances, into an open, comfortable living area. In the middle of it all, next to a long wall of exposed brick, sat a baby grand piano.

"Whoa," Alexei said when he saw it.

"*Right?*" Dahlia tossed over her shoulder as she walked toward the kitchen island. "Picture me, the first time I walk into this place, and London has somehow neglected to mention they own a *baby grand*. Like it was normal."

"You can move out anytime you want, you know," London said.

"True, but Gary down the hall would miss me. You know he needs someone to remind him to take his pills. Does anyone want anything to drink? Snacks?"

"Dahlia," Julie groaned, flopping onto a love seat. "We literally, only moments ago, stopped stuffing our faces."

Khalil, Reina, and Laynie had other responsibilities they had to get to after brunch, but Alexei hoped he would see them all again soon. He wasn't sure what exactly had made him so comfortable at brunch. Maybe it was the fact that he was a person who danced to pop music at parties now. Who had rough, satisfying sex afterward. Who had a beautiful man who was in love with him.

Maybe it was simply because all of Ben's friends had been so kind. They had asked him questions, included him in the conversation. They were all so interesting, so different from each other. Alexei had gathered they all connected from different points in Ben's life—Julie and London, from childhood; Khalil from high school and then as roommates after; Laynie had worked with Ben at the coffee shop before nursing school. Reina and Dahlia were new. But they all still seemed so intrinsically linked, if only from enjoying each other's company. Alexei had never experienced friendship quite like that. Friendship that wasn't dependent on shared faith.

Alexei did miss that. Being around people who shared his faith. When he'd stopped going to church after coming out to his parents, he'd dropped out of the church community entirely. Assumed no one he knew from that circle would want to associate with him anymore anyway. He still wasn't exactly sure how to find that kind of community now, at least in a way that felt healthy.

But he had liked Ben's friends. Alexei had liked brunch.

"Incorrect," Dahlia said. "We stopped eating at least an hour ago. Totally room in our stomachs for snacks now."

The group congregated in the kitchen. Alexei leaned against the granite-topped island. Almost immediately, the back of his neck prickled. He turned his head. And almost jumped.

"Oh," he said.

A small creature with long hair in a mixture of colors stared dully back at him. With one eye. And an abundance of teeth.

"You found Schnitzel!" Julie said.

Dahlia turned from where she'd had her head stuck in the refrigerator and hustled back to the kitchen island. "Schnitzel!" she admonished in a loud whisper. "Daddy London's going to make us give you away if you keep doing this!"

"Just"—London raised an exasperated hand to their forehead—"how does he even get up there?"

"I feel like 'Daddy London' is a phrase I'm not supposed to hear," Julie said.

"Yes," London agreed. "Let's all pretend that never happened."

"Oh my God." Ben leaned down to the floor, where Dahlia had placed the furry, profoundly ugly dog. "He's amazing."

"Oh, I wouldn't—" Dahlia warned as Ben reached out a hand. Schnitzel growled. "He needs some time to warm up to strangers sometimes."

"I helped name him," Julie said, smug, as she scooped the dog up in her arms. "London hates it," she said in a similarly loud whisper as Dahlia had used.

"I don't *hate*—" London pinched the bridge of their nose with a sigh. "It's just a little...off-putting."

"Why didn't he growl at you?" Ben asked, a bit indignant.

"We love each other," Julie stated. And to London, "People name their pets after foods all the time."

"Yes, but normally it's like, Waffles. Something cute and fluffy. Not an ugly piece of fried meat."

Julie gasped. "Don't listen to what they say about you," she whispered to Schnitzel. Schnitzel stared back at her with the same dead-eyed look he'd given Alexei.

"Good Lord." London turned to Alexei with a sigh. "*Anyway.*" They nodded toward the piano. "It's all yours," they said, voice gentling. "Get it warmed up."

And so Alexei did, while the rest of the group bickered about Schnitzel and consumed snacks around the kitchen island. A small pattering of butterflies took flight in Alexei's stomach as he sat on the padded bench, as he lifted the lid and ran his fingertips over the cool keys. It had been so long. And he didn't think he had ever played an instrument as fine as this one.

It also felt immediately familiar. It felt a little like coming home.

Soon, too soon, Dahlia, London, and Julie had pulled up chairs to be closer to the piano, munching on cheese and crackers and grapes. Ben leaned against the brick wall behind the piano.

He had been quiet since his phone call at the end of brunch, and Alexei was curious as to who had been on the other end of the line. But he smiled at Alexei now, stuffing his hands in his pockets, and it was the reassurance Alexei needed.

"Um," Alexei said when he realized he had everyone's full attention. "I feel like Ben misled you with the 'Wonderwall' story. I actually don't have much popular music knowledge. All I really know is . . . churchy stuff."

"Churchy stuff is okay, Lex," Ben said quietly.

London nodded in agreement. "All music is music."

Alexei closed his eyes and thought about the keys under his fingers. This felt different than Big Bear City, when alcohol and bravado had taken over his system and he'd borrowed that guy's guitar. Sitting in this apartment, surrounded by people Ben loved, people Alexei could see himself loving one day, too, about to play the music he'd played back when he thought he knew where he belonged—this felt even more intimate and frightening. More real.

When he opened his eyes, he felt Ben's gaze on him, steady and loving. He found himself thinking about Alina. She had always loved listening to him play. He thought about how it always felt, playing the piano at church. How it made him feel like he was doing something important. How even if the rules of his faith often made him feel constricted, bound to a world that possibly didn't want him, possibly didn't believe he could be made of goodness and light, too, when the music started, it unraveled all the ugliness and made it beautiful. Made it okay to feel whatever Alexei needed to feel.

Alexei rested his hands on London's piano, and he began to play.

He wasn't sure how long he played, blending one hymn into another, but he played long enough that he almost forgot where he was, who he was, resting in that perfect, weightless space music took him to when he got it right, that space that always felt closest to God.

When he stopped, he blinked, looking up. His face flushed as self-awareness returned. But all the other faces around him were smiling. Ben tilted his head at him, eyes crinkling.

"That was lovely," Dahlia said, her voice hushed, like she didn't want to break the spell.

Alexei looked down, pleased, until he felt Ben's arms wrap around him from behind. He let himself absorb this moment, in this place with these people, and he had to agree.

It was lovely.

CHAPTER TWENTY-THREE

Y ou sure you're okay with this?" Ben asked as he picked up the keys to his Jeep. "Sorry to abandon you. I swear this wasn't in the plans."

"And I swear I'm fine." Alexei tried to reassure him with a smile. "Go. Your sister needs you."

Ben nodded, lips set in a grim line, and walked out the door to where Carolina waited on the drive.

Alexei watched him throw his arm around her shoulder, watched how Carolina seemed to collapse into him as they walked toward the car, her legs unsteady. And then, feeling like he had already seen more than Carolina probably wanted him to see, Alexei shut the door and walked back to the living room.

He truly was fine with a night in with Ben's parents. The plans for the beginning of the week had always been quiet anyway, before the hectic graduation schedule took effect.

They had spent the last two days exploring Nashville together. Alexei had been to Ben's favorite coffee shops, tried his favorite ice cream, been to the Ryman. He had seen Ben's elementary school, looked through old photo albums. Khalil had cut their hair.

Every moment had been enjoyable, letting his body rest, letting his mind capture so many new things. He loved learning about Ben's world most, more than the sightseeing: who he had been, who he was outside the trail, this full, wondrous feeling that made Alexei's head spin.

The humidity had been hard to handle.

And there had been moments, over the last few days, when Ben had seemed distracted. Staring into the distance with an odd look on his face, disconnected from the world around him. Which wasn't like Ben, who was always present, always excited for the next moment. He'd snap out of it eventually, when Alexei put a hand on his arm, returning to Alexei with a smile. But Alexei hoped Ben would talk to him about whatever it was soon. He wondered if Ben was having some conflicted feelings about all the talk about Carolina and Boston University, since he knew Ben felt insecure about his own educational experiences. Even though Alexei wished he wouldn't.

Even if Ben hadn't gone to nursing school, even if he worked at the coffee shop for the rest of his life, he would still be Ben. He would still help people. He would still be the best person Alexei had ever known.

But other than the heat, other than whatever was on Ben's mind, Alexei was almost surprisingly comfortable being here now, more familiar each day with Ben's family. Iris and Luiz, in particular, welcomed Alexei with open arms, never once making him feel his presence was distracting from Ben's visit home. On the contrary, Iris acted thrilled Alexei was there, one more person to ply with her food and bubbly conversation. Luiz was quieter, but his eyes were always smiling. Alexei felt calm around him. He would be happy to be a Luiz Caravalho one day, content to be surrounded by the noise and love of his family, the legacy of his small but important life.

So when Carolina had returned home from school today, red faced and in tears instead of being elated about almost being done with high school, Alexei was neither surprised nor disappointed when she had requested a Ben and Ben Only night at their favorite local pizzeria. Iris looked like she was having a harder time with not being invited. But when Carolina had said, "I'll talk to you later, Ma, I promise, but Ben's leaving soon. I just want a night with Ben," she had relented.

"Well, Alexei." Luiz clapped him on the back after they had finished their dinner of leftover casserole Iris had made the night before. "I know it's only Tuesday, but since you're our special guest, I'll roll out the full Friday night Caravalho experience." Luiz moved to kneel in front of their TV stand as he spoke, riffling through a number of DVDs in one of the lower cabinets. "I'm thinking maybe *Cover Girl*? Haven't watched that one in a while. Unless you have a favorite musical of your own?"

"If you don't like musicals, you can say so," Iris muttered in Alexei's ear before she settled into an armchair with a glass of wine and a library book. "No other genre of film exists in my husband's mind. But I presume most young people have an appreciation for things set after the 1950s."

"*Cover Girl* is '40s, not '50s," Luiz said.

"That doesn't actually change my point, amor."

"Musicals are fine," Alexei said, sitting on the couch. Delilah jumped up after him, nuzzling her head in his lap. "Although I don't know if I've ever actually watched one."

"Ever?" Luiz looked over at him in shock, hand frozen over the DVD player. "Not even *Singin' in the Rain*? *West Side Story*? *The Sound of Music*?"

This was all more than Alexei had previously heard Luiz say at one time. Which inspired him to ramble a bit himself.

"Maybe?" He shrugged. "I didn't watch TV or movies growing up. Even now, I mostly watch documentaries. Maybe one of those has been on PBS at some point?"

"Well," Luiz said, "this makes me rethink the whole thing. We should probably start you on *Top Hat*. Or *Guys and Dolls*, at the very least."

"Luiz," Iris scolded. "You already have *Cover Girl* out of the case. And if you make me watch *Guys and Dolls* one more time, I just might scream."

"Fine," Luiz sighed, but there was no heat in it, just as Alexei suspected Iris wouldn't actually scream at her husband. Considering she likely wasn't going to watch whatever they chose anyway, as she already had her library book cracked open, reading glasses perched on her nose.

"I am sixty-five percent sure I've seen at least part of *The Sound of Music*," Alexei mused, trying to reach through his memories to find a tenuous connection with Luiz Caravalho.

"I'm sixty-five percent sure most people alive have seen at least part of *The Sound of Music*," Luiz said, pressing Play on the remote. "*Cover Girl*, though, is Gene Kelly and Rita Hayworth. You can't go wrong."

As the opening credits began, Luiz unfolded the legs of a card table that had been hiding behind Iris's chair. He set it in front of the couch before retrieving a rolled-up swath of green fabric, also from behind Iris's chair.

"And now for the real entertainment of the evening," Luiz said grandly, or at least as grandly as Luiz Caravalho probably said anything. "Like I said, Friday night special."

That was when the unease started to creep into Alexei's good mood.

"You don't have to do that, either," Iris said from behind her book. "Those things drive me batty."

"No," Alexei said faintly as Luiz arranged the mat on the table. He cleared his throat. "I like puzzles."

Truer to the point, Alexei loved puzzles.

Alexei used to do puzzles with his family all the time. In particular, with his mother. They drove Alina batty, too, and their dad simply never tried that hard. But Alexei and his mother could sit and work on puzzles for hours.

Sometimes they would talk as they worked; sometimes they listened to classical music; sometimes they sat in silence. She always let Alexei work on the border first while she sorted, quietly pushing the right pieces his way. Later, once the border had been completed, they would each attack different parts of the picture. But she would keep finding pieces for him, always keeping an eye out for what he was doing while she worked on the clouds, the more difficult splashes of solid color. They were a team.

"Just started this one last week," Luiz said as he sat next to Alexei on the couch, placing the box of unused pieces between them.

It was a grid of vintage posters advertising America's national parks. Alexei had completed one almost exactly like it before. The Lebedevs loved a national park.

For a few minutes, Alexei focused on Rita Hayworth and Gene Kelly, hoping the panic threading through his veins would subside. He could watch the movie. Luiz didn't seem to mind that he wasn't working on the puzzle. This was okay.

But out of the corner of his eye, he could see the piece that completed the top of Half Dome in the poster for Yosemite. He had seen it ever since Luiz opened the box. Luiz was happily working on the poster for Big Bend in the opposite corner, oblivious.

That piece would not leave Alexei alone.

Eventually, he picked it up. He clicked it into place. Like every puzzle piece Alexei had ever successfully placed, it was satisfying. He picked up another.

"That's a good man," Luiz said with a smile. He reached over and gave Alexei's shoulder a small squeeze before returning to his own part of the puzzle.

It was just like how Ben had reached over to squeeze his mother's shoulder while they were looking at the slideshow of pictures that first day, when they had sat on this same couch.

Like Ben's friends, the Caravalhos were always touching each other.

Life with the Caravalhos felt so easy.

Alexei held the next puzzle piece in his hand.

His mind quietly stepped outside of his body.

And suddenly everything felt wrong.

Suddenly, any hints of comfort or familiarity he had felt these past few days seemed obvious for what they were. Tricks of the mind. Small fantasies.

This wasn't his life. He wasn't a Caravalho.

And he couldn't quite grasp why he was trying so hard to be one.

Alexei Lebedev didn't belong in Nashville, Tennessee. He belonged in the Northwest.

And he wanted to do this puzzle with his mom.

He let the piece in his hand drop to the table.

He had been play-acting, pretending this life could be his own. Like just because his own family had left him, he could walk right into the first friendly one he met. Shame curdled inside his stomach.

It didn't matter that the Caravalhos were welcoming and warm. That wasn't how this worked. They weren't his. They would only ever be Ben's.

"You okay, hon?" Iris looked up from her book, brow creased. "You look a little funny."

Alexei swallowed. He needed to get out of this room, and quickly, yet he didn't want to appear rude.

"I'm not feeling very well all of a sudden," he managed to say.

Iris frowned.

"I hope it wasn't the casserole; it seemed to sit well with everyone last night."

"No, no," Alexei said, already standing. "Ben and I got some ice cream earlier. Maybe that's it. Or maybe I'm just tired. I'm so sorry; it's hit me all at once."

"Of course," Iris said, her face smoothing back into comforting reassurance. "Gosh, this has all been a whirlwind for you, I imagine.

And you and Bento are working yourselves so hard out there on the trail; I should have demanded you two take a day just to sleep."

"Sorry about the movie," Alexei said. He felt his head nodding nonsensically, unable to stop.

"No problem." Luiz waved a hand. "We'll finish it another day."

"Sure," Alexei lied.

Everything about this was a lie.

Somehow, Alexei found himself on Ben's bed, Delilah curled up next to him. Absently, he scratched her back.

He stared at the ceiling and waited for Ben. He tried to fall asleep. He thought about his journals, sitting at the bottom of his pack. He had gotten complacent on the trail lately, he knew, getting so used to his and Ben's daily rhythms. He hadn't written in his Good Things journal, the journal that was supposed to help him let go of the past, in a very long time.

There simply hadn't seemed to be room for his grief these last few weeks, what with how happy he had been. No time left at the end of the day to work at writing about his profound sadness, a sadness he had buried, somewhere along the line, beneath Ben's kisses and his laughter and his soft hair.

Alexei had been so terribly irresponsible.

Everything he had worried about when he'd first started walking with Ben—that Ben was a distraction, that Alexei wouldn't have enough time alone to work through things, to make his plans for Alexei 2.0—it had all come true, hadn't it? Alexei hadn't rebuilt himself. He'd only rebuilt himself around Ben.

And now the weight of his grief crashed over him all at once, sat on his chest like an anvil.

What would happen the day Ben eventually left him? Because surely, Ben wouldn't want to be stuck with someone like Alexei forever; he would find someone more fun, someone more like him. Would Alexei even see any of these people again? Why, instead of working at getting over the greatest loss he'd ever known, had Alexei simply collected more people to lose?

Every minute that he sat in someone else's home, thinking about how he'd never again be able to enter his own, the one where he had learned to walk, to read a compass, to listen to birds, to imagine with Alina, to solve puzzles with his mom, to track stars through a telescope with his dad, to play the piano and the guitar, to love and belong and pray—it felt like his skin was on fire, carpeted with ants, an itch he'd never be able to relieve.

Alexei didn't belong here.

And he was no longer welcome in the place that had raised him.

Maybe the only place he truly belonged—the only place he had ever truly belonged—was the woods.

Alexei waited for Ben, and he waited for the moment he could leave here, this city that wasn't his, that he possibly never should have come to in the first place.

Alexei wasn't sure how late it was when Ben stumbled down the stairs to the basement. He was still flat on his back on Ben's bed, Delilah still at his side.

When he woke himself enough to sit up, Ben was pacing, hands clutching at his hair.

Something was wrong.

"Hey," Ben said, coming to a pause in front of the bed. His limbs moved restlessly, like they weren't ready to be still.

"Hi," Alexei said.

"So," Ben said on a long breath, "we have to talk."

Alexei waited.

And when Ben said "Alexei," Alexei's stomach dropped, like it already knew exactly what Ben was going to say next.

"Lex, I'm not going back to the trail."

This is what it feels like, then, one part of Alexei thought. *The other shoe dropping.*

Another part of him started a long, frantic, embarrassing wail inside his head that made it hard for him to hear anything else.

"Was this the plan all along?" Alexei heard himself ask. "You were just waiting to tell me?"

Because when Alexei thought about how happy Ben had been here, how full and alive he'd been these last few days around his people, it all seemed so clear. Of course Ben had never been going to go back. Alexei had been fooling himself, believing he and Ben would actually get on a plane again and head back to the wilderness together.

Ben sank to his knees and put his head in Alexei's lap. Alexei stared down at him, his mess of dark hair, resisted every urge to touch him.

"No, Lex," Ben said. "I promise. I only decided for sure tonight, like an hour ago, and I had to tell you right away. It's not..." Ben's voice got thick. He leaned back, grinding the heel of a palm into his eye. "I didn't plan this, but some things have happened."

"Okay," Alexei said, even though it wasn't, even though he found he didn't care about whatever had happened. He just wanted this all to be over, now. He wanted to be back on the PCT.

"Carolina's boyfriend broke up with her," Ben said, and Alexei almost laughed at how irrelevant this felt. "They had a whole plan about how they'd stay together, do long distance between Georgetown and BU, and Carolina has spent her whole life *planning*, knowing what's coming next, and it's sent her into a tailspin. I could kick that kid's ass for doing it during finals. What the hell." He looked down at the floor. "I've never seen her like this. She's scared. She's spent her whole life acting like an adult, and now she's about to start this journey she's wanted for so long. But tonight she was just...a scared little kid."

Ben was quiet a minute.

Some part of Alexei knew this was kind of funny.

That he and Carolina were the same.

"I can't leave her, Lex."

Alexei didn't have a response to this, although he knew he probably should. He waited while Ben tapped his fingers nervously on his knee.

"But that's not the only thing," Ben said slowly. "It helped make my decision clear, but..." Alexei could tell Ben was biting the inside of his cheek. "I got a call from the nursing home where I did my geriatric rotation." He took a deep breath, his voice changing from the certainty that had been there while he was talking about his sister to something higher and shakier. "They have an opening. For an RN. They want me to do a residency there."

Alexei thought about Ben treating Thompson's cut at Deep Creek. About Ben examining the old man's arthritic joints at the hot springs. And he thought about Ben in Big Bear City, asking what would happen if it turned out he wasn't good at being a nurse after all, the vulnerability that had been in his eyes.

"That's great, Ben," Alexei said softly, and it sounded like his heart breaking.

Ben glanced up at him, his eyes surprised, or maybe panicked.

"Yeah," he said, voice still unsteady. "It's...it's really unexpected, and I should have told you about it as soon as they called me, but I've been processing it, trying to figure out what to do, and...I guess they liked me when I was there before, and..." He wiped his palms on his pants. "I liked it there, too. A lot. I feel like I can't pass this up."

As soon as they called me. It clicked then. When Ben had gotten the call at brunch on Sunday. How distracted he'd been ever since. The nursing home had been the call.

All this time, while Ben had paraded Alexei around Nashville, he hadn't told him. This monumental piece of news. Even though Alexei had told Ben, he'd told him, so long ago, about how he needed Ben to be clear with him. Hurt slashed at the last of his defenses.

A silent beat passed before Ben looked at Alexei again.

"Can you tell me what you're thinking? Lex?"

No, Alexei answered immediately in his head.

"You'll miss the High Sierra," is what he said eventually.

Ben hung his head. "I know," he whispered. Looking up, he attempted a smile, eyes wet. "Although let's be honest, I probably wasn't going to survive the High Sierra anyway."

Alexei's chest constricted. *You would have been fine*, he wanted to say. *I would have kept you safe.*

He would need to get out of this room soon. He was having difficulty breathing.

"Lex." Ben finally got up and sat next to Alexei on the bed. "Look, I don't really care about the High Sierra right now. I mean, I *do*. You have to know I do. I wanted to reach Canada, Lex. God, my bear canister and ice ax are waiting for me at Kennedy Meadows. You should go through my resupply box there, take what you want. I...I've wanted to do something like this forever, and the fact that I'm not finishing it, just as I was really getting into it, is..."

Ben shook his head, trailing off. Alexei stood, unable to sit calmly next to Ben on the bed, thighs touching.

Of course Ben would stay and take care of his sister.

Of course the nursing home wanted Ben. He would be wonderful.

"Anyway, what I'm saying is, I'm devastated about the trail but I don't *actually* care about the trail right now. I care about *you*, Lex. I care about us."

Alexei stared straight ahead at the washer and dryer, the colorful rooster painted on a blue ceramic plate hanging on the wall above them, his back to Ben.

"We can work something out, Lex. I'll wait for you to finish the trail if you'll wait for me to finish the residency. We'll wait for each other. Lex, Julie was right the other day, I'm kind of a slut, I've dated a lot of people, but you...you have to know this is special, right? That we found each other on the trail? We're special, Lex. Being with you has been so *easy*, from the moment I met you."

Shut up, Alexei thought. *Shut up, shut up, shut up*. Maybe if Ben shut up, this wouldn't hurt so much. It was all clear now. Ben was staying in Nashville. Alexei wasn't. Ben had a bright future ahead of him. Alexei didn't know a single thing about what his own future entailed, except that it wouldn't be here.

There didn't seem to be a lot else to explain.

"Can you talk to me? Please? Get mad at me? At least look at me? Something?"

Strangely enough, Alexei *did* feel himself getting a little mad. If Ben called him *Lex* one more time, he might explode.

After a long moment, he heard Ben sigh.

"Tomorrow, before all the graduation stuff starts..." Ben's voice was soft now, close to defeated. "Will you let me take you on a date, Alexei? A real one? Please. I'll make it nice, I promise. I'll..."

Ben trailed off. Alexei's neck started to feel sore. He realized he had been clenching his muscles, his shoulders bunched, his hands curled into fists in his pockets.

He waited. For Ben to finish, for this miserable night to be over.

But Ben didn't speak again. Alexei turned only when he heard the soft rumble of Ben's snore.

He was slumped over on the bed, body twisted, legs still hanging over the side from where he had been sitting moments before. His mouth was open, his cheek smashed onto the pillow.

So here's kind of a weird thing about me, Alexei remembered Ben's words from that morning so long ago, after the coyotes. *Sometimes, when I'm really stressed, I...fall asleep.*

Alexei slumped with relief. He was glad Ben's body had taken over. That he had stopped talking. That he looked relaxed. At peace.

He didn't have the capacity to truly examine everything his heart felt about Ben Caravalho right then, but he knew, on a cellular level, that he always wanted Ben to be at peace.

And now, Alexei had to move quickly. And quietly. He did not want to wake Ben. But Alexei was good at being quiet.

He had not felt it when he met that first rattlesnake, back in the desert. When he first met Ben.

But now, all his body could feel—the only thing his mind understood—was the need for flight.

He gathered his things from the bathroom.

He folded the new clothes he had bought at the mall, left them in a neat pile on top of the washer. Maybe Tiago could use them; they were about the same size.

He stared at the pocket Portuguese-English dictionary he had purchased earlier today at Parnassus Books.

He had hoped Ben could help him with the pronunciations.

At the last minute, he stuffed it into his pack.

Carefully, he zipped the last zipper. He eased the pack onto his shoulders, making sure his trekking poles didn't clang together.

He allowed himself one last look at Ben. He had shifted onto his back in sleep, one arm hanging over the edge of the bed, one resting on his chest. His face was turned away from where Alexei stood, his jawline smooth in the dim light of the room.

Alexei went upstairs.

He was grateful Ben's parents still had a landline. Mindful not to bump into anything in the dark, he made his way to the old peach-colored phone in the small nook in the corner of the kitchen.

He dialed 411. He picked up a piece of junk mail from the counter to confirm the address. He asked the taxi not to honk, told them he would be waiting.

He didn't linger. Didn't take another look at the family photos on the walls.

Alexei walked out of the small but well-lived-in home of Iris and Luiz Caravalho, and waited for a taxi to take him to the airport. He counted the minutes until he could fly back to the single-track trail where he belonged, a wilderness he understood, a place for his heart to finally learn to protect itself, where he could once again be alone.

II

Kennedy Meadows to Cascade Locks

Miles 702 to 2,153
Summer

CHAPTER TWENTY-FOUR

Somewhere over America
June 15

Mom and Dad,

All the articles I've read about grief said anger was a natural part of all this, but I haven't been strong enough to feel it, even after all this time. I was never angry at you, just disappointed in myself. That I didn't expect you to react how you did, like I clearly should have. That I couldn't be who you wanted. I didn't know how to move on from that. Sad for you, sad for all of us.

Well, guess what. I think I fell in love with someone. And then I got scared, and I left. And I'm angry now.

I always did every single thing that was asked of me—from you, from the church, from God. Except this one thing. And you can't get over it? It doesn't make any sense. I know it makes sense to you. But it just...doesn't. It doesn't make sense, Mom, and I think you know it.

I spent time with another family this week. They were kind, and friendly, and acted like their gay son was totally normal. They welcomed me with open arms. I should have loved it, that kind of acceptance. And I did, for a while. But the more I think about it, the more it only makes me feel like a freak. Because it was so different from what you did. Because it was so new to me. Because it *didn't* feel normal.

You raised me to believe that family and faith were everything.

How can you take that away from me and not expect me to crumble?

Because I feel like I'm crumbling, Mom and Dad. I thought I was okay, but I'm not. I'm hiking on the PCT, a dream you grew in me, Dad, and I feel so close to you when I'm on the trail, so close to all the hours on other trails we spent together growing up, but my body feels broken, my heart feels broken. I don't know where I belong, and everything hurts.

So fuck you.

There, I finally said it.

And it felt awful.

I hated it.

I hate everything about this.

Your son,
Alexei

Unsent

June 16

Dear Ben,

I am so sorry. To be honest, the events of the last 48 hours are all a little hazy in my mind, and I can't truly remember what I said or didn't say to you that night. Which isn't an excuse. I am sorry I left without saying good-bye. That was selfish of me, and I hope you can forgive me someday. But if you can't, I understand that, too. I hope I didn't ruin Carolina's graduation. How is Carolina doing, and how was the graduation party? Carolina is going to be just fine, but I'm glad you're with her.

I wanted to say congratulations. Because I can't remember if I said that or not. About the job, I mean. Of course they wanted you. I hope it puts all of your unfounded doubts to rest. You are incredible, and are going to help so many people, and they are going to love you.

I wish I could explain myself better, why I had to leave. I'm so sorry if I hurt you in any way. Mainly, I am sorry for getting so attached to you when I knew the whole time that I was broken. Getting to meet you, and seeing a part of your Nashville world, was so special for me. You have so much love in your life, and you deserve all of it. Even experiencing a fraction of it was truly enlightening, and I can't thank you for it enough.

I should go now, before this gets too... I just wanted to apologize, and let you know I'm back on the trail, and that I'm safe. I'm forwarding your resupply box that was here at Kennedy Meadows back to you. I'm thinking about all the homemade meals you'll be able to eat now that you're home, all the real food and flush toilets, and it makes me smile. I hope you eat all the Raisin Nut Bran your heart desires.

Alexei

PS. I stole a piece of junk mail from your kitchen, for your address. Please tell your mom she's pre-approved for a Capital One credit card, and that I'm sorry I didn't say good-bye to her, either. I wish I could tell everyone that I'm sorry.

Sent from Kennedy Meadows
Mile 702

June 23

Alexei,

I showed Julie your letter. I didn't know what else to do with it. She read it three times and was quiet for a long time. Which proved to me I must really be in a pathetic place because Julie never holds her tongue. Anyway, she eventually gave it back to me and just said I should write you a letter back.

So, whatever. Here I am, writing you a letter, although I don't really know what to say to you, Alexei. I don't really want to tell you about Carolina's graduation. I don't really want to tell you anything. I want to say something about that bullshit about you being broken, but clearly I can't change how you feel about yourself, Lex. Which is a lesson I thought I'd learned a hundred times before, with boys before you, but I guess I'm just a fucking idiot. Anyway, good news is that I've finally decided I'm done. For real. I've thrown my heart out there too freely my entire life, and yeah, maybe that was all my own doing, but I'm really fucking tired of it being broken all the time. So, no more relationships for me. Maybe I had to go out to the PCT and meet you to finally get that through my thick skull. So thanks, I guess.

The residency is going great, though. It's hard and interesting and sad sometimes and great other times and makes me so tired by the end of the day that I barely have energy to think about how mad I am at you. Or worried about you. Or something. Or about how it felt that morning when I woke up and you were gone. I pick up every extra shift I can, hoping I am one day so wiped that I can never again dwell on the fact that when I told you I loved you that night, you never said it back, did you? I've been a fucking idiot my whole life, haven't I?

Anyway, I'm not going to send this. Obviously, I'm not going to send this. But fuck, Alexei, I hope you're still safe out there. I wish I could forget you. But mainly I really wish you had a fucking phone.

Ben

Unsent

CHAPTER TWENTY-FIVE

June 29

Alina,

Do you remember that Christmas when I bought you socks, or something boring like usual, but my *real* present was every variety of Little Debbies I could find? I sneaked into your room on Christmas night and clamped my hand over your mouth so you wouldn't scream, and you kicked me in the balls, which looking back, was warranted. Then we sat up eating so much sugar our stomachs hurt. Zebra Cakes were your favorite; I loved the Strawberry Shortcake Rolls. I can still taste that sticky strawberry-flavored goo as I write this. I had never felt more rebellious in my life than when I bought those at Fred Meyer for you.

Or do you remember when we used to run through the woods when we were kids, and you always pretended you were something odd, like a sloth, or a narwhal? And I was always a fox.

I saw actual foxes on the PCT, back in the desert, in the middle of the night. Kit foxes, to be exact. They were playful and had adorable ears. I wish you could have seen them.

I miss you, Alina. How's the new apartment? Do you have it decorated like you wanted? Is work still okay?

You know I want to ask about Mom and Dad—or maybe I don't—but either way, I've decided I'm not going to anymore, Alina. I hope you know by now that it's not your responsibility, choosing between them and me. They will always be our parents, and I will always be your brother. I probably haven't been a very good big brother lately, but I would like to be. I'm in the middle of the High Sierra as I'm writing this, and I'm going to be honest, it's pretty scary out here. It's ridiculously pretty, but…well, there have been some sketchy moments, and let's just say it's made me think about some things. We've always been siblings, but when I get back to Portland, Alina, could we be friends? I would really like that.

I fell in love with someone out here. I don't know if you want to know that or not, but he's not here anymore, and I'm trying to move on from it. I guess I thought if I told someone, it would feel easier, and the only person I really want to tell is you. It's hard to describe what it felt like, falling in love with Ben, but it was like he…loosened me. Like I didn't know how stiff and uncomfortable I had been before, until I started walking with him. Like I had been clenching my jaw for so long and never fully knew until I met Ben, until I discovered the relief of my muscles starting to let go.

And now that I'm trying to walk without him, it's like all of my loosened limbs are confused, trying to snap back into place again but not finding the right joints, disconnected and bruised.

But I've been thinking about some of those small things we did when we were kids. Running around the woods, sneaking sugar. Trying to remember that my body has been fluid before.

Do you remember how easy it was to convince Mom to let us quit Russian school? In my memories, our childhood was so strict, but when I look deeper, we got away with so much stuff, and it makes me laugh. I'm trying to hold on to those memories, to remind myself I can reshape myself again.

Have you ever been in love? It occurs to me I've never asked you. Maybe you have secrets, too. You don't have to share them with me, of course. But you always can, if you want. I hope you know that.

It's late, and I'm writing this by the light of my headlamp, and I forded three scary rivers today. I might be a little delirious. I won't even be near a post office for another few days, so we'll see if I actually get the courage to send this when I'm in town.

I miss you. I think I already said that, but I really mean it. I hope you don't hate me too much for everything that's happened. Maybe when I reach Cascade Locks, I could meet you there and we could get those ice cream cones that are five feet tall at the Eastwind Drive-In. That's what I'm going to think about, anyway, for the next few hundred miles.

Alexei

Sent from Mammoth Lakes, July 6th
Mile 902

July 8

Ben,

Today was really hard. The last three weeks, actually, ever since I got back on trail, have been really hard. I wish you were here, but I'm glad you're not, too. You would be so stressed. I'm stressed. The scenery is gorgeous, like postcard perfect; I can't even describe it. Of course Ansel and John liked it here. But maybe they were also a little out of their heads.

There are so many switchbacks, Ben, so many steep climbs. Some of the passes...I've survived them, but barely. There is so much snow. And so, so many river crossings. Sometimes it feels like I have to walk forever to find a spot to cross that feels even remotely safe. My feet are wet all the time and my nerves are shot.

I'm so tired, Ben.

What if I die out here?

I don't want to die here.

I feel so far from God.

It's made me realize how, even though we never really talked about my faith, you and me, how close I actually felt to it, while we were together. Like God had been hovering over me the whole time, saying *See? This is love. Like I love you. Do you understand?*

And now all I want is for God to talk to me, and I can't even hear him. Which is strange, because you'd think if there was anywhere I could find him on the trail, it'd be here, where every view takes my breath away, every day a testament to the wonders of this world. But I can barely feel him.

All I can feel, most days, is missing you.

It's such a generic phrase, *I miss you*, simple and meaningless.

What strikes me about missing you is how specific it is. I miss your sweatshirt and the smell of your instant coffee in the mornings. I miss the feel of your hands, how you scrunch up your entire body in your sleeping bag so when you fall asleep all I can see is your hair sticking out, the lines of your forehead. I miss the feel of your chin right after you shave. I miss how you smell, the gap between your lower front teeth when you smile. I miss being quiet with you. I miss how you made me feel like I could be anything I wanted to be.

I've been studying this Portuguese dictionary I bought back in Nashville, at least on the nights I have the energy to. I test myself as I walk. *Árvore. Rocha. Céu. Trilha. Pássaro.* It makes me feel closer to you, even though I know it's silly and unhelpful. But it helps pass the time, and honestly it feels good to learn something new, to use my brain for something other than merely walking and surviving.

I am so glad you're safe in Nashville. You better be safe in Nashville. You better be asleep, in your laundry-warmed basement that smells like lilacs, with Delilah at your feet. Or maybe you've moved into a new apartment? Either way, please never leave the house or do anything remotely dangerous ever again. Picturing you safe and happy is the only thing that gets me through days like today.

I came to the PCT to find this new version of myself. But sometimes, since coming back here, I only feel more lost.

I don't know what I'm doing here.

Lex

Unsent
Mile 917

July 8

Lex,

I never told you about Paul Salopek, did I? It's funny; we spent so much time together, but there was still so much I didn't get around to telling you.

The truth is, there were lots of reasons why I came to the PCT. I told you about most of them. But one thing I've been thinking about lately, that I never talked about with anyone, is when I first learned about Paul Salopek.

Maybe you already know about him. But he's on this walk

called Out of Eden, where he's walking across the entire fucking world. He started in Africa, following the path of historical human migration. And he's just…walking, and talking to people. Hearing their stories. Trying to figure out who we are. And then writing smart shit about it in *National Geographic* and books and stuff. But I think when I first read about him a few years ago, some part of me thought, *I want to do that.* I know you went to the PCT to be alone, but I went to hear people's stories.

I miss it, Lex. I think that's part of what's been hurting so much. You left me, like I probably always knew you would, but…you got to go back.

I lost you. But I lost the trail, too.

I thought starting this job, the career I wanted, would finally help ground me. Make me grow the fuck up. And I love it, Lex. I really do. I lucked out, working at this place; it's such a good facility, such good people. I get to help people. It's rewarding.

But I still feel restless. All that stress and debt of nursing school, the good fortune of working the exact job I wanted— and I'm still that antsy kid, always wanting to be outside. Always wanting to hear a new story. If anything, I feel that restlessness even more, since getting off the trail. Like instead of getting it out of my system, the PCT only amplified it.

I wish I knew where you were. What you were seeing. I wish you would write me again, Lex.

Ben

Unsent

July 10

Dear Ben,

I told myself I wouldn't write you again—as in, write you something and actually send it—but I've reached Tuolumne Meadows, and I'm staying here for a zero day, and keep thinking about the mailbox here, and how you had hoped to make it this far, and...I don't know, I hope it's okay if I tell you about some of the things I've seen. Because I think you really wanted to see them, too.

The High Sierra has been scary at times. But there are meadows, and trees, and wildflowers, and panoramic views everywhere. And the birds! They are everywhere. I really wish you were here taking pictures of it, Ben. I think about that every day. I wish I was like Ruby, that I could capture the beauty of all the plants in my notebook, to keep forever. I'm just passing it all by, just trying to keep my body together, to reach the next mile, the next landmark.

Except when I sit on the shore of a lake. There are so many lakes here, and I love them all. At least, until the mosquitoes start to eat me alive. Which they are doing these days with increasing regularity. But still, I love the lakes.

And there have been waterfalls! There are so many waterfalls in the Northwest, Ben. Maybe you'll get there on your own sometime to see them.

There is water everywhere, really, in the Sierras. So much less stress about having to plan things around making it to the next water source in time. Although I can't wait until I don't have to carry around this bear canister anymore. It's hard to remember the desert, sometimes.

There are also people everywhere, so many extra section hikers who are doing the John Muir Trail. I've heard a lot of different accents, different languages. I talk to people, sometimes, when I can. But mostly I just think about how much you would have loved talking to everyone.

Anyway, I just wanted you to know that I'm okay. I hope you are, too. More than you know.

My next big stop will be at Echo Lake, in about 150 miles. If you want me to not write to you anymore, just send me a short note there, okay? Tell me to fuck off, or whatever, and I will. I have a resupply box waiting, so I'll check to see if I have any other mail when I'm there. I know it's probably selfish, wanting to keep writing to you. Just tell me not to and I'll stop, promise.

Give Delilah some scratches for me.

Lex

Sent from Tuolumne Meadows
Mile 941

———

July 15

Alexei,

Keep writing.
Please be safe.
Delilah misses you.

Ben

Sent from Nashville
Received at Echo Lake
Mile 1,094

CHAPTER TWENTY-SIX

July 23

Ben,

It was so good to see your handwriting. I can't even describe how good it was.

I still wish I knew how you were doing. I think about how you're doing all the time. But I understand if you don't want to tell me. I'm glad you're okay with me writing, though. Because there's a story I need to tell you.

The first thing you should know for this story is that I've gotten better at hitching. I still don't love it, but it's necessary to get to supplies here in the Sierras, and every time I successfully climb into someone else's vehicle without vomiting, I feel a little proud of myself. And I think about that first hitch with you, to the dinosaurs. Thank you for taking me to the dinosaurs, Ben. I never would have gone by myself.

Anyway, I hitched here to Tahoe City with a woman named Jenn. You would have loved her. She smacked my arm as I was waiting on the shoulder of the highway and said, "You hitching to town? Let me borrow your white male privilege and take me with you so I don't die alone in some creep's car." She called herself a happily fat hiker and told me about all the condescending advice she'd gotten so far on her section hike, how people come up to her and talk to her about dieting before they even ask her name. It made me think about Ryan, and some of the stuff he said had been said to him. Different stuff, obviously, but all stuff I don't have to experience, you know? Stuff I should think more about.

Jenn told me a lot, too, about some of the racist stuff John Muir said and did, especially against Indigenous peoples. How we should call the John Muir Trail the Nüümü Poyo instead, or Paiute Trail, to honor the native names. Even though I'm done actually hiking that section of trail now, I'll try to call it that in the future.

I kept thinking about how Carolina would've liked Jenn, too. How I wanted to tell Carolina about Nüümü Poyo.

We even got dinner together in town, me and Jenn. She mostly talked and I mostly listened, but she's funny, kept making me laugh. Every now and then she would randomly say, "I like you, Alexei," like Dahlia did at brunch that day. It was nice.

Anyway, for some reason I wanted to tell you about it. We probably won't ever hike together back on the trail; Jenn is, quote, "slow as fuck and anyone who has a problem with that can eat my ass." And I am doing pretty high mileage these days, at least when the trail allows it. But I've been mostly keeping to myself, since I got back, and it felt good to laugh with someone again.

And I wanted to tell you about the John Muir thing, but maybe you already knew.

Okay. I guess that's all. I have some other letters I want to write, before I leave here.

Tell Delilah I miss her too.

Lex

Sent from Tahoe City
Mile 1,126

July 23

Dad,

These last few weeks have been the most technically difficult hiking of my life, and I've only survived them because of you.

Knowing how to read a topographic map, how to balance my weight on a thin log crossing a perilous river. How to dress basic wounds. How to stake a tent on difficult ground. How to notice when I'm dehydrated. Recognizing animal tracks. Knowing bird calls.

The last one isn't an essential skill to survival, but it's the one that brings me the most joy. And I realized the other day it's also what drew me to the man I love, and it's all because of you, and maybe there's something ironic in there, but it only makes me sad.

I have to admit to myself, at some point, that I'm only here because of you. I told myself, through all the prep I did for this trip, all the training and research, that I was doing it for myself, to help myself find peace and a new path forward. But you're the one who started bringing me to trails when I was only a kid. You're the one who brought us to national parks.

You're the one who constantly talked about your dream of hiking the John Muir Trail.

So maybe subconsciously, I set out to do this in order to prove something. To you, to myself, to God, who knows. I did your dream, Dad. It's been more difficult than I ever could have imagined, and you will never know about it. Because I know, Dad. There's no point in me trying to be optimistic about it. I know you're never going to change your mind.

For so long, I felt empty, and then guilty, and then sad, and now I've reached this anger stage I hate most of all, but I'm coming to terms with the fact that it might not ever go away. I might not ever stop being angry and hurt by you, Dad, and that sucks. It's not fair.

But one thing I can do is stop feeling guilty. About my pain, about your decision. Your decision was yours and yours alone. And I'm not going to punish myself for that anymore.

You would love it out here, Dad. I've never been in wilderness so pure. Every day, you feel close to God. I lost him for a while out here, but I feel him again now.

So maybe you *should* hike the John Muir Trail one day.

Because you might have been the one to bring me to church, Dad. But I got to know faith on my own.

And your interpretation of God is a tragedy.

Alexei

Unsent

July 24

Alexei,

I've been talking to this patient, Charlene, at work. She's pretty near the end, can't talk or walk anymore. Doesn't get a lot of visitors. I don't know if she can actually hear me. But whenever I talk to her, her vitals always stabilize. So I think part of her, somewhere, can. I swear sometimes she makes this grunt at the exact right part of my stories, and I always say, "Right, Charlene?" and I like to think it makes her laugh.

I've been talking to her a lot about you. About our time on the trail, and when you came to Nashville. It's been really help-ful, actually. And just today, I was talking about Uncle Jaco's party, and brunch, and how things had seemed to be going so well. How it really seemed like you were having a great time in Nashville. Because I still try to puzzle it out, sometimes. I'm not angry anymore—at least, mostly not angry—and I always knew you'd want to go back to the trail, but I don't know why you didn't at least leave a note. I have to tell you, Lex, it hurt Ma's feelings that you didn't. I think it hurt Dad's, too. And Carolina might punch you if she ever sees you again, just as a heads-up.

But Ma did mention how you had acted a little off that night, before I came home. How you were watching a movie and doing puzzles and suddenly looked sick.

So I was telling Charlene all this, about how great your visit had been, and suddenly, it hit me.

It must have made you miss your family so bad, Lex, being around mine.

We should have talked about it, before we left the trail, how it would affect you. We should have talked about all of it so much more.

I wish I had better words to say about all of it. And I'm not going to send this letter, either—I'm sorry I can't make myself write a real letter to you; I can't exactly explain it, but I'm still trying to be careful with my heart here, I still want to keep it intact from now on—but I just wanted to write it down. That I'm sorry.

I'm sorry if being here was hard for you in any way.

I'm so sorry your family left you, Lex.

And I'm sorry I didn't make it more clear. That my family would never replace yours. But they would've been yours, too. There are so many ways to find family.

The Caravalhos loved you, Lex. Some of them always will.

Ben

Unsent

July 27

Mom,

Writing this one is harder. I thought I could get both you and Dad out of the way in Tahoe City, but it's taken me a few more days to gather the courage for you.

I know you miss me. It's something I feel in my bones.

Part of me wishes I could see you when I get back to town. I'm almost to Northern California now. I have seen so many amazing things. And that part of me wishes I could tell you all about it. I think you would say yes, if I asked. We could meet secretly, without Dad, and you'd get to hug me, and I'd get to tell you about my life.

But that doesn't seem fair, Mom.

I want you to love the whole me.

I don't want you to love me in secret.

I think if you really wanted to know where I was and how I was doing, Alina could tell you. I think you could have written me.

I don't think any of this is what our faith is about, Mom.

And I think you know it, too.

I'll never send this, but at least I've said it.

I love you. I will always hope you're okay, that you're healthy and safe.

But I'm not going to wait for you anymore.

Alexei

Unsent
Mile 1,255

July 29

Lex,

I got your letter, the one about Jenn and John Muir, and showed it to Carolina. I watched her read it. She smiled, and bit her lip like she does when she's concentrating. When she was done, she just sighed and said, "Let's get ice cream and watch a sad movie." So we did.

A lot of this summer really hasn't been that bad, Lex. Work has been helping me. I feel more confident, I think, knowing that I'm learning things there, that I'm doing a good job. Ted is a really good boss. And I've gotten to spend so much time with Carolina. I'm still sad I didn't get to finish the trail, but it's getting easier each day, letting it go, and I wouldn't give up this time with Carolina for anything. I can't believe she's leaving in just a few weeks. I don't know what I'll do when she leaves. Finally move out of my parents' basement, probably.

I've gotten better at letting go of the trail. But the one thing that hasn't gotten any easier is missing you.

There's another patient at work, Sana. He can still talk, just chooses not to most of the time. Kind of like you. Anyway, any time one of his family members comes to see him, they bring him origami. And his eyes light up every time. I had his sister show me how to make a few things. I was pretty bad at it at first—it made Sana's sister laugh a lot—and I still can't do the more advanced shapes, but I've at least mastered the crane. At night, sometimes, if I'm having trouble sleeping, I've been staying up and making all these cranes. Every time Ma comes down here and sees all these paper cranes everywhere she looks at me like maybe I'm unwell. And maybe I am.

But every time I make one of these silly paper birds, I wonder what birds you've been hearing lately, and it makes me feel a little better. A little lighter, just like your birds.

Ben

Unsent

CHAPTER TWENTY-SEVEN

August 15

Ben,

The most amazing thing happened today! I ran into Ruby!

I almost didn't believe it, when I saw her hunched over her sketch pad on the side of the trail, just like always. She skipped the High Sierra, got back on trail near Lassen here, said she wanted to see "the weird volcanic shit." (And some of it is *so weird*, Ben, but so interesting. I wish you could see it.) I sat and looked through all the drawings she'd worked on since we saw her last, and I swear, Ben, it felt like a piece of my soul was restored.

She says hello. She asked where you were, and I told her you'd gone home. And then she asked if I was okay. I said not really, because it always felt right, being honest with Ruby. And then we were quiet a while, and a Steller's jay flew to a low branch right across from us. I don't know if we ever got to see one of those together, Ben, but they are gorgeous. Just the most brilliant blue. It took my breath away. Even Ruby was impressed.

And then I asked her if she wanted to walk with me for a while. And she said, not really. And we both laughed. And it felt so incredible I almost cried. To be around someone who gets me again. Someone who knew me when you were with me. Even if five minutes later I said good-bye, even if I probably won't ever see her again. She's getting off the trail again soon, she said. Said she was feeling ready to go home. That she'd listened to her body enough. That it had helped.

But seeing her was really important for me, I think. Just like knowing you was important, too, Ben, even if we never see each other again either. I still don't connect with 80% of the people I pass on the trail, like I had a hard time connecting with people in the real world, too, before this. But I met Ruby. I liked Faraj and Ryan and Leon and still think about them sometimes, how they're doing. I met Jenn. I met you.

There will never be anyone else exactly like Ruby. And there will never, ever be someone exactly like you, Ben Caravalho.

There will also never be anyone else to take the place of my parents. Some parts of myself will always be missing.

But you taught me I can find people. That there will be other people I meet in my life who will understand me. Who will love me. Who will show me how wonderful and surprising the world can be.

That is a gift I could never possibly repay you for, Ben, no matter how badly I want to.

I think of how it felt to let you in, to meet Ruby and admire her drawings, to play the piano in London's apartment, to laugh with Jenn. It makes my soul feel vast and full.

And then I think about how many people you let in. Every single day. Whether they are the people in your permanent circle, or the people you only meet for a few minutes. I've been thinking about the new patients you're working with in your new job, the stories they probably tell you, how comforting it must be for them to know you are listening with your whole heart.

I think about all the people you let in, and I think you must feel like the sun.

That's what it felt like, knowing you. That you were as bright as the sun, and now I'll always have a little piece of the sun with me from those weeks I was able to walk next to you. So how lucky am I?

I wanted you to know that even though I told Ruby I wasn't okay, I feel closer and closer these days to the idea that I will be. My mind has been quieting the closer I've gotten to Oregon. I'm walking faster than I ever thought possible back during those first days. The miles pass by, and I watch the ground and listen to the birds and don't think much about anything at all, and I feel calm. Like finally, the trail and I understand each other.

Did you know that some scientists call the paths animals and humans make all over the world, that divert from the carefully planned and constructed roads of civilization, *desire lines*? The paths that beat through the heart of the jungle, that draw shortcuts through city parks. People can destroy desire lines, try to train us to use the better developed paths, but we'll keep making our own desire lines, again and again.

It finally feels like the PCT is my desire line. Like the PCT and my own internal compass are finally, temporarily aligning. It feels right now, following it until I get home, until I figure out what happens next.

But I don't think I would have even come close to feeling anything the trail has given me now, if I hadn't met you along the way first.

I know you always talked about how I saved your life. But I really think, Ben, that you were the one who saved mine.

I keep hoping you'll write me again. I check for letters from you at every post office I pass. But it's okay that you haven't. I understand, Ben.

I just want you to know. How much I hope you always get to walk along your desire lines, too.

Obrigado, Ben.

Te amo.

Sempre,

Lex

Sent from Castella, California
Mile 1,505

August 24

Alina,

I'm getting close to Oregon now, and I've been trying to think about what I'm going to do when I get to the Bridge of the Gods. I was so determined to make it to Canada, but I'm getting pretty tired, Alina. I have *loved* Northern California; it's been such an interesting combination of the desert, the Sierras, and home, too.

But my knee has been hurting me; the skin on my left foot has started to crack. Maybe once I make it through Oregon, once I reach the Columbia River Gorge, I'll just come home. Since I didn't technically start at the Mexican border, I've never been a true thru-hiker anyway, and 2,000 miles still isn't bad. God. I can't believe that when I get to Cascade Locks, I'll have walked 2,000 miles. The trail hasn't been anything like I expected, but I do feel stronger. And grateful I've made it through safely so far, even with all the aches and pains.

I still don't really know what will happen when I get back to

Portland. Where I'll go. I never told you that was part of my plan. Going somewhere new after this, somewhere far away. I hope that doesn't hurt you too much. But I think it might be good for me, Alina. Starting over. I hoped I would know by now, where exactly I'm planning to go, but I'm telling myself it's okay. That I don't have to have every single part of my life planned out. That maybe I'll never have it figured out. That maybe I just need to keep doing my best.

Whatever happens, wherever I end up, I think I'm going to try to find a new church. I don't know yet, if any church will work for me anymore, but I might try.

Because the way I've been feeling on trail as the weeks have gone by lately is how I think I used to feel in church. It's a kind of smallness. When you feel so connected to the universe, and realize how insignificant you are. And it's never sad. It's comforting. Because it's kind of amazing that we're here at all. I can be quiet and small and insignificant, but I'm still here. I still get to see all of it. I get to listen. It feels so peaceful, getting to be small.

Once I leave the trail, maybe I could find that in a church again, somewhere. Or maybe somewhere else entirely that's not a church at all, I don't know.

I'm not telling you this because I want you to find this new church with me, or anything, but because I think you might be the only person who understands.

Hope you're still doing okay. I miss you. Meet you for pizza when I'm back in town?

See you soon,
Alexei

Sent from Seiad Valley
Mile 1,662

August 28

Alexei,

Well, damn. You really pulled out all the stops in that last letter, huh? Like, holy shit. If there was a hall of fame of love letters, *desire lines* would definitely be in there.

I didn't show that letter to Julie, or Carolina, or anyone. I've read it about a million times, though, just for me. You haven't written again since then, and I have this feeling you won't. Like that letter was your way of saying good-bye.

Which is unfortunate. Because while I couldn't find the right words to say to you earlier in the summer, I finally have things I want to say to you now, Lex. More than could ever fit in this letter. But I figured trying to write down at least some of them would be a good start.

It made me really happy, what you said about letting in good people, Alexei. That was what I had hoped for, what I had wanted to show you—that there's so much good in the world, that you can normally find it in your friends—when I made you make that pact, back in the desert. Before things got complicated between us, before I let myself fall in love with you.

I am not the sun, or however you put it. I know there are so many shitty people out there. I've seen it, over and over, from those fucking guys at Deep Creek Hot Springs, to the families I see sometimes at Lakeview, who fight over who's getting their parents' or their grandparents' or their uncle's most prized possessions before their family members are even fully gone. I mean, shit, I spent the majority of my twenties working customer service; I know people aren't always good.

But there *is* always good somewhere, Lex. And you deserve as much of it as you can find.

What I've really been working on this summer, though, in between all the working and the missing you, is trying to believe that I deserve it, too.

I didn't tell you a lot about my past relationships, Lex, and that's on me. But they weren't always great. I always threw myself all the way into them anyway. There was one boyfriend in particular, Robbie...

I made a lot of bad decisions in my twenties, but staying with Robbie too long was probably the worst one.

By the time I got out to the PCT, I had gotten kind of burnt out on it all.

I was supposed to be taking a break from men, from making bad decisions, when I met you. But then you kept saving my life. And I couldn't walk away.

What I've been wanting to tell you, though, is that I've been going to therapy. Julie suggested it a few times, and I finally stopped being defensive about it and tried. I've been going most of the summer, actually. Therapy has been good for me in lots of ways, depending on what I need to get off my chest that week. My mess of feelings about you, and the trail. Or helping me work through shit I see at work. (Charlene passed away, and while she isn't the first patient I've lost, for some reason it hit me hard.) Or working through grief I guess I still have about my aunt Birdie. Because watching someone die of Alzheimer's is hard, and I guess I sort of went right into nursing school instead of really processing that.

A lot of the time, though, we talk about my exes.

Ruth, that's my therapist, has helped me recognize how toxic a lot of my past relationships were, for various reasons.

And that letter from you, Lex—that letter was kind of a

lightbulb moment for me. All that stuff you said about loving how I let other people in. Because Robbie—well, Robbie sort of hated that. But you never did, did you? Even with everything that was going on with you and your family, you never got mad when I wanted to talk about mine. Never got upset when I texted on my phone for hours. It was like...it just made you happy, whatever made me happy. Whatever I loved, you loved, too.

So many of my past partners wanted me to change something about myself. And I always believed them. That I needed to be better, different, grow up.

But you never wanted to change me. You were always just you. Wanting just me.

I think, for a long time, I kept letting people break my heart because I didn't know what else to do. Letting them leave, or hurt me, because I grew to expect it. Because maybe I thought I deserved it.

But I think maybe I have to try more. To stand up for my own happiness, you know? Unbreak my own heart, sometimes. I think I've been so obsessed with all of my bad decisions that I haven't truly given myself enough chances to make good ones.

And you know, Lex, it really isn't fair. That you always got to decide. When you said (or didn't say) good-bye. I think it's time I had a say.

Plus. I hear there are some waterfalls in the Northwest I need to see.

Ben

Unsent

III

Oregon–Washington Border

Mile 2154
September

CHAPTER TWENTY-EIGHT

The path from Mount Hood down to the valley of the Columbia River Gorge, the lowest elevation of the entire PCT, pummeled Alexei's knees for mile after mile of brutally quick descent. As he approached Cascade Locks, the last stop on the PCT in Oregon before the Bridge of the Gods delivered hikers to Washington, Alexei almost laughed at how anticlimactic it felt. This could possibly be the end of it all, the last day he walked the PCT, at least for now. He was approaching the lands he knew well, the vistas and trees and mosses that had raised him.

Home.

He had walked 2,000 miles to get here.

Revised his plan over and over again.

And all he wanted was to sit down and take a hot bath.

Alexei left the trail at a junction that delivered hikers onto a quiet street of Cascade Locks, a few blocks away from the bridge. He was halfway down the street, contemplating what, exactly, he should do from here—maybe see if there was a room available at the Best Western, rest his bones before deciding for sure whether he was completing his journey here or walking on to Washington—when he heard someone call his name.

"Gosh *darn* it, Alexei!"

Alexei half jumped out of his skin.

His eyes widened when he saw her.

"Alina?"

She ran up the street toward him, golden hair streaming in the wind.

"*Ugh!*" she groaned, stomping her feet when she reached him. "I *knew* you would walk too fast and beat me! You are the *worst*, Burr."

"Beat you?" Alexei repeated, still dumbstruck.

He had last written to Alina hundreds of miles ago.

"How did you even know I would get here today? Like, at this exact moment? Are you a sorcerer?"

"I've been following your GPS tracker ever since you stepped foot into Oregon, you dummy." She shook her head at him, hands on her hips. "Well, before that, too."

"Oh." He blinked.

"Yeah, it doesn't work great all the time, but I can usually get a vague read on where you are. And I saw that you were getting close, that you were near Timberline a couple days ago, and *ugh*, I was supposed to be waiting for you! As soon as you stepped off the trail! And you beat me by, what, five minutes? This is so typical. I'm going to hate you forever for this."

"Um. I'm sorry?"

"You should be. Also I love you."

With that, Alina jumped forward, throwing her arms around Alexei's neck. This show of affection threw his brain into gear, cemented that this was real. He had a funny desire to twirl his sister around in a circle, if only his pack wasn't so damn heavy, and his knees didn't hurt so damn much.

"Alina," he said into her hair, fighting off tears. Russian slipped out without thought: "Ya skuchayu po tebe, Alinachka."

"I missed you too, Alyosha." She gave his neck an extra squeeze.

He added, in English, getting a hold of himself: "Thank you for coming to see me."

"Of course I came to see you!" She stepped back and squinted at him. "You told me to. We're getting ice creams at Eastwind, right?"

"I didn't…" Alexei shook his head. And smiled. "Yes. Yes, let's go."

And so he walked down Moody Avenue toward Wa Na Pa Street with his sister, and his knees hurt just a little less with each step.

They had to wait in line at Eastwind, which wasn't surprising, considering Alexei had managed to hit Cascade Locks in the middle of a weekend, the type of warm September afternoon that had everyone wringing out their final dreams of summer. And nothing said summer in the Northwest like a soft serve from Eastwind Drive-In, where even the small size seemed to run as tall as a toddler. Alexei had never once seen someone actually finish the large size. It seemed a colossal waste, but at the same time, there was something pure and fun about it. Alexei felt deliriously happy, waiting in line for one right now with Alina.

Once he and Alina had ordered their cones, both simple chocolate-vanilla twists, with a side of cheesy potato rounds for Alexei, they found a picnic table where Alexei could rest his pack, where they could hear the rush of the river. They both took their first bite. Alina went all in, one big chomp at the top, while Alexei always started with a careful lick around the edge of the cone, preemptively beginning the battle against drippage.

Alexei thought, if he had a phone, he would take a picture of this moment, his sister and the ice cream and the Columbia River, and maybe it would be his first ever Instagram post.

"So," Alina said after a few quiet minutes of solid ice cream consumption had gone by. "I came to make sure you were alive, obviously. But I also wanted to tell you you're a good brother. Because that first letter you sent made it sound like you weren't sure. Which is ridiculous."

Alexei huffed out a breath.

"Alina. I literally, like, exploded our family apart."

"What are you even talking about? Alexei, *you* didn't do anything. Our *parents* exploded our family apart. That's not on you, okay?"

Alexei looked down at his feet. He knew she was right. The last 2,000 miles had been for Alexei to tell himself that exact thing. But he still didn't know how to navigate this with Alina.

"I know," he eventually said. "But thank you for saying it."

"Alexei..." Alina bit her lip. "I know things were awkward before you left. Like, super-duper awkward, and I am so sorry. I wish I could have been there for you more. It was just a lot for me to process, too, and I didn't know the right thing to do, but Alexei...first of all, I should have said this right away, but you know I have absolutely no problem with you being gay, right?"

Alexei shot her one quick glance.

"I thought so, but I wasn't completely sure." He scratched at the scruff on his chin. "It didn't *feel* like you had a problem with me, but at the same time, we were raised in the same church, under the same parents...I don't know. I wouldn't have held it against you, if you disagreed with it even a little."

"Well, I *don't*, okay?" Alina followed her defiant statement with an angry huff. "God, our parents, our church—they're just so backwards about it all. Like..." She waved her free hand through the air. "Come on! You know?"

Alexei smiled, his insides warming. "Yeah, I know."

"And anyway," Alina said, a decibel or two quieter, swinging her legs, "I kind of always...wondered."

"Yeah?" Alexei asked, more curious than anything. "For how long?"

"I don't know. Like, since you were in high school and I was in middle school, maybe? I always thought you maybe had a crush on Mikhail, from youth group."

Alexei leaned his elbows back against the table, stunned.

"Oh my God," he said. "I *did* have a crush on Mikhail from youth group."

Alina giggled. "He *was* pretty cute."

Alexei grinned. "Yeah, he was."

"Actually," Alina said, "I wanted to talk to you about that, too. I know you've cut yourself off from…all of us, and that totally makes sense, I get it. But word has gotten around about you, what happened with Mom and Dad. And yeah, some of our old friends, some people in the church, are being real assholes about it."

"Alina," Alexei half gasped, half laughed at Alina saying *assholes*.

"*What?*" she cried. "I'm an adult now, Alexei! I curse sometimes! And they *are* assholes; there's no other word for it."

"All right." Alexei smiled. "Fair enough."

"My point was that some of your old friends feel really awful, Alexei. They're *not* assholes, and they want to reach out to you, make sure you're okay, let you know they don't think homophobia is what our faith stands for, either."

Alexei absorbed this. He appreciated it, of course. It did make him feel glad.

At the same time, there was a reason Alina had called his old friends from youth group *your old friends*. He would let them know he was doing okay, maybe. But they had been drifting apart for a while. When he thought about them, it didn't give him the same sensation in his chest he had felt at brunch in Nashville with Laynie and Khalil, the same comfort he'd been able to access in London and Dahlia's apartment. He wanted to chase that feeling again.

"And I'd love to help you in your search for a new church if you want," Alina said after a moment of silence. "If you want to do it on your own, I understand. But…it might be good for me, too."

Alexei nodded.

"I would love that, Alina."

A few moments passed before Alexei took a breath and asked. He asked because he sensed Alina was expecting it. Because maybe if he asked one final time, out loud, they could move on.

"They're doing okay?"

Alina looked down, answered as quietly as Alexei had asked.

"I don't go see them as often anymore. Maybe every other week, if that. I don't...I don't go to church with them anymore. Things are strained. I think Mom's close to breaking. I can tell in her eyes, you know?"

Alexei exhaled.

"But she won't do anything without his permission."

"Yeah," Alina whispered. "I don't think so, either."

"I'm not hopeful, Alina," Alexei said after a beat. "That kind of hope, for something that might not ever come, it's draining, you know? I'm not going to waste my life on hope for them."

Alina was quiet a moment. Then she nodded.

"Yeah." She looked over at him, a blaze of defiance in her eyes. "You shouldn't. I won't, either."

She reached over and twined their fingers together.

"Yeah," she said again softly, as if she were talking to herself. "Good."

Alexei squeezed her hand.

"You're never getting rid of me, though," she added. Alexei smiled. Let the promise wash over him, until it settled deep inside.

Their cones were half done, their fight against dripping vanilla-chocolate twist now firmly in favor of the ice cream. They battled on for a few minutes longer until Alina removed her hand from Alexei's to wrap the sticky remains in a napkin, walking away to dump it in the trash can. Alexei finished his last bites in triumph as she returned, throwing his chocolatey hands in the air.

"You do know," she said, "that you are a massive dork. And yet, somehow, you will still always be the coolest person in the world to me."

Alexei almost choked as the last bits of cone made their way down his esophagus.

"You think I'm *cool*?"

"God, Alexei, are you dense sometimes. You're my big brother! I've always worshipped you, and it's wild that you don't know. *Of course* I remember when you bought me those Little Debbies. That was the coolest Christmas of my entire life! You were always way smarter than me, way more talented with music stuff; it was always a struggle to keep up with you. And, like, now? Not only did you have the courage to come out to our dumb parents, but then you hiked the *Pacific Crest Trail*? I mean, I'm only telling you this because you look like hell and you smell really bad, so don't make me ever repeat any of this stuff again, but I'm so proud of you, I could cry."

She didn't cry.

But Alexei did. And he laughed, which somehow felt right, too.

"Don't worry." He sniffed into her shoulder as she wrapped him in another hug. "I will never make you repeat any of that again."

She squeezed him harder.

"I will if you need me to."

"I know. You know I'm proud of you, too, right?"

"Yeah," she said, and Alexei thought maybe her voice sounded a little stuffed up, too. "I know."

Eventually, Alina stepped back. They both wiped at their eyes, laughing a little more.

"Anyway," she said. "Not to rush you off or anything, but you have to cross the bridge now."

"What?" Alexei laughed harder. "Just because you made me cry doesn't mean you're the boss of me now. I was thinking I'd take a little break here. The trail here from Mount Hood was brutal, Alina. I'm serious; I can barely walk."

"No." She shook her head, smiling. "*I'm* serious, Alexei. You have to cross the bridge now."

Alexei's smile dropped.

"Alina," he said. "Why do I have to cross the bridge?"

"I'm not telling," she said, bouncing on her toes, her grin stretching from ear to ear.

Wait.

What—

But before he could protest further, she gave him one last hug, quick and light this time, yelling "I love you!" over her shoulder before she ran through the parking lot, leaving Alexei alone at the picnic table, confusion on his face, chocolate-vanilla soft serve roiling in his stomach.

It took Alexei a long time to leave the picnic table.

His sister had been here—and then she was gone. It took Alexei time to process it, to assure himself it had been real.

He had been feeling so at peace these last few hundred miles. Proud of what he'd accomplished, how far he'd come. Looking forward, tentatively, to the future.

But seeing Alina again—knowing, definitively, that she was still here, still his sister, his friend—

He released a quiet sob. Oh, God. He had been ready to face his future alone. But it felt so good. Knowing he didn't have to.

Alexei sat a bit longer. Processed it all a bit more.

And then he kept sitting.

In his defense, his knees really did hurt.

But eventually, he peeled himself away from the table. Took a deep breath. Shook out his arms.

Picked up his pack.

Alina had told him to cross the bridge. Alina had a secret. Alexei only had one guess about what that secret could be.

Even if it seemed completely implausible.

It almost hurt even to think it.

But he supposed he'd have to walk a bit more either way, to find out.

Alexei's breath grew tighter in his chest with each step he took across the Bridge of the Gods. The Columbia River flowed beneath his feet, blue-green and majestic in the September sun. The cars crawled carefully around him.

Alexei had been here before; knew exactly what the other side looked like. The green-and-white "Welcome to Washington" sign, the acorn-shaped PCT marker, the arrows pointing right to Stevenson, left to Vancouver.

Except this time—

Oh. Oh good God.

There he was. Leaning against a black rental car, parked in the dirt right off the entrance to the bridge.

Alexei stopped short, rested his hands on his knees. He hadn't talked to a soul in, like, 300 miles, and then Alina, and now—

He was going to faint. Except this bridge was ridiculously high, so he would definitely die if he fell off it, and if he swayed the other way, he'd only get hit by a car, and Ben Caravalho already saw too much death.

At least, Alexei assumed Ben hadn't come all this way to watch him die.

For a long time, Alexei hadn't been sure if Ben hated him or not. That one letter he'd sent had been so short and indecipherable, hardly a letter at all. He hadn't sent anything after that, which had been fair. There likely wouldn't have been any easy way for Ben to know where Alexei was at any given time anyway, even if he had wanted to write.

Even though he apparently knew, like Alina, where Alexei would be today.

Because Ben and Alina must have been in cahoots.

And you wouldn't be in cahoots with someone's sister if you hated him, right?

Still. Maybe Ben was here only because he wanted to yell at Alexei in person about everything, which again, would be reasonable. It was awful, how Alexei had left that night. He deserved to be yelled at.

Maybe—

Ben finally turned his head. Pushed off from the car, turned toward him.

Jesus, Mary, and Joseph, as Iris Caravalho would say.

Alexei breathed deep.

He took a step forward. Walked into Washington. Toward the man he loved.

Ben wiped his palms on his shorts as Alexei approached, stuck them in his back pockets. Looked at Alexei from under those dark eyelashes.

Alexei came to a stop when he was five feet away, trekking poles dangling from his hands.

"Hi," he said.

"Lex," Ben said, and Alexei almost fell over from the impact. "Hey."

Ben looked down then, shuffled his feet.

"I thought...you came to my hometown, where I'm from. So I thought it only fair that I met you here, in the state where you were born."

God, Alexei thought. He looked good. Alexei had forgotten for a bit there, how good Ben looked.

"I wanted to make some kind of big gesture to welcome you home, but I can't play the guitar, and I can't write like you, so..." Ben glanced at Alexei. Took his hands out of his pockets. He looked almost shy.

"I was just wondering, Lex, if you'd take a walk with me."

CHAPTER TWENTY-NINE

B en white-knuckled the steering wheel. It was only a few miles to the tiny village of North Bonneville, just past the Bonneville Dam. He'd been there all morning, while Alina texted him updates from Alexei's GPS. Had gotten everything ready, practiced what he was going to say, before Alexei finally walked across that bridge.

Alexei had gotten in the car. Things were going as smoothly as they possibly could, in terms of surprising-the-man-you-loved-who'd-abruptly-left-your-home-without-saying-good-bye-several-months-ago kind of metrics.

Still, as they drove down the road in silence, as Ben wound through North Bonneville and parked behind the dugout of a Little League baseball field, he wasn't entirely sure he wouldn't be sick at Alexei's feet once they got out of the car.

He looked so good. So strong and calm. His beard was even scruffier than before. He smelled awful. Ben wanted to kiss him so badly.

Alexei left his pack in the car. It was clear he knew where they were, smiling when they approached the entrance to the trail. Strawberry Island, it was called. Alexei smiling was another good sign.

And to Ben's great relief, once they began walking through the open, breezy grassland of the island's interior, past the waving wildflowers and the rush, it took only a few moments to get used to it again. Walking next to Alexei. Wrapping himself in Alexei's quiet. Letting it soothe his heart.

And as they walked, as Ben kept stealing glances Alexei's way, he could see it. Feel it. That Alexei Lebedev was at peace now. His shoulders were relaxed, that little smile never quite leaving his face.

Ben swallowed past a lump in his throat. He had stuff to say. He couldn't cry yet.

He led them to a side trail that wound through a patch of cottonwoods, toward the tip of the island. His heart pounded in his temples.

As they neared the bench at the end of the trail, Ben exhaled when it came into view, exactly as he had left it.

Alexei's steps faltered. He stopped a few feet from the bench, staring up into the trees. At the strings of battery-powered white lights Ben had placed there this morning, using the stepladder Alina had let him borrow, currently hiding behind a fir tree. At the hundreds of paper cranes, strung among those lights, that Ben had carried in a large box, somewhat ridiculously, on his flight across the country.

He had worried the effect wouldn't be as impressive if Alexei arrived in the middle of the day, as he had, but it was dim enough in this patch of trees, and it had turned cloudy over the river, where the blue-gray caps of the Columbia were visible from the viewpoint, the deep green hulk of Hamilton Mountain to their right, the monolith of Beacon Rock. And they were all alone here, and it felt—

Alexei's forehead was furrowed. That little line there Ben loved so much.

It hit Ben then. That while Ben had hoped it would be romantic, it might also be a lot for Alexei, who didn't like surprises, who was easily overwhelmed.

"Hey." Ben stepped forward. "Lex. Are you okay?"

When Alexei didn't say anything, only kept looking around above their heads, Ben started to panic. "I'm sorry," he blurted out. "I know it's a little extra. Our sisters thought it was a good idea, but—" He glanced over to the bench, where a basket sat, full of Fruit Loops and gummy bears. Part of him was thrilled it hadn't been stolen by a gang of squirrels, but also, maybe he should have just met Alexei and, like, talked quietly over tea.

But when he turned back, Alexei was finally looking at him. And he was smiling again. Small, but there.

"Cranes," he said.

Ben breathed out. "Cranes," he agreed. And then, "Do you need to sit down?"

"Yes," Alexei answered immediately. "Yes, that would be good."

Ben tried to shove the basket behind the bench before Alexei saw it, but he was too late. Alexei whisked it out of his hand, placing it on his lap as he sat down. Ben sat next to him, careful to give him space, trying not to fidget too hard.

Alexei stared at the treats before he asked, "Why?" He turned toward Ben. "Why do all this for me? I'm supposed to be the one apologizing to you."

Ben waved this off. "You apologized in the letters. And I wanted to."

Alexei frowned. "The letters weren't good enough. Ben, I'm so sorry."

"I know, Lex." Ben turned, unable, in fact, to sit still, propping a knee on the bench. "I keep thinking about you leaving in the middle of the night like that, all alone, and..." Ben shook his head. "It wasn't about me, was it? You must have been hurting. You must have been hurting so much."

Alexei breathed in, slow and deep, returning his stare to the Fruit Loops.

"No, it wasn't about you. But I still should have thought about you, when I left, how it would affect you. I didn't mean to hurt you."

"I know." Ben had to curl his fingers into his palms, to keep from reaching out and taking Alexei's hand. "And I'm sorry, too, by the way. For not telling you right away, as soon as I got the call about the job."

It almost felt silly even to talk about this; it all felt so far away now. But Alexei nodded gravely, like he was grateful. "How is your job?"

"It's good." For a second, Ben forgot that he hadn't actually told Alexei about it yet. That he'd never sent any of those letters. "It's great, actually."

"Good." Alexei gave another of those grave nods. "And Carolina?"

"She's good, too, Lex. But—" Ben took a deep breath. "Can we maybe talk about us?"

Alexei froze. Looked out at the river. From somewhere above them, there came a sweet, whistling song, rising over the distant roar of the highway.

"Hermit thrush," Alexei said quietly.

Ben almost cried again.

"Alexei," he said instead, "I'm sorry we didn't talk more, first of all, about how coming to Nashville, being around my family, would affect you. Because it was hard, right? It must have been," he filled in before Alexei could answer, do another one of those sad nods that were slowly killing him. "And I hope it doesn't feel like I'm talking down to you when I say this, but I just need you to know that my family will always be yours, too, Lex. Doesn't mean they'd replace yours. But no matter what happens after today, you'll always have a home with the Caravalhos in Nashville. I promise. And—"

Ben pushed up the sleeves of his shirt. Was about to press on when Alexei interrupted his thoughts.

"Ben." Alexei's voice was so quiet, it made Ben go still. "Ben, what is that?"

Ben looked down. Oh. Alexei must have seen the beak.

He pulled his sleeve up to his elbow so Alexei could see the full tattoo, done in grayscale. The puffy body, the black head. Intricate patterns shaded down toward the soft belly and tail feathers. The ink was fresh but healed now, the lines crisp, the dark ink of the bird's head stark against his skin. The artist, a buddy of Khalil's, had done a fantastic job.

Ben felt a bit embarrassed about it, though, in the here and now. He hadn't meant to reveal it this way. Hadn't actually thought about it much at all in his planning of this trip, even though he should have. Of course Alexei was going to see it.

"It's a dark-eyed junco."

"I know," Alexei said, voice still quiet as a desert morning.

Ben ran his fingers along the small *700* tattooed just underneath the bird's breast.

"I wanted something to remember the trail by. I know seven hundred miles isn't close to twenty-six hundred, but it's still more miles than I'd ever walked in a row before."

"But"—Alexei frowned—"I don't . . . we didn't even see that many juncos."

Ben was quiet a moment, still staring down at his arm. It had felt right, when he'd talked about the design with the artist. When the needle had bit into his skin. It really had felt like something he'd done just for himself. He smiled every time he looked at that damn bird.

But eventually, he went with the truth.

"You think they're pretty," he said.

Alexei gaped at him.

"You remember I said that? That was . . ." Alexei shook his head. "Ages ago."

"Of course I do, Lex," Ben said. "I remember everything you say."

He pulled the shirt back down over his arm. A second passed; Ben tried to remember what he'd been saying.

"Is it okay if I stand up for this next part?" He was already standing as he asked, shaking out his hands, ready to do this now.

He stood in front of Alexei, holding that basket of candy in his arms, and part of Ben worried about this next part. As he had worried during the entire plane ride here. As he had worried all morning while he set up his lights and his cranes. That this *was* too much. That Alexei might have moved on at this point. That he might not want Ben back anymore.

But then he thought about that *te amo* in Alexei's last letter, that *sempre*, and he pushed forward.

"Lex," he said, "I didn't tell you a lot about my history with relationships before, but it hasn't always been great. I've been going to therapy this summer, working through some things." Ben licked his lips, swallowed. "I'll be honest, when you left that night in Nashville, I went to a dark place at first, because...I was so tired of it, Lex. People breaking my heart. But all summer, and in therapy, I kept thinking about how you made me feel when we were together. How it was the total opposite of Robbie. He was—" Ben scratched the back of his head. "The worst one. But I started to feel like maybe I should start...taking charge? Of my own heart. Work at it more, keeping the love I want. And what I really want is still you, Lex."

Alexei's face was doing...so many things. He was totally crushing that cheap Dollar Store basket in his hands.

"I don't regret telling you I loved you that night, Lex, after Jaco's party," Ben pushed on, feeling stronger now. "Even though, in retrospect, I should've chosen a better time to tell you, than when we were...you know. But I don't regret telling you then, because I was just so fucking happy that night, Lex." Another annoying lump in his throat made him pause, take in a short breath before he could continue. "So happy. But—you never gave me a chance to do it better. You never let me take you on that date. So I came here, and I did this"—he waved a hand at the trees—"because I love you. But

I did it for me, too. Because like I said, I wanted to. And I've been punishing myself for too long for wanting things. So I'm going to try to stop doing that now."

He placed his hands on his hips. Let them fall. Unsure how to end the speech.

"So. That's about it," he said. Even though it wasn't. He had more to say. But he needed to hear Alexei's response first.

"Ben," is what Alexei eventually said. He put the wrecked basket on the bench next to him, leaned over as if in pain, hung his head in his hands. Ben watched his back rise and fall a few times as he inhaled, exhaled through his fingers. Finally, Alexei sat back on the bench and said, exasperated, "God, Ben, would you come here?"

Ben hesitated for only half a second.

And then his knees were hitting the old wooden bench, resting alongside Alexei's hips, his hands cradling Alexei's face, Alexei's beard scratching Ben's thumbs. Alexei grabbed Ben's thighs, anchoring him, so they didn't both topple off this bench into the Columbia.

And before Ben could hardly catch his breath, Alexei's mouth collided with his. One of Alexei's hands reached around, gripping Ben's ass, and as their tongues collided, it reminded Ben so much of that very first time back in Big Bear City, when Alexei was so sure and confident and Ben had wanted to sink into him forever. It was surreal and achingly familiar all at once, kissing Alexei Lebedev again. It filled Ben up, left him dizzy and breathless and hot.

Alexei broke away too soon to kiss Ben's forehead, his eyelids, the tip of his nose.

"I love you, too, Ben Caravalho," he breathed into Ben's neck, just below his ear. "I love you so much. God, I'm so sorry I didn't tell you that before I left."

Ben's entire chest seemed to cave in. Maybe this was what swooning felt like.

"Okay," he said, breath hitching as Alexei's hands traveled under his shirt, his mouth sucking on Ben's neck, and shit, fuck, Ben was dying. He put a hand on Alexei's chest, forced himself to push back. Alexei looked at him, eyes bright and hungry, mouth still open. "Okay," Ben said again. "Here's my next question, then."

Alexei blinked, closed his mouth with a swallow.

"How's Alexei 2.0 coming along?" Ben asked. "Has he decided where he's going to move?"

Alexei blinked some more, brow creasing.

"I saw your lists, in your journals," Ben explained, voice gentle. It almost felt like a dream, remembering falling asleep next to Alexei in his tent as Alexei wrote his lists.

Alexei nodded, eyes clearing. He took a deep breath before he answered.

"Oh," he said. "Yeah. Actually." Another swallow. "Turns out I'm not moving at all."

Ben's eyebrows rose. Something in his heart rose, too.

"No?"

"No." Alexei relaxed his back against the bench. "I'm staying in Portland. I finally figured it out when I reached Crater Lake." He looked down, ran a hand down Ben's thigh. "Remind me to tell you about it sometime."

"Can you tell me about it now?" Ben pleaded, overcome with a sudden need to hear Alexei talk. He ran a hand down Alexei's arm. "I just...I've missed you so much, Lex. I want to know how you're doing. I want to know about Crater Lake."

Alexei looked at him a moment, that quiet, serious, thoughtful Alexei look. And then he stared at Ben's shoulder, and started talking.

"It's in Southern Oregon, not long after the California border. It's the deepest lake in the US, one of the clearest lakes in the world. As soon as I entered the national park boundary, it felt like—" Alexei pursed his lips, a hand playing with the hem of Ben's shirt. "Like the woods were trying to tell me something. My heart was pounding the whole way to the rim. That's the thing about Crater Lake; it's in a literal crater, so you have to walk all the way to the rim to actually see it. But when you get there, it's—"

He paused, looking Ben in the eye again.

"It's incredible. You would love it."

He dropped his gaze back to Ben's shoulder and continued.

"I found a quiet spot, past all the crowds, and just...sat there. For a really long time. I'd been there before, was the thing. I remembered the first time we'd visited, when I was twelve years old. I could remember, all of a sudden, these vivid little details. My dad spreading a map across the steering wheel. My mom spraying this awful-smelling mosquito repellent everywhere. How she was always wiping my hair away from my forehead, because I had this awful bowl cut back then, and it was so hot."

Ben smiled. He wished he could see it. He wondered how many childhood photos Alexei had been able to save. He wished he could break into Alexei's parents' house and steal every photo they owned.

"But when I remembered all these things, it didn't feel like an open wound anymore. It felt like...scar tissue. Because it felt different, being there this time, as the person I am now. The person who had walked hundreds of miles through the desert and survived, who had walked away from my parents and my church and survived, who'd fallen in love with you, who'd let myself be happy, for a while. I was back in this landscape that I loved, that I had never really wanted to leave, not really, and I was okay. It felt okay—it felt *good*, being back in Oregon again. Staring at this crater that had been turned into a jewel, feeling like it was welcoming me home. And I suddenly wondered if I had walked almost the entirety of the PCT just to get back here again."

Finally, Alexei's eyes met Ben's once more.

"I'm still not a hundred percent sure if it's the right thing. Maybe I'll still move someday. But for now...I don't want to let them push me out, you know? I'm ready to go home now, in a way that's just mine. I think it can still be mine."

Ben waited until he was sure Alexei was done. And then he reached down and drew Alexei in for another kiss. It was slow this time. Quiet. Important.

Fuck, he was in love with this guy.

"Alexei," he said when he broke away, "that was the best story I've ever heard."

Alexei's eyes shone. "Thanks," he said. "I've had a couple hundred miles to put it into words in my head, so that helped."

Ben bit his lip, running his knuckles over Alexei's face.

"I have to tell you, I'm sort of relieved," he said. "I hated that Alexei 2.0 list."

Alexei tilted his head. "Yeah?"

"Yeah. I never knew what it meant exactly; I just hated the idea of you thinking you needed to change yourself. I like Alexei 1.0, Lex."

Alexei grinned, running a hand down Ben's chest. "Well. There are still some things I'd like to change. I just realized I don't have to move to the other side of the country or become a totally different person to make them happen."

"Good." Ben was about to kiss him again when he remembered he still hadn't gotten to his final questions. "Speaking of running away to the other side of the country, though." He ran a hand through Alexei's hair. Alexei's eyes drifted shut. "I have...a proposition, let's say."

"Mmm," Alexei said.

"How would you feel about me coming to Portland?"

Alexei opened one eye. "Like, to visit?"

Ben's nerves woke up again, fluttering around in his stomach. "Well. Yes. To start with. But then I was thinking...more permanent-like? If you would be open to that?"

Alexei's eyes were fully open now, that crease deep in his forehead, shoulders tight.

"What about Nashville? All your people are there. Wait. What are you saying?"

"I'm saying I want to be with you."

"I want to be with you, too, Ben, but—" Alexei shook his head. "I couldn't take you away from the place you love, from the people you love."

"That's the thing, though," Ben said. "You wouldn't be. I've talked it out with them, and Ma has assured me that what she and Dad want, more than anything, is for me to live my own life. She's felt guilty, apparently, ever since my aunt Birdie got sick, that I helped so much with her instead of doing 'young people things,' as she put it. Point is, Ma and Julie and everyone, they've made sure I know that even if I don't stay in Nashville forever, they'll always be my home. Just like I told you that you'd always have a home there. And I do plan on staying there until I'm done with my residency at Lakeview, because I don't want to let Ted down, and I want to see it through for myself."

He took another deep breath.

"I thought the PCT would be this one last adventure to get my restlessness out of my system. But Lex, ever since leaving the trail, I just feel it even more."

He found Alexei's hands, gathered them in his own.

"I want new adventures, Alexei, and I want them with you. The beauty of it is, people need good nurses everywhere. And I know it now, that I'm a good nurse. I would've followed you anywhere, if you would've let me, but I really am glad you're staying here. Because I've only been here a day, but I can already tell it's special. I can't wait to get to know it, know all the things you love about it. I mean," Ben reeled himself in, "if that would be okay with you."

"Ben." Alexei's voice sounded funny. When Ben finally let himself focus on Alexei's face again, he realized Alexei was crying. "Literally nothing in the world could make me happier. Ben, please, come to Portland. You'll love it."

"And you don't mind that you'll have to wait a year or so for me to finish the residency in Nashville?"

"Ben," Alexei said again. "I've been waiting my whole life to find you. One more year is nothing."

Well. Now Ben was finally crying, too.

"Honestly." Alexei brought a hand to Ben's face, wiped away a tear with his thumb. "That might be for the best anyway. I still have a lot to work out for myself. The trail has helped, but I want to go to therapy, too. I have to find a new job. And I might try to find a new church."

"That's great, Alexei," Ben said, trying to discreetly wipe away snot with his sleeve. "We can talk about it, how casual or not casual you'd want to be while we're apart. We could do visits, like you said."

Alexei's eyes lit up, his hands curling in Ben's shirt. God, Ben could pass out with happiness when Alexei's eyes looked like that. "Yeah? Like I could come to Nashville again?"

Ben laughed at the excitement in Alexei's voice.

"Of course you could, Lex. And I'll come here when I can; you can start showing me around."

Alexei smiled, bigger than Ben had possibly ever seen him smile before. "Cool," he said, and Ben's heart melted.

"Te amo, Alexei," he whispered.

"Te amo, Benedito."

Ben's grin sparked across his face. "Oh, you said that *good*, Lex." He pinched Alexei's side.

"Thank you." Alexei blushed. And then, "I can't believe this is real."

"Me neither," Ben said. "Honestly, I was so stressed the whole time Alina and I were waiting for you to get here, I'm amazed I didn't pass out while I was setting this up. It's possible I could still fall asleep at any moment here, just as a warning."

Alexei laughed. But after a moment, his laughter died away.

"I'd like to hear more about Robbie," he said, voice quiet. Measured. "Someday. If you're able to tell me more."

"Yeah." Ben released a slow sigh. "Sort of figured that."

After a beat, Alexei said, "Let me see the tattoo again."

Ben yanked his sleeve up once more. Alexei cradled Ben's arm in both hands, running his fingers along the bird's feathers. Ben sucked in a breath. "I'm glad you like it."

"I fucking love it," Alexei said. And then he grinned, and blushed, and Ben's insides exploded.

"Alexei," he said. "I am so turned on right now."

"Good," Alexei said. "Me too. Where are you staying?"

"The Best Western, just across the bridge."

"Oh, thank God." Alexei kissed Ben's tattoo, then rested his forehead against Ben's neck. "How long?"

"Just a couple days. Ted was happy to give me a little time off, but between the flights and everything..."

"A couple days is amazing."

"You don't have to stay the whole time, if you have to keep hiking," Ben said. "Isn't it getting tight, if you want to reach Canada before the snow? It's okay if you need to keep walking, Lex."

Alexei was quiet a long moment.

"I actually wasn't sure if I'd keep going," he said into Ben's chest. "My body's starting to hurt. Maybe I'd just stop here."

"Oh. Well, that would make sense, too." Ben shrugged. "It's your hike, Lex."

Alexei's arms wrapped around Ben's back, suddenly capturing him in a tight hug.

After another beat, he said, half muffled into Ben's shirt, "But I think I'm going to go for it. I'm so close. Might as well try. Right?"

Ben's heart twisted. Half in pride. Half with the need to hold Alexei so tight, he could never do anything dangerous ever again.

He nuzzled his face in Alexei's hair.

"Yes," he said. "Except I actually do have one condition."

"Hm?"

"Before you get back on the trail, you have to let me drive you to Portland so you can get your damn phone."

A laugh. Alexei snuck his hands under Ben's shirt again. "Stop." Ben smacked Alexei's fingers. "That tickles. Oh, and you have to keep writing me. At every single post office. And you have to make them extra sappy now. So I guess that's two conditions."

"Ben." Alexei shifted, pressed his mouth against Ben's neck again. Ben shivered. "Does your hotel room have a king bed?"

"There weren't any available," Ben lamented on a half wheeze. "Only queens."

"I suppose that works, too." Alexei sucked at his earlobe.

"It does have a shower, though," Ben said. "And I have to say, Lex, you smell quite horrible. God, I forgot what the trail smells like. Is it weird that your BO makes me feel sentimental?"

Alexei smiled against Ben's cheek.

"Ben?"

"Yeah?"

"Take me there."

EPILOGUE

Portland, Oregon
One year later

Rex popped his head into Alexei's office at 11:00 a.m., right on schedule. If anything, Alexei was surprised he hadn't seen him already today.

"Is it Ben time?"

"An hour left," Alexei replied. Technically fifty-eight minutes now. Not that Alexei was counting.

"How much longer 'til it's Ben time all the time?"

"A little over three months."

Rex knew this. Ben would be moving to Portland just after the New Year. The actual best Christmas present ever. Even better than Little Debbies.

Rex just liked to ask Alexei about it, because according to Rex, it was entertaining to watch Alexei blush. Sometimes, annoyingly, he would even pinch Alexei's cheeks, if they were in the break room and Alexei was distracted enough to let it happen.

Alexei wouldn't have expected it, that Rex would be his best friend at the office—Alexei's friend, full stop—but he had worn Alexei down with his affection over the last year. And Alexei had learned by now that the unexpected things often were the best things.

Alexei had gotten this job at the Forest Service's Portland offices a month after returning from the trail, late last fall. The job itself dealt mostly with budgets and memorizing more federal codes than Alexei had ever previously known existed. He did get to make lots of spreadsheets, though. Many satisfying charts.

Mostly, he loved coming to work every day and seeing the Forest Service logo on the wall. Even if he was still in a steel and glass office building, it always made him feel a little closer to the woods, to memories of the trail. He got a bit of a thrill, too, each time he was able to talk with scientists who worked in the field, who did the real work to help protect and manage those woods Alexei loved.

It made him daydream lately about going back to school for something more science based one day, something that would qualify him for more field work here, something that could combine his love of data with his love of the land. It was a quiet, consistent pull, this new small desire to do something more.

But for now, he was going to pick up Ben Caravalho from the airport in fifty-five minutes. He was out at his stable job, where sometimes, he got to learn a little bit more about trees. He got dinner once a week with his sister, who he swore got funnier by the week. There was a church he attended sometimes that displayed a rainbow flag in front of their doors, that might eventually become a place he could feel a part of.

He had not talked to his parents again. He had never passed them on the street.

But there was also a therapist he saw every other Tuesday. Who listened to him on the days when their ghosts haunted him more than he'd like. Who gave him coping strategies. Who had smiled last week and told him he was doing "so, so well."

His therapist, early on, had also recommended Alexei for a referral for an autism assessment. When he'd first received the diagnosis, it had sent him into a tailspin of questions, mostly about his parents.

Had they known? Had his teachers ever recommended an assessment for him when he was young that they rejected? What would it have been like if he had known earlier?

For the most part, though, when he was able to quiet his questions about his past, understanding his autism had only been another way for Alexei to learn how to love himself.

He had more dreams these days than he'd ever allowed himself to have before. But for now, having a job and a therapist and a sister and a boyfriend and a brain he understood better was all enough. It was more than enough.

Alexei spent the next fifty-three minutes reading his email and not comprehending any of it, mindlessly clicking in and out of a report he was not going to finish. At 11:59, he closed down his computer and left the office early for the day.

Ben had taken an early morning flight. Alexei would arrive at the airport entirely too early, as he always did.

Alexei could not wait for Ben to be here full time, to *live* here. It was too much even to contemplate sometimes. There were nights Alexei couldn't sleep from the excitement. He would text Ben lists of questions—What kitchenware was Ben bringing? What kind of dog food did Delilah prefer? Should Alexei buy a new bookshelf?— or sometimes, lists of things he knew about himself that Ben might find irritating. His need to place shoes in perfectly straight lines by the front door. The fact that, inexplicably, he *always* bought spinach at the store, even though he had never, not even once, used an entire bag before it went bad.

Ben typically texted him back one of two things:

i love you so much

or

please go to sleep, you handsome nerd

What Alexei didn't text, what he kept secret, were his dreams of buying a house with Ben one day. With room for a garden. Room for Delilah to run and rub her back in the grass. Room to plot their next adventures.

He knew Portland might not be permanent for him and Ben, that Ben might want to keep roaming after getting his taste of the Northwest. They had talked about it, and Alexei felt comfortable with whatever happened. He'd be okay leaving, he thought, if it was with Ben. Moving forward was different from running away.

Either way, even if they moved one day, Alexei still wanted to buy Ben a house. He would buy Ben a hundred houses, if he could, wherever Ben wanted them.

Despite his fantasies about the future, Alexei had to admit, as he drove to PDX, that there was something slightly bittersweet about this, Ben's last trip to Portland as a temporary visitor. Alexei would be traveling to Nashville for Thanksgiving, as he had last year. But other than that visit and this one, Ben would be busy wrapping up his residency and his Nashville life this fall. He wouldn't be back until January, when he arrived on a one-way ticket.

And as hard as the distance was sometimes, the anticipation of these visits was always heady, an all-consuming rush. By the time Alexei was actually en route to the airport, the excitement would fill his veins, fizzy like champagne, until he felt like he could float away. He would miss that.

And *this* visit. Alexei had been looking forward to this visit for months.

Ben had never visited in September before. The few days they had spent in Cascade Locks last year didn't count.

Alexei stopped at a store to buy flowers.

And then he parked at PDX and worried the stems of those

flowers, pacing in front of the terminal until Ben was there, with his eye crinkles and his hair in a bun, a gap-toothed smile that was just for him.

When they got to Alexei's apartment, a one-bedroom in a small complex in the Hawthorne neighborhood, the routine was always the same.

Carry Ben's bags to the door.

Open door; try to act chill.

Drop bags. Close door. Wait half a second for Ben to push him back against it.

Let Ben have his way with him.

It was Alexei's favorite routine in the world.

This time, he asked the question first.

"What do you want," he asked between kisses, his hands roaming underneath Ben's shirt, whatever small talk they'd been making in the car already far away, the pads of Alexei's fingers familiarizing themselves with Ben's skin once again, coming home to it.

"Nuh-uh." Ben nipped at Alexei's neck. "You know the rules. Your city, you get to choose first."

"But it's going to be your city, too, soon," Alexei said, already breathless. "I want to pretend it already is. You choose."

Ben leaned back to look at him, contemplating. The corner of his mouth tilted.

"I mean, if you're going to twist my arm about it. I want the chair."

Alexei's stomach swooped. Ben leaned back in.

"Me on your lap." He completed the request in a whisper, his lips brushing the shell of Alexei's ear, making him shiver.

The chair was a little physically difficult, far from the luxuries of a king bed. Oversized and sitting in the corner of the living room next to the bookshelf, Alexei had purchased it at a vintage store two years prior. It was the one thing in the room that didn't come from IKEA, that allowed Alexei to feel like he could be hip. Maybe.

Previously, it had been Alexei's reading chair.

Now, even when Ben wasn't there, Alexei could barely sit in it without squirming.

Clothing was dispensed with in due haste, and soon, Ben was in Alexei's lap, skin on skin, mouths everywhere they could reach.

More tender moments would come later, before the out-of-towner had to return home. But post-airport-pickup sex was always an almost humorously fast, deliriously hot affair, and Alexei loved the clear boundaries of it all, the mutually understood consent that they each needed release as quickly as possible.

Alexei would miss this urgency, on the off chance it went away once they lived in the same place. Even though it was hard imagining that now, Alexei still chasing Ben's mouth as he grabbed for the lube. He couldn't quite picture any scenario where he wouldn't relish ripping Ben's clothes off, making his mouth drop open and his eyes go glassy, when given the chance.

"Lex," Ben breathed as he sank down onto him, "I missed you."

Alexei leaned forward, kissing Ben's chest, twirling his tongue around Ben's nipples, groaning as Ben worked himself over him again and again.

"You're so beautiful," Alexei murmured, a hand digging into Ben's hip, "Ben. I love you."

"So fucking much," Ben panted, moving faster, hands clutching at the back of the chair behind Alexei's head. "God. So good. Fucking want this all the time. *Fuck.*"

"Same," Alexei said, and Ben laughed for half a breath until Alexei took his dick in hand, wrapping his fist lightly around the base.

"Lex," he grunted, hips bucking. "Don't—tease—need—*yes*, like that, just that, *Lex.*"

"Missed you," Lex mumbled, starting to lose coherent thought, everything crashing toward that place, constricting, hard and bright. "Te amo, Ben, *Ben*, my—"

And then there were no words.

Minutes later, after Alexei had cleaned them up, Ben lay cradled in Alexei's arms, knees curled toward his chest, head resting in the crook of Alexei's shoulder. Languidly, Alexei traced circles on Ben's back.

"Those *te amos*," Ben said sleepily. "Even when you're about to come. Iris would be impressed."

Alexei's shoulders shook.

"Would Iris actually want to know that?"

"Ugh, gross, you're right; please forget I said that. My brain still isn't functioning properly."

Alexei kissed the top of his head.

"How is she doing?"

"Well, she is *far* less annoying now that she's substituting." Ben laughed into Alexei's chest. "She lasted all of, what, three weeks of retirement? As expected. But she's happy now. She gets to go in when she wants, still gets to see people but doesn't have to deal with the constant stress. I think she and my dad are planning a vacation, actually. A big one, like, to Europe. They've never done anything like that before."

"I'm so glad," Alexei murmured, closing his eyes as a ray of afternoon sunlight slanted in through the window.

It had taken only a bit more convincing on Ben's part—and some help from Alexei's therapist—for Alexei to believe Ben's people truly were Alexei's, too. But once Alexei allowed himself to open the door to the idea of letting new family in, it wasn't even that hard, keeping the door open.

"Okay." Ben pushed himself off Alexei's chest, stretching. "That was worth waking up at 4 a.m. for, I suppose, but is there any chance I have time for a nap before the bird show?"

Alexei nudged Ben's side.

"*Swift watch*, you mean. And…" He double-checked the time. "Yes. We have about an hour before we have to leave."

"Done," Ben shouted, scrambling from Alexei's lap before Alexei had even finished the sentence, running naked into Alexei's bedroom. Alexei heard the loud *thud* that signaled Ben's flying leap onto the bed.

Alexei slipped his underwear back on and walked into the kitchen, checking once more that everything was ready in the cooler and tote bag he had prepared the night before.

Every September, thousands of Vaux's swifts rested each night in the oversized chimney of a local elementary school, a stopping point on their migration south. They gathered around the chimney at twilight, circling lazily until they coalesced into a teeming, fluttering dark mass. A tornado of tiny heartbeats, swirling closer and faster around the chimney with each rotation. Until finally, whenever their leader communicated the signal, they flew into their nighttime haven all at once, a vortex of beautifully orchestrated feathers and wings.

The swifts were small, but together, they put on a show. Hundreds of Portlanders showed up nightly in September to watch, bursting into applause when the last swift had made their way home. Or at least, their home for now. A place to keep them safe on their journey.

Alexei had been waiting for months to take Ben to see it. It still pinched that there was so much of Alexei's history he wasn't able to show Ben, like Ben had been able to show Alexei in Nashville. He couldn't take Ben to see his childhood home or the church where he had spent so many hours of his life. Couldn't look through photo albums, or have his mom cook Ben his favorite childhood meals.

But Alexei had attended swift watch since he was small. Remembered sliding down the big hill near the elementary school with

Alina on beat-up pieces of cardboard as they waited for the birds to arrive, as the sun slowly set over the West Hills. Swift watch was a part of him then, and a part of him now. One more precious piece of his life he still owned, that he could still show Ben.

Although even swift watch had been changing over the years, the number of swifts who showed up each year steadily declining as they found different chimneys to rest in, different flight paths to take. Like everything, even the patterns of birds shifted over time.

It wouldn't be exactly like it used to be, but it would still be a good show. Alexei still couldn't wait to have a picnic, maybe rest his head in Ben's lap, while delicate creatures danced above them, fearless and beautiful.

Alexei double-checked everything: the chips and hummus, the cheese and crackers, the chocolate-covered strawberries for dessert. The wine he had discreetly hidden in two small thermoses. It wasn't technically allowed at swift watch, but Alexei was getting better at breaking the rules these days.

He refolded the blanket, rested it on top of the cooler.

And then Alexei walked into his bedroom to rest awhile next to his boyfriend, whose hair was lit under the rays of a warm autumn sun. Ben hummed a happy, half-asleep sigh when Alexei cuddled up behind him. But Alexei didn't feel like closing his eyes yet.

After a moment, he reached behind him for his phone. Pointed the camera above Ben's shoulder to the window, where the leaves were beginning to fall, where the birds were beginning their journey, the world preparing, once again, for another cycle of change. Another opportunity to be renewed.

When he finally chose a filter—Ben always laughed at how long it took him—Alina gave it a heart right away. Followed by Ruby, and Carolina, and Rex.

Alexei put his phone down then. His follower count was small, but loyal. He knew all the hearts that would come next.

He settled back onto his pillow and reached out a hand, wrapping it around Ben's side. It felt as familiar now as anything ever had, reaching for Ben. Like touching the smooth keys of a piano. Like braiding Alina's hair. Like the soft leather of a well-used hymnal.

Alexei stuck his nose into Ben's hair and, when he breathed in, held the breath in his chest for a long moment. Treasured it like it was holy.

Loved it like it was home.

ACKNOWLEDGMENTS

Thank you so much to my editor, Junessa Viloria, and her assistant, Sabrina Flemming, for turning this book from a heavy sigh to a well-earned smile. Your belief in Alexei and Ben's story, and your tireless work to make it better, has meant the world to me. Thank you also to Leah Hultenschmidt, Estelle Hallick, Dana Cuadrado, Jeff Holt, Joan Matthews, and the entire Forever team for welcoming me with such open arms, and as always, to my agent, Kim Lionetti.

Thank you to Hattie Windley for once again rendering my characters with such talent and care. I am the luckiest author in the world to have covers like yours.

Thank you to the very first readers of this book: Manda Bednarik (who deserves extra thanks for also driving me to trailheads so many times, including that time we almost died), Jen St. Jude, Gabe Fleury, CJ Connor, and Elora Ditton. Thank you Danielle "Uncle Dan" Rosen for answering my nursing school questions, and to Meredith Moran for Portuguese inspiration and letting me steal Tiago's name. Thank you also to Anna Kopp for her crucial Russian help. Any language mistakes contained here are my own.

Thank you especially to Ellie MacGregor, whose help with this book in its later stages was invaluable, as well as to KT Hoffman, for insights, encouragement, and kindness when I needed them most.

Thank you to Jenny Bruso and Unlikely Hikers, whose mission is so important to me, along with every other person and organization working for more inclusive outdoor spaces, including but not limited to Fat Girls Hiking, Brown People Camping, Indigenous Women Hike, The Great Outchea, Melanin Base Camp, The Venture Out Project, and Wild Diversity. I encourage everyone to follow their important work.

Thank you to my family, especially my mom, who went on many grueling hikes with me as I prepared for the PCT, and my dad, who understands the need to roam. A special thanks, too, to the cousins, who like the Caravalhos, know how to party, especially when there are Whitney songs and hats shaped like food.

Thank you to Cliff Lyddane, the best hiking partner there ever was, for always being patient with me when I was slow and/or needed to cry, and also preinstalling water source locations in your GPS. Thank you to Cheryl Strayed and Bill Bryson for helping me dream about trails from an early age. Thank you to the Pacific Northwest for existing.

Thank you to The Writing Folks, especially Sami, our fearless leader; Chandra, my soul sibling; LC, who always makes me laugh so much; Lani, who always helps me believe slashing word count is easy; Brighton, whose fierceness and talents helped inspire the creation of Ruby; and Gigi, who helped me figure out Alexei was neurodivergent and supporting me in that journey more than she knows.

Thank you to every reader, blogger, Bookstagrammer, BookToker, and member of Romancelandia who was so very kind about *Love & Other Disasters* (and Moonie's, too). I cannot express what your support means to me.

Finally, thank you to Kathy, for always saying yes to my restless adventures, even when it makes you nervous—like leaving for weeks to hike sections of the PCT, or quitting my stable job to spend more time writing romance novels. I love you.

SOMETHING WILD & WONDERFUL READING GROUP GUIDE

AUTHOR'S NOTE

Several years ago, at a dusty trailhead outside of Ashland, Oregon, near the California border, my friend Cliff and I said good-bye to our wives and walked onto the Pacific Crest Trail. We planned to walk the full length of Oregon, but about 150 miles in (after many tears and small triumphs), I was lagging behind Cliff during a pleasant, mellow stretch, when a sudden sharp pain ricocheted up my foot. The pain didn't go away. I collapsed onto a log and cried again, consumed by a feeling of failure. By the time I finally limped my way to Cliff, he already understood what was happening: we needed to get off trail. And he was…totally, completely fine. He missed his wife, anyway. His absolute lack of disappointment in me made the following painful miles back to civilization surprisingly light and happy; we'd walked a while on the PCT, and we were going home.

The following summer, foot healed, we went back for another fifty-mile stretch. This section, through famed Jefferson Park, was even more stunning than the stretch we had walked through the previous year. There were also things that truly scared me, this time: a river crossing where one slip could have been the end; sandy, steep switchbacks; and rocky cliffs that made my heart pound in my ears, and not in an exhilarating way. We woke up at dawn one morning, on a forest ranger's advice, to outwalk a raging nearby wildfire. I hadn't prepared enough this time, physically, and my body was in rough shape most days.

When we finally made it through, we waited at a trailhead to be picked up by Cliff's wife. I was dirty and exhausted, thinking about how I should probably never get on the PCT again, even though I knew I would want to. Thinking about how I got through what I did only because of Cliff. A man walked up to say hello, asked how our hike had been. After a minute, he climbed into the back of his truck and handed us both an ice-cold beer. A little bit of trail magic, to say good-bye.

Trails, like life, are about making boundaries and occasionally breaking them, about understanding our bodies and learning how to keep going, about finding good partners and kindness in strangers. Psychologists have a better understanding than I do about why we do dangerous things on purpose, why we are pushed to do things that scare us. What I do know for certain is that Alexei Lebedev is braver and stronger than I will ever be. I could never hike his hike. But he was pushed into that bravery out of necessity. It's a kind of strength that never feels quite fair. And I hope the next time he and Ben step onto a trail, it's just for the sake of taking a walk for a while, before heading back home.

Thank you for reading their story. If I could, I'd hand you an ice-cold beverage of your choice for making it to the end.

DISCUSSION QUESTIONS

1. One of my favorite things I did when preparing for the PCT was walking the Wildwood Trail, a thirty-mile trail through Forest Park here in Portland, Oregon. I completed it over the course of several weekends, and I saw such a fascinating range of landscapes in those thirty miles even though it was always only minutes away from downtown, proving you can find bits of wilderness and adventure everywhere. What's the best walk you've ever taken?

2. A comment I received from early readers of this book was that they wished Alexei would have sent those letters to his parents. For me, it was the writing of the letters that was important for Alexei, not the actual sending of them. What would you have done? Why do you think letter writing can be so powerful?

3. Alexei's fear of the desert and Ben's appreciation of its beauty are things I feel deeply and simultaneously. (I could never live in the desert, yet I am endlessly fascinated and inspired by it—there is probably a reason my first two books take place largely in Southern California. If you enjoyed the Nashville chapters, though, get ready for far more Nashville in book 3.) Is there a landscape or location that has always intrigued you? What kind of landscape feels like home for you?

4. On a scale from 1 to 10, how likely do you think it is that London talks to Schnitzel in baby talk when no one else is around?

5. Early readers were also split about Ben and Alexei's abrupt separation in Nashville. Some were upset with Ben, and some were upset with Alexei. (I imagine many readers will just be upset with me.) What were your feelings about how their visit to Nashville went down?

6. Faith is an experience that is often fraught for queer people. It's also an extremely personal experience for all people, so please ignore this question or discuss it at your own comfort level: What were your feelings about Alexei continuing his own journey with faith, and possibly finding a new church? Would you have done the same?

7. Spending months on a trail is a privilege many people don't have as it's often not possible to get months away from work or family obligations. If you could escape your daily life for a few months, what would you do?

8. Much of this book is about the meaning of *home*. What defines *home* for you?

ANITA'S FAVORITE HIKES
IN THE PORTLAND-VANCOUVER AREA

Trail of Ten Falls

Silver Falls State Park, Oregon
Loop
7.8 miles

Who could say no to ten waterfalls?! Truly stunning. (Note: doggos not allowed.)

Wahclella Falls

Columbia River Gorge (Oregon side)
In-and-out
2.4 miles

One of my favorite hikes that I've returned to again and again. Anything in the Columbia River Gorge these days is completely overrun, so if you want solitude, this won't be where you find it. But if you can get there early or on a weekday, it's so worth it.

Trillium Lake Loop

Mt. Hood, Oregon
Loop
1.9 miles

Another popular spot you have to get to early, but the view of Mt. Hood over the lake simply can't be beat. An easy, nonstrenuous stroll.

Cape Falcon

Oregon Coast
In-and-out
4.8 miles

Like most Oregon coast hikes, this one is often muddy and often crowded but features a lovely walk through towering Sitka spruces before arriving at a remarkable, if somewhat terrifying, viewpoint in the middle of the ocean.

Tom, Dick, and Harry Mountain

Mt. Hood, Oregon
In-and-out
7.7 miles

Am I including this one just because the name is really fun to say? Possibly. This is one of the tougher hikes on my list, but the payout at the end is worth it. This hike begins on the uber-popular Mirror Lake Trail, but trekking on past the lake to this rocky outcrop makes you feel like you're king of the world.

Catherine Creek, Coyote Wall, and the Labyrinth

Columbia River Gorge (Washington side)
Loops, many options
2–8+ miles

Okay, I'm cheating a bit here, but these are all in the same area and all offer fascinating views of the basalt cliffs that line the much-drier Washington side of the Columbia River Gorge, along with abundant wildflowers in the spring. Note that Coyote Wall in particular is also very popular with mountain bikers, who careen down some of the same trails. I have also seen rattlesnakes in these areas before. As a heads-up, keep an eye out for handsome quiet men who might offer protection.

Siouxon Creek

Gifford Pinchot National Forest, Washington
In-and-out, lollipop loop
4–8.2 miles

Another one with many options. Just hiking to Siouxon Falls and back (four miles) is an incredible way to spend a day. The clear turquoise of Siouxon Creek will soothe your soul.

Falls Creek Falls

Gifford Pinchot National Forest, Washington
Out-and-back with a longer loop option
3.4–6.3 miles

In a land of many waterfalls, this is one of the most impressive—high, multitiered, and in the wet season, thundering.

Clackamas Lake, Timothy Lake

Mt. Hood, Oregon
Loop and in-and-out options
3–10+ miles

Whenever I'm missing the PCT, I go to Skyline Road on Mt. Hood, where there's a beautiful PCT trailhead with multiple hiking options. A nice loop on one side of Skyline will take you to peaceful, marshy Clackamas Lake, while following the PCT on the other side of the road will lead you to large, sparkling Timothy Lake. Both are lovely options; I honestly love going to this area and just wandering. (It's also usually uncrowded, as opposed to other spots on the mountain.) For an added bonus, stop at Little Crater Lake on the way, a tiny but magnificent wonder.

Strawberry Island

Columbia River Gorge (Washington side)
Loop
3.2 miles

Also called Hamilton Island. I have long considered this my favorite hidden gem. An easy stroll around this largely open island of wildflowers and waving grasses provides views of the Columbia River and surrounding mountains, and it is almost always quiet whenever I'm there—except for the occasional birdwatcher as it's also an excellent location for birding. There's a small trail through cottonwoods to the tip of the island, where you can rest a while on a crooked bench and perhaps look for the ghosts of paper cranes.

*Don't Miss
Anita Kelly's Next
Swoonworthy Novel!*

COMING SPRING 2024

Discover London and Dahlia's story in

Every recipe needs a little chemistry . . .

Available now from

HEADLINE
ETERNAL

FIND YOUR HEART'S DESIRE...

VISIT OUR WEBSITE: www.headlineeternal.com

FIND US ON FACEBOOK: facebook.com/eternalromance

CONNECT WITH US ON TWITTER: @eternal_books

FOLLOW US ON INSTAGRAM: @headlineeternal

EMAIL US: eternalromance@headline.co.uk